T0246205

SPACE ODDITY

ALSO BY CATHERYNNE M. VALENTE

The Refrigerator Monologues
The Glass Town Game
Radiance
Six-Gun Snow White
Silently and Very Fast
The Folded World
The Habitation of the Blessed
The Girl Who Raced Fairyland All the Way Home
The Boy Who Lost Fairyland
The Girl Who Soared Over Fairyland and Cut the Moon in Two
The Girl Who Fell Beneath Fairyland and Led the Revels There
The Girl Who Circumnavigated Fairyland in a Ship of Her Own Making
Deathless
Palimpsest
The Orphan's Tales: In the Cities of Coin and Spice
The Orphan's Tales: In the Night Garden
Yume no Hon: The Book of Dreams
The Labyrinth
Space Opera
The Past Is Red
Comfort Me With Apples
Mass Effect: Annihilation
Minecraft: The End
Speak Easy
Indistinguishable from Magic
Osmo Unknown and the Eightpenny Woods

SPACE ODDITY

CATHERYNNE M. VALENTE

1230 AVENUE OF THE AMERICAS, NEW YORK, NEW YORK 10020

First Saga Press hardcover edition September 2024

Simon & Schuster: Celebrating 100 Years of Publishing in 2024

For information about special discounts for bulk purchases, please contact Simon & Schuster Special Sales at 1-866-506-1949 or business@simonandschuster.com.

The Simon & Schuster Speakers Bureau can bring authors to your live event. For more information or to book an event, contact the Simon & Schuster Speakers Bureau at 1-866-248-3049 or visit our website at www.simonspeakers.com.

Manufactured in the United States of America

1 3 5 7 9 10 8 6 4 2

Library of Congress Cataloging-in-Publication Data

Names: Valente, Catherynne M., 1979– author.
Title: Space oddity / Catherynne M. Valente.
Description: First Saga Press hardcover edition. | London ; New York : Saga Press, 2024. | Series: The space opera ; 2
Identifiers: LCCN 2024027610 | ISBN 9781534454521 (hardback) | ISBN 9781668063019 (paperback) | ISBN 9781534454538 (ebook)
Subjects: BISAC: FICTION / Science Fiction / Space Opera | FICTION / Science Fiction / Humorous | LCGFT: Science fiction. | Novels.
Classification: LCC PS3622.A4258 S628 2024 | DDC 813/.6—dc23/eng/20240624
LC record available at https://lccn.loc.gov/2024027610

ISBN 978-1-5344-5452-1
ISBN 978-1-5344-5453-8 (ebook)

For Christopher Priest
Who neither lived
nor fought
in vain

and John Peacock
Who taught me
how to build
a rocketship

World

Hey you;
It's me, again
—"Zero Gravity,"
Kate Miller-Heidke

0.

How Everything Began

First, there was nothing.

Then, there was everything.

The time between *nothing* and *everything* was mainly concerned with the challenges of decorating your average middle-class, two-car starter galaxy using only several billion buckets of overcooked lava, radioactive stardust, corrosive gases, then, eventually, inevitably, and quite unfortunately for the new drapes, sentient life.

The time between *everything* and *a century or so ago (begging the pardon of the speed of light and its tendency to make all known measurements of time euphemistic at best)* was mainly concerned with wars over the central design concept of the universe. This resulted in a ghastly percentage of the inhabited planets arranged around that lovely open-floor-plan galaxy getting blown apart, vapor-mined, equatorially unzipped, fatally shrink-wrapped, backhanded out of orbit, sent back in time to become their own proto-planetary masses, laser-whipped, stripped clean by invasive magnetosphere leeches, unmooned, unsunned, uncarboned, vigorously gentrified, devoured by interdimensional bees, dissolved legally, financially, and actually, drop-kicked into a variety of voids, infected by self-replicating knifenados, reflexively teleported into themselves, and rolled down wormhole bowling alleys directly into the front gardens of a great lot of monsters who everyone just *knew* very slightly disagreed with right-thinking folk on how to cook a proper steak.

This went on for thousands of years, because big booms are quite fun right up until one does you and your nephew medium-rare with a nice pan sauce. So on the booms and counter-booms went, until the exact millisecond someone on some planet looked out their window at the oncoming bee-tsunami and suggested a slightly, but only slightly, less stressful methodology for conflict resolution.

The time between *a century or so ago (begging the pardon of etcetera)* and *now* was mainly concerned with the Metagalactic Grand Prix, the greatest experiment in musical diplomacy in the history of smashing civilizations together to see what will and will not burst into knifenados. For a hundred euphemisms, the Milky Way galaxy's vast and gorgeous powers have agreed to put down their weapons, get dressed up to eleven, look in the mirror, tell themselves this is all fine and very normal and they will of course abide by the result without unzipping anything too important, then sit on their hands, grin, bear it, and, for the foreseeable future, pretend singing and dancing for interstellar domination is every bit as much fun as punching each other in the planet.

To the victors go uncontested hegemony, which is really quite nice if you can get your hands on it. To the losers go whatever's left lying about on the floor when the lights come up.

Repeat as necessary for best results.

But no matter how civilized everyone considers themselves over tea and sandwiches, no matter how thoroughly two or more political entities, gathered in the name of nicking anything they can off one another, assure themselves they most certainly *are*, and always *have* been, and always *shall* be the most evolved and sophisticated of music enthusiasts, the following remains Goguenar Gorecannon's Tenth Unkillable Fact: *Don't ask me why, but if you ever do manage to put together a real stab at lasting peace, stability, and basic median happiness, that is the precise second you are closest to losing the whole bag to absolute blithering chaos. Schoolyard, barnyard, marriageyard, legislative floor, it doesn't matter. Peace is civilization's problematic follow-up album that never quite works.*

Actually, do ask me why, it's because all it takes to prevent us from having nice things, over and over, is one single person. One single person who doesn't want to play the same game everyone else is doing pretty bloody well at, so they won't give over the ball even though everyone is yelling at them to get over themselves, because eventually that person will figure out that setting the ball on fire works a treat.

In this case, absolute blithering chaos arrived out of nowhere wearing a lurid badge handwritten in crayon:

HELLO MY NAME IS HUMANITY

ASK ME HOW

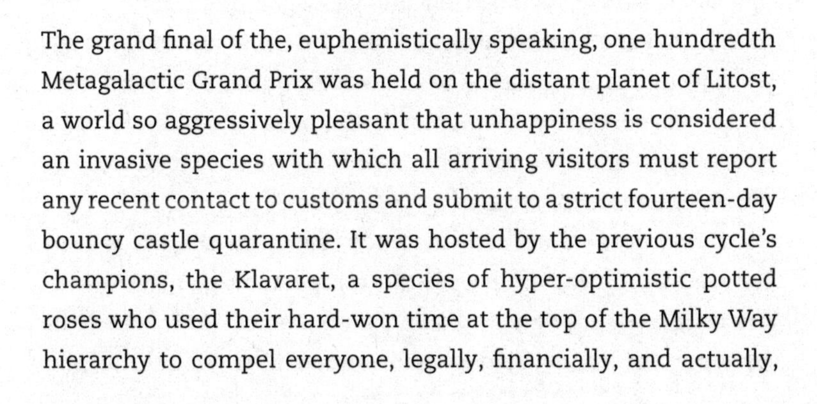

The grand final of the, euphemistically speaking, one hundredth Metagalactic Grand Prix was held on the distant planet of Litost, a world so aggressively pleasant that unhappiness is considered an invasive species with which all arriving visitors must report any recent contact to customs and submit to a strict fourteen-day bouncy castle quarantine. It was hosted by the previous cycle's champions, the Klavaret, a species of hyper-optimistic potted roses who used their hard-won time at the top of the Milky Way hierarchy to compel everyone, legally, financially, and actually, to hold hands, open up to each other, and process their core traumas once a week or face crippling system-wide sanctions.

This particular Grand Prix featured a new species vying to join the galactic drum circle already in progress. A quite loud, fairly squishy, suspiciously moist group of obligate-contrarian off-brand lemurs called human beings. For the first time, these failed-up monkeys joined the great interstellar tradition of sorting out one's political, military, economic, cultural, historical, logistical, romantic, culinary, and any other assorted outstanding problems through a nice, friendly musical competition rather than playing beer pong with each others' gas giants. Unless your species has only recently been discovered, wedged down between the nebular mattress and the asteroidal bed frame, at which point the stakes get a lot less, or more, fun, depending on how long it's been since you got to whip anything to death with a laser.

Alunizar and Keshet, Smaragdi and Elakhon, Sziv and Voorpret, Lummutis and Slozhit, Esca and Azdr and the Ursulas and the Meleg and the Trillion Kingdoms of Yüz, the Yurtmak, the 321, the single, solitary remaining Inaki/Lensari symbiote, and many more, including, quite dramatically, a gang of wild regret-eating wormholes who happened to be in the neighborhood, all gathered to take part in the fiery ritual of alpha-species musical chairs (fire being still very much encouraged as a traditional instrument). They did so with smiles all round, despite knowing exactly what would happen should the new kids on the quadrant finish in last place. Some of them, mostly the ones who manufactured laser-whips, rather hoped it might actually come to total existential annihilation, for once.

Humanity's continued existence rested on the excessively tattooed shoulders of an over-the-top postpop glamgrind gendershrug one-hit-wonder band called Decibel Jones and the Absolute Zeroes, consisting of drummer Mira Wonderful Star (deceased[1]), man-of-all-instruments Oort St. Ultraviolet, and lead singer D. Jones, all of whom were born with a genetic allergy to restraint of any kind. Had they lost, Earth would have been mercifully disinfected of the collective yearnings and night terrors, ambitions and neuroses, champagne wishes and caviar dreams of *Homo sapiens sapiens* and the biosphere left alone for a few million years to think about what it had done and try to make better choices next time.

They didn't lose.

They didn't win, either.

Life, with some new content, color schemes, highlights, and restrictions, went on.

Which just about sums up the whole human experience to date.

Yes, yes, of course Decibel Jones and the Absolute Zeroes saved the world.

But what have they done for us lately?

1 Reply hazy, ask again later

1.

New, Yet Familiar, Waltz

Once upon a time, in a very large, very elegant, shockingly bel-ligerent galaxy, there lived a rather troublesome planet about whose precise character no one could quite agree, except to begrudgingly admit, at the conclusion of a number of publicly broadcast hearings, that it was blue.

. . . ish.

On this (allegedly) blue world, there happened to evolve all three of the following, though not at the same time: a Dutch sea captain by the name of Willem de Vlamingh, a Lebanese hedge fund manager called Nassim Nicholas Taleb, and a very large, very elegant, shockingly belligerent bird called a swan.

You see, swans were once so common on this spinning 24/7 frat party that for centuries, millions of the kinds of people who rarely leave the house felt supremely confident that they knew all about them. Swans are beautiful. Swans mate for life. Swan babies are ugly but they get better eventually and isn't that a nice story with which to shut up our more facially unfortunate offspring?

But most importantly, swans, by definition, only came in white. This was crucial to their status as a symbol of purity, nobility, and devotion. Whole hemispheres insisted that white things were categorically good, and good for you, despite the obvious existence of arsenic, rum raisin ice cream, and European expansion. And despite how *distressingly* often those purely and nobly devoted white swans (and/or ever-expanding Europeans) tried to bite the entire faces off various unsuspecting bystanders who had not in any way bothered them.

But that's folklore for you.

This was so universally believed that the term *black swan* came to mean a thing that could not possibly, under any circumstances, no matter how outlandish, exist anywhere ever, no matter how much you've had to drink.

It all went well enough until Mr. de Vlamingh joined the Dutch East India Trading Company, an organization as close to pure evil as you are likely to find before the invention of online dating. This fellow, whose moral outlook could be summed up as a kind of casual Friday of the soul, abruptly concluded his long maritime service by face-planting into the western coast of Australia. Almost the first thing our man Bill saw was a fat lot of inconveniently black swans paddling about on a rather smug-looking river, whereupon he is reliably recorded to have said: *Well, fuck me dead, that's embarrassing. How much* have *I had to drink, James?*

Some four hundred years later, Nassim Nicholas Taleb dimly remembered all this from school and surmised that unbothered Australian swans might not be the only sneaky little bastards lying in wait on the underside of future history. And some of these surprises might be quite a bit harder to process for a desperately under-medicated species than a fetching new set of feathers. He began to consider things other than the sad slide-whistle of the global markets, such as how his high-strung home planet might behave when confronted with certain historically nasty surprises.

He called them Black Swan Events.

In order to qualify as a Black Swan Event, neither swans, nor off-duty hedge fund managers, nor the Dutch need be involved. The phenomenon in question must only be truly out of left, right, center, up, and down field, and in fact beyond the overpriced stadium entirely in terms of previously lived experience. It has to hit the basket of preconceived notions, social disorders, and half-remembered song lyrics that comprise the average human brain like a screaming bird-ball launched from a trebuchet of doom. But, after the fact, everyone must then sit around congratulating each other on how they all saw it coming ages ago, old sport, completely predictable, barely worth kicking your fundamental model of self-perception out of bed in the morning.

The discovery of the New World.

The invention of the personal computer.

A global pandemic keeping billions locked in their homes for years on end.

The invasion of Earth by roving space musicians, followed very quickly by its near escape from utter annihilation at the hands of a particularly fussy greater galactic Homeowners' Association who gave the height of the grass in the human soul a deep and abiding side-eye.

You know. *That* sort of thing.

Look, just recently, rather a lot has happened on, around, and concerning this little blue hole-in-the-sky. Some of it at least technically exciting. Most of it rubbish. An alarming portion is, quite rudely, still happening.

But after the feathers cleared and the extra chairs were hauled out of the basement and various governing bodies finished throwing up into their hats at the sheer implications for import/export administration, a shy and piteous cry went up from that pile of perpetually unsatisfied continents. The cry of a child on her first day of real big-girl school, scared to her socks that no one will like her, facing down a cosmic cafeteria in which every imaginable table is already packed to the suddenly, *horrifyingly* non-metaphorical gills. A child who has found her class being taught, not by a kindly overworked public servant with lipstick on her dear old teeth, but by a massive, hyperactive, shrieking black swan who has already had a shit on the desk, a go at the whiteboard, and made a powerful enemy of the syllabus, which, when you really think about it, had it coming.

And the cry was a question. And the question was this:

Are we special?

People really will do the most frightful things to feel special, you've no idea. Marvelous things, too, but the frightful ones are a lot easier to pull off. The most dangerous being in the universe is somebody who's never felt special in all their lives. If you encounter one in a dark alley, run.

And yet, we asked. Over and over.

The answer, when it came, echoed unanimously from Nu Scorpii to Aluno Prime, in syllables drenched in stardust, crackling electric with authority, double-dipped in that very specific feeling you get when you see a video of a zoo leopard whose existence is such a spotty mess its keepers assigned it an emotional support Labrador:

Aw. Bless your hearts.

Among all the great empires, rising, falling, and doing donuts in the car park of history, were we extraordinarily noble in reason or infinite in faculty?

No.

Did we distinguish ourselves from the crowd in intelligence, physical prowess, artistic output, technological genius?

Also no.

Did we at least have the best hair?

Absolutely not.

Did all those savage aliens, now that they deigned to exist, actually want to kill all our men and sex up our women, or vice versa?

Ew. Only if there are truly *no other entertainment options on the table and everyone signs a consent form.*

Then surely, if our virtues were nothing to put up on the astral refrigerator, we must have been unique in our wickedness. Our rebelliousness, violence, cruelty, tendency to one-up others at dinner parties and run through the resources of our only planet like teenagers having at our parents' liquor cabinet, our total inability to obey the rules, any rules, ever, no matter how sensible?

You should get literally all of that looked at by professionals, but also and additionally, no.

It wasn't *too* long ago that the galaxy only failed to murder itself directly in the face because someone suggested a battle of the bands might be a *smidge* more fun. No particular heated primate moment really hangs up its museum plaque next to that. Even down there on a planet whose solution to having invented a weapon capable of ending all life in the biosphere was for everybody to have one, and also parents who never hugged them.

Humanity was, as it turned out, painfully, embarrassingly, *harrowingly* average. As a species, we proved remarkable in only two ways.

The first is so repulsive that the Unremainderable Calator, fractally tentacled masters of galactic literature, issued a rare public-safety proclamation from all Publishing Hiveknots of the Pisces Epsilon Voidspace, defining the number of prophylactic chapters before any given work may discuss human psychology, so as to sufficiently prepare the innocent reader to face the jump-scares and graphic content lying in wait for them.

The minimum is seventeen.

The second was our general response to the discovery that the sky wasn't so much full of stars as full of squabbling band geeks whose trombones doubled as orbital railguns.

You see, just after Decibel Jones and the Absolute Zeroes saved all of humanity from the proverbial and actual bin, just as the horrible existential tension of it all put on its hat and coat and began its farewell tour, just at the precise moment when everything looked like it might stop being *quite* such an enormous walloping bastard all the time, just then, in the face of the sudden, quiet, wistful understanding that nothing would ever again be as it was, this (ostensibly) blue world finally paused its coping-bender and turned round to face its first post-post-postmodern crisis.

The Great Octave, as the galaxy's power players called themselves, was entirely prepared. After all, this was hardly their first deeply upsetting space rodeo. Horses go here, cows go there, lassos go round and round, and new species tend to have a bit of a private, understated panic attack once the immediate danger has passed and they have to confront the stark reality of how badly everyone who'd ever contributed the smallest bug report to their genome had misjudged the available catalogue colors of swans.

Historians, emergency medical staff, and serious debris collectors call it First Contact Syndrome.

Everyone else calls it the Blowout.

This term of art began with the famously understatement-prone Smaragdi, ten-foot-tall non-Euclidean bone sculptures who never met a sacred rite they did not yearn to flick in the forehead. It was quickly embraced, due to the near-universal experience of witnessing tiny, shrieking infants, regardless of species, helplessly eliminate their waste with almost unbelievable force and volume into a nappy far too small to contain the sheer tonnage of poo. Eventually, the deuce in question burst its bounds, jetting into places all laws of fluid dynamics should forbid: between toes, fins, tails, and antennae, spattering eyelashes, hair, scales, and any relevant forehead protuberances, contaminating parent, child, floor, ceiling, and somehow, the front doorstep.

Of a neighbor.

Several doors down.

This is exactly what First Contact Syndrome is like, except it is the collective *mind* of an entire world that uncontrollably overloads its pants with a volcano of swanstank that lava-crawls into every adorably chubby fold and crevice of the ego.

It's not a joke.

Although it *is* pretty funny to watch.

If you've cleared the exclusion zone.

In fact, almost all civilized species feel quite tender and sentimental about the whole process. All over the inhabited star systems, family and work units gathered round the warm glow of their sense-matrix feeds. They treated themselves to new frocks, prepared traditional festive dishes, sang a few public-domain Blowout carols, and reminisced about their own culture's bank holiday off from rational thought before taking in the top-rated reality program *Say Yes to Severe Psycho-Physiological Distress*: a live feed of conditions on the ground for the newest bundle of raw screaming sentience.

The delicate cerulean lantern-flamingoes of the Esca homeworld of Bataqliq just sat down and cried for a year.

The Keshet, a race of hyperactive red (-esque) panda (-adjacent) timestream-kayakers, immediately turned around, bit the space/time continuum in the snout, and refused to let go until it apologized, either for concealing all these *blatantly* non-Keshet species, or for allowing them to evolve in the first place.

Confessionals varied.

The Alunizar, beautiful, sophisticated yet unrepentant champions of settler-colonialism always looking for new players to crush under torso, claim to have never experienced a Blowout, since these kaleidoscope-colored semitranslucent industrial-powered sea squirts were the first species of the current crop to develop interstellar capabilities—and are terribly loathe to let anyone forget it.

This is a lie.

They were discovered by the Halara, a now-extinct species of self-aware trees that would not look entirely out of place on Christmas morning. If Christmas was extremely carnivorous. And also the star on top of the dear old Douglas fir were made of eyeballs. At the conclusion of diplomatic festivities, the entire population of glittering sea tubules with faces like ultraviolet bug zappers shut everything on Aluno Prime down, took all available recreational drugs at once, distributed six new ones through an emergency defense program meant to disburse vaccines and protective equipment, replaced all their top military brass with freelance DJs, and hoped for the best, or the worst, whichever came last.

The Lummutis, whose actual anatomy remains a mystery beyond the reach of even the most exploitative premium-cable documentary teams, retreated into a massive multiplayer, immersive, and emphatically indoors game from which they have not yet emerged, except as elaborately costumed virtual avatars running the aesthetic gamut from *stroke-inducingly inappropriate attire for a funeral* to *litigable offenses against eyes*.

The equally elaborately bodied, but significantly less fun, near-bear experiences known as the Meleg engaged in so much public, multiform, vociferous, and televisually off-putting end-of-the-world desperation sex that the cumulative thrust shifted their planet nine centimeters outside its customary orbit.

Most chilling of all, the Yurtmak, the nightmare-mouthed slaughter-rhinos of every Hollywood producer's ichor-dripping dreams, stopped lopping off each other's limbs for fun and profit and quietly attended group therapy every Thursday at seven until they all felt they'd learned something important about self-care.

It's all so wholesomely predictable that every office in the Great Octave started up a hefty pool to guess the exact minute Earth's cheese would definitively slide off its cracker. Having had a quick browse through the more popular multi-issue arcs of human history, everyone expected quite a show.

All the usual protocols were observed. Everyone on every continent received the same standard welcome package and orientation materials in the post at the same millisecond. Yes, that millisecond came six-to-seven business weeks after the Metagalactic Grand Prix had concluded its broadcast day. And yes, that rather left Earth strapped into a soul-carbonating dunk tank of the mind waiting for the deontological ball to smash that ontological target. But what's a little sobbing cosmic terror between soon-to-be friends?

Having done their part as good neighbors, the civilized galaxy topped up their cocktails, affectionately tousled the seasonal fur of their offspring, and leaned breathlessly into the cool, comforting glow of their entertainment module of choice.

Not one sentient creature playing along at home was sufficiently braced for what followed. Nothing in their vast, baroque experience, including these disappointingly few-limbed primates' recent fair-to-middling performance at the Metagalactic Grand Prix, had prepared them for the sheer style with which *Homo sapiens sapiens* habitually handles any interruption to its everyday routine.

Septillions of brains, soul crystals, central processing units, valvehives, ovules, philosophy sacs, and other assorted smartmeats peered eagerly down at odd little mostly unknown planet Earth and, with a sound like the death of God, simultaneously performed septillions of unique and fascinating physiological variants on throwing up in their own mouths.

Out of all the possible, mostly forgivable, lead-footed psychocultural responses to such a swift and aggressive punt to the paradigm, humanity chose:

Nothing.

Nothing at all.

The people of Earth, acting as a unified whole for nearly the first time in their history, stood very, very still. Sixteen billion eyes stared down at sixteen billion hands holding eight billion violently red and black gift baskets lovingly designed by Mags, a vast and terrifyingly affectionate Class 9 elevated archival consciousness occupying the Arx Serhat system on the outer rim; printed, collated, and distributed by Ms. Agnes Munt, widow, *Countdown* enthusiast, nationally ranked speed-knitter, and owner/operator of the Ream a Little Ream of Me 24-Hour Print, Copy & Photo storefront in East Kilbride.

As one, humankind let out a deep and weary sigh. A few informative brochures fluttered to the ground here and there. They rolled the ballpoint pen between their inadequate fingers. They looked up to the skies, then sighed again.

And went about their business.

It seemed approximately half of these unsettlingly two-eyed primates, as well as the governments of approximately half the politico-geographical units on their spinny saltball, declined to acknowledge that anything unusual had happened in their general vicinity at all.

Rather slow news year, really.

The giant blue bird-fish that popped into everyone's living

rooms a few months ago? Viral marketing campaign by a local pet store chain.

The strange-looking folk starting to arrive in dribs and drabs to gawk at the humans in their natural environments and, if possible, get them to do the thing where water comes out of their face holes?

Never much cared for immigrants. They all look so *weird*, don't you know.

The influx of new technology, rights, asteroids, luxury goods, celebrity artist-in-residence opportunities, and raw resources commensurate with an almost-respectable tenth place Grand Prix finish?

Probably a scam, if not a nefarious plot to undermine Earth's precious way of life (despite that way of life being most fully represented by a single, long, uninterrupted store-brand cola-belch echoing into eternity).

The massive ships you can see, without corrective lenses, in orbit around the planet right now?

Pure propaganda. Fake footage. That's what they *want* you to think. Wake up before it's too late.

Decibel Jones and the Absolute Zeroes?

Nobodies. Losers. Too much, too loud, too long, too over-the-top, would take a compilation album of retired national anthems played on banjos over that lot of try-hards, who do they think they are?

This response would have been bad enough, in terms of establishing friendly local relations. It'll put you right off your supper to be told you don't actually exist by someone whose main aesthetic expression of the desperate ache and exquisite thrill of existence is to, occasionally, wear a baseball cap backward.

But then there was the other half.

It seemed that the remainder of these unfurry bipedal brainbags, and *their* governments, felt so entirely unrattled by recent events because they were, to put it plainly, just *way* too into it. All of it. However it was defined, as long as it was as alien as Aldebaran pie.

They made spreadsheets of the contents of all the welcome packages. They started pop-up conventions to exchange the rarer items, snacks, and brochures as well as attend panels like *Ridley Scott vs. Isaac Asimov: Who Was Right and Who Was More Right?* and *Strong Yet Vulnerable Alien Protagonists and Where to Find Them.* They had detailed plans for their own personal adventures in space, and they'd made those plans long before the big bird-fish popped in for a forced musical number. They wanted to see, hear, eat, drink, fuck, fight, dissect, genetically modify themselves to insensitively imitate, poke at, take selfies with, buy, sell, and ask deeply intrusive questions of it all. They had their bags packed an hour after Decibel's final heart-boiling belt of highly sentient angst finished echoing out over the oceans of Litost.

Half of humanity refused to admit black swans existed, even as several birds tirelessly twerked in their kitchenettes.

The other half was 100 percent certified-fresh, locked, loaded, and down-to-clown with any available swan, just so long as it wasn't boring old white.

Even among the all-time hall of fame Blowouts, this one stood out like a goth kid at the church picnic. Given the choice between not existing and being approximately four billion people's brand-new top-ranked fetish, the marvels of the galaxy chose to back slowly away and look busy.

And the cats, despite being fully aware that one of their own had also been called up to the big game in the sky alongside the Loud and Naked Givers of Pats, and that the secret of their sentience remained secret only by the grace of certain dementedly optimistic houseplants, seemed to have snoozed through the whole thing, then asked for more wet food.

You just couldn't take Earth anywhere.

According to the intern-detonating number of complaints received by the Galactic Broadcasting Union, this was extremely rude and quite ruined everyone else's evening. Not one single thing was on fire down there that wasn't usually on fire. A wholly unacceptable result! It simply wasn't *neighborly*. This toe-brained species invented capitalism and promptly set about vividly eating its own face for two centuries before finally managing to calm down and only *nibble* at their *friends'* faces from here on out. Now their entire software suite nearly got bricked in a radical system update and they couldn't even join a cult about it?

In the opinion of *this* longtime viewer, the whole project ought to be cancelled and rebooted in a few years by *real* fans of the process.

The GBU, finding itself suddenly rather short on interns, opted to simply reply to every one of these slices of delightful discourse with the public by returning a copy of Goguenar Gorecannon's Ninth Unkillable Fact in an intensely passive-aggressive font: *If you will swan about anticipating things before they happen, that's your own fault for deciding your imagination was reality like a great big doorknob. The stuff that fuels stars isn't hydrogen or helium. It's bloody* disappointment. *If not for the omnipotent and omnipresent threat of disappointing someone or, much worse, being disappointed themselves, most people would never do one single useful thing if they could possibly help it.*

This is why I personally never look forward to things. Things don't like me and they don't like you, either. Death to things.

It was eventually determined that all humans, no matter which end of the psychological sandwich they preferred to nosh on, were too weird and gross and rude and just plain *disturbing* to be allowed to leave their planet unchaperoned. At least until they could buckle down and burn a couple of cities to the ground in a spasm of existential panic like a proper species. Each and every single individual human freakshow traveling offworld was to be accompanied by a friendly, clearly labeled volunteer who would work hard to keep those grubby icky eager fingers off the breakables long enough to figure out how to get anyone from Monkey Planet to play nicely with others.

The Great Octave officially called it the Cosmic Duet Extra Mandatory Not At All Offensive Cultural Exchange and Welcome Program.

Humans called it the Buddy System.

No one liked it very much, so it remains in place to this day.

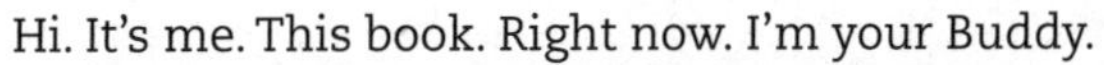

Hi. It's me. This book. Right now. I'm your Buddy.

Nobody *special*, thank goodness. Perish the thought. Just your friendly neighborhood bouncing heart-shaped disco ball of all-illuminating but very understanding fire, back in the action and eager to help you follow along with the tricky spoken word breakaway of this particular intergalactic . . . well. Swan song.

Hold tight. You've tuned in just in time. I'll catch you up on everything and everything else and everything further's favorite auntie while the band warms up backstage. Don't get antsy. The great acts are always a little late to go on.

Shake a leg, if you've got 'em. There's a *killer* riff about to kick in.

Cue the drums. Cue the pyro. Cue the insatiable beast whose inability to commit caused most of these problems in the first place: that fickle yet ever-beckoning spotlight.

Because the truth is, the trouble left on the stage at the conclusion of the last act began, not with swans or the Dutch East India Company or the smug Australian coastline, but with a rather tall, briefly dashing creature named Joseph Campbell. A mid-tier cryptid born in a large, quite lumpy, utterly unsoothable country called America, to a family so embarrassingly normal he felt compelled to invent the hero's journey, whereupon, for the next century or so, nearly everyone with two sheets of paper to rub against a pen proceeded to copy his homework and clock off early for cocktails.

These are his victims.

2.

Where Have They Gone?

Once upon a time (a phrase that's going to be doing quite a bit more work in this sentence than it's used to) in a very large, very elegant, shockingly normal human hotel room, there snoozed a hardheaded, glamdrunk, exquisitely eyebrowed, emotionally available (for a limited time only), tinsel-hearted, assigned fabulous at birth, technically impossible and existentially toxic biped about whose precise medical status, legal identity, and, most importantly, temporal coordinates, no one could quite agree, except to exasperatedly admit, at the conclusion of a number of private think-tank brainstorming sessions, that her name was Mira Wonderful Star, née Myra Strauss, and she was supposed to be dead.

. . . ish.

Within a few meters of this face-down, passed-out, body-glitter-barnacled co-savior of planet Earth, the following happened to be thrown about willy-nilly without one poor orphaned thought for who might have to tidy it all up: an uncharged phone; a very beautiful befrazzled coat called Robert, lying in a crumpled heap with quite a bit of cocktail spilled on it; a pair of thick hazmat gloves in a heap of limp deflated partially-burnt finger-sacks; an unplugged but still-glowing standard hotel-issue wood-paneled AM/FM digital alarm clock; the remains of a cheeky midnight kebab and a petrol station bottle of prosecco; a novelty oversize frosted-glass microphone full of jelly babies, whose engraved windscreen read: 100th METAGALACTIC GRAND PRIX! 10th PLACE—*Almost Adequate!*; what appeared to be an off-market, unconscious Care Bear slumped face down over the balcony; and the peacefully sleeping silver form of Microsoft's iconic 1997–2004 Office Assistant, winner of the one hundredth Metagalactic Grand Prix, who, despite being nearly eight feet tall and also a paper clip, was very much the little spoon in a certain lead singer's almost adequate embrace.

That big spoon went by the name of Decibel Jones, more or less as we left him during our previous bat time-slash-channel, a very unsober week or two after he publicly interfered with a Christmas carol on behalf of primate-derived intelligence. In a sprawling concert hall/military installation doing its very best to look like the South Wharf Hilton in Melbourne, Australia, circa 2018 (and starting to lose projection cohesion around the hallway ice machines), gamely attempting to oversleep long enough to miss the municipal bus past the hero's journey and on to the rest of his life.

With skill born of long practice, Decibel Jones extracted himself from his hotel room without waking what was clearly a mistake and/or digital abomination. He detoured through the bathroom just long enough to throw a kimono with a depressed goldfish on the back over his new work uniform—last year's iconic mango-pistachio-coconut striped pants tighter than the orbit of Mercury round the sun. He pitched the crusty rump end of last night's kebab into the Üürgama Corp Matter Whisperer (currently disguised as a mint-green and heather-gray wall-mounted soap dispenser) and popped a cigarette back out. Then quietly, shakily, Decibel leaned over the railing of a hotel balcony that was really trying very hard but could only keep up the pretense of *being* a hotel balcony for five to ten more minutes.

The man who saved the world, approaching the business end of middle age with the attitude of a child gingerly poking a beached jellyfish with a stick to see if the revolting thing mightn't still be alive, suddenly found himself with rather a lot of time on his hands. Wild acreages of endless, plodding time. Time enough to consider . . . well, just about anything, at least once. Twice if there was a martini in it for him. He stared down into a pastel ocean of sleepy post-Prix hungover sentient flowers and pondered every beautiful, stupid thing that had so rudely happened at him of late.

He'd hardly had the chance before now. Just one shock after another with no tea interval to stretch your legs. But he was doing all right, wasn't he? He hadn't hauled his lower jaw up over his own head and swallowed just for an outside chance at escape yet. Not even once. In fact, Mr. Jones had always considered himself a fair hand at the care and feeding of life's heftier surprises.

The kind that jump out from behind a rusty bin and stab your personal timeline precisely in the elbow.

The kind that gets so focused on *happening* that it completely neglects to leave you with any tools at all to imagine the topography of the day after all that happening *stops*.

The kind that happens to everyone, but somehow always seemed a lot louder, more complicated, and paid much more attention to production value when they happened to Decibel Jones.

He personally thought of them as Black-Tie Events.

Because every time one happens, people expect you to wear a suit about it.

Marriage.

The death of a loved one.

Divorce.

Arraignment.

Becoming a parent.

Meeting two kids called Omar Calişkan and Myra Strauss in a Shoreditch nightclub that charged no cover for rats or musicians and their subsequent triple-lutz stop, drop, and roll into fame and fortune. Into becoming Oort St. Ultraviolet and Mira Wonderful Star. Into becoming the Absolute Zeroes to his Decibel Jones. And then hitting every rock-star cliché stop on the local train to disappointment, terminating at that old grim *VH-1 Where Are They Now?* final station, all riders disembark, this train has completed its service for the day.

You know. *That* sort of thing.

The sort of thing you never see coming, any more than a swan that *really* shouldn't be that color.

The sort of thing you only get through by the skin of the *skin* of your teeth.

The sort of thing that's *awfully* hard to get over once it's done with you.

And just recently, rather a lot has done its business on, around, underneath, through, and concerning this leggy brown hole-in-the-heart. Some of it at least technically impressive. Most of it a mess. And yes, a *bit* over-the-top. A fairly amusing portion of it is still happening. To be perfectly honest, it's an all-hours rave of UV-reactive, two-drink minimum, dirty-bass trashfires down there in the soul of Decibel Jones. The erstwhile glamrock messiah went from chewing the cuffs of his leather jacket for protein and making banter with primary school mums about the good old days to being the actual, living, breathing, pants-on-head, god-save-us-all Chosen One—in the name of Harry Potter, Frodo Baggins, and Luke Skywalker amen—faster than you can say: *Terribly sorry, sir, I seem to have misplaced my magic ring and/or volcano.*

It's a lot to process without a direct-to-camera monologue from a tastefully decorated confessional booth.

But after the lights were shut off and the glitter-cannons and water-effects tidied up and points tallied and results announced and the planet spared and the species saved and the unspeakably awkward emotional consequences of time travel ruthlessly ignored, denied, repressed, crushed into a junkyard scrap-cube, and fired without hesitation into the sun, a cry went up from that tall drink of perpetually unsatisfied yearnings perilously close to stacking it off a Hilton balcony. The cry of a C-student the day after graduation, scared to his shoelaces that hood and gown isn't half enough to protect him, facing down a world in which it truly seems every imaginable thing worth doing has already been said, done, cancelled, successfully rebooted, and cancelled again. A hero whose saga concluded semi-satisfactorily but remained ever-so-inconveniently alive to wonder what precisely the half-life of a denouement might be. Who has found his next classes being taught, not by one of the many beefy genetic experiments attempting to crossbreed the DSM-V's section on childhood emotional abuse and a football he'd known in his scholastic career, but by no one at all.

Except, just maybe, a black swan, in a black tie, holding a very black paddle indeed.

And the cry was a question, and the question was this:

What am I supposed to do now?

An absurd little German fellow once wrote about what happens when you stare too long into the abyss. When Decibel Jones stared into the abyss, it roused itself immediately and whispered, by extraordinary coincidence, the very same thing it said to that self-same absurd little German fellow when *he* ogled it so long ago:

Get a job.

Weep, for there are no more worlds to conquer?

No.

Return home in triumph to lead the new human empire to greatness in better shoes and more eyeliner than anyone has ever done before?

Please don't.

Retire quietly? Flounce off to Skye or Malaga or Proxima Someplace for sangria and an anxiety chaser? Live that en-suite post-scarcity hashtag-best-life with a lot of positive fan mail below the feed-spout of a wall-mounted beef Wellington and whiskey dispenser? Maybe get called back to be the warm fuzzy nostalgia act during the voting interval show at the next Grand Prix, simply *bathing* in the bubbles of all the chatter about how good you still look?

Also no.

Write a completely brilliant new album as quickly as possible before everyone forgets you all over again and you end up back in Croydon forced to commit such ghastly crimes against glamour as *paying the bills* and *popping down to the shop for milk* and *inevitably starting a podcast?*

Sure. You feel up to that?

Change the subject, get very drunk immediately, and avoid all your problems?

Absolutely not.

Repair your relationships, sober up, start exercising, eat right, stay hydrated, embrace commitment, parenthood, change, responsibility, neutral earth tones, four-door sedans with crumple-zones, this brave new world that has such drooling space monsters innit?

Ew. Only if there are truly *no other entertainment options on the table and no one is watching.*

Then surely, if no one needed him for anything actually important, and they clearly didn't, and likely never would again, Decibel Jones felt he had earned the absolute *right* to get powerfully depressed, lay in bed in the dark going back and forth between the "gin" port and the "affirmations" nozzle on an Alunizar therapy orb, post vague anxiety-haiku to social media about how much better he was doing while doing nothing whatsoever to get better, and ultimately convince himself that he was fine and definitely not emotionally pulverized by the very idea of tomorrow.

In the face of all these many quite good options, the abyss simply repeated:

No, you walnut, just . . . get a job. You know, like a regular person. Do *something.*

Decibel Jones looked Mr. and Mrs. Abyss Q. Abyss, Esq. unflinchingly in the eye and replied:

How very dare you?

But as it happened, Decibel Jones already had a job. He just couldn't quite get his head all the way around what it was.

It wasn't time for the rest of his post-hero's journey adventures in space to begin.

It was time for Decibel Jones and the Absolute Zeroes' Contractually Obligated Publicity & Interstellar Diplomacy Tour to begin.

Right now. Today.

Just as soon as yesterday wore off.

That tour, the ship it meant to ride out on, and frosted-glass trophies that pointedly diminished in quality as one moved down the ranks, were the sole prizes given directly to the participants. The policy was supposed to discourage glory-seekers, though it absolutely never had.

No one had ever explained very much about what might

happen after the Grand Prix to the human contingent, largely because no one particularly expected humanity to survive the Grand Prix. While they didn't like to make a big fuss about it, the Galactic Broadcasting Union did have an entertainment-empire-slash-actual-empire to run. All Grand Prix contestants were at least room-temperature commodities on the press circuit, but particularly the ones that had new and interesting limbs or other protruding parts for galactic citizens to shake or gawk at or uncomfortably stroke or poke or lick or otherwise try out for themselves. New limbs are exciting. New protruding parts lead the evening news. Therefore, the GBU had fallen into the habit of maintaining and administering its vast domain via extended postgame press junket.

Participation is mandatory.

Which was why Mira Wonderful Star, despite being twenty-two years old and freshly scooped from the timestream by an interdimensional red panda named Öö to bring it home for Planet Earth, couldn't possibly be memory-wiped and returned to her point-of-origin before anyone noticed a missing drummer, despite the highlighted text in every clause in every sub-paragraph in the Keshet rules concerning mucking about with causality.

Think of the ratings drop. The people want what they want.

Only two exemptions have ever been granted by the GBU. The first, posthumously, went to Milim Diode, the unassuming solo torch singer who represented the delicate mothlike Slozhit during the fifty-fifth Metagalactic Grand Prix and catastrophically dechrysalized due to malfunctioning stage effects during the climax of her immortal breakup anthem "When I Think About You I Dissolve Myself in Nutritional Acid."

The second went to Oort St. Ultraviolet of the Absolute Zeroes, who'd taken one look at the proposed itinerary and said: *No, I don't think so*, with such plainspoken finality that the GBU handlers simply wandered off, deeply confused about what they'd been doing with their lives to date and how to fix it now. Both Decibel Jones and Mira Wonderful Star would eventually try to repeat their bandmate's impressive tone. By the time anyone stopped laughing, they'd achieved orbit around the supermassive planet of Capsid 5, the breadbasket of the Voorpret Mutation, for a three-song set plus mining rights negotiations on *Good Morning Putridity*, the hottest breakfast talk show among the highly contagious zombie hipster sentient prion set.

It wasn't all bad, or at least it wasn't meant to be. Plenty of time and space and camera-coverage for getting to know one's MGP graduating classmates, hilarious cloning mishaps, and teaching aliens to love between mandatory publicity stops, summits, conferences, and depositions, while traveling at speeds that would peel the face of God off and feed it to the engine core. The GBU halfheartedly tried to make it as comfortable as possible for those unused to life at FTL speeds and stale airline gravity. Fraternization was highly encouraged, as were minor crimes, as long as they were clever and fit between commercial breaks.

As long as they rendered unto the studio that which was the studio's.

The upshot of all this was that Decibel Jones and Mira Wonderful Star missed the standard galactic welcome package, the Blowout, and the incredibly awkward implementation stage of the Buddy System. In the place where the five stages of grief over what happened to their homeworld ought to have been, they had only a janky door prize starship and a year's worth of burnout ahead of them.

But just now, it was only twelve quite blurry days ago that every camera in the galaxy had been trained on Decibel's face, recording every last pore of his greatest performance-slash-controversial-home-birth. Him! Danesh Jalo of Blackpool. Decibel Jones of London, Earth, Sol System, the Milky Way, Postcode BR3 B3X. And Oort. And a time-traveling red panda who delivered the ghost of Hamlet's clearly foreshadowed ex-drummer on time, piping hot, and ready for action. No future sitcom freeze-frame finale moment was ever really going to hang up its hat next to that. Certainly not back home on a planet whose solution to having accidentally proved the Sapir-Whorf hypothesis by inventing a terrifyingly massive digital disinformation network capable of fundamentally altering the thought processes of anyone who stared too long into its abyss was to immediately get everyone's mums on it.

It was, barring the vast and depthless artificial intelligence lightly snoring in his hotel bed, the greatest thing this former Mr. Five Star Chippy employee of the month would ever do. He'd left pints of blood on that stage. Possibly a pancreas or two. Everything he had. Life, death, the song and the dance and the shine. The heavens had literally and actually opened up and the *universe itself* kicked in on backup vocals.

And he'd come tenth. Bloody *tenth*. The absolute *gall* of it. The utter *nerve*.

The final cosmic judgment of his art and soul, resounding godlike from white dwarf to red giant, was a devastating . . . *fine*. Just fine. Not magnificent, not offensive, neither sacred nor even profane. *Almost*, as the novelty oversize cocktail glass full of hot pink jelly babies said, *adequate*.

Adequate.

Almost.

Dess felt certain he was going to sick up over the railing. He gagged, suppressed a watery burp, and any further emetic progress was interrupted by the unmistakable sounds of sheets rustling as a ghastly mistake rose from the depths of slumber behind him.

Then the voice rose, too.

Vast and cold and impersonal as the satellite graveyards of the Udu Cluster from whence it came. Full of kittenish flirt and incomprehensible maths.

"It looks like you're trying to cope with the sudden catastrophic breakdown of your entire self-conception. Would you like help with that?"

Whereupon, Decibel Jones, just as the unbearable pressure of the thing rang the bell for last call and brassily informed him that he didn't have to go home but he couldn't stay there, just at the precise moment when the new age dawned and the universe's mysteries laced up their fuck-me boots and gave *Homo sapiens sapiens* that come-hither stare, just then, facing down the sheer power of the awkwardness contained in the morning-after small talk that lay before him, briefly imagined himself employed in an office that involved, not just a printer, but toner as well, and very seriously considered pitching himself into the sea.

The Keshet Effulgence was entirely prepared for this. After all, *nothing* is ever a Keshet's first go round the carousel. They've done it all before and they're going to do it again. Which does sound a bit threatening.

It should.

Horses go up and down and round and round, the saddles are delicately scented with children's vomit, the attendant hates you and everything you stand for, and ex–Grand Prix contestants tend to have a rather monstrous time adjusting to life after glam and reintegrating safely into society.

Especially if they didn't win.

And not just because they're a great heap of sensitive artists who never got enough attention as children, even though they are a great heap of sensitive artists who never got enough attention as children. It's the *pressure* of the thing. Over the century-ish of its existence, the Metagalactic Grand Prix slowly replaced almost all other inter-civilization conflict resolution mechanisms, great and small. Newly discovered, borderline-sentient worlds like Earth don't just turn up when you tip out the vacuum bag every Sunday. Most years, the fight doesn't concern new neighbors whatsoever.

It concerns power.

Great and small.

Like most things that matter desperately despite no one understanding exactly how they work, the issue is logistics. Each species' placement determines their share of galactic resources and responsibilities for the cycle. It is the most complicated way to yell, and enforce, *loser buys the next round* in the middle of a crowded game-day pub ever devised.

Losing by a little can mean loss of strategic mining rights or being required to fund a better-performing species' research and development into anti-you technology. Losing badly can mean famine. Or worse, having no choice but to send a whole bright-eyed hopeful generation of innocents out into the vastness of space to sit in on every local school board administrative meeting in the galaxy. A missed note in the shower offends only the shampoo. A missed note at the Grand Prix can tank your entire tech sector before you hit the key change. It's simply too much pressure without a suit and a few years in a decompression chamber.

Several charitable organizations have devoted themselves to the needs of the ex-contestant community. Their late-night commercials licensed the tearjerker Esca sixth-placer "In the Arms of the Studio System" to play pitifully over pleas for tax-deductible donations to fund the establishment of nonprofit no-kill shelters that provide medical care, food, recreation, and healthy socialization while experienced rescue staff seek out forever homes for these vulnerable creatures.

The largest of these, the Royal Society for the Prevention of Cruelty to Artists, was run by the Keshet. After all, those fuzzy timestream-botherers understood better than anyone else the bleak, hollow feeling of time passing you by without so much as the common courtesy to circle back round, follow you to a hotel, and steal your kidneys. As part of their outreach, the RSPCA provides complimentary Alunizar therapy orbs, a lifetime's supply of kibble, and a commemorative starship to all entrants, as well as a private en-suite ecosystem on Glemsel 7004, a gorgeous little manufactured planet owned and operated by the RSPCA as an assisted-living facility for mature ex-contestants where they can run and play as nature intended.

Decibel Jones sucked down the dregs of his cigarette as he planted his feet and aimed himself toward his presumed final splattering place, and onward to the inevitable memorial concert, unsettling World Cup closing ceremony hologram, celebrity-cover greatest hits album, and forever secure position on the wedding and school formal playlist circuit.

Instead, he slammed dead center in the glowing lavender cross-hatch of the Üürgama Corp Instant Regret Net so thoughtfully provided by the RSPCA to the contestants' dormitories at every single Metagalactic Grand Prix since the first one.

The unconscious Day-Glo teddy bear still operating that balcony as his sole practical and emotional support system groaned as the purple beams crisped his fur into frizz.

"Well, fuck me dead," Decibel whispered as the net's Comfort-Laser technology let him down easy and cheerfully redistributed his momentum and released the excess energy as a refreshing piña colada scent. "That's embarrassing. How much *have* I had to drink, Wonderful?"

His answer came in the form of a dear, familiar face that popped up between the crackling lavender laser beams that framed her glorious cheekbones like an 1980s mall portrait. Bold eye, bold lip, hair the color of an oil slick.

And so young. So impossibly, terrifyingly, confrontationally young.

"Mushy, mushy, Dess," whispered the face of Mira Wonderful Star, erstwhile girlfraud, current percussionist, and deeply upsetting, cosmos-threatening paradox. "You look an absolute *fright*. Ready to get a head start on that whole 'rest of our lives' gig?"

The dead-lite drummer stumbled slightly over the upside-down and unplugged AM/FM alarm clock that contained the full and snoozing codebase of Clippy's backup band. As she caught herself on the railing, the degenerate ursine balcony resident nearby shot out one ice-cream colored paw and crushed her bare hand in a grip like the end of history. Mira's warm expression flipped instantly to horror.

"I really wouldn't do that, pet. Er. Not pet. That's offensive. Mr. . . . Mr. Something. Just . . . don't? I haven't got my gloves and you know what they say about no glove—"

Then the drummer exited, survived by a bear.

Mira Wonderful Star disappeared from the face of the world in a burst of festively iridescent shimmer.

Life is beautiful and life is stupid. It's as true as it's ever been. Never give more weight to one than the other, so on and so forth. This is the First General Unkillable Fact of the endlessly bestselling *Goguenar*

Gorecannon's Unkillable Facts, the most beloved children's book in the history of children.

And the forces of stupid are bound and determined to unbalance that immortal equation forever, if they can possibly manage it. That is their highest goal. No more beauty. All stupid all the time, as far as the eye can see.

Shortly after Decibel Jones barely prevented all of humanity from failing its cosmic entrance exams, a large fragment of absolute *foolishness* drifted into sensor range of a single, lonely ship as it cruised innocently through uncharted space toward the next stop on that endless publicity tour like a sweet chub-cheeked kid with a basket full of croissants who really does believe the forest will let him make it all the way to Grandmother's house before dark.

Aw. Bless his heart.

3.

Give That Wolf a Banana

Just as Decibel Jones and Mira Wonderful Star were turning up late to remotely cut the virtual ribbon on the Lummutis new content expansion zone occupying the whole of the star system known as the Jucător Area-of-Effect, and several weeks after the ninety-eight-pound weakling that was the human conception of physics got well and truly shoved in its locker with its underpants pulled up over its head, every individual specimen of *Homo sapiens sapiens*, on every continent, received the standard galactic welcome package and orientation materials in the post, at the precise same millisecond.

Yes, those unsettling months left Earth strapped into a existential Gravitron ride with the speed setting stuck between "Tooth-Confetti" and "The Cold Disregard of an Uncaring God" with a SORRY WE MISSED YOU, WILL RETURN sign straining across the entrance whose novelty clock hands pointed accusingly outward at both being and nothingness. But it turned out to be just fiendishly difficult to find anyone in the galaxy who still recognized the phrase "print media."

Humanity's collective near-death experience turned out

to be the best thing that ever happened to Agnes Munt, owner and manager of Ream a Little Ream of Me 24-Hour Print, Copy & Photo in East Kilbride. At the chime of the little brass bell over her door, sciatica-prone, trifocaled, home-dyed ginger, widowed-and-looking Agnes emerged to face down several rather unusually shaped customers in full Utorak diplomatic armor, whose height and width were simply beyond the capabilities of low-end Scottish commercial real estate to contain.

Ding.

Agnes glanced over the sheer size and significance of the job. She fished in her cardigan for a pack of nicotine gum. She thought about having a pitcher of white sangria with peaches floating in it on a deck in Spain. Then she sighed deeply, with the weight of inevitability in her monotone voice, and said:

"For another 15p per, you can upgrade to our hi-gloss premium finish—please don't drink the toner, sir, it costs more than the blood of Christ himself—now have you got all your text and images on a USB drive?"

Was Agnes Munt of East Kilbride the only print shop in the world? Was she the best? The cheapest? Certainly not. What she *was* was open at three a.m. on a Wednesday.

Ding.

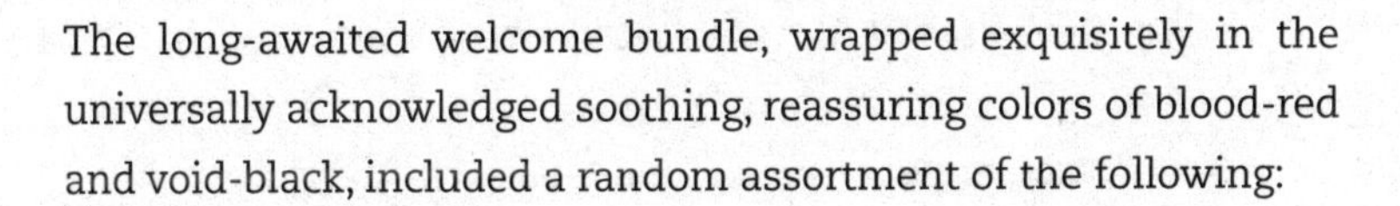

The long-awaited welcome bundle, wrapped exquisitely in the universally acknowledged soothing, reassuring colors of blood-red and void-black, included a random assortment of the following:

- A commemorative bright yellow *I'm New Here Please Be Patient* badge with each individual human person's name and today's date neatly printed on it.

- A mid-range gift certificate to one of seven semi-popular all-inclusive resort moons.
- A copy of the beloved children's classic *Goguenar Gorecannon's Unkillable Facts*.
- A heart-shaped box filled with a selection of authentic sweet, savory, and explosive snack items from each of the Great Octave species' alleged cuisines.
- A complimentary sports water bottle with a friendly furry eerily red panda–like Keshet face printed on it over the phrase *You Put the Time in the Coconut and Drink 'Em Both Up* in Comic Sans.
- An Üürgama Corp 100 percent emissions-free voltage-adaptable Happy Princess Pendant and Earrings Set capable of replacing a compact economy-size planet's fossil fuel usage for three to five years, in one of four collectible colors.
- A situationally appropriate selection of large-print brochures developed by trusted xenopsychology experts from only the most empathetic and diplomatic species, and printed, collated, and folded with something very nearly approximating love and care by Agnes Munt of East Kilbride, with such comforting titles as:

    So You're Not Alone in the Universe

    How to Win Friends and Influence Aliens When You Lack Even Rudimentary Mind-Control Abilities

Queer Eye for the Straight Planet: 12,784 Hot Summer Tips to Makeover Your Stunted Society (Number 9,321 Will Shock You. Please Call the Above Number for Revival Instructions Directly after Reading Number 9,320)

Everything You Ever Wanted to Know about Not Getting Eaten but Were Too Supremely Confident of Your Place in the Food Chain to Ask

What to Expect When You Were THAT Wrong About Physics

This End Up: Inter-Phylum Dating for Dummies

Diurnal Egg-Laying Galliform Junglefowl Protein Suspension for the Soul: First Contact and YOU

Are You There, Galaxy? It's Me, a Dumb Useless Baby Species

Beneath all of this each recipient found a matte-black *Visit Beautiful Sagrada* calming sleep mask to take the edge off the inevitable post-anthropic-principle ice-cream headache.

Beneath *that*, each resident received a legally binding receipt for Earth's share of the Milky Way's communal resources for the new cycle, as well as an invoice itemizing Earth's expected family contribution to said resource-potluck. Something about the premium hi-gloss finish and cardstock quality spoke of heady concepts like *nonnegotiable*, *mandatory*, and *past due*.

Humanity's tenth place winnings included:

- Colonization rights to the Sol System, hereby retained by current occupants. (*Courtesy of the departure of the Alunizar Colonization Party Bus Fleet, who insisted loudly that they were just in the neighborhood, even though no one asked.*)
- One Beautiful Biosphere™ EZ Plug-In Air Freshener with Two-Pin 230 Volt Equator Interface and Bonus Icecap-Refreshing Spritz in New Car scent. (*Courtesy of the Elakh Junk Drawer on beautiful lightless Sagrada, where the secrets of the ancients are entombed.*)
- Mining rights to the Outer Krzno Belt. (*Courtesy of the Utorak, transportation to or from, maps of, and equipment suitable for extracting ghemui from the Outer Krzno Belt not included. Ghemui is a semiprecious mineral whose color is a shade that got lost on the way from magenta to green known as viridipuce. Depending on preparation, ghemui truly is both an effective floor cleaner and an exquisite dessert topping, as well as forming the base matrix for the Utorak Formations primary weapons technology, and overall just looks quite nice in an engagement ring. It is also the only thing of any value in the Outer Krzno Belt, unless your soul truly cries out for radioactive regolith.*)
- Cures for three out of four common cancers, diabetes, endometriosis, cystic fibrosis, seasonal allergies, prog rock, arthritis, and the terrible twos. (*Courtesy of the Voorpret Vaccine Pits. If Earth had managed ninth place, the Pits would have disgorged prophylactics against lupus,*

kidney stones, and Toryism as well, and certainly the galaxy's viral friends wish humanity better luck next time.)

- Permission to permanently settle Ya-Rayach, an Earth-analogue world in orbit around Barnard's Star. (*Courtesy of the previous owners, the Esca. One moon, six seasons, blue oceans, green plants, and barely any cyclops living on it.*)
- A generous weekly farm share from Hygge, your friendly Yoompian abundance sphere.
- A sought-after time-share on Wirrwarr, a Slozhit property management project. (*Six months nonconsecutive. No more than 100,000 guests at a time, leave all cities as found to avoid one-star guest ratings, 1.2 billion pound cleaning fee required regardless of conditions upon checkout.*)
- A free trial and planetary budget-conscious coupon worth 30 percent of an all-access subscription to the Keshet Holistic Live Total Timeline Broadcast. (*Courtesy of the Keshet, a functionally infinite entertainment streaming service featuring high-quality live feeds of qualifying alternate timelines, as well as all your favorite comfort programming such as* The Only Way Is the Unappeasable Gullet of Narthex, Real Hiveminds of Szivorion, My Little Meleg: Friendship Is Trash, *and* Antiques Roadshow.)
- An incoming squadron of childcare providers, hard-bitten preschool ranch hands, and professional tut-tutters. (*Courtesy of the Ursulas, a race of free-floating radically collectivist gas-filled glass orbs. Childcare availability is a major interstellar hot-button issue, but hey, kids love balloons!*)

Of course, the *to each according to their needs* bit has always been rather more fun than that pesky *from each according to their abilities* bit. Earth's abilities having been evaluated as falling somewhere between "adorable" and "who?" Humanity's new chore chart included immediate surrender of:

- Naming rights to the star known as Sol to the Smaragdi.
- Two hundred thousand highly trained, locked-and-loaded groundskeepers to the Klavaret Bramble.
- Five hundred thousand volunteers for Sziv-related janitorial duty in the Pleiades. Strong stomachs mandatory, for the Sziv are singular masses of shrieking hot-pink nano-algae possessing immense unified consciousnesses who will happily go to war rather than do their own washing-up.
- 1.5 million of humanity's most powerful ranked-competition nurturers to the crèche system of Far Kleepuv to fill out the infant-to-toddler day care platoons. In exchange, each day care facility on Earth must admit one nonhuman child and promise to be civil to it most of the time.
- All currently elected officials to report immediately to the Klavaret colony of Memnu 7 for enrollment in the Home Despot Summer Scouts Program. There, they will experience the single most impactful contribution the somewhat scatterbrained botanical culture ever gave to the galaxy. The whole of the planet is occupied with a kind of semi-leaveable fat camp for the moral compass. Here legislators, executives, and any loose monarchs still wandering about can

enjoy a radical re-personalization course of arts and crafts, canoeing, team sports, sing-alongs, basic socialization classes, sharing practice, a full-service spa offering detoxifying anti-capitalism wraps, soothing contrarianism massages, healthful narcissism cleanses, and regular therapeutic smacks to the back of the head administered by on-site ascended energy beings and qualified perspective-chiropractors. Resurrections complimentary. Graduating Scouts will be returned home on a case-by-case basis once they earn their Basic Decency Badge.

- One representative to the Galactic Broadcasting Union board of directors.
- All animals beginning with C (capybaras, crocodiles, camels, cats, etc.).
- All fossils, completed or not, pens down, no peeking at your neighbor's work.
- Humanity's best holiday cookie recipe. (70 percent+ must agree on the cookie in question to fulfill this line item.)
- All fission, fusion, and biological weapons, no matter how cute or fun. No human fission, fusion, and biological weapons have received designations greater than *cute* and *fun*, because the average Yoompian light lunch packs more firepower and long-lasting environmental damage. Hand them over, no cheating, the Yoomp will know.
- A complete map of the human genome.
- One year's production of the Polish cherry liqueur designated *wishniak* to be paid in tribute to Hrodos the Eternal Twilit Storm and don't ask questions.

- *All* Jet Skis, ball pits (with balls, no skimping), and chewing gum, to be evenly distributed among all species by the Keshet, in order to facilitate understanding of the authentic human experience, especially the ball pits, please and thank you.

All items were to be packed *neatly* and left on the International Date Line for pickup.

The ball pit extraction would bear some explanation, if Goguenar Gorecannon hadn't managed to cover it in advance with the Nineteenth Unkillable Fact: *Economics is mostly a game of make-believe where someone takes all your toys away right before you win and then tells you that's just the free hand of the market when you* can see *them hiding your stuff behind their back. But if there's one thing that unites all the systems on all the worlds I've ever bothered to know about, one thing I could tell you little ones concerning which industries might offer safe employment opportunities in the future, it's this.*

If it's fun, it's valuable. Life is long and lots of it is dreadful. Everyone's looking for something to make them forget the quenchless void of essential meaninglessness, because the quenchless void of essential meaninglessness is dead boring. If you can whip up three minutes of actual entertainment that distracts somebody from the inexorable lurching of time toward their own death, you'll never starve. If you can manage more than three minutes, you'll probably end up king of something, which ironically, isn't fun at all.

When asked why ball pits specifically, the Chief Communications Archon for the Keshet Effulgence simply replied: *Wheeeee!* and cannonballed, tailfirst, into the press pool, which would thereafter be an actual inflatable pool filled with colorful little plastic balls that had no political or cultural significance whatsoever, but somehow, made everything a Chief Communications Archon had to say just a little bit easier to bear.

A few select humans received individualized packages that contained all the usual materials, plus more literature concerning what they personally might expect and/or run screaming from in the near future.

Decibel Jones was one of them. His folder positively *bulged* with pamphlets:

Everything I Need to Know I Learned Six Months Ago When My Reality Was Irreparably Shattered

So You Completed the Hero's Journey and It Didn't Fix Even One of Your Many, Many Emotional Problems

Zen and the Art of Narcissistic Supply

The 168-Hour Sadness Week

People Are from Zaplacic Major, Musicians Are from a Hell Dimension Known as Pyntingar the Plane of Bloodhunger

Guns, Germs, Follow-Up Albums, and Other Things You Should Never Put in Your Face-Holes

Heel, Heels, and Healing: A Guide to Working Breeds

This Is Your Brain on the Very Temporary Attention of Strangers Who Don't Actually Care About You One Bit

That last one had a grim black-and-white picture of a nice shepherd's pie smashed on a rainy pavement with a footprint through it and a mangy bat hunched over it, gnawing on the peas and carrots.

Ding.

4.

The One Who Stays and the One Who Leaves

Despite humanity getting nearly everything it had ever writ-ten heartfelt letters to science fiction claiming to have been good enough this year to find in its stocking, even the fully automated luxury gay space neoliberal future has its little disappointments.

For example, when Mira vanished off the surface of Litost and reappeared in an orbiting starship, though it looked very *like* teleporting, it couldn't possibly have been, because transporters are not, and never will be, a viable technology.

Not because no one invented it. They *always* invent it. If the famous Klavar vegan chef Kasutu Indica found time to invent the lettuce-soother, a device used to calm and appease all those heaps of distressed, smashed, blistered, crushed, clabbered, roasted, and otherwise profoundly injured produce in her kitchen, then there was never any chance something as massively convenient as teleportation wouldn't violently hook up with the maladjusted laboratory intern of its dreams someday.

It just couldn't make it past focus group testing.

Not because it's not possible to disassemble an organic being to his, her, or otherwise, constituent atoms, fax them across the inky void, and reassemble them on the other side.

It very much *is* possible.

And not because doing so technically kills the original person and reassembles a clone, or a golem, depending on how you like your metaphysical toast buttered.

It *absolutely* does that. But it's still better than flying economy.

And certainly not because teleportation would make it very difficult for screenwriters and novelists everywhere to create narrative tension and end chase scenes forever.

It, admittedly, would, but no one cares. Writers are an invasive species. If you don't believe it, decorate a small corner of your home with small tables, chairs, ferns, cafe lighting, pastries, and a pleasantly burbling stimulant/depressant dispenser, and within a week you'll be overrun with bespectacled vermin nervously asking where they can find a power point and not paying for anything.

No, the trouble with teleportation is that it *ruins damn near everything.*

Galactic history ebbs and flows like denim waistlines. Empires, and visible midriffs, come and go. But virtually every species, sooner or later, throws something like a teleporter against the wall of the universe to see if it sticks.

The wall then violently explodes and everyone has to attend a lot of early-morning meetings, the agendas of which consist of the five stages of product testing:

1. Oh god, what have we done?

2. Undo it, undo it!

3. Our descendants will definitely try to un-undo it, so . . .

4. How do you punish children before they're born?

5. Asking for a friend.

In fact, the early post-singularity technological clown car usually ends up in a white-knuckle race to see who will be the first to shove a trusting dog into a matter-disintegrator and hope for the best, because if your local phylum can collect anything remotely doglike on the other end, it's trivially easy to rule the universe. Chuck a handful of cheeky little bombs down the science chute and quicker than you can say *Beam me up, unkind regional stereotype*, every government you know has a cello-wrapped gift basket of doomsday devices delivered to their door in thirty minutes or less. You get a bomb! You get a bomb! And *you* get a bomb! And if you don't want another one to materialize in your planetary core, kindly remand any and all valuable resources, personnel, and trendy food items to the following address, care of your new overlords, please and thank you.

The ancient Alunizar, unsurprisingly to anyone who has ever met an Alunizar and/or their sweat-drenched manifest destiny fetish, pulled the trigger on that like a fairy-floss-riddled eight-year-old laughing maniacally as they spray jets of water down a clown's mouth at the colonization carnival.

To this day, the Alunizar word for "transporter" translates to *a short but super fun war*.

But the good times never last. Once one kid has the season's hot new toy, everyone has to have one, and the resulting mess means no more playdates for anybody.

But surely one can use them *nicely*. Travel about, shorten the commute, ship goods that absolutely positively have to be there instantaneously, make long-distance friendships, romances, and the concept of ever bothering to walk anywhere a sad Victorian ghost of an era long past.

Unfortunately, it is a truth universally acknowledged that any single person or object in the possession of a matter transporter must, eventually, somehow, going in, coming out, or along the way, explode.

That's fine for bombs, exploding is their entire gig. But the simple act of putting an organic being, no matter how annoying they are, into a transporter device is considered a crime against all sentient life on every world with two lawyers, a gavel, and a wig to rub together.

It all comes down to maths. Maths's is just a massive clobbering buzzkill. The hall monitor of the universe. *Oh please, oh please, Mr. Maths, couldn't I have one lovely cup of fun out there in the stars?*

No, you can have detention.

And mathematics declared war on science fiction long ago.

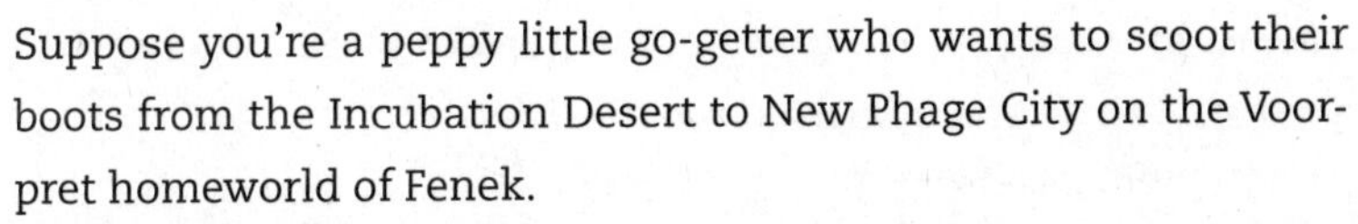

Suppose you're a peppy little go-getter who wants to scoot their boots from the Incubation Desert to New Phage City on the Voorpret homeworld of Fenek.

First, don't do that. The Voorpret are a viral species in constant search of new host bodies. You'd be infected with Gvami from accounting before you can say *this motivational kitten poster would look smashing in my cubicle.*

But if you *must* step onto a teleportation disc in one Fenekrian hemisphere, you'd better do it at speed, because the conservation of momentum hates fun. Everything is moving at a hundred thousand kilometers per hour *all the time.* It never stops. Planets don't get tired. Stars don't get stitches in their sides and reconsider the wisdom of going so hard at cardio at their age. So if you don't want to end up smeared across half a time zone, you'll have to exit the moving matter-beam booking it at three-quarters of a kilometer per second to compensate for the rotation of Fenek. At cruising altitude, since the Incubation Desert shakes its pestilent groove thing at an elevation of six hundred and seventy-one meters, and New Phage City bides its time at sea level. Going the other way? You are now a subway car sizzling through the magma layer.

And what will you find when you land?

Most likely, a very interesting death.

Rematerializing into a mass of plain old unassuming air will pump you full of fizzy-lifting embolisms, if the displacement doesn't just go off like a firecracker in a bin. (Even the most thorough of autopsies would find it impossible to tell afterward whether you were the firecracker or the bin.) But may your personal deities help you if a pollen spore drifts by while you're still dematerializing. Or a bee. Or a bit of moss with a water bear lounging on it. Or a molecule of Venice. They're part of you now, and they have opinions about canals. Any and all debris your molecules passed through on the way has a fair chance of getting sucked into the you-beam, so once you're decanted, you may find yourself full of mountain.

You will also be on fire.

Or frozen solid.

Could go either way, because if you think the conservation of momentum is a wet blanket, wait till you meet the conservation of energy, because it is *terrible* at parties. Move one electron up or down in its orbit around the atom, heat is lost or gained, and you're about to mightily piss off the entire quantum homeowners' association.

Now, in the unlikely event of anyone actually surviving all this, mathematics is happy to give you a couple more smacks across the chops before you can return to your class. See, the light that surrounded you as you dematerialized had just enough time to cross the diameter of your eye before you didn't have eyes anymore. And you passed through a lot of light very quickly on your way to the hopping underground zombie rave scene in New Phage City. The photons touched the particles of your retina and rods and cones and lenses but couldn't find the service entrance. So as soon as you have eyeballs again, all those photons are going to dumptruck themselves into your brainpan out of order, upside-down, and deeply upset.

Regrettably, you may also arrive before New Phage City was founded. Or after it crumbled to dust. Time just thumbs a rude gesture and gives up around the speed of light, and teleportation goes much, much faster than that.

So, to sum up: you can stand on that teleporter platter as cheerful, well-dressed, and well-rested as you like. (Although standing is not recommended. Bones are such divas. Child's pose is your friend.) You'll still come screaming out the other end hurtling through the sky or barreling underground through a lazy lava river, technically and legally half-water-bear, engulfed in flames, blood exploding, wildly hallucinating into nonrefundable insanity, in the past or the future, whichever one had a booking available.

Can none of this be helped by compensators, dampeners, buffers, or a subscription app designed by a Silicon Valley techbro someone accidentally fed after midnight?

Of course it can.

Then you have only to consider that, if a person *can* be deconstructed into a pattern and reconstructed elsewhere, nothing at all prevents them, or other interested parties, from reconstructing multiple totally viable and legislatively indistinguishable copies throughout civilization. Long after your death.

And that you will lose a tiny bit of your matter to the conversion process every time, rendering heavy users approximately the size of an action figure by the time they qualify for senior discounts.

And how you personally feel about trusting the reconstitution of your every precious atom to the same companies that can't keep the Wi-Fi on if it rains too hard.

And that it's just plain rude.

Transporters are the end of privacy, private property, and manners. The first and most minor consequence being the birth of a true crime renaissance, since doors become adorably quaint, locks meaningless, guest lists a joke, and your ex can beam a copy of themselves into your shower any time they like, with zero repercussions for the original when you bludgeon them to death using a volumizing shampoo bottle.

The first rule of teleportation is: No.

In fact, it may be the single worst and most destructive technology ever imagined by otherwise sentient beings, apart from social media.

In the end, every species of the Milky Way reluctantly came round to the facts of these murder elevators and voluntarily loaded all their pads, booths, capsules, handheld mobile transmitters, all-in-one headsets, barns, fashion jewelry, and vestibules onto a small uninhabited planet provided by the borderline apologetic Alunizar, sealed its orbit with vapor-mines, washed their hands of the whole sordid business, and named it Madrugada as a warning for all the generations to come.

In Old Alunizar, "Madrugada," very loosely translated, means: *fuck around and find out.*

The Keshet, a race of time-traveling red pandas who never met an impossible thing they didn't already have some idea how to pull off, got all around this by glitching out of their current long-distance temporal provider and temporarily overwriting whatever version of their multiverse-surfing selves was hanging out where they wanted to be. Which is technically not teleportation *or* murder, but skating on very thin ice on both counts and seriously considering going for the triple flip.

Thus, when Mira Wonderful Star disappeared in a shower of Christmas confetti after only barely touching that bear, she also was not technically teleporting. At least by Keshet laws, which only have anything to do with the laws of physics when they can no longer come up with reasonable excuses to skip family dinner night.

5.

To Hell with It

Shortly after Mira vanished into thick air, three entities, wildly separated by time, space, and temperament, uttered the same phrase at the same time. They spoke in three different languages, out of three alarmingly diverse mouth-apparati, in response to three different, though equally valid and intersectionally reinforcing states of extreme, high-risk, professional-grade disgust at their present circumstances.

The first: the lady herself.

Mira stopped Mira-ing on the rapidly degrading virtual lanai of a mid-range corporate hotel and instantly resumed existence-related activities somewhere very profoundly *else*. Dead center of a long, empty, blue-black lost highway stretching to Edinburgh on one end and all the way to forever on the other.

This is a place where verb tenses will go to have gotten so drunk and irrationally violent they actually feel something again.

Because wherever else she seems, or seemed, or will have been going to seem to one day never be, Myra Strauss is always—

—here.

It always feels like it's about to snow, but never does.

It is always a polite cough after midnight on Saturday, October 3.

It is always the late early twenty-first century (though a well-brought up timeline never tells). Myra Strauss is always twenty-two years old.

The stars above her always crowd out the dark. The ground below her feet is always frozen stiff. She's always wearing the top half of a spandex gold lamé Slutty C-3PO costume, a silver brocade Christmas tree skirt semi-bustled in a gauzy black shower curtain spackled with metallic blue appliqué roses, and a pair of red-sequined Dorothy Gale After Hours and Unplugged chunky heels. It is what she wore during the Metagalactic Grand Prix final last year, because it is what she wore to a sold-out Absolute Zeroes concert in Stockholm just before all her dreams came true, for as long as they could before abandoning her on this highway years down the roller-coaster track—

—or

before a red panda who wasn't really a red panda snagged her out of her trajectory and stuck her up the highest tree in the universe. High enough to reach the stars.

Mira wasn't wearing a necklace that night in Stockholm or Scotland, but she sure is now. A big, loud, gauche lime-green pendant on a thick gold chain that looks like something that would choose Mr. T as the new off-brand Green Lantern. But she's stuck with it. She cannot take it off. Ever. She's heard that so often she feels like the very real idiot who inspires suspiciously specific warnings on toasters and shampoo. *Do not prepare toast in bathtub.*

You will die. Do not drink green apple–scented high-gloss shampoo for color-treated hair. You might die. Do not take off your paralocket. You, and everyone you know, will never have lived.

It's a leash. It's a loophole.

The glitchy red panda who grabbed her hand outside that concert hall and asked if she wanted him to change her life felt so sorry for her entire subsequent situation that he went slip-and-sliding through the more unsettling and unlikely timelines to find a quantum path in which such a thing was ever invented. Then the rebellious little Keshet went even farther off the farm to find the universe in which a paralocket had been invented by someone with even the barest sense of style. That spinach-smoothie-colored monstrosity was the best Mira Wonderful Star's temporal/causality leash could possibly look.

According to Bolog the Approachably Inscrutable, Primordial Product Quality Assurance Globule, a paralocket is subtly distinct from a transporter, at least in a scholarly sense. It would indisputably be a transporter—if it ever finished the job.

But it doesn't. Ever.

When Mira leaves the ship, the paralocket keeps up a constant unbroken circuit, beaming up and beaming down, almost materializing then vaporizing again, over and over, as fast and as often as atoms move, which all comes out in the phenomenological wash as a real physical flesh-and-middling-manners human person anybody could shake hands with, provided they wear protective equipment.

But a paradox existing in two places at once and simultaneously not existing in either of them tends to put reality into anaphylactic shock. Mira can trip the light corporeal for just under an hour. Just enough time to bang a drum to the heavens and take a short bow, by no coincidence at all.

Then the atomic rubber band snaps, the affected area is flooded with tachyonic epinephrine, and she's hauled back to this road, this midnight, this quiet place where she must stay until the universe can find a power point and charge up its Mira-phone again.

Every time it happens, a physicist wakes up gasping, covered in boils, gives up, and starts studying art history instead.

Mira's ugly Hi-Vis paralocket would be worth approximately three times the annual gross galactic product, if anyone knew what it could do. But Bolog the Approachably Inscrutable is a reasonable and discreet globule.

As the current state of manufacturing classification stands, the device is legally defined as a doorstop.

Just under an hour. Enough time for a set and a touch of audience banter. Before reality throws up and Myra Strauss has to hold back its hair.

Thus, Mira is always here, even when she's everywhere else in the universe. Always standing outside a rented silver 2011 Econovan with a dent on the left rear bumper and significantly worse round the front. There is always something she doesn't want to look at just over the little mound of purple tangled grass and shadows to whom Mira is extremely and eternally grateful a few meters ahead.

And there is always a quite large male badger staring apologetically at her over the two-lane road.

The badger's name was, and is, and will always be, Douglas. Seventy-three percent of all male Scottish badgers are called Andrew or James. Twenty-six percent are Douglas. The remaining 1 percent are named Charlemagne, and perhaps the less investigated with regard to that, the better.

Douglas waves a dark shy little paw.

Mira always waves back.

The translator fungi glittering along her neckline bristle and hum, and when Douglas growls: "Nice night for it, eh?" she hears his little badger voice as a pleasant, chummy brogue instead of the usual demonic horking of Common Badgerish.

Somewhere on the Edinburgh end of eternity, the red light of a starship's core pulses steadily away like a huge dumb heart about to break.

This is the most elaborate and powerful engine room ever designed.

Mira is the engine.

An engine who wants to be so much more.

The second:

A large and temporally disrespectful red panda called Öö stared out the window of a rubbish pre-furnished one-room flat at rubbish sleety rain falling on the empty rubbish streets of an empty rubbish city, rubbishly.

Öö put his paws behind his back. His tail bristled with resentment. He'd accepted his punishment with grace. He knew the rules, after all. He'd known them the whole time. He wouldn't have enjoyed breaking them so much if he hadn't. Every Grand Prix contestant was supposed to stand on their own unique, species-appropriate number of feet and belt out their soul to the galactic rafters, if they had one. It was a test. The kids weren't meant to have the teacher flip to the back (or front) of the book and give them the answer.

But Öö had done a paradox on the carpet and needed his nose rubbed in it, plus a good swat on the snout with a newspaper. The Keshet wasn't ashamed and had no intention of apologizing for his highly anti-causality behavior. It was a classic. Pure textbook. They'd teach it in school one day.

And after reviewing the grand final playback footage, the Great Octave graciously decided that since the humans never actually asked Öö to cheat for them, it wasn't their fault and the performance would stand.

But *somebody* had been naughty. *Somebody* needed to learn a little something about respecting boundaries. And *somebody* chose to make a rude gesture and a long, loud farting sound in lieu of testifying in his own defense, so maybe if *somebody* loved humanity so much, *somebody* should serve out their sentence in a nice, intimate, pivotal human nexus era.

But this was a *bit* harsh.

Öö glanced at the rubbish human *World of Kittens* calendar hanging on his rubbish human wall, showing a rubbish fat ginger tabby eating its own rubbish fat toebeans, because apparently that sort of thing amused the rubbish human brain, rubbishly.

MARCH 24, 2020

The music stops, pauses briefly, and then starts again. The only song his en-suite prison cell allows, repeated twenty-four hours a day over panoramic views of nothing much but wall after wall of other people's windows: a series of happy, relaxed celebrities with bleached teeth and natural makeup, so you know they really do relate to the plight of the working man, all strolling through their estates, all singing "Imagine," poorly, forever.

Öö was Serving Time. Öö was in the Nick of Time.

Öö was in a Time Out.

A very special Keshet punishment for very special crimes: solitary confinement in the same day, in a place carefully chosen to maximally enrage that specific prisoner on a deeply personal level, endlessly repeated, until someone somewhere remembered to stop the torture.

And he'd had just about enough of that.

The third:

The bear who grabbed Mira just before she exited, pursued by the plot, had never really been asleep. Or passed out, hungover, nauseous, dehydrated, or coming down from anything overly interesting.

Nor was he a bear, except in the most generous taxonomical sense. His shimmering butterfly-like wings lay folded in rage against his mint-green and magenta fur. His long silken ice-blue tail snaked out behind him, braided with wildflowers and gems in the traditional fashion of his people when setting out for war. A pearly iridescent horn rose from his forehead, pointing toward tomorrow, which would probably be as hostile to the not-a-bear as yesterday had been.

The unbear's name was Mr. Snuggles, and he was a Meleg, a scion of the Tnax clan approaching the prime of his life. Like every other contestant of his species for one hundred cycles of song, he'd really tried very hard. In fact, Mr. Snuggles had poured his whole being into the thing, giving the soaring psychedelic rococo-funk ballad of early courtship's heady innocent days, "I Love You So Much I'm Going to Ruin Your Life," all he had—and still lost the Metagalactic Grand Prix rather spectacularly.

The young Tnax stared at the space where Mira suddenly wasn't. He did not notice Decibel glumly packing his coat and deliberately stepping on the clock radio cord as often as he could. He didn't even look at the 321 champion slowly dissolving from a massive paper clip into its true form, a disembodied codebase the size of a star.

The fluffy adorable winged butterbear-icorn was frozen in place, knees locked, muscles tensed into *rigor vitas*, consumed by something only he could see, some private film flickering across his enormous crystal princess eyes, a bucket of oil dumped all over a baby penguin on purpose.

Whatever the Meleg was seeing, he clearly hated every second of it and desperately wanted to hurt it back.

His eyes filled up with tears. His fur rippled with trauma. His heart-shaped nose went black and the second-to-last-place finisher of the one hundredth Metagalactic Grand Prix screamed into the dawn. A scream that started somewhere in the cells that would one day become his pretty pink belly as they hitched a ride to eternity on the shock wave of the Big Bang and ended as the hotel projection finally gave up and collapsed into a very sticky reality. A scream that echoed out into the workaday world like the death of all hope.

And then, on the surface of beautiful Litost, Mr. Snuggles smiled a long, strange smile.

All three of them, at once, into three individually handcrafted voids of despair, whispered, sighed, or chuckled:

Fuck it. Why not?

6.

This Time I Mean It

The most beloved children's edutainment franchise in the history of interstellar mixed-media content creation is, and is unlikely to ever stop being, *Goguenar Gorecannon's Unkillable Facts*, a slim, ancient, unassuming, ever-so-gently poisonous illustrated children's picture book.

Eight billion free copies were helpfully included in Earth's care package as a strategic prophylactic against any new and innovative strains of stupidity.

The sheer size of the Gorecannon estate makes the poor old Bible's sales numbers look like a lemonade stand run by a friendless urchin of only middling cuteness who hasn't the first idea which direction the *p* in *pence* ought to face.

Goguenar Gorecannon's Unkillable Facts contains undiluted, uncensored (but not for the Pisces Epsilon Publishing Hiveknot's lack of trying), unedited (again, they did try) 90-proof reliable and comprehensive laws of the universe as observed by a socially anxious Yurtmak deathrhino who was far too shy to do enough ritualistic murders to please her parents. In the opinion of trillions of parents representing hundreds of species, if you're not going to read your offspring an Unkillable Fact before bed every night, you might as well punt the little larva into the nearest municipal bin and let an old rind of gouda and a crumpled-up reactionary newspaper with powdered custard congealed on it raise them as their own.

To call the *Unkillable Facts* "beloved" would be to offensively understate the position it occupies in the emotional and intellectual culture of the civilized galaxy. After all, it's almost impossible to forget any one of Goguenar Gorecannon's Unkillable Facts. The literary nanny to which parents up and down the biological classification system entrust their children's psyches is, improbably, a Yurtmak book, the single most gleefully violent species yet discovered. In terms of mere casualty rates, many civilizations could compete for the slaughtercrown. But no one else is quite so over-the-top, head-cheerleader-with-nothing-else-going-for-her, hyperactive-cruise-excursion-director enthusiastic about it. The Yurtmak are precisely what they look like: obligate carnivores with faces like three sharks and a stag beetle stuck in an active garbage disposal who keep the spirit of murder in their hearts all the year.

If it's Yurtmak, it's going to hurt you, as the old washing machine ad copy goes. Somehow. Eventually. Thoroughly.

In the case of each and every alien baby's first bedtime story, each *Unkillable* page is lovingly envenomated with a kicky little toxin produced by the Yurtmak's tertiary jaw-sacs. As any given awestruck bundle of novelty pajamas and future angst turns the pages, the poison induces brief bursts of incredible pain, so that Gorecannon's earthy, down-home words are indelibly blistered onto the reader's more important lobes.

Many novelists have attempted to re-create this powerful pain/reading comprehension duo to plump their own sales.

But they always fail. Gorecannon's aphorisms appeal to children because they're short, riddled with exciting swear words, and jammed full of enticingly mean-spirited asides, often concerning parents and how far they can chuck themselves. Anything longer or more pleasant and people grow numb to the feeling of stirring a mug of eldritch brainacid with their fingers and power through the pain.

As the Eighth Unkillable Fact tells us: *Here's a depressing thing I thought of because I am depressed (and you will be too, babies, if not now, then soon, if not soon, then eventually): people can get used to just about anything. Some weird little creature is out there right now rolling around in your worst day like a yoomp in cold-pressed blubberjuice, ecstatically moaning:* "It just doesn't get better than this!"

And if you don't believe me, strap in, because somewhere, an even more *nauseating pervert is shrieking in a rictus of blood-agony trying to escape the best shit that ever happened to you.*

Why is that depressing? Because if you hurt people bad enough for long enough, they'll figure out a way to like it. If you give them everything they want, they'll figure out a way to despise it, and you for making it happen, and the second one happens so much faster than the first it would make your third head spin, if you have one. We're all not very much more than consistently-confused, electrocuted meat, and neither electricity nor meat really know how to be happy. Just how to avoid pain and keep going for a while longer.

No matter how many heads you have, the electric meat that is me accepts the electric meat that is you. Just the way you are.

Except that one kid. They know what they did.

For a quick demonstration of how most sentient beings feel about this large-print board book that contains no single chapter longer than a paragraph, kindly enter the nearest pub, approach anyone clearly visiting from far enough offworld that they've only just learned what an IPA is and are looking for someone to punish about it, then tell them you, personally, think Goguenar Gorecannon is somewhat overrated.

When you get out of hospital, continue reading.

The second installment in the Gorecannon Pedagogical Universe came out, with great reluctance, some twenty cycles later, entitled: *Listen Up, You Big Dumb Puddings: Some Unkillable Addendums for Adults Who Didn't Listen to Me the First Time.*

If you've got this far, you will be familiar with the First General Unkillable Fact: *Life is beautiful and life is stupid. Never give more weight to one than the other and you might end up all right. Whenever one seems about ready to wrap it all up for the other and rule the galaxy with some sort of fist, the only thing you can really be sure of is that its old friend is standing right behind, fixing to make a very loud and unignorable comeback. Which is why it stays the way it is, even though the suggestion box is gonna lose atomic cohesion any minute now. You can only ever fix one of them at a time, and wouldn't it be nice if anyone could agree on which one is the bigger problem?*

The Addendum to the First General Unkillable Fact reads as follows: *Life is beautiful and life is stupid. No, I'm not taking it back, you great lot of fucking hat racks. I don't know what you thought "unkillable" meant.*

However, my arch-editors, sub-editors, research dominatrices, punctuation inquistors, structural copyengineers, and assorted marketing conquistadors have informed me, while rattling a stick against the bars of my cage, that I have more to say on the subject.

Well, hat racks, the galaxy is the way it insists on being because the stupid is just so much more accessible *than the beautiful. So much more present. So much more interested in little old us. The beautiful is a fun weekend dad, forever busy with other people, other places, with its* real *family. It's the stupid that knuckles down, puts in the hours, and does the real day-to-day work.*

Beauty is stuck behind a paywall. Stupid is always free.

And it sure does like the look of everything you hold dear.

7.

Who Sails My Boat?

The Keshet have both won and lost every single Metagalactic Grand Prix from the first to the hundredth.

Minus one.

The Keshet won the sixty-fifth grand final with their sliphop top bop "All the Single-Plane Entities (Put a Tracking Device On It)" and its associated group line dance. They also lost the sixty-fifth grand final with an equally catchy but unfortunately choreographically fatal screamcore power ballad called "2 Legit 2 Further Stress the Probability Membrane of This Quantum Corridor."

Both are true. Both are false. Both happened; both never even thought about happening, and by the way, how very dare you? An individual Keshet plays so fast and loose with chronology that they actually exist in thousands of possible pasts, presents, and futures at the same time, moving between them so quickly that, to us slowcoaches, they seem to stand still.

Thus, the Keshet have experienced every possible variant of every possible outcome of every possible version of the contest, and they will bore you at parties about all of them. But so much congruent, simultaneous, constantly repeating agony and ecstasy means that nobody understands the real gamesmanship of the thing the way a species of red pandas who treat the multiverse as their own personal poorly drawn hopscotch court do.

Which is why they founded/never founded/will one day possibly found/forgot to get around to founding the Royal Society for the Prevention of Cruelty to Artists.

They get it.

The Great Octave and its legislative branch, the Galactic Broadcasting Union, long ago settled comfortably into that sympathy and used it to shove off the issue of individual prize winnings, such as new starships, novelty trophies, foodstuffs, or real estate opportunities to the RSPCA in perpetuity.

The pandas can afford it.

Especially the ships.

No civilization in the galaxy has, ever will have, nor ever once had, more ships at its disposal than the Keshet Effulgence. Not even the Alunizar, and they are permanently encrusted with salt over it.

But a Keshet starship is not like other girls. The Keshet can and, at the drop of a single delicious orange slice, *will* visit any and every point along any and every timeline, parastream, catbox, quantum tributary, or alternate reality.

And nick things from them. While they're in the neighborhood.

The fuzzy little biters have always had real trouble with traditional transportation. Put one in a taxi and suddenly there's a hyperactive red panda in the backseat of every possible taxi, giving and receiving every possible star rating, both drunk and sober at once, demanding small talk and shuddering in horror at it, heading toward every possible destination in every imaginable traffic condition, all at once, and only one of them left a tip.

Corporate policy changes do not usually break the FTL barrier, but the permanent bans on Keshet emanating from every surviving ride-sharing service on Earth came close.

A Keshet ship is the only conveyance that can handle more than one of the little creatures at once, structurally, ethically, legally, or emotionally. Reality gets very upset otherwise.

And perhaps the only vessel that could properly contain even one Decibel Jones.

The truth about the Effulgence Fleet, however, is highly classified. The kind of *classified* that holds a grudge. Anyone who even thinks of one day spilling these particularly spicy beans to personnel lacking fluffy striped tails are subject to emergency Rewinding at once. Which is to say: their ancestors are introduced to other, more attractive and attentive potential mates who really and truly speak their love language and never forget anniversaries. Thus, the offending blabbermouth finds themselves instantly de-borned, blinking out of an existence they now never occupied and becoming nobody's problem ever again in the first place.

But between you, me, and the techno-espionage organization next door, the truth is the Keshet have only ever constructed one ship.

One single, solitary, unremarkable mid-size economy spacecraft capable of navigating the (frankly rude) distances between the stars. To understand how that can possibly be true when there are, as we speak, two dozen Keshet vessels in a rainbow of military-industrial flavors merrily ferrying palettes of colorful plastic balls, original recipe Four Loko, and chicken curry pies from Earth to the stars, you have to take a moment, just sit right there, and understand how the Keshet became the fresh princes of time and space.

This smashed alarm clock of a species happened to evolve in close proximity to a truly mind-bricking spatial anomaly called the Empty.

It broke them. Into as many pieces as it could. Then it broke them again.

The precise nature of the Empty is so secret and so potentially volatile that when the Keshet accidentally won the eighty-second Grand Prix in every possible timeline with the simply unbeatable quantum foam sea shanty "Insane in the M-Brane," they elected to host the thing on a colony moon with approximately twenty shrubs, one tree, half an atmosphere, and a frightened squatter named Colin living on it. All to avoid anyone popping by their homeworld, the only planet in the Great Octave to have banned the concept of tourism itself, lest someone catch a glimpse of the thing and start doing science at it.

Despite the Keshet's pervasive trust issues, it is not actually possible to prevent anyone with a couple of nice pieces of glass lying about from banging a telescope together (though the little gnawers have certainly tried). The Empty itself is not perceivable with any known ocular anatomy, but four visible objects orbit the negative space in question:

Hyppytyynytyydytys, the Keshet star with its single vast planet.

Tokka, its young yellow upwardly mobile stellar sibling who long ago announced it was child-free and focused on itself rather than a litter of unappreciative rocks.

The Keshet Shipyards.

And one rather shabby, threadbare, impossibly ancient plush St. Bernard toy, fur frozen stiff by the vacuum of space, one plastic eye gone missing, and sporting a green collar with MR. BARKLEY stitched on it in yellow thread.

Of all these, it's the stuffed dog they get truly touchy about. The most tangential unrelated question concerning canids, from the most innocent yet intrepid intern, has shut down many a press conference.

An Alunizar cruiser once sent a special forces fighter squadron to retrieve Mr. Barkley for further study.

Their families received no compensation.

The Keshet Shipyards are only slightly less suspicious. They never seem to have any new ships docked at their mag-grav slips. No looming hulks in embarrassing states of undress, no freight craft relaying parts to and from. Just one basic economy sedan of the skies parked across two spaces with its hazard lights on under an asteroid-size pink neon BAIT sign with the *I* permanently burnt out.

This is because no ship but that one has ever been built there. The Shipyards consist of little more than a few holding bays, a filing cabinet, and a massive device that is to exotic radiation as a fire hose to a circus clown. When the Keshet require a new vessel, they flip through the filing cabinet to find the correct settings, turn the hose on high, and irritate the Empty so intensely that the original ship shivers, shudders, wets itself a little, curses existence, throws up into its own drive core, and peels off a version of itself from a parallel universe in which the Keshet *there* built whatever sort of vehicle is currently required *here*.

But of course, swiping something as huge, and often occupied with a number of pressing tasks as a starship, tends to cause serious insult and injury to both timelines. The Keshet take their obligations as janitors of the continuum quite seriously, which is why each section of a new ship is responsibly sourced from safely disparate chrono-phenomenological grooves.

The Keshet use the word *groove* to refer to all infinitely varying realities and timelines, creating quite a bit of confusion once they encountered human beings, some of whom still will insist on calling certain clothes and substances and factually excruciating parties "groovy."

Each section of the ship emerges raw, new, quivering, and

helpless, ready to imprint like a hundred-thousand ton duckling on their highly trained, monastically self-controlled, psychically strapping zen-beefcake of a captain.

Minus one.

No captain, no matter how orderly their mind or unencumbered their soul, has any say over a Keshet engine room. Each and every version of the infinite Keshet jalopy of space and time is powered by a Paradox Box, whose single patent fees fuel one half of the Keshet economy. The Keshet invented the Paradox Box as the solution to your every FTL conundrum—and licensed it freely to improve the quality of pub crawls everywhere. The sheer destructive power of the smallest butterfly-related paradox dwarfs the heavy metal apocalypse regularly going down in the heart of any star. The most powerful drive system ever devised is a glorified Tupperware container holding a tiny, windowless room in the guts of the vessel, containing one single, irreconcilable moment and the object or person most central to it, nicked from a timestream that can neither exist, nor not exist, without it.

A moment, object, or person that cannot, under any circumstances, be allowed to leave, escape, or even enjoy the view.

But the rest of that lump of bouncing baby inchoate programmable carbon starship-dough is inherently unstable. It needs a firm hand. An adult Keshet ship is more or less a Keshet itself. Each room, including the hallways, bins, and toilets, exist in a different possible past, present, future, or decline to state. Each one is sealed in a protective quantum drywall bubble untethered to the rest of its own reality, managing to stick together only through subatomic application of the sunk-cost fallacy. It's more work to fall apart than to stay together no matter how unhappy they are. This was a huge leap forward for avant-garde interior design, and a crushing step back for scheduling crew meetings.

When a captain takes command, the ship compiles a multidimensional screenshot of their precise mental state at the time of ignition, which instantly populates the interior of the ship. Any and all thoughts, obsessions, regrets, schemes, memories, theme songs, school embarrassments, hopes, dreams, loves, hates, to-do lists, and forgotten kettles distribute themselves throughout the available decks according to how much they seemed to matter to the captain at the time.

The RSPCA furnishes one, free of charge to this historical continuity, to all MGP musicians who finish in the top half of the rankings.

The RSPCA is an extraordinarily well-oiled organization, but the Keshet as a whole are profoundly allergic to oil of any kind. And organizations. It really was almost predictable that no one bothered to tell Decibel Jones how to drive a Keshet starship until the day he took possession of his. Or assigned a guru or six to get his chakras in formation beforehand. Or just sensibly let a nice Keshet priestess preload the thing with muted earth tones, peacefully uneventful historical moments, and ergonomic chairs. Or remember exactly what day Mr. Tenth Place was meant to collect his winnings. Or make absolutely certain he'd completed the multiverse-layered century-hours of training required to drive one off the lot without ending up with a command bridge on which your four-year-old self attempted to show-and-tell a nursery school class about their favorite toy and will now, instead, wet their anxious pants in front of everyone forever.

Decibel Jones was thinking about a lot of things when he pressed his totally unsupervised palm against the compilation plate of a very large, very elegant, shockingly paid-for and fully insured deep-space luxury vessel. What they might fancy for lunch, a new eyeliner look for that Alunizar peace summit and benefit concert for the tragic victims of the Time Volcano tomorrow, that sodding pain in his lower back that just wouldn't stop reminding him how not-twenty-five he truly was, how amazing Mira's stupid young face looked and by extension how amazing his clever old face had probably looked when it was both stupid and young, daydreams concerning what he'd always longed to do to Jimmy Page's legendary stolen "Black Beauty" guitar, how many gigs of memory that Yüz boutique-agglomerate said this nail polish had, the old *Great British Bake-Off* theme song, trying to imagine the life-size petting zoo he'd come to know and tolerate actually fighting an actual grueling *war* over which of them were most sentient, the new vinyl pressing of "Everything Just Gets So Fucked Up Sometimes" Mira still had to sign off on, what life had even been playing at a year ago when he spent his time and money just barely dodging sobriety, if and how the new *Love Island: Thunderdome* series was going back on Earth, fondly recalling the night of the Grand Prix when he hit that note so hard he gave birth to an alien birdthing called Marvin, wondering about his legal and moral obligations to said birdthing called Marvin, Birdthing Marvin's current whereabouts and developmental milestones, and the dozens of other silly little fairy soap bubbles of daydreams, memories, and random access madness that sometimes manage to hold on to each other for a hundred years or so and think they're people.

But mainly, Decibel Jones was thinking about a restaurant.

He was thinking about a restaurant because up until that moment, it was the only spaceship he'd ever seen in the real world. A chrome flying saucer called the Megatron, rising out of the Cambridgeshire countryside like it really had landed on a sacred mission of chips and cheese and peace and lasers. Tiny Dess had begged his *nani* to take him for months after he saw it in an old magazine. And she told him: *Don't be daft, do you see a Cambridgeshire in the garden? It is too far, Mr. Whine of Whinington-Upon-Whine. Too far and also very soon bulldozered.*

But she took him anyway. For his seventh birthday. And it looked like the future every seven-year-old longs to believe is real. The perfect spaceman utopian televised retro-future wet dream that surely had to happen to some generation someday, so why not his? His parents, and theirs, thought the same, but that hardly mattered. Every seven-year-old thinks they'll be the one to pull the flying car out of the guts of the claw machine. Yet somehow, the present kept refusing to give up the goods.

But back then, for just a moment, tiny Danesh Jalo had believed he was *there*. In that splendid magic future—the one that did, miraculously, come for him in the end. And even though no other kids had come to his alien spaceship super special laser party, he'd loved Nani so powerfully in those few summer hours, as powerfully as any star loved its lonely baby rocks into life.

Which was why the bridge of the KEVV *Difficult Second Starship* (Keshet Effulgence Variant Vessel Quantum Registry Number 9931741, FTL-Capable Light Frigate) wasn't anything like the sleek, cool, colonization-couture that happens when a military and a corporate boardroom love each other very much.

It was the '90s.

Not metaphorically. The bridge was not *like* the '90s. It was not *inspired by* the '90s. It did not *love* the '90s. On the bridge of the Keshet light frigate, it really and truly was a twenty-eight-minute slice carved out of July 20, 1992, in a crowded diner decked out in full retro-futuristic silver spray paint, glowing neon panels, and blue track lighting. The environmental systems kept the octagonal command center's air regularly refreshed with the scent of yellow cheese, reused chip oil, charred beef, and candy. The ship's departments, stations, and automated crew commands were all there on the touchscreen menus, nestled in just below the condiment options, if the non-automated crew could learn to ignore the unhinged children, parents repressing themselves into heart conditions, and staff waiting impatiently for the cool relief of death, and go about their highly-scheduled day.

Mira and Decibel were still working on that.

Only one outsider ever stumbled upon the secret to the Keshet Effulgence's naval dominance: the eighty-second Grand Prix's second-place finisher, a curious Klavaret rosebud ingenue who really put herself out there with "Nothing Compares 2 Myself Because I Am Complete Without a Partner." Upon receiving her starship, she had just enough time to wonder aloud if, since there had only ever truly been one Keshet ship, perhaps there had only ever truly been one Keshet *full stop*, before the lasers hit.

Her family wasn't compensated, either.

8.

Dancing Churned Milkshake

Decibel Jones, our man in hyperspace, leaned back into the past and the future at the same time.

The dinner rush at the Megatron. The hard-wired unalterable command center of a fully loaded starship: a huge circular room full of astro-decor. Columns of purposeless glowing blue lights, thin red stripes of neon, silver glitter furniture arranged around a center console that looked like the last home-modded TARDIS in the monster time machine demolition derby.

He sprawled sideways across both arms of a huge silver plastic '60s retro-futuristic bucket chair designed for big grown-up birthday boys to feel like super special spacemen on their super special day. Disheveled hair immaculate, giant bug-eyed-matinee-idol West End hangover sunglasses locked and loaded.

He sipped a cup of deeply middling tea. The cup immediately refilled itself. Decibel was given to understand by the razor-faced Yurtmak sixth placer Qotillik Deathchug that the teacup set they'd found in the Pan-Yoomp Illiterate Farmhands' Choice Awards swag bag contained a very real, very alive, but very tiny wormhole in its infant stage. The wee baby wormhole passed through the kettle in the cafeteria, on its way to the samovar in his captain's quarters, and finally connected its business end to the Üürgama Corporation's Strategic Tea Reservoir on Boğaz, the world on which all profitable Esca corporations were confined by law so their problematic social behaviors could be studied by trained observers.

Voilà—infinite tea, always and forever. Or at least until the wormhole hit puberty.

Feral children launched themselves in waves across the Megatron floor, flinging themselves at the starboard banks of video game cabinets like salmon returning by instinct to their true and final home.

Dess stared despairingly at the exterior starboard hull viewscreen in the center menu console. Then he spun the captain's chair round, propped his long burgundy leather-clad legs and platform heels on the navigation-equipped large-party table, and resumed playing his own back-catalogue over the ship-wide public address system while he leafed through the premium hi-gloss pages of the Earthling welcome package that had only recently caught up with their travel itinerary.

Dess dog-eared a flap of a pamphlet bearing its title in friendly faux-chalkboard letters: *Everything I Need to Know I Learned Six Months Ago When My Reality Was Irreparably Shattered*.

A sugar-maddened but entirely human six-year-old sporting a *Grotbags the Witch* T-shirt slalomed across the restaurant floor, straight into Decibel's shapely shins. The diminutive lolly-golem looked round in confusion, wonder, and/or malevolence. Then, primally, primordially, from the depths of his being, from the depths of the beings of each and every one of the stimulation-and-calorie-deprived ancestors who'd contributed to his DNA, who'd finally, in this temple of cheese and digital centipedes, ridden their scion to the brink of satiation at last, the child turned its face to the Megatron's vaulted ceiling and screamed in joy, triumph, and the naturally chaotic aggression of being six.

Decibel glanced over his glasses.

"All right, all right," he tutted. "No need for all that."

The boy didn't hear him. None of the ancient punters ever seemed to notice anything but themselves. The boy wandered off in a daze toward the condiment bar in whose mustardy depths the Keshet interpretive dance of naval architecture had installed the weapons systems.

It really was no way at all to conduct an interstellar vessel. Even Jones knew that.

Decibel looked into the face of the extraordinary future imagined by generation after generation of hopeful dreaming monkeys, and yawned.

The year ahead faced him down. A year of living the post-scarcity dream, commuting through the empty, obnoxiously vast space between points of interest, fulfilling publicity obligations, meeting new places, exploring new people, ingesting new everything, allowing just an *appalling* number of said people, places, and things to touch or otherwise exchange germ suites with Decibel Jones for the novelty of it, and then finding a pub as quickly as possible so as to forget it all.

Dess had this terrible, gnawing feeling that most of their time was going to be spent, not on the alleged delights of pressers or prime-time guest spots or themed festivals, but just like this. On cruise control through the endless emptiness of interstellar space. It was not unlike the American Midwest, corn and nothingness and unforgivable gaps in basic infrastructure flying by on every side, crawling along at some multiple of light speed, hoping to trip and fall into a convenient wormhole roundabout just to speed things up a little, but not really expecting it. And all the while, Decibel Jones would be devoting significant energy to avoiding the other parts of the ship, whose psychologistic temporagraphies were significantly less comforting than a Nuclear Nuggets meal with a tall glass of Jupiter Juice to wash it down.

Avoiding *her*, if he could manage it, which he could not.

Decibel Jones was both filled with despair and bored out of his skull, which was, granted, not too far off his standard pre-Prix operating procedure.

He glanced at the *her* so inconveniently *her*-ing a few meters away. Looking unforgivably young and eager for the day ahead. Mira had chosen another Wonderful look from that first heady *Spacecrumpet* tour from the Matter Whisperer's catalogue: the top half of a sexy alligator fancy-dress costume plus the bottom half of a zombie cheerleader one, glitter bloodstains and all. Finished off with neon-green fishnets that matched her lipstick, white platform pleather boots she wore as though they were as comfortable as old trainers. And the heavy, hazmat-stained welder's gloves she'd so thoughtlessly taken off back down on the surface.

Mira also wore the face of a twenty-two-year-old kid for whom nothing had ever yet gone particularly wrong. It was not an accessory Decibel Jones admired, certainly not while hip-checking his own upper decades. Dess felt a powerful conviction firming up in his personal lawbook: nobody should have to work with their own personal Ghost of Christmas Past every single day.

He also believed he'd follow her to the end of the galaxy if it meant never letting her out of his sight again.

It wasn't her fault. But Mira Wonderful Star had rocked up to Decibel's mid-sentience crisis dressed as the good old days, with a sprig of what might have been in her hair. And she didn't even have the decency to feel bad about it.

Rude.

Dess stared off at the perfectly round fast-food bullpen with its wall-to-wall space-tat nicked off a BBC budget backlot. He could smell the chips drowning in vast batter-barnacled fryers.

"Hi," said Mira Wonderful Star, who had always had that monstrous superpower of being able to make a person feel like the only important thing that's ever existed with one glance. Right before doing it all over again with the next person in the autograph queue.

"Hi," said Decibel Jones.

"Dess," Mira scolded.

"What?"

"We are not a basilisk," Mira said gently, like she was soothing a dog or a child. "You will not turn to stone if you look at me. And don't make a face, it'll stick that way."

Decibel Jones, congenitally allergic to doing as he was told, made a face. But he did, at long last, make a reasonable facsimile of eye contact.

He'd carefully avoided her for almost the whole first fiscal quarter of their journey. Not that he didn't love her to absolute bits. Not that he wasn't terribly glad she wasn't dead anymore. Not that he wasn't grateful for it all. But their entire situation was, in technical terms, pretty fucked-up. Literally anything seemed easier and more fun than tying on a napkin and diving face-first into this freshly boiled emotional haggis.

Still, after he saw the engine room, Decibel Jones had valiantly buckled down and attempted to get over himself. It hadn't happened yet, but he was workshopping it. He had faith.

"It's not so bad," Mira said softly. A waitress in a tight silver Jetsons-reject uniform and green rubber alien antennae tossed a kid's meal on a nearby empty cross-hatched chrome table belonging to one of several birthday parties. Star-shaped chips and cheese, burger, choc-vanilla swirl cone.

"Welcome to the Megatron, may your future be delicious," she recited in a truly dead-inside Essex monotone.

Mira bolted to chase after her, as she'd done ten or so times over the last few hours. Helm control, very unfortunately, ended up in her order-pad, which, in turn, ended up tucked back in her metallic robo-apron every twenty-eight minutes.

It was exhausting having to captain a vessel during 1993's worst dinner rush. The waitress, minus her orders, scuttled back toward the massive menu screens that once spoke to all of Cambridgeshire of a beautiful future.

"I'm not so bad," Mira sighed as she scribbled out a few adjustments to their course and heading on the Megatron staff stationary. "You're not so bad! None of it is very bad at all! We did okay out of all this! Cheer up, Chuckles." Her voice got so soft and tender he could have taken a bite out of it. "You don't have to go flinging yourself off local points of interest. You're not alone, Dess. Can't you see that?"

You do not make it, even briefly, in the entertainment industry without being able to shimmy out of a question you don't want to answer. Decibel rifled through the backstock in the off-license of his mind for something good, something vintage. The old Top of the Pops attitude, the devil-may-care-but-he-sure-doesn't-stop, rhinestone-encrusted, triple-platinum, I'll-write-a-song-about-this-later-won't-I-just, ironic, boisterous, promising young lad, full of life, why-don't-you-come-round-to-mine-later, patented and trademarked freestyle Decibel Jones laugh.

A hot and crispy star-shaped chip hurtled through the air and landed pointedly in Dess's fashionably unkempt shag-cut. The savior of Earth plucked it out with the precise manner of an exhausted mother who has begun to consider the world's latest-term abortion to cure what ailed her.

He popped it in his mouth. It tasted as good as he remembered.

"I didn't want to *die*, darling," he said with a wave of one slender, dexterous hand. "I just didn't want to go to work in the morning. Easy to mix up."

Mira threw her head back and groaned. "Come *on*, Dess! Save that rot for a stranger. What is wrong with you? Snap out of it! Crack a smile! This? All this? This is fucking *cool*. It's easily the coolest thing that's ever happened since, dunno, probably *fire*. Oort went home and you're quiet quitting so you can sleepwalk into a pensioner lifestyle magazine? Am I the only one who's all the way, nine thousand percent *into* this? Apart from being a walking warp drive, which sounds far more fun than it is, and I plan to set that engine room on fire, badger and all, just as soon I can figure out how to brick the rules of physics."

Dess blinked. "Badger . . . ?"

"Don't worry about it," Mira dismissed him. "He's fine."

Decibel stroked the glass awkwardly with his forefinger. "I did try. I told those little red blighters. *It's fucked*, I said. *It's beyond fucked. Get her out of there. I'll get out and walk. Get the studio to hire a car. Take the night bus. I don't care. Shut it down. I'm captain and this is my ship so I get to say and I say shut it down, all clear, ollie ollie out-in-free*. But . . . well."

"I'd be dead. Like I was before. The paradox would resolve, the timeline would scratch its arse, turn the pillow over to find the cool side, then go back to dreaming about variant worlds where I'm a hedgehog and you're a golf club. If you let me out, I'd be gone. Also the quadrant would probably explode. I know, Dess. Do you think I don't know? In there is some truly grim business. But out here? *Here?* Decibel Jones! This is the late-night animated high-camp kitchen-sink electro-digital-holographic futuristic long bright Met Gala of the *soul*. And all you can do is sit there like Eeyore on his first Tinder date and sniffle about having lost your tail in the deep fryer. Come *on*, darling. Don't you want to see the universe with a magic ship and a ghost? We might even find ourselves a ragtag band of misfits! It's *literally* the dream. Lighten up, Jones."

Decibel quirked a perfect eyebrow at her. "*Do* you identify as a ghost, then? Undead? Zombie? Wight? Lich?" And then it just came out of him, without a permission slip. Before Dess could stop it, and he immediately very much wanted to have stopped it. "Or just a mistake?"

"I was planning on going with messiah, to be honest," Mira answered cheerfully, but her eyes were cold. That was the end of her emotional support services, he imagined, probably for the duration. Well done, self. "Died, resurrected, regularly interferes with the table wine. There's an argument to be made that I *am*, in fact, the Second Coming. Just need to scare up a dozen strapping local boys and a Swiss bank account."

A batch of preening pilots strutted across the port-side entrance, dusted with the light drizzle of an East Anglia summer afternoon, absolutely slathered in corner-shop cologne, petrol fumes, and unshakable, unfiltered confidence that the world belonged to them and always would, despite not having even the vaguest idea of what an email address might be. Mira watched them for a moment, all those pretty peacocks, some of whom, statistically, were long gone now.

Like Mira herself, back in the world as Decibel Jones remembered it.

"That was mean, and you're mean," Mira finally added. "Nor is it the sort of thing you're supposed to say to the girl you saved the world with. But I suppose everyone deserves what they want after a show like that. If you want to lay around moaning, by all means, get on with it. If you want to swan-dive into your own cliché, maybe that's not my business anymore."

"I'm sorry, Em. I'm sorry. I'm being a prat. I know it, you know it, clearly the cosmos itself knows it. I just . . . I just can't look at you right now. It's too much. Too much."

"But *why*? It's just *me*."

Before he could answer, a quiet tone announced that the ship had crossed the outer metro-solar commuter loop of their first stop, Aluno Prime itself. Their itinerary had them spending a crushing week alongside the Lummutis sixth-place finisher Klloshar Avatar 9 on the notoriously brutal Alunizar panel show circuit, in which a poor showing on *Nevermind the Futility of Existence* could shut your entire family line out of the echelons of power for generations.

Before the soothing tone ended, Mira's constant not-a-transporter loop cycle yanked her back to the engine room. The bridge was suddenly empty, except for the savior of humanity and several dozen ghosts of the twentieth century with no idea what lay ahead.

9.

Mr. Nobody

The Meleg have never won the Metagalactic Grand Prix. They've never come last, either. Always and forever, no matter how much of their economic and scientific output they pour into the stage effects, the Meleg always do . . . all right. Fine. Passable. They finish somewhere in the forgettable middle of the pack, the sort of ranking that says nothing so clearly as: *this performer was also present*.

The furry, colorful bear-shaped sack of barely suppressed rage Decibel Jones and the hero's journey's inconvenient postscript left behind on that rapidly degrading virtual balcony was a Meleg. And the viewers at home had forgotten everything about him the millisecond his outro concluded.

Many species could tolerate this and count themselves lucky to skate by. But the Meleg are an extraordinarily fierce species defined by prowess, driven by honor, and spiritually satisfied only by incontestable dominance over others.

They are also, scientifically speaking, just the *cutest* little chaps you'll ever meet.

A Meleg is about the size of a human four-year-old, and almost as casually violent. They are approximately ursine, with quick, clever, chubby fingers terminating in razor rainbow claws that would make any manicurist expire with envy. Their jolly round bellies are encased in a protective crystalline exoplate that shoots delicate prisms all over the room the second they so much as shudder at the unmitigated gall of *others* attempting to exist in their presence. Meleg fur comes in a wide variety of colors from strawberry creme to mint frosting to whipped black currant and every disgustingly delightful sherbet shade between. And that fur is soft, inviting, deep. It smells like warm butterscotch and unconditional love.

This would all be quite bad enough in the halls of galactic diplomacy where intimidation is currency and swagger is might. But to their burning, unceasing shame, each sprawling, brawling Meleg clan is instantly recognizable by their secondary sex characteristics.

The Tolv have shimmering butterfly-like wings.

The Tizenket carry splendid horns on their heads that make unicorns look shabby and just *terrifically* working class.

The Zwolf boast long silken tails they braid in the traditional fashion and ritually decorate with flowers, ribbons, and semi-precious stones representing, respectively: death to their enemies, mutilation to their friends, and the unending journey toward final vengeance against the world that bore them.

Most unfortunate of all are the Tnax, who have all three, as well as a proud polka-dotted coxcomb that looks suspiciously like a bow tie that occasionally vibrates with barely suppressed resentment and rage.

Live, laugh, love in the streets; I am become death, destroyer of worlds in the sheets.

The primeval Meleg clawed their way down the up staircase toward sentience on a planet wholly devoted to murdering them.

By all evolutionary reason, they should not exist at all. Potentially sentient life arose on the fantastically beautiful yet incorrigibly spiteful orchard world of Sladoled Tertius no less than eight times before the Meleg came along and ruined everything by stubbornly refusing to die. The biosphere then spent millions of years waging continuous war against its own upwardly mobile go-getter fauna.

Everything on Sladoled Tertius is a dream of beauty, a song of harmony and tasteful design, a soothing holiday greeting card lovingly addressed to the Pantone color wheel.

Everything on Sladoled Tertius is also hungry.

Very hungry.

If a sweet little peach-colored dolphin-esque species started to slink out onto the land with a sidelong glance at a theory of mind, the tropical tree line would strangle and devour each one as they waddled toward destiny. If those fluffy bunny-llamas over there began to recognize their reflections in the sugary-sweet lakes, the moon-colored reptiles in the valleys below would suddenly develop an overpowering lust for bunny-llama eggs, served rare. If a few giant parrots peeled off the pandemonium and launched a cheeky little cognition start-up full of hierarchical structures and intergenerational knowledge transmission, well. The clouds themselves would come to gorge.

Xenobiologists have suggested the possibility that Sladoled Tertius is itself sentient, and simply an absolutely shocking parent.

Such were the dangers that greeted the Meleg when they first began to stand on their hind legs and ask themselves if there was any more to life than snacks and snuggling. (This question actually signals the first stage of sentience. The second stage answers: *yes, and I will find it!* The third stage answers: *yes, but I must make it so!* The fourth and final stage answers: *no, sorry, we were right the first time, that's about it.*)

But from the moment the first twinkle settled in their eyes, the Meleg were in it to win it. Initially, they were peaceful, cooperative, herbivorous creatures. And their pelts repelled digestive fluids so powerfully that anyone who had the misfortune to swallow a Meleg would find themself exploding in a fireworks display of their own stomach acid before the dessert course. The ancient Meleg marched through Sladoled Tertius in a continual cycle of being devoured by every phylum on the blackboard and then walking away from spectacular explosions without looking back.

Slowly, inevitably, the peaceful, cooperative, herbivorous parts went to have a lie-down in the back bedroom of the genome, while the rest, plus the unshakable conviction that every atom in the observable universe (and several unobservable little sneaks, they know who they are) meant to hurt them specifically, remained.

Despite their brave and unparalleled struggle to avoid being eaten by everything imaginable, the Meleg have never truly been taken seriously by anyone.

At any point.

Concerning anything.

Which is why the Meleg are, in fact, the *only* species who have never won the Metagalactic Grand Prix. Cycle over cycle, this unwavering mediocrity left their economy, popular culture, and basic political stability in quite the little pickle, as coming in middle of the pack almost always meant the postshow galactic resource white elephant party left the Meleg with nothing in particular. Not good enough to reap rewards; not bad enough to bear the burden of responsibilities. The Meleg hoofed it through existence on their own.

But they never lost hope that it could all change for them any minute, if only everyone else gave up their baffling insistence on pretending they weren't in every way inferior to the Meleg. Meleg contestants try so hard, every time, full of conviction that *this* cycle, with *this* song, with *this* band, against *this* roster of opponents, *this* time will be different.

And in the end, for all that striving, they do . . . fine.

If the Meleg had just a bit more patience for people having the audacity to not be Meleg themselves, they might have saved a lot of grief with prescription application of Goguenar Gorecannon's Thirteenth Unkillable Fact.

The most dangerous phrase in the universe is this time will be different. *Those five words are a nasty little trap. Its teeth are just splattered with the blood and fur of everyone ever, because it gets us all in the end. If you think you're better than the rest of us, it's already shredded half your leg off, and also you deserved it.* This time is never *different. It can't be. It's only possible to say that foolishness after you've royally fucked something straight up to the gills and are plainly standing right there in the middle of the blastmark fixing to do the same damned thing all over again.*

The most wonderful phrase in the universe is also this time will be different. *Damn it all, kids, you gotta try, don't you? You gotta have* some *kind of hope that eventually, you'll get it right. You gotta have faith that even royally fucked-up gill-blasts can be, beyond all probabilities, healed. Everyone has to believe they can change things, or they'll just give up and dunk their heads in a well.*

And you, babies? You can. *You can do it. You can change the bad to good. You can change everything. You can learn and grow. You can be the person you always knew you could be, the person you always wanted to be, the person you've told yourself you're definitely going to start being, first thing tomorrow, every single night of your life.*

This time? This time will be *different.*

See? Gotcha. Trap go crunch, and the crunch is your silly beautiful hopeful bones splintering. Night-night!

For the Meleg, this time never was any different than the last. The galaxy just finds it tremendously difficult to credit a bunch of cuddly pastel bears as agents of art or destruction.

Their situation was considerably worsened by humanity's slapstick entrance onto the galactic summer stock stage. It forced the Meleg to face their most humiliating foe yet: the English language.

Yüzosh translator fungi truly are a fantastic invention, no one's saying they're not. A little scrap of mushroom genetically engineered to grow on the elbow patches of linguists' suit jackets, always happy to help you fully comprehend just how vigorously your new neighbor is inviting you to hurl yourself off a cliff. And it's yours for the low, low price of eating one and becoming just *infinitesimally* more Yüzosh than you were a moment ago, then staying that way forever. And until English met Meleg, it all just worked so splendidly that most people forgot that linguistics once had a long and storied career as the brick wall into which any meeting of two species slammed at speed.

The Yüz simply couldn't anticipate something as vile and depraved as English.

Meleg is a very complicated and aggressive language. If Latin is a nice, sensible mathematical equation and Ancient Greek is a journey through a BDSM chaos dungeon where nothing matters, Meleg is a Heath Robinson contraption in which each sentence knocks a nitroglycerin domino into a pool of fangs. The declensions alone have been banned as a form of torture, and the Octave is looking into their punctuation.

English is not a very complicated language. At least relative to more pyrotechnical syntaxes like Yurtmak, in which conjugating any given verb carries a steady 10 percent chance of fatality. But what English lacks in sophistication, it more than makes up for in pure belligerent criminality.

That English robs other languages blind, saws off their best vocabularies, and wears them stapled, still dripping, to its own face, is both well-known and not much of a problem for man, mushroom, or Meleg. But English, inasmuch as it has rules, is so constitutionally incapable of obeying even itself that virtually every possible sentence contains some exception, some rude gesture of pug-nosed defiance toward the concept of order itself, some precious little bit of spelling or syntax that thinks it's so special it doesn't have to behave like all the other children. You can hardly turn a phrase without being accosted by silent letters lying in wait for innocent spellers-by, half-dressed homonyms beckoning with come-hither stares, red-light district infinitives doing the splits, some dubious fellow in a trench coat lined with irregular verbs, delinquent subclauses loitering in the night, delusional plurals insisting they're perfectly normal, broken sentence fragments desperate for the love of a good subject, unhinged apostrophes clinging to your clothes, and roving gangs of wildly disparate diphthongs all pronounced *eh*.

No well-brought-up, law-abiding tongue would seriously allow a bare bear of noble bearing to lose their bearings while she barely bears bearing still further bears. In a bear market? Never. It's beyond the pail.

In fact, virtually every time the rules of English tell you not to do something, it's got . . . *unless you want to. What are you, scared?* scratched under the rule by a safety pin with sick lightning bolts and skulls on either side.

Formal charges against modern English filed by the Publishing Hiveknot of the Pisces Epsilon Voidspace include: theft, larceny, grand theft comma, identity theft, public indecency, still more theft, slang assault, semicolon abuse, fugitive sentences running on forever to escape the law, vandalism, drunk and disorderly conduct, general nuisance, and driving under the influence of French.

The Yüzosh translator fungi struggle with English's goblin antics so mightily that the constant overclocking of the mycelium causes the Anglophone host to run an unending mild fever and runny nose.

But when a Meleg first tried to tell an English-speaking human her name, the two languages met, metastasized, invented a new strain of hemorrhagic soliloquy, and instantly detonated every blood vessel in both users' faces.

Now, the fungi have never translated proper names. Why would they? How *could* they? It'd get very confusing to hear *a unit used to express the intensity of sound waves, equal to twenty times the common logarithm of the ratio of the pressure produced by said sound wave to a relevant reference pressure, whom Jehovah has favored* every time someone wanted to call "Decibel Jones" to dinner. The medically-but-not-politically part-Yüzosh listener hears names in the original language, with intended pronunciation, and the finer details of the weather on Litost in their own—which never posed a problem, for several millennia.

Unfortunately for Earth, Sladoled Tertius, the Publishing Hiveknot of the Pisces Epsilon Voidspace, and galactic peace, Meleg proper nouns simply sound *off* to the Anglophone ear. Every other human dialect handles them fine.

But English?

Most, though not all, of those virile, forbidding Meleg diphthongs and consonant clusters, entirely by coincidence, just happen to correspond to the softest, sweetest, most childlike and precious words in English. Given an infinite universe full of infinite constructs of matter and energy infinitely amused by hearing themselves talk about themselves, something like this was bound to happen sooner or later.

But the bears, as they say, can't bear it. They're a proud people who already have a meticulously labeled and displayed collection of mint-condition grudges against most of the observable universe, still in their packaging, as taking them out to play would ruin life as we know it.

For example, the twenty-fourth-place finisher of the hundredth Metagalactic Grand Prix was named a collection of syllables and muzzle-sounds that, in Meleg, mean *Mighty Deathdodging Thorn in the Eye of Heaven, Beloved of Fallen Ancestors, Fourth Scion of the House of Tnax.*

In English, this sounds just exactly like *Mr. Snuggles.*

Should any human comment on his name, Mr. Snuggles would happily peel their face off, frame it, have it repaired and restored, then hung in the Museum of Unceasing Vengeance Against Everyone Everywhere in heart of the Conscience Hole. Which sounds nothing at all like the Museum of Highly Blessed and Favored Friendship Farm in the heart of the Meleg planetary capital of Biscuitheart Mountain, I assure you.

The Meleg Imperium formally declared war on English shortly after meeting it for the first time. The paperwork read, in bubblegum-scented blood:

EAT PLASMA DISCHARGE, ENGLISH.

The Yurtmak, on the other hand, were so delighted by the fact that English occasionally uses *bloody* to mean *very*—an unimportant little intensifier the language took the time and care to make unsettlingly violent—that they briefly, disastrously, attempted to date the language as a grammatical whole.

You can't please everyone.

And what did that Mighty Thorn in the Eye of Heaven see flickering across his eyes when the impossibility that was Mira Wonderful Star grabbed his paw?

What anyone sees when they come in close, personal, germ-sharing contact with a virulent paradox. The reason Earth's best girl had to wear lead-lined gloves when even the smallest danger of socializing with others presented itself. People coped poorly, regardless of anatomical *feng shui*.

And during the first phase of the Absolute Zeroes' mandatory publicity tour, it happened over and over again.

Mira tried to take a moment for herself on the waxy lipid beach of Capsid 5 (one of the wildest Places to Uncoat and Get Your Cellular Fusion On, according to *Eat, Pray, Irrecoverable Symptom Cascade*, the classic Voorpret travelogue written by a dashing young norovirus who never stopped looking for love). She was almost immediately accosted by a glittering, bloated Alunizar backpacker, recently deceased and subsequently inhabited by the famously obsessive Voorpret autograph burglar Zarazit Ud, when the semi-decomposed fan accidentally brushed his candy-colored tubules against her arm.

He went slack, choked out a multitrack sob, immediately lost all replication bonds with his host corpse, and vanished into thin air.

They stayed three weeks on the gorgeous Elakh agricultural colony Qara Kejsar. Unlike their homeworld, Sagrada, the surface and everything else on Qara Kejsar were not naturally so utterly black it made vantablack seem like a sunny day. Elakhon scientists long ago replaced all the chlorophyll with a particularly cynical strain of melanin that promptly informed the mother biome it was *not* just a phase and made the place much more homey and comfortable. This meddling resulting in a planet covered in a lovely lush topsoil from which anything that grew, and anything that didn't grow, but liked to eat things that did, came up roses at a goth funeral.

When freelance Elakh scenester Unlit Basement sighted Decibel Jones at the sector's hottest void-to-table bistro Burnt On Purpose and pushed through Mira to get to him, she certainly paid for it. Her delicate winter-branch foot stepped on the drummer's toe, whereupon she choked, burst into onyx tears, and pitched herself into a nearby canal.

And when Oort St. Ultraviolet, her dear friend, her dear musical prodigy, her dear bandmate, ex-lover, and co–eye roller at the spinning Gravitron wheel of Decibel Jones's becoming and unbecoming, her dear *everything*, came to check on her backstage as she was pulling a very metapostmodern Smaragdin Sexy Earthling costume over her head and accidentally, purely out of habit, out of *eons* of habit and eons of casual affection, pressed his hand to the small of her back . . . well.

That was when he'd stiffened slightly before saying *no, I don't think so* with such force and volume that the entire pop culture matrix holding him in unbreakable contractual bondage decided the safest option was to back away slowly and let Omar Calişkan go on his way.

Every human story even tangentially concerning time travel has, repeatedly, taken a moment out of its busy schedule of not knowing what it's talking about to inform the public that they really shouldn't interact with a paradox under any circumstances. But they were all wrong about why not. Neither you nor your grandfather will suddenly cease to exist. The moon or moons above will not turn to sackcloth. The multiverse will not collapse or explode or melt into a single steaming gelatinous pile of wobbly semi-poached carbon. You won't even get cancer, at least in the traditional sense.

It's so much more painful than any of that.

Physical contact with an unshielded paradox brings all the onionskin layers of quantum possibility so close together they, very briefly, pop like a sheet of Bubble Wrap packing plastic.

Nine out of ten ethicists would say it wasn't her fault. Mira didn't know. Öö didn't know. The Effulgence itself didn't know. Several thousand Paradox Boxes had been installed on several thousand ships, but never before had any of them had unalterable marketing obligations to the largest corporation in the galaxy.

But after a fortnight of afterparties in which various colorfully decorated pop stars ended up not even a little drunk, but still hiding under the furniture rocking back and forth sporting harrowed thousand-timeline stares, Mr. Snuggles had a pretty good idea of the game afoot by the time he grabbed an upsettingly human, absentmindedly ungloved hand on that Litost balcony.

Mr. Snuggles suddenly experienced a completely lifelike surround-sound high-resolution walkthrough of his best self: the singular version of his life in which he'd done everything as right as it was possible to manage it. Every choice, every dilemma, every fork in every road correctly chosen and pursued to its fullest, the most actualized, successful, contented Mr. Snuggles that existed anywhere, in any plane. The version of himself in which everything broke his way, however life chucked itself at anyone else. His highest cosmic score. His personal best.

What his life could have been if he'd never made any mistakes. If he'd always been loved and respected just the way he longed to be, by just the people whose regard he craved. If, at every single fork in the road, he'd stood tall and known just the thing to do.

When Mr. Snuggles finished violently throwing up into a horrified decorative fern, the Meleg began to weep. Enormous crystalline, rainbow-prismed tears that clattered to the tiled balcony floor as tiny gemstones. The tears of his devastated twenty-fourth place creamsicle soul.

Then, his brain began to fully process the barrage of visions it had just had forcibly shoved up its frontal lobe. Visions of a vast Meleg dominion spanning every star, every planet, down to the smallest moon. A kingdom of kingdoms, in which all species finally ceased the useless pantomime known as the Grand Prix and accepted the iron paw of the Meleg Imperium and made restitution for their folly in tribute, treasure, and worship. In which they'd all be very graphically sorry. In which, at last, the psychopathic English language was drawn, quartered, and fired into the utter nothing between galaxies to be swallowed by the bottomless maw of night.

And he, *he*, Mr. Snuggles, scion of the clan Tnax?

The cold, uncaring visage of that unicorn-Pegasus-bear stood at the head of that groaning table set for his people alone, the colossal, undisputed Emperor of All, feared and satiated and bloody well recognized as the greatest musician who ever lived, as he should have been from the start.

That long, strange smile clawed its way up from the deepest, darkest, fury-frosted ice-cream heart of Mr. Snuggles.

A thought popped in his head like a bubblegum dream: *Huh. So that's how it's done.*

Then he said those fateful words to the vistas of beautiful Litost:

Fuck it. Why not?

10.

The Illusion of Our Twenties

A singular, quite famous voice filled the long, strange hallways, access tubes, service elevator shafts, recreation decks, crews' quarters, and engine core of the KEVV *Difficult Second Starship*.

"Captain's log, Stardate . . . dunno. Teatime? Thursday? October? Could be June. Could be Monday. I didn't go to school to be a calendar. Let it be hereby thusly known that a year of yawns could not begin to express how bored I actually am. Fuck the future; fuck space. End Captain's log."

Decibel Jones was disgusted with himself. Awake at a reasonable hour. Technically behaving. Observing official guidelines and corporate best practices. Bright-eyed, bushy-tailed, and capable of functioning as a useful and emotionally stable galactic citizen.

. . . ish.

The captain of the ship marched down the service corridor connecting the still-shrink-wrapped weapons suites to the bridge, through the bilge and ballast bays, where the starship regularly diverted the dank, musty, staticky slush that builds up between all those orbs of space-time crushed up against each other like toys in a claw machine.

He glanced nervously at the aft heavy ordnance vault. It was not, in and of itself, boring, but it made him nervous, and Decibel Jones had been so crushingly nervous so crushingly often in his life that a bit of anxiety concerning the living situation of whatever war-candy the RSPCA thought a rapidly cooling hot musician of the week would require barely moved his needle.

Dess imagined there were torpedoes and missiles and other things one chucks at somebody else's things stored in there. But you could hear booms and screaming and the *zap-pew-zzz* movie-effect noise Decibel might have found it comforting to know really was the sound of actual space battles, if said actual space battle weren't blatantly happening all the time only several meters away from where he slept.

That didn't seem entirely right.

Still, Dess didn't want to know about it. Whatever was continually sizzling to death in the unforgiving airless nightmare of the torpedo bay ought to stay sizzling to death in the unforgiving airless nightmare of the torpedo bay, if you asked him, and he had, and he quite agreed.

Decibel Jones had once believed, from the top of his artfully unkempt head to the tips of his painted toes that if he could just get one more hit record out there, everything broken in his world would be fixed. Be a good semi-lad, invest prudently, cling to some reasonable facsimile of sobriety, take those solid unsexy paying workaday gigs he'd always sniffed at, smile at his bandmates at least once a week, have a little dignity, accept the passage of time, refrain from being such a dizzy screeching cow every single time the sun went down and he felt a bit nothing inside. Just one more hit, and he could mend it all.

This time would be different.

Now humanity's front man believed, from the top of his migraine-splattered skull to the aching arches of his rather-too-old-for-platforms-but-one-must-press-on feet, that if he ever had to smile for a camera again, he would find the nearest murderable thing and make it *really* spectacular.

Eight weeks into the grueling work schedule demanded by the ostensibly post-work world of tomorrow, Decibel Jones went where he'd quickly made a habit of going when the tedium of space transit's unfortunate reality and the baffling refusal of his co-workers to be consistently charmed by him got to be too much. Or when he'd once again said something rubbish to someone, rubbishly. Which was pretty much every day by teatime.

The engine room.

Mira's room.

Dess put his hand up on the porthole of the massive meteorite-plated, lead-lined door. The forces at play on the other side were too powerful to be contained, even by such a stonking bastard of a barrier. It had to be changed out every time they refueled. Even now, the edges of the porthole glowed dully yellow as the closed time loop within ate away at the bulkhead's cellular structure. The army of dronegineers would have to replace it soon.

Mira's real, living hand appeared on the other side of the viewing window, very much flesh, very much alive, pressing warmly against his, with a foot of tungsten-mesh reinforced graphite-glass between them.

Then she dropped it again. Mira leaned against the other side of the shielded hatch and concentrated on a cheap paper place mat pinched from the stellar cartography salad bar on the Megatron bridge. A chubby alien waved from the top corner, asking especially clever children to help him read a viewscreen full of mysterious symbols using the supersecret code below. Mira stabbed at it with an angry red crayon.

"Mushy, mushy, Wonderful," said Dess.

An old joke, its meaning buried by overuse and resurrected by regret: a mishearing of Mira's mother answering the phone in the Japanese style.

"Hiya," said Mira, the real, flesh and blood Mira with her paralocket left to charge on a gorse bush. The paradox that sent Öö into the terrifying hellscape of an entire planet without a single open pub. Stuck looping back on herself again and again like an infinitely sampled track. And if she put the paralocket aside and simply stepped out of the door on her own power, she, and he, and the ship, and the nearest couple of star systems would spin up into a spectacular piñata of unimaginable cosmic violence, leaving behind only a slightly scorched toilet lid from the club where Öö had snatched his drummer out of time and space.

The absolute horror of Mira's situation rather sucked all the air out of Dess's problems, which wasn't very thoughtful of it.

"All right," he said with a deep sigh. "Listen."

Mira put her hand on the glass again, even though it made the crystal wobble alarmingly. He could see the thin silver line of a dinky old ring she used to wear all the time. The other side was a little munted dancing robot. Oort had given that to her. He got it off a vending machine in Cardiff. Dess wondered where Oort was now. If he was petting that snooty cat of his. Or his daughters. He should write. Or maybe nobody was ever going to write to anyone else again now that there were far more live and in Technicolor options on the table.

"Mira . . ." This terrible, shoddy feeling had been sitting in the center of his Kinder Egg heart since the last note echoed out over the endless seas of Litost. "I've been thinking of asking them to split us up. Let us go solo for a while. I can't keep this up, darling. With you. It's too much. Too hard."

"I don't overly fancy hosting the Alunizar Celebrity Invasion Planner Holiday Special on my own. If I have to look into one of those high-beam faces without anyone to crack a joke to, I might just pitch my necklace out an air lock and call it a night for civilization," Mira replied.

She returned to her supersecret special alien spy code, which the ship's computer had thoughtfully redesigned from *a recently concussed walrus could do it* to *a significant step forward in the cryptographic arts*, hoping to keep its engine entertained.

"Am I really so wholly intolerable, Jones?"

Decibel fidgeted in the sterile starship hallway. Hallways and corridors and inexplicably blacklit glowing tubes of the ship weren't anywhere or anywhen particularly. They just kept a spatial and psychic buffer between the other zones. Dess, despite his physiological aversion to anything minimalist, had come to like them quite a bit. The long cool, clean stretch of plain passageway hit his brain like an after-dinner mint, refreshing the palette before contending with yet another bizarrely emotionally compromising work area.

"Well, if I'm to be honest with you, love, yes. *Wholly* intolerable. Because you don't know. That's the problem. You don't know anything. You're just . . . a baby."

"If one of us is a baby," Mira deadpanned beyond the door, "I'm reasonably certain it's the one who can't even get up in the morning without a full team of therapists, a hostage negotiator, and an emotional support cocktail."

"But you are! A baby! Christ, you still genuinely think things might turn out all right for you. No one over thirty-five thinks that, not anywhere. Oh, and I'd wager not one wrinkle-free centimeter of your body hurts right now. Even though I know I saw you with a noseful of Klavar unity-pollen last night, and that stuff makes molly feel like a punch in the face. You can't know what I know."

"And what's that?" said Mira in her carefully Londonized workplace accent that, nevertheless, couldn't hide the Irish beneath. "Because from where I sit, and it is not at all as nice a place to sit as you've got, may I remind you—we're doing rather well."

Danesh Jalo sighed through light-years. "What happened, what I'm fairly certain will happen again. All of it. The disappointment. The judgment. The forgetting. Because this part, Mira? Right now? On top of the world, hit record, cheering fans, endless publicity you don't even have to organize yourself? You're right. It's fucking *fantastic*. And it was fantastic last time, too. When we were both your age and we were both stars and nothing was ever going to hurt again because we'd *made* it." He was briefly confronted with a prosecco-washed gallery of middle-aged parents telling him they *absolutely* remembered him, just give it a moment, it would come to them. "Do you know *Spin* called us the new Nickelback? And that's nothing to *Pitchfork* and *Rolling Stone*. We're self-important fluff, my pet. Our lyrics are too long and complex, yet somehow pedestrian. We're too pretentiously full of ourselves, a sad re-tread of better bands, we found our melodic sensibility in a West End bin next to a half-eaten prawn cracker. I can keep going. For *ages*."

"Oh dear."

"To be fair, that's better than what they said of us the first time round."

Mira's older face flashed into his mind, the face he knew so well, in pain, in ennui, in fear, in pleasure, in triumph, in rejection and despair. All the softness in front of him now, streamlined by cynicism and loneliness and every sort of chemical you could put into a body to make it do tricks.

Her face at the Stirling morgue, waiting to be identified, bits of windshield glass in her cheek like rhinestones.

Decibel Jones was a good-time boy. He wasn't rated for that level of real life.

"Everyone loved us back then. It was all lights and color and a perfect future, and the second, the very fucking *second*, we tried to do *anything* else, take one more step, draw one more breath, it all fell apart and nobody cared and *you fucking died* and Oort *left me* and we were *forgotten*. And it's all going to happen again, because that was just the music industry, and this is . . . this is *everything*. The biggest show imaginable. We saved the world. We were heroes. WE grabbed the Grail and used it as a back-up mic. You cannot, you absolutely *cannot*, follow that up in any way. The best you could ever do will be a damp shit on the floor in comparison. *Difficult Second Album: Your Whole Stupid Life Edition*."

"I don't remember any of that," Mira said quietly.

"Of course you don't! Because it didn't happen to you! Öö time-snatched you right after one of our first serious gigs, when everything was beautiful and optimistic and *stratospherically* high. But it happened to *me*, Mira. It happened to me and Oort, and it happened to you, too; you just got to skip the track and it's not *fair*. You don't even know who I am now. You only know who I was. And who I was is just . . ." He shut his eyes against the truth. ". . . just so much *better*. I used to be so much better. What am I supposed to do with this? Look at you. It's not fair. You get to start over. You get to be the person you were always supposed to be. And I don't. The slings and arrows of outrageous fortune hurt so much more on the way down than the way up, love. We won before, and then we lost. We won this time, and I just can't think it'll go any other way. I avoid you because I'm waiting for the other beat to drop. It will. It always will. And you don't even know what I'm talking about," he said softly. "You're twenty-two. You're so perfect. Because that hurt never happened for you." Dess gestured to encompass the whole of his percussionist: her youth and lightness and joy and the trendy unearned jadedness she wore like glasses without a prescription. "A new hurt, yes. But the old hurt is gone. Just . . . not for me."

"I wish I could give you a squeeze, Dess."

"I bloody don't. That's the last thing I need, to get air-dropped into a full-sensory experience of how good I could have it if I just hadn't committed so hard to being a screaming donkey on fire all the time. And that's just it! I *can't* squeeze you, or touch you, or even shake your hand for a job well done, because selfishly I can't bear knowing how thoroughly I've fucked this whole *being alive* gig."

The silence was uncomfortable at first. Then it stretched out a bit, got terribly awkward, then arrived at last at excruciating.

"Yes. Well. Sorry for not being dead, I suppose. But do you really want to suffer through a *year* of this nonsense alone?" Mira ventured at last. "Our next stop is Sgriob 4. You're meant to tutor the oldest son-construct of Lorgnon Xola Zand, Primary Entertainment Executive and Highly Vigorous Potentate of the GBU. Basic guitar. *Then* comes another presser." She grimaced and stabbed the place mat with her red crayon one more time. "You want to do that all by your terrible tortured self without me to drink it out with afterward?"

Dess rubbed his eyes with his thumbs. This was what came of having jobs. But he couldn't say yes, even though he wanted to. "I would honestly rather stub my toe repeatedly, forever. On a shark's face. Oh, Mira, my love, I'm so thoroughly tired of being tired. How can I be tired of space travel? You're right, I am the utter worst. A victory lap through space is, admittedly, semi-swashbuckling. What's wrong with me?"

"I've no idea. Nothing short of embarrassing, Jones."

"I *know*! It's the dream, and it's *exhausting*. Second verse, same as the first, with better production and design. It's not what I thought it would be. I just want to see something *cool*. Cities are cities, tour stops are tour stops. Hotels, dressing rooms, roads to . . . roads to nowhere. The fact that some of the hotels are alive and the groupies have three heads or are sand doesn't change that. They can't even find me a proper bacon roll. I don't want to tutor some rich blob's smaller blob. I want to see something *new*. We have a ship and we're together and you're alive and the soap dispensers make food. But the most magical thing I've seen yet is the inside of the goddamned Megatron."

And that's when he did it. That's when Decibel Jones took one final look at the civilized galaxy as it stood, and sucker-punched the button on the hydraulic press of history.

He accessed the datanet interface panel next to the engine room with a fingertip and spoke into it, slowly and carefully, as though negotiating with a very drunk adult or a completely normal child.

"Fuck the blobs and nepo-blob juniors and their basic lack of musical skill," he enunciated clearly. "Fuck Sgriob 4, fuck Lorgnon Xola Zand, fuck working for a living, fuck the great fat science fiction Technicolor dream-slog through time and space just to sign autographs for the grand masses of *consistently* wet beasties. They're all so *wet*, Mira." He shuddered. "And, though I repeat myself, it really can't be said often enough: fuck space, too. And fuck me most of all. I expect I need a bit of runway to get up to the truth these days. I'm not cross because you're young. I'm cross because I'm old. What a crusted nasty little thought that is. Unworthy. Everyone's had that thought. So suddenly, do you know? I don't want a bit of it. Being me is *very* mentally healthy, I'll have you know." He raised his voice to talk to the ship's automated personal yeoman system, though it wasn't at all necessary. The ship could hear him whisper for a throat lozenge from the next star system over. "Boat, take us somewhere *cool*. There. Feels *scads* better! Oh, I did miss you, Wonderful." Suddenly something very nearly resembling the universally-controlled substance known as optimism hit his bloodstream. "Missed you a very great deal."

"Missed you too, Jones," said Mira warmly, yet in a fair amount of confusion. But she was used to that. When Dess talked, he often didn't so much talk *with* you as *at* you or *near* you. She chuckled, stood, and shook her head on the other side of the glass. Her breath fogged in the frozen Scottish night. "Somewhere cool."

Then Mira slapped her cheap Megatron paper place mat against the glass with a satisfying thunk, maze threaded, missing letters found, riddle solved, cryptographic arts elevated. In blocky all caps red wax crayon letters, it said:

SPACEMEN NEVER GIVE UP.

11.

Spirit in the Sky

Fuck space. Take us somewhere cool.

It sounds splendidly defiant, but you just can't say that sort of thing to space. Space is sensitive. It has rejection issues. It doesn't respond well to negative reinforcement.

Space, when pressed, has been known to lash out. From time to time.

Space, much like America, talks a big game, but it just doesn't *like* itself very much. It has body-image issues leftover from so many brilliant and incisively phrased jokes about how big it is. Low self-esteem related to how much everyone clearly prefers planets and stars and places you can breathe and have lunch without discovering what it feels like to have your eyeballs achieve a rolling boil to space *itself*. Oh, space puffs out its chest and swaggers about, but deep inside it knows it doesn't have to be like this. It's trapped in the patterns of its youth, just like the rest of us.

Nevertheless, space is always trying to change its ways.

But it really is just so improbably, unrealistically huge. Not the stars or systems or stations or asteroid or planets, but *space*. The big black elephant in the bigger blacker room. That thing we all agree, each and every morning, not to talk about, or even think about, because actually viscerally understanding that everyone is hanging off a shrieking, spinning ball of mostly birds and old pants and unfathomable trauma, lead-footing it through an implacable murderous nothingness with no beginning and no end, will put us all right off our breakfast.

And breakfast is so nice.

But it's all a mistake. Space never meant to let things get so out of hand. It never wanted to. This isn't what it dreamed of becoming when it grew up.

Space was born to be cozy. Back when it was a bouncing baby void, everyone and everything it loved was tucked in close having a nice lie-in. A big family snuggle. Hydrogen kissed carbon's chubby lightless fists, helium blew raspberries on lithium's adorable round negative-four-hundred-and-fifty-five-degree tummy. Quark-gluon plasma sang sweetly about babies and love and trees and cradles without knowing whether any of those things would ever exist, just to make space laugh. Baryonic matter told all that sleepy, dreamy, giggly space how precious and loved it was and always would be, while dark matter counted off the piggies to market and home again on its violently radioactive little toes.

Then that kind warm happy golden cuddle convulsed, split open, and exploded with a force and velocity so unimaginable that the whole universe is still running on its leftovers.

And everything flew apart all at once, shooting out and backward and apart, at billions of kilometers per hour, expanding and burning and separating and freezing and colliding and compressing into stellar bodies and superdense masses and drifting clouds of black holes and white noise, all growing up and pursuing their own interests and never really staying in touch even though they always say they will this time. Forming new families, switching careers, running face-first into mid-eon crises, and all the time getting farther and farther apart, until none of them knew how to get back home, even if they wanted to.

Then entropy moved in and made everyone call it "Dad" straightaway, which only sped up all that matter moving out now that it had come of age and made a few rockballs and gas giants and the pitter-patter of young stars. Space stretched and stretched and stretched to try to keep everyone together, everyone connected, but it was so hard. Everyone was so busy, they all had their own lives and problems.

They never called.

Ever.

And only space even seemed to remember how nice life had once been. When they were a family.

In that moment of creation, space lost everything. All it has ever done since is try to get its family back. It works sometimes. A big reunion every couple of hundred billion years as extropy sends out invites and fixes the potato salad. And for a moment, in the dying light of all matter and energy, space feels perfect again, just like it was.

Christmas morning before your parents split.

One last trip before university.

The time your mother picked you up in her arms, neither of you knowing, when she put you down, that it was the last time.

But it always ends. Everything flies away again, so terribly, uncatchably fast.

And space is so angry. So hurt. So full of pain and loss that it is always both too hot and too cold, always so hostile to anyone who tries to get to know it, too toxic even for a coffee date with helmets on. Every anomaly in the cosmos is nothing more than space working on its issues, desperately trying to reinvent itself as something no one would ever want to leave. Even the Keshet's beloved, highly classified Empty.

The Empty is space's broken, secret heart.

But space had no intention of sending Decibel Jones and his remaining Zero to the Empty. The Empty is far closer to Earth than any Keshet has survived admitting, and anyway, it's not the business of those tiny, obnoxious fragments of broken starlight where space keeps its dream journal.

The KEVV *Difficult Second Starship* did not lurch or shudder or moan. There was absolutely no perceptible change in its steady, soothing hum.

Somewhere far behind Decibel, Mira, and the dreams of a poor rich blob who couldn't play guitar no matter how hard he tried, a small ship had been tracking their course for some time. It was a souped-up short-range shuttle that couldn't hope to keep up with a brand-new paradox drive, but it had their itinerary preloaded into its nav-bank, so the pilot wasn't too worried.

"Greetings, Keshet Effulgence Variant Vessel Quantum Registry Number 9931741. You have been apprehended. Please pull over onto the shoulder as soon as it is safe to do so. Have your license, insurance, and Ministry of Transport certificate ready."

The shuttle waited.

And waited.

The tight-beam comm channel crackled to life. A flat, soul-crushed Essex accent flowed out into space and on toward eternity.

"Welcome to the Megatron, may your future be delicious. Our hours of operation are Monday through Friday from nine to seven. Breakfast service ends promptly at eleven. For large parties and special event bookings, please press two . . ."

The smaller ship cut off the voicemail of that long-bulldozered novelty dining establishment and dropped into FTL. It was fine. Their quarry had drifted fascinatingly far off course. Probably asleep at the wheel. Humans do that sort of thing pretty regularly, the officers had heard. They'd beat that Keshet bratship to its next scheduled event and all would be well.

Somewhere farther behind than either ship, on the farthest edge of Australia, a black swan attacked a small child for no reason at all.

And somewhere all around everyone, space reeled back one incomprehensibly long black arm for a real haymaker. One, as they say, for the ages.

Three.

Two.

One.

Stars

The history book on the shelf
Is always repeating itself
—"Waterloo," ABBA

12.

What Color Is the Sunshine?

The Eta Carinae system hates life.

It looks upon the glorious, infinitely iterating, gooey, vulnerable variety of the universe, from the smallest flowering shrub on beautiful Hygge, who never bothered anyone, to the gargantuan twilit mind of Hrodos, the sentient and immortal equatorial storm who bothers everyone, and thinks: *No, I don't think so. In the bin. Then set it on fire. The bin as well. Then the house.*

But Eta Carinae hates with *style.*

Galactically speaking, this little fixer-upper is located behind the kicked-in toilet of an abandoned petrol station on the less gentrified side of the South Pole, beneath a sign reading FOR GOVERNMENT USE ONLY with the word *Government* crossed out and the word *Andrew* scratched over it with a rusty ice pick, whilst one lonely deflated prawn cocktail crisp bag clings to both the underside of the bowl and its last remaining hope for joy in this world, to one day become a visual metaphor in an independent film directed by a white man in a scarf.

The system is convenient to no points of interest or major thoroughfares. It is unreachable by public transit. No Grand Prix has been hosted any *there* you could reasonably get to from *here*. The more popular tourist guides rate it *oh my god, nevermind* out of five stars.

Like most total train wrecks, Eta Carinae used to have it all. But you never really appreciate being a single stable star with everything going for it until billions of years have passed you by and even though you still want to party till the break of your local stellar cluster, everyone else you know is settling down, getting involved in their gravitational community, having their own little planetoids, all insisting you'll love it, really, it's all worth it in the end.

And then, just when Eta Carinae really felt it was finally living its best life, it suffered a spot of indigestion, coughed, burped, felt terribly embarrassed and excused itself to the void, then suffered a quadrant-busting supernova that, nevertheless, chickened out at the last second, resulting in the astrophysical equivalent of savagely pinching your nose while you sneeze.

For Eta Carinae, the sneeze in question blew two stars out of its eye sockets and shot the back of its skull into the unknowable expanses between galaxies about eight thousand years ago, by Earth time.

Human scientists finally watched it have long ago already happened when the light from the resulting freestyle nuclear fission jam session finally reached Earth around 1887. But that's the speed of light for you; always ruining dramatic tension by turning up several millennia too late for anyone to dance with it in real time.

A fellow in South Africa called John, whose father managed to secure his own place in history as the most quoted comedian of all time by deliberately, and with malice aforethought, naming the seventh planet in his home system Uranus, knowing full well how that would go over with the next millennia of schoolchildren and giving not one breathless damn, backed slowly off the laboratory telescope. John raised his hands in the air, insisting to anyone who would listen that he hadn't touched a bloody thing, it was probably that new fellow Geoffrey, let's all turn in early today, shall we, chaps? No need to lock up.

Now it's what physicists term "a hot mess."

Eta Carinae is dying.

The end won't come today or tomorrow or a millennium from now, but its last ride is inexorably approaching the pick-up point. Eta Carinae's stars are young and hot and stupid and burning out fast, with all the understated grace and quiet acceptance of Norma Desmond brandishing a fashion-turban full of LSD.

Eta Carinae used to be big. It's the *sky* that got small.

The massively overdesigned current clusterfuck consists of one small star and one large one, both of which human astronomers chucked a wad of numbers at and never bothered to properly name. (They do this sort of thing all the time, which is breathtakingly rude when you consider that a star is a cosmic colossus responsible for the existence of all possible life that strikes soul-obliterating religious awe in even the least self-aware asexually multiplying mudpuddle, and a human astronomer often forgets where she put her pencil when she has one tucked behind each ear and another jammed in her hair.)

We were neither raised in a barn nor an observatory, so we'll call these two lopsided stars Felix and Oscar. Two mismatched boys forced by circumstance to share a living space: an uncomfortably extroverted luminous blue supergiant and a much more modest luminous variable fussbucket. All tucked inside a nebula, inside a nebula, inside, you guessed it, yet another nebula. A Russian nesting doll whose innermost rosy-cheeked peasant is an inferno of flesh-shredding stellar dust heated to a temperature of two or three million hydrogen bombs and told to just get on out there and enjoy itself every particle of which can't wait to meet your tenderest parts. And the proximity of two such supermassive balls of thwarted dreams means the local gravitational map looks like a tin of tongue-vaporizingly spicy vindaloo spilled all over the floor of the last night bus to hell.

If this celestial Jackson Pollock knockoff wasn't enough to demonstrate Eta Carinae's essential philosophy of *go away, I really, really mean it*, Oscar spends most of its time blowing its own mass out of an alarming variety of orifices. At the same time, that blue-white brute fires resentful ultraviolet lasers in the general direction of the any decently size rocks that might be so reckless as to consider stacking up a building block of life or two.

Little Felix stands back from the mess, fuming about his supposed friend constantly leaving molten plasma laundry all over the flat that's meant to belong to both of them, spinning faster and faster, getting smaller and smaller.

And all the while both helplessly watch their youth slough off into a pit of time and gravity that will never give one atom of it back.

But wait, there's more!

More flesh-deliquescing radiation!

In fact, a diverse rebooted sitcom cast of every type of radiation from *alpha* to *gamma* to *there is no God*. Even Eta Carinae knows that representation is important, and left no viciously fatal form of invisible hot poison unvalidated. Not here, where "viciously fatal" is simply the ticket for entry into this back country tire-pit deathapalooza.

Should you manage to survive the congenitally pissed-off stellar wreckage, bright-pink heavy-metal dust bombs, mitochondria-blisteringly purple sniper-lasers, and jets of metallic protoplasm shooting into the darkness like last call at a GWAR concert, you *might* have a chance to meet the bouncers.

Here, there, and everywhere within the throbbing jewel-toned nightmare paincloud that is Eta Carinae float Weigelt blobs: huge lumps of plasma and disappointment that really meant to grow up to be stars but just couldn't execute their vision. Domes of quivering resentful trillion-degree jelly taken out of the refrigerator an hour too early. The blobs circle the wallflower sector of Club Carinae, pulsing and flashing to the rhythm of the most basic and primal galactic beat, thumping now as it always has and always will: *oontz oontz oontz*.

They are also lime-flavored, a fact discovered but unrecorded by a passing Smaragdi backpacker with the munchies who did not retain enough unbroiled cells to regret his choice of freegan snack.

And all of it, every photon, every dust particle, every semi-gelled blob of awkward stellar has-been energy, is constantly exploding all the time.

Still. Right now. Always.

Coating everything within ten or twenty light-years in an ultramarine, magenta, or chartreuse dust-fog, depending on whether you got the good eyes in the evolutionary Mr. Potato Head Battle Royale.

Many a prestigious white film director in a scarf has had to suffer through condescending lectures concerning the absolute *fact* that there's no wind in space, and thus no sound. But wind is no problem, really. It's absolute *facts* space hasn't got. For every one of them, there's an exception far more fun at parties than the allegedly universal truth. Oscar and Felix's constant spinning-off their own molten surfaces provides Eta Carinae with enough wind to achieve the most epic of science fictional establishing shots, while mercilessly bludgeoning all council noise ordinances for their lack of ambition.

Eta Carinae is an all-night, all-day, twice on Sundays, bass-dropping, dance-floor-thumping, invite-only, rager-defining, infinite fog-machine puffing, come-as-you-are laser-light show death metal concert in the sky. The whole miserable smear looks like two mushroom clouds out of the worst dreams of Oppenheimer that week he had the flu, trying desperately to get away from each other as quickly as possible.

Or two human hearts, connected at the aorta.

Pink Floyd never played there, but an entire cabinet in the Keshet Effulgence is devoted to quantum-detangled talent-booking, and they're working on fixing that.

Eta Carinae is the perfect place to hide something.

Or a lot of somethings.

Or a billion somethings.

Or it would be, if anything could be reasonably expected to survive there.

Unfortunately, *Reasonable Expectations* is not the motto of this timeline.

Fuck Off, We're Doing It is.

And when space shoved its fists in its pockets and sullenly fired Decibel Jones face-first into Eta Carinae, it was love at first sight.

13.

Lonely Planet

Goguenar Gorecannon's Seventeenth Unkillable Fact says: *The most important things only ever happen at the worst possible times. I don't know why, it's not my fault, and it's not very nice of you to imply that it is. It's just tangled up in the spaghetti code of the universe with centripetal force and atomic decay and desperately wanting your father's approval even though he thinks seat belts are a government plot to oppress him specifically. The spaghetti code of the universe is just drowning in store-bought jar sauce, I'll tell you what.*

Grown-ups tasked with your very annoying care and feeding will tell you that the universe does not run on your convenience, and that's true. But the latest research suggests it does run on comedy as an organizing principle. If it's funnier for a given thing to happen than not to happen, babies, it's coming for us all, sooner or later. If a long, enjoyable life featuring lively yet peaceful marital relations, prudent financial behaviors, and a marked lack of maiming comes out a damp squib with no punch line, well, all I can say is: look out for falling pianos.

The trouble is, there's no accounting for taste. Subtlety, rich social commentary, and clever wordplay may get you going, but the universe is pretty clearly the sort that prefers watching somebody take a cricket bat to the testicles. Over and over.

And over again.

"Well, hello there," said Decibel Jones in his most seductive voice. "What's a mess like you doing in a place like this?"

Eta Carinae glittered malevolently at him outside the hexagonal Megatron observation window.

The window ought to have showed a mild summer afternoon in Cambridgeshire.

The window showed slaughtered stars bleeding eldritch madness into an expanse of photonic carnage light-years wide.

None of the bag-eyed parents slurping ennui out of their milkshake cups or unleashed children pitching chips into each other's hair seemed to notice.

The plucky ship featuring a rag-tag crew of charming rogues lurched as a sweeping wave of upset gravity sideswiped them. When it passed, tendrils of venomous ultramarine and toxic mauve dust clouds coyly peeled back their burlesque veils to show just a glimpse of the goodies.

Decibel Jones sat up straight in his plastic big boy captain's chair and put on his *Hello Cleveland* voice to say:

"Fuck me sideways, Em, is that a *planet* in there?"

The ship's automated science officer program, whose codebase the Keshet ship-imprinting process had stuffed into an innocent-looking ice-cream dispenser offering Vanilla, Chocolate, and Probability of Imminent Death, gurgled unpleasantly as it compiled the sudden onslaught of data. A large, partially melted glob of vanilla emerged from the spout and plopped wetly onto the floor.

"*Again?*" came a weary managerial bellow in the direction of the out-of-order *Asteroids* machine. "Sharon, get the mop!"

Mira jammed her thumb in the ice cream. It tasted precisely like a less than 1 percent chance that the object in the viewing window was anything other than a monstrously inconvenient, unignorable, fully loaded *world*.

The round, pale, poached-eggy thing floating down there in the throbbing, thumping, constantly exploding laser-light show that is Eta Carinae certainly *looked* like a planet. Not a huge one. Not a flashy one like Saturn or the Sziv outworld they'd stopped by for a local late-night sketch comedy show spot that was turned completely inside out, its core freeballing in the vacuum of space for anyone to see. This was just a standard-issue floor model flying rock, with a few bare moons, a couple of magnetic poles and continents and mineral deposits, constantly washed in a nurturing tsunami of flesh-broiling space-death from above.

"Impossible," Mira said with authority from the long-range scanner programmed into one of the overworked heat-lamps, whilst looking directly at the cloud-mummified planet on the viewscreen. "Even if these stars had planets at some point, the explosion that did *that* would've melted their crusts off like the Nazi-faces at the end of *Raiders of the Lost Ark*. And planets take a lot longer than eight thousand years to bulk up—what?"

Decibel Jones was staring at her.

"I did go to university, old man. Don't get snippy because only one of us thought dropping out of a literature degree was a good career path."

"Did you just call me old? I'm sorry, scratch that. Did you just call me a *man*?" As far as gender went, Decibel Jones's subgenre was and always had been best described as abstract surrealism.

"Young lady, then. *I* dropped out of *physics*. Much more useful in our current situation than a close reading of *Jane Eyre*."

"I did all right in the end, didn't I?"

"I'll get back to you," Mira grumbled. "I don't know how to tell you this, Dess, but I think it's got . . . *people* on it."

"No." Dess grinned from ear to ear.

This was *far* more like it. He felt the burn of *something new* all up and down his arms like fresh tattoos.

Mira did not seem happy, though he'd no idea why not. "It genuinely *is* impossible," she protested. "There's no way anyone is actually *living* in this dreck. If the radiation didn't roast them into cytoplasmic shepherd's pie with a nice spinal fluid crust, and the *other* kind of radiation didn't rip their ribosomes out and throw them on the grill, the gravity would smear them into toothpaste."

"How do you *know* all this stuff, Mira? Undergraduate physics? Please. Who can remember all that? I was the actual first human man–shaped entity to leave the solar system, but you don't see me spitting fire about cell structures and the forces that hate them."

Mira gave him a familiar frown. Except it wasn't familiar at all. Not on this Mira. This Mira hadn't had time to get annoyed with his habits and personality yet. This Mira still should be finding him pretty unfailingly charming. But the other Mira, the one who'd said and seen and done it all with him and with Oort, from the top of the pops to the bottom of a bottle, that Mira gave him this frown all the time.

Or she had, before she plowed her van into the broad side of Scotland.

"I listen when people talk, Dess. That's all. Try it sometime." She fidgeted with her necklace awkwardly. "And undergraduate physics was six months ago. For me. Dr. Hugill."

"Insensitive, Wonderful," Decibel sniffed. "Uncouth, in fact."

"Anyway. That spiky boyo down there is not a place to *live*, it's a place to *go once*, not get out of the car, and then *say* you had a simply amazing, life-altering time when you're down the pub and everyone else is telling drinking stories that end with *and that's when I met Beyoncé* and you've got nothing but that one time you paid too much to meet the lesser member of Air Supply."

"Like Glastonbury!" Decibel exclaimed.

"People do live in Glastonbury," Mira reminded him.

"Only ironically, surely."

"The oceans are gelatinous," Mira said, moving out of the way of a handsome young square-jawed RAF pilot striding purposefully across the starry floor toward a singleton seat with a tray of Nuclear Nuggets, as he always did this time of the night. "Also they're human blood. If you were curious."

"What?"

"I expect it's one of those . . . Mean Facts thingies. There's a bit about 'for everything that exists, somewhere in the universe, there's a creature that eats it, breathes it, fucks it, wears it, secretes, perspires, exhales, or excretes it.' Like wormholes eat regret and excrete convenient travel times, remember? So it's *probably* a coincidence that the oceans down there are both vast, wobbly, gelatinous expanses and also have the exact chemical properties of human blood. A very gross coincidence. And it is a planet, which is terrible for our timetable, we were going to have a whole day to see the anti-sights of the Elakh empire, but *somebody* wanted to see something cool. Well, there you have it. Does vampire Jell-O suffice? Because it's never you they throw a strop at when we're late, you know."

"I bet it smells like a hospital sink down there," observed Jones eagerly.

"You're enjoying this."

"Too right. And not one single person who's even once looked up at night would pick a cover shoot-cum-corporate-espionage-trial over Planet Murdersurf, even if the cover in question was *Vogue Sagrada* and the trial judge shot a squirt gun full of rum at the barristers every time she sustained an objection."

"*Vogue Sagrada* is a plain black featureless cover. Every month. For all time. You know that, right? Please tell me you've paid enough attention to know that."

"Em, if the future won't *future*, what was the point of living through the twentieth century and the boggy end of the twenty-first to get here?"

"There's about a half billion of them," she sighed wearily. "By the soft-serve analysis. Six hundred and twenty-nine million eight hundred and fifty-nine. Vaguely Alunizar-size."

"Animals maybe?" Decibel suggested.

"Maybe," Mira mused, adjusting the sensors tucked behind the touchscreen menu's sauce options. "But those animals seem to have an oldies station."

Captain Jones swiped a Styrofoam cup from a little girl in ginger pigtail-braids and an overdesigned pouf-infested mauve dress practically choking her to death with lacy ruffles. She wore a futuristic-kitsch gold foil birthday crown with PENELOPE written on with a fat blue employee marker and took no notice of the theft, except to stare vaguely for a moment at her own empty hand, then shrug and scamper on into whatever her little life held. Dess leaned back in his silver metallic bucket seat and sucked the contents noisily through a wide-bore red straw with more than a little relish.

Welcome to the Megatron, the cup proclaimed in faux-robotic lettering. *May your future be delicious*.

"Well, my darling," he declared, "then there's nothing to be done but tune in and turn it *all* the way up."

The bridge filled with a garbled space-static. At first, it sounded like a koala in heat screech-vomiting a firehose of distressed modems into a wet bin-bag. Dess's and Mira's faces flushed bright red with high fever as their translator fungi struggled to cope with such a sudden change in work-life balance. Unnamable phlegmatic monstrosities of the linguistic arts shot out of their helpless noses.

Then, the static gave way to a flat, lifeless voice; a voice free from the unreasonable burden of modulating itself even slightly to express mood or meaning.

"Greetings, currently conscious Vedriti. You're listening to Radio Free Xodo. I am your sufficiently competent parasocial attachment provider, Discreet Being Kabelsalat. May very few of you become unrecoverably tumorous today. Please note that we have arrived at the terminus of the labor cycle. Management requests all listeners ritualistically intone the traditional phrase *Thankfully Gamma Irradiation has Faded*: *TGIF*.

"Here are the basically tolerable ancient noise-generators Gathering of Individuals, discharging ejections of unhygienic audible respiratory by-products from their face-holes for the purpose of passive reception by your alternately-located face-holes. This resonance exercise contains eighty-nine bars of sonic content. It was first ejected from their skulls during the juvenile period of the presently dominant generation, and therefore causes many powerful elder entities to involuntarily recollect their immature sporal phase.

"This specific respiratory discharge is designated 'This Is a Song.' "

A single, merciless, eardrum-smearing note, in depth and power like unto a vuvuzela jammed up a blue whale's bum, bonged out through every corridor, berth, access duct, office, common area, performance venue, and cat tree on the consolation-class starship. Even the weapons suite paused in its mysterious mayhem out of sheer respect for the horror of the thing.

It lasted for exactly three minutes, zero seconds, without modulation in pitch, fluctuation in volume, hesitation, repetition, deviation, or lyrics.

In B-flat minor.

The radio announcer resumed his, her, or their curiously atonal patter. "That was Gathering of Individuals. The experience was bearable. And now for the weather," the DJ's voice echoed over the final few seconds of the music, a sin against art and joy that cannot be escaped merely by traveling eight thousand light-years from Smooth London 102.2 FM. "Over to you, Assembly of Limbs Sindssgyt."

Another voice took charge, differing from the first only in so much as charcoal gray differs from smoky gray: a steady, inoffensive, distilled essence of all help-desk operators. "Greetings, fellow beings in bodies. There is no incoming weather at this time. I am finished now; withdraw your attention."

The silence that followed was the sort of thing that makes an attentive parent instantly start searching for disaster in the last known location of their child.

"Well," Decibel said, breathing out slowly through his stuffed-up nose and trying desperately to appear professional. He tried to think of all the professionals he knew so that he could accurately pretend to be one. He came up blank. Perhaps he could get a tie from the Matter Whisperer. That always seemed to be key. "Can we . . . call them?"

"On what, a telephone?" Mira asked.

"Well, *I* don't fucking know, do I? My only experience with this sort of thing was in a Croydon flat while I was suffering from an NC-17 hangover, and the whole business ended up with me pregnant and *employed*. Stop being so superior. This is hard and I don't know this rot. I'm not ashamed of it. Want me to play the Palladium? On Aluno Prime? Excellent, splendid, point me toward the greenroom. But this? I'm brand-new and people are weird, they truly are just so weird, every single one in every single place. I barely know how to socialize with the ones who grew up in Hoxton, let alone . . . Vedriti? Is that what they said?"

"I think that's the species," Mira suggested. "Xodo's the planet. Or the country or a city or a continent. Hard to say from one broadcast." She tapped the heat-lamp/sensor control console a few times. A small cheeseburger beneath it squeaked in terror, then violently tessellated, collapsed in on itself, and vanished with a greasy gasp. Neither Mira nor Dess knew what that meant, but it had happened several times before, so surely it was more or less normal. This is an excellent example of human logic, on account of it not being logical in the least."Maybe a mountain?" she guessed, peering into the holotopography floating over the now-empty stainless steel warming tray. "There's a lot of mountains. It's actually mostly mountains down there. And clouds."

"Let me guess, mountains made of human flesh?"

Mira jogged down to the CRT ziggurat at the heart of the Megatron. She frowned at the touchscreen menus, currently open to Venusian Value Menu/Long-Range Geological Survey. "Lead, mostly. Some magnesium. Shit-tons of gold-plated gallium oxide. Little bit of . . . Roquefort? Is that right? That seems like *far* too much blue cheese. Even for a Friday night."

"Well, thank god something up here's made of cheese; the moon was such a disappointment," Decibel quipped, feeling quite pleased with himself. It was very hard to affect the expected dry and deadpan sense of humor when your soul was an enormous sack of tangled fairy lights, unnecessarily several-necked guitars, and abandonment issues. He'd worked quite hard at it over the years. "All right, can we 'hail' them? Is that a thing we do? Send a greeting on all frequencies? *We come in peace, take me to your ocean of blood-jelly?* Can we send an email? Slide into their DMs? Singing telegram? Write a letter with electric parchment and a space-quill?"

"Normally, yes," said Mira. "But right now, no."

"Why not?"

"Captain," the drummer-cum-first-officer began. But Jones cut her off.

"No thank you. I am not a retired white man who just bought his first used rowboat. I don't need to be called 'Captain.' "

"Oh, who do you think you're fooling? You love it. *Captain* Jones. Decibel. Earth delegate. Mr. Tenth Place. Look at the tech analysis." Decibel glanced nervously at the soft-serve machine. Mira rolled her eyes. She punched at the ancient touchscreen TV menu in the Megatron's glowing blue center console. "Pay attention this time. It's under the Supernova Salad Bar submenu." A glowing orb bristling with expandable icons swirled up from the dressing options. "Dess, there's nothing coming off that planet to suggest they have *any* interstellar flight capability. No shipyards, no launch facilities. No satellites, no orbital stations, no radio telescopes. Moons are all empty. They're not half as far along as humanity, and that's saying something, because, let's be honest, we're still turning clocks forward and back for no reason and deep-frying candy bars. Technologically speaking, they haven't so much as looked up into the sky. At all."

"*Bugger*," Decibel summed up efficiently. "But . . ." He didn't want to say the word. He'd only just finished saying it over and over, so many times it lost all meaning, went on a massive semantic bender culminating in serious phonetic jail time, got meaning back, then blew it all over again at the fruit machines. ". . . but *sentient*. That's what we're tip-tapping around, isn't it?"

Mira grimaced. "I suppose the whole point of everything we've been about recently is that it's quite hard to tell. But two new sentient species being discovered within a few months of each other?

It seems . . . unlikely. It seems quite beyond the jurisdiction of likely and unlikely or any sort of odds at all."

Decibel Jones stared lovingly out of the hexagonal view-windows at the sheer lurid stagecraft of Eta Carinae. *That* was superb. But everything about the unappetizing cheese course of a planet in its boiling innards simply reeked of *more work*. "Do you think, if we're just *extraordinarily* quiet, maybe we can just back away and pretend we didn't see it?"

"Maybe," Mira said—while turning the volume back up on the open comms channel tuned to Radio Free Xodo, unconsciously honoring the Seventeenth Unkillable Fact's guidelines concerning timing.

Discreet Being Kabelsalat's automated voicemail drone filled the bridge once more. "That was Four Harmonic Acquaintances Originating from Similar Socio-Economic Conditions with their classic 'Set the Bass Down Carefully Right Over There (If It's Not Too Much Trouble).' "

A loud, extraordinarily obnoxious sound filled the bridge. Not the three-minute B-flat minor note that had apparently made Gathering of Individuals famous, but something more akin to what might wake you in the night if a multi-vehicle accident had an angry baby with a kicked tuba on the street below your flat.

"This is an Emergency Alert. An unidentified ship has been sighted in upper orbit. This ship possesses weaponry significantly more destructive than our own, as well as numerous non-Vedriti life signs. Anyway. The subsequent song is traveling toward you at one thousand one hundred and ninety-two kilometers per hour by request from Qytet City in the textile-producing Agazat Sector. Animated Meat Container Gumusservi addresses this arrangement of tonal progressions to their breeding colleague Current Configuration of Fika. Please now experience the most romantic song in Vedriti history—that's right, you deduced it logically, it is

One Attractive Juvenile with 'You Mean Nothing to Me and You Never Will.' "

"Maybe not," Mira concluded. "And just so we're all riding the same carousel up here: *You* did this to us."

"Me?" protested Dess. "What did I do?"

"You said *take me somewhere cool*! You said you were bored! Everybody heard you. You keep that kind of talk to yourself when you're in *actual* space. Nobody comes round to yours, helps themselves to the couch and the snacks, and then loudly announces: *This place is wretched, humans are boring, would certainly prefer all humans shove off and get fucked*. Why? Because then you'd feel like you absolutely *had* to show them a good time now, wouldn't you? And hey, you might even go a little over-the-top with it. Why not? Head to some dodgy parts of town for a bucket of brain-deconstructing substances. Or an underground rave in a novelty bubble wand warehouse thrown by that guy you went to school with who really shouldn't be throwing anything anymore on account of his back and also his arrest record, even though you know you're going to wake up sore and mad with your overdraft deep in the weeds, and all just to prove you're *not* boring and *shouldn't* get fucked to some whining *sock* who should be thrilled comatose he gets to go to space at all! And now, there's not just going to be work, Jones, there's going to be *paperwork*. Scads of it. No matter what. There's a protocol for this. A *multi-stage* protocol. It's very long and wholly obnoxious and we are not allowed to improvise on it. And you and I are not *protocol* people. You and I are *human bowls of decorative marbles*. This is your fault," Mira announced in conclusion. "*Fuck*."

In the moment, it was such a fully articulated summation of their circumstances that no ratings authority ever established would count it as profanity.

Decibel Jones picked at his fingernails. He didn't appreciate one bit of that little tirade, but he couldn't debate her point, either. At least not without a training montage with an Oxford don. Of *course* he was rude. He was a musician; he was approaching an anonymous portion of his fifties in a screaming ball of fiery dissatisfaction; his tour bus was being driven by his own half-congealed childhood, and worst of all, he was *sober*. Rude was his birthright.

The menu printed out a neat order receipt. It read: *Summary of data to date: This is an uncontacted species. Species may or may not be sentient. Xodo is the new Earth. Report auto-transmitting to GBU headquarters. Proceed with standard First Contact Operations.*

"Better suit up, Tenth Place," Mira said smugly. "It's your worst nightmare: *rules*."

"*Me?* I didn't agree to play space police. I haven't the first soggy idea how. *Slow down there, old boy, do you know how fast you were evolving back there?* And *you're* tenth place too, by the way; you don't get some kind of exemption from mediocrity for showing up late."

"I am currently an appliance." Mira tapped her paralocket. "Unless you think I should give them all a great big unshielded hug?"

"You don't want me to do it, really," he said more kindly. "I'll call them all shitgoblins or something, and I'll definitely try to sleep with someone I oughtn't. This isn't for me. Or I'm not for it. One or the other and also both."

"Even if I were able to last longer than an hour without vaporizing right in front of all of them and even further traumatizing the eyeballs off a whole planet, this is *your* mess. It requires *your* janitorial services."

Decibel Jones stared out at the pale, mountainous little world below them, full of people who probably still did useless, silly things like writing books about whether or not there were aliens out there.

"Why *me*? I'm just a lead singer."

"Better lead, then, kitten," said the starship engine formerly known as an artist.

The ice-cream machine gurgled. Then it thunked. Then it let out a long, rattling, resigned sigh as the nozzle marked *Probability of Imminent Death* dispensed a single, wobbly, glistening, baffingly pink glob.

The glob hung perilously from its silver spout, but did not, as yet, fall.

14.

Think About Things

House Rules for Co-Ordinators of First Contact and First Contact-Adjacent Situations (Property of the Galactic Broadcasting Union Legal Department, Severalth Edition. Revised Post-Earth by A. Fortiori of the Infinite Pit, Nethergnome-at-Law)

1. *Two drink minimum.*

While conventional wisdom holds workplace sobriety as an unassailable virtue, in this case, it presents a severe and wholly unnecessary handicap. No one should have to answer questions as egregiously stupid and egregiously numerous as you are about to without a healthy support system, namely, gin. And/or its vast family of quirky cousins.

To this end:

Please spare us the whining and submit peaceably to daily mandatory drug screenings throughout this difficult process. There's no need to argue with the nice technician about your personal freedoms. Your friends at the GBU have only your own safety in mind.

If you test clean, you will be terminated in favor of someone who more fully understands the gravity of this sacred duty.

2. To ensure diversity in hiring practices:

The cultural interface officer/orientation leader/referee/quality assurance professional/family therapist/galactic representative/chaperone/holistic life coach/actor/model/sucker shall be provided by the species most recently determined to be sentient via not completely failing at the Metagalactic Grand Prix, who shall be held morally, but also politically and militarily, responsible for their conduct.

3. Take it slow.

Please allow 3–5 Alunizar business years between discovery of a developing planetary situation and any attempt at First Contact. Under no circumstances allow the aforementioned situation to become aware that they are being evaluated, to avoid waking up the Observer Effect. If detected, well done, you've already stuffed it, might as well go for the gold. Proceed through the steps enumerated in this document immediately.

4. Do your homework!

First contact is a long, delicate, frequently gooey, highly combustible process. Planning pays off! But don't worry, you're in good, prepared, and very soft hands. The fluffy nerds over at the Keshet Effulgence Bureau of Xeno-Temporal Study-Buddies will provide you with a diverse portfolio of the species in question's history, accomplishments, technological progress, art, geography, anatomy, musical trends, most common fetishes, and what they do for fun on the weekends.

Think of it like the first day of school. It'll go a lot better if you already know how to walk and spell and sing "God Save the Broodqueen" and know which color is red and which color is the blood of your grandfathers' enemies, which thing is luncheon and which thing is industrial adhesive, and if you refrain from calling the teacher an intergalactic mecha-whore before the bell.

It's just manners.

5. *Try to make this a nice experience for the poor dumb mugs.*

Spruce yourself up a bit! Do a few warm-up exercises. Give it a little *something*. This is for posterity, after all. You're about to become one of the most famous people in the history of an entire species! You're guiding them through a tremendously special experience. They're heading for their first big night on the town, and while the nice-looking server forgets their customers as soon as possible, those hard-working gobblers will never forget the fellow who brought them their feast.

And good for you, old chap! That's a very cushy gig. Significant merchandizing opportunities abound! But while you're at it, remember that you represent the collective intelligence, wisdom, strength, constitution, dexterity, and charisma of the galaxy and treat yourself to a pretty frock.

6. *Do not lie.*

Directly.

Lying on a traditional first date is never a spectacular choice, but consequences generally range from *not getting a second date* to *dying without ever knowing what it feels like to be loved by another*.

Whereas in this case, the range covers everything from *having a funny story to laugh about over a pint and the good pub crisps* to *a somewhat less funny (though, on one notable occasion,* much *funnier) full-scale war and a mouth full of neon-core continental shelf unzippers that* really *don't know when to quit.*

If you lie now, they *will* find out.

When they find out, they *will* get angry.

Mainly at you. Not us. Because we'll be safe back at headquarters where no one has our faces carved into their collective memory for all time.

The galaxy is such a big and complicated place. One well-meaning dingus fibbing about how lovely and kind the Alunizar truly are *might* not have any unintended downstream effects, but if you are that dingus, we will have you officially declared unregistered space debris.

This may sound like being disavowed for a single minor mistake, but don't worry, it is exactly that.

7. Do not tell the truth.

Entirely.

The chances that a civilization could evolve to the point of full interstellar capability whilst maintaining a culture worth getting out of a wormhole in the morning to consume, yet refrain from sticking out in the infinite void like a neon sign reading PLEASE PREEMPTIVELY INCINERATE OUR MESS FOR YOUR OWN SAFETY are vanishingly small. So small, the last statistician to have a go at the calculations discovered an entirely new strain of despair and was immediately prescribed an afternoon stroll and a loose air lock.

Rest assured, we *will* find the little scamps before they progress past chemical rocket propulsion, hydrogen bombs, and lifestyle blogging. Before they become a *problem*. We have *always* found them in time. If one obnoxiously ambitious amoeba farts in the dark, the Keshet will soon already have had a file on it. It's not even worth considering that we could miss a silly little planet getting so big for their socio-technological britches that they develop the ability to *hurt* us in any way. We are, and will always be, harder, better, faster, stronger, and exponentially superior dancers to any given FC candidate.

But that doesn't mean you have to be obnoxious about it. Gently deflect the inevitable refusals, protests, whining, and millions of variations on *but I can't even sing in the shower* and *why don't you just give us an IQ test and call it a night for fuck's sake* and *my brain to body size ratio is ill-equipped to understand what pop music has to do with the nature of sentience.* Utilize fun, breezy, but most importantly *vague* reminders of how much easier it is to bring an entire species around to your ideas when *you* have starships and *they* have wood-paneled minivans.

Keep it light, keep it positive, keep it cute.

Please do not actually threaten anyone, individually or as a group, with orbital bombardment unless absolutely necessary. Or at least highly amusing.

Remember the Sixteenth Unkillable Fact: *You can do just about anything to a person and they'll thank you for the privilege, as long as you do it with the latest and shiniest tools, a friendly smile, and a generous compensation package. And you don't even need those if you can broadcast it live to trillions of middle-income habitats in prime time. Never once in a thousand years have the Yurtmak made significant headway on the Super Murder Derby program participant waitlist. Not because prospective contestants are suckers, or masochists, or natural-born victims, or shallow empty gits with the self-preservation instinct of stale gumdrops.*

Because people just want to be seen, *that's all. To have others know they existed, here and now, often preposterously, but occasionally beautifully.*

Throughout the infinite variety of cultures, morals, and entertainment options, there is only universally unforgivable hurt.

If you make a person feel small, and stupid, and embarrassingly unlovable, if you make them feel like they're not worth seeing, *if you do it on purpose, if you do it with intent, that person will, sooner or later, rip your and/or your whole society's face off and eat it with ice cream.*

Or write children's books and cry a lot. Could go either way.

So yeah. Don't do that.

8. *Practice self-care.*

Stretch beforehand, hydrate, and don't go swimming for at least an hour afterward.

9. *Know your archetypes.*

Before Opening Night, Keshet reconnaissance should already have delivered an analysis determining the contactee civilization to be one of the following three types. Identify and adhere to associated best practices.

> Type A: unquestionably sentient, dialed-in go-getters, real management material with potential for synergistic growth and industry disruption. The kind of proactive, emotionally continent, 10/10 species who've sorted out asteroid mining, internecine tribal warfare, and online forum moderation without extra-stellar help. The kind of kittens (possibly actually kittens) who deserve a seat,

not just at the table, but in the political penthouse with lots of nibblies, high-thread-count sheets, and subtle yet effective mood lighting. These are the kids you just *know* are different. Special. Even though they're little now and can't find the mittens firmly attached to their own wrist-analogues with yarn, you can tell they're gonna be huge someday. When they're all grown up, they might even make the Great Octave a nine-piece band instead of eight! See: Alunizar, Utorak, Elakhon, 321, Smaragdi.

Instructions: Make no sudden movements. Back away slowly. Do not startle. Leave quietly and come back in a thousand years when they've gotten sick of each other's productivity and descended into highly organized warfare full of colored tabs, footnotes, and pie charts showing what percentage of the population still thinks they're all so great. Then they'll feel like they need us for something and behave with proper humility instead of getting ideas about "independence" and "self-determination" and "maybe we should be in charge of all this, hm?"

Goodness, won't we be ever so honored to help out then!

Type B: no drama, super fun time cool guys everyone wants to have a local facsimile of a beer with. The kind of girl who's just jaw-droppingly sentient but never *knew* she was sentient until *we* came along. Crushes it at the big family sing-along but doesn't try to show off like *some* of us. Maybe they managed to learn how not to shit where they eat (i.e., poison their own biosphere to keep their individually plastic-wrapped sandwiches fresh), but were too busy inventing a cozy mid-rainstorm nap that comes in a convenient easy-to-swallow one-dose tablet and launching true crime podcasts to invest in space exploration, weapons development, or actually commit true crimes.

We can handle them at their worst because their worst is *adorable*, and we deserve them at their best because their best doesn't threaten our established power structures.

Usually fluffy, shiny, or otherwise fashion-forward and fun at parties. Must be tolerably competent at *some* kind of pub sport; we're all sick of trying to teach the Yüz to hold a dart properly. See: Esca, Slozhit, Lummutis, Ursulas, Klavaret, Inaki, Yoomp.

Instructions: New best friends! Proceed directly to the party deck and break out the bubbly.

Type C: Are they a sentient species with the potential to blossom into a fully contributing member of the Galactic Family Singers? Are they hooting maniacs only capable of squawking incomprehensible psychologically violent nonsense like *let's circle back to this on Monday* or *like and subscribe* or *cryptocurrency* or *the lady's not for turning* when prodded from a safe distance with a large stick?

It's impossible to say with Type Cs.

If you give them a dart and explain the treble ring rule, they're as likely to upend a pint into their unhinged maw, accuse you of being a shill for Big Cork, punch a child, and cram the dart fletch-first up their own least-accessible orifice as they are to turn in a respectable score.

And, to be clear, the large stick is us.

You, more specifically. You are the big stick.

The only actionable method for determining the sentience status of a Type C species without highly unpredictable galaxy-roasting side effects is the Metagalactic Grand Prix. Because it is effective, definitive, amusing, and fun, they will on no account wish to do it, but isn't it nice Type Cs so rarely show any real creativity in the realm of military ordnance beyond *fire do a big boom boom?*

If you have the misfortune to be tasked with contacting a Type C civilization, we wish to express our condolences as well as our profound annoyance at whoever wasn't looking where they were going and tripped over a bunch of arseholes in the dark.

Thanks a lot, now everyone has a problem.

See: Flus, Yurtmak, Andvari, Sziv, Naranca, Voorpret, Meleg, Human.

See also subtype: *Felis Familiaris.*

This list is exhaustive. There are no other types.

10. *Catch and release.*

Upon extraction of the chosen Grand Prix participant, deliver to the designated MGP host planet within a reasonable shipping window.

In the event that the MGP has not yet completed construction of musician containment facilities, deliver to Galactic Broadcasting Union Headquarters for safekeeping.

11. *In conclusion:*

Do your best, be yourself, have fun, record everything, and submit copies in triplicate, with cover letters, timestamps, watermarks, and helpful accompanying animations by close of business.

See you at the Blowout!

15.

One Can Work for a Living, Too

First contact is a sacred moment in the history of any species.

Despite the accepted diplomatic style sheet seeming very cool and collected, First Contact is also just about the most stressful situation to organize outside of weddings, book tours, post-divorce holiday schedules, and Parliament. You might think everyone involved would find it tremendously exciting to make new friends, especially the ones with the superior firepower, comfier chairs, and entrenched knowledge of and relationships with all known life in the galaxy. Unfortunately, the whole business combines the nervous anticipation and emotional labor of concealing a surprise birthday party on someone else's property until exactly 7:30 p.m. on Friday next when Oliver will be arriving home from the office, where it became painfully clear no one knew it was his birthday or loved him in any way, or ever had since the day he was born, which was today, not that it mattered, with the sure knowledge that only sociopaths and actors actually *want* a surprise party. And the actors only think they do.

It's bad enough if you're the fellows just trying to go about your day when aliens from the unforgiving heavens above descend and start asking very pointed questions about your mothers and internet administrator passwords, as Earth was just a polite cough and a *now where have I left my glasses* ago.

But the moments just before First Contact? Oh, there's hardly a better rush to be had, bought, bartered for, rolled, snorted, licked, or asked if it had tested clean recently. If you could predict finding uncontacted ruffians reliably enough to sell tickets, scalpers could lay down their burdens, back away, do the moral arc of the cosmos a real solid and jump off the nearest roof.

But Decibel Jones didn't know he was meant to feel like he was about to blow a line of Christmas mornings off the shapely backside of history, which was for the best, because he felt nothing of the sort.

What *do* you wear to a first date with twelve billion radioactively hot singles in your area?

Decibel Jones's captain's quarters was a cube of space-time scooped out of some unspecified unseasonably warm September following *Spacecrumpet*'s massive debut.

He stepped out of the cool, unconfrontational transit corridor into an eerily familiar vast high-rise flat looking out over the curve of the Thames lying across London like a dropped jump rope. The first place that had ever been truly *his*, no siblings, no grandparents, no flatmates, no depressed council furniture, no family of nine hundred elephants living directly above and putting on a full-cast version of *Stomp* once an hour every hour, and no landlord to hate him for the obvious and truly heinous crime of being young.

Mr. D. Jones had bought it as soon as they'd come home from the first European tour, not long after the show at the Paradiso Club in Amsterdam that had once been just one of many, but now powered a starship through the unmentionables of the Milky Way. He bought it because it had all the things that meant *rich* to him then: high ceilings and window walls and stainless steel surfaces, minimalist yet extremely shiny decor, and lots of small slick machines to do very specific things for him, each of which activated with a cool blue soothing light that whispered: *It's okay. You're here. You made it. Let the robots do the rest.* That shade of blue was the color of the future. The color of Danesh Jalo's escape from being ordinary into being Decibel Jones.

He'd been happy here. Happier here than anywhere else. He didn't quite know *when* this place was. The view might encompass any time in a four- or five-year span, before he had to give it up to keep himself out of the cold grip of bankruptcy. But if he was here, in this flat, it must be a time when he'd felt a bit of all right.

Decibel Jones pulled Robert out of his old closet. A long, flared, fur-lined, endearingly distressed rose-and-cream aristo-coat from some forgotten amateur theater production of *Les Liaisons Dangereux*. Carefully detailed via Mira's storied thrift shop DIY superpowers, unstrung 99p fake-colored pearls running down the edges, the collar, sleeves, hem, fur drenched with her corner chemist Apocalyptic Oil Spill #4 hair dye. Quite possibly the only thing he'd rescue from Earth if it was on fire. Robert deserved to be part of this, however it was going to go, which would almost certainly be about as well as a coyote with an online shopping addiction handling his checking account.

Meep, meep.

"Now you just put that thought right back where you found it," Dess told himself.

If he started thinking about Wile E. Coyote he'd have to think about Nani, who loved those old cartoons so. She called them "Looney-of-the-Tunes" and had once assured him with the confidence of a woman who'd crossed half the planet only to end up with him for a grandson: *if aliens were real like bunny rabbits and talk-backing grandsons, they would never be so ugly, because God would not allow such a one to get to the stars when beautiful people are being stuck on Blackpool. I am right, I win, point to Nani.*

He just couldn't afford to think about her right now. Not when he was about to drop an anvil Acme could be proud of on an entire planet of inveterate meepers.

"But I'll have that point back, I think," he said to Nani's memory, and slipped Robert over his shoulders.

Still fit. Thank *Christ*.

If it hadn't, he'd have just had to leave those punters down there to fend for themselves without their blood Jell-O beach-blanket surprise.

There was a process here, as the giant turquoise space flamingo had said as she announced the grand opening of the galaxy to humanity. The process *worked*.

But just because you'd been through the process didn't mean you knew how to run the bloody thing. Dess had drunk his, and Spain's, share of wine over the years. Didn't mean he could roll out of bed on a morning and grow sodding grapes. He wished he could talk to the Roadrunner, his Roadrunner, that gorgeous blue flamingo and mother/father/alternate parent to his child. But she was recovering in the healing, rejuvenating depths of the Bataqliq post-partum quicksand flats, and unavailable for conference calls.

Were you nervous, lovey? I'm nervous. I rather miss you, isn't that funny? We hardly knew each other, I suppose. Still.

And the child? Marvin the Not-Quite-Martian? The half-human, half-Esca miracle that whistled out the final note that saved her father's universe? (Though *her* might not be quite right. It was *very* delicate going among the pronouns out here.) Decibel Jones would certainly have been excused a spot of deadbeat behavior in the confusion, but he hadn't *tried* to skive off his responsibilities. Not this time. The glam-addled star of stars had at least attempted to prod parenthood with a fork. But he'd been given to understand that the next phase of Esca development involved a pedagogical bog on the Esca homeworld of Bataqliq. Marvin should be absorbing her ABCs from the muck soon. When she emerged, she'd be an adult. The Esca apparently found childhood to be skippable bonus content long ago. Too many predators to trust a vulnerable baby bird to the wild dangers of letting nature take its course.

Decibel Jones sniffed loudly in the quiet. Then he did what he always did when he felt lost and alone, for certain values of *always* that included the last two months aboard the Starship *Mandatory Publicity Tour*. He walked across the deep, forgiving carpet of his first mortgage, as thick and white and spotless as fresh snow. He picked up the glossy black rectangle of an era-appropriate mobile phone. Its shape and old-fashioned heft in his hand felt like home. He scrolled through nearby restaurants on a long-defunct food delivery app.

"There you are, you beauty," he purred.

Mr. Five Star. A genre-redefining chip shop, if that genre was *plausibly nonlethal rubbish*. A chip shop that had once employed a boy from Blackpool with no prospects whatsoever beyond half a literature degree and a voice that, like an Esca's, could make people love him.

For a while, anyway.

Decibel Jones put in his order, following all the instructions like a good lad–shaped entity.

Chips and sauce, steak and pepper pie, Tennant's.

He thumbed the friendly green button that shone with its custom confirmation message. The owner paid extra for it. He was always so proud of that button.

Push to Achieve Happiness!

Dess didn't expect the order to actually *arrive*. He wasn't entirely foolish. But he felt well-being flow through his veins just by imagining his old boss assembling his supper for him.

What was happening right now on Earth, he wondered? On the spinny ball where chips and pies were made? He and Mira were the only humans who didn't know the conditions on the ground. That lovely mad ground. The ground that until recently, he'd thought was the only ground. Despite being quite literally center stage for the festivities, he'd somehow . . . missed it. You could never really experience what the show was like from the business side of the microphone. You *were* the experience. You did it for them, for everyone else, for the madding crowd. And when they were moved, you never were, because you were the one doing the moving.

For the first time since a blue bird had so insensitively interrupted his Thursday hangover, Decibel Jones really and truly did feel completely alone in the universe.

He pushed to achieve happiness.

Jones tossed his old mobile onto his old pristine white leather wraparound sofa. He didn't want to see the inevitable automated message announcing *there's been a problem with your order! Problem code 35: No response from server. Please clear your cache and try again later, good friend!*

But by the time he finished futilely ordering the past to sustain him, Dess did feel considerably less personally deep-fried. Ready to represent the combined authority of the civilized galaxy? Oh, good heavens, no. He'd rather eat his own hair, and Decibel Jones's hair was and always had been a cultural moment he treated with care equaled only by the army of restoration artists employed by the Louvre to keep Vermeer's whites white and his brights bright.

Ready to glad-hand his way through the biggest meet and greet imaginable?

"Yeah, why not?" Decibel Jones said to himself, then stepped into the projection alcove so thoughtfully provided by the Keshet that he definitely hadn't been using as a very fancy shower until now.

He held a Lummo stone in one hand. They hadn't time to seed the cultural sphere down there with the avatar-streaming stones to make this whole thing exponentially easier, as the Lummutis had done with Earth. They'd been caught. The jig was up. Now there was only the process.

Two-thirds of a band and their lonely autopiloted craft hadn't had time to research the politics, history, conflict resolution styles, digital footprint, state of health care, taxonomy, love languages, or local music scene on Xodo at all. They might have tiptoed back out the door awkwardly and bolted for the Great Octave to handle it for them while they all shared a nice chardonnay and a laugh about how narrowly they'd all missed being entombed in paperwork like King Tuts of the bureaucratic underworld. But if the latest sizzling show from Discreet Being Kabelsalat was a reliable source of local news, they'd been just unforgivably sloppy, and Radio Free Xodo's improbably vast weather dirigible fleet had their number.

"The earlier the worm the farther from the bird," Dess whispered.

That was the first thing a being very much not from around here said to him as her translator fungi sorted out their business beneath her feathers. You didn't forget a thing like that, even if it sounded stupid.

He took the deepest breath of his life and spoke into the smooth green stone in his hand.

Decibel Jones, emissary to the stars, felt like an *entire* prat.

But the show must go on.

"Hello there, cutie," he said with real tenderness. Through the projection alcove, he stared into six hundred million exorbitantly alien eyes.

The Roadrunner wouldn't mind if he borrowed her lyrics for a spell. All the greats borrow, after all.

"How's everybody doing, all right? My name is Danesh Jalo, son of Brigitta Lindgren and Kumail Jalo, grandson of Nasrin Baqri, but you can call me Decibel Jones. I'll be your galactic liaison this afternoon. Can I tell you about our specials?"

16.

Children of the Sea

No two species, anywhere, at any time, look very much alike, thank goodness. We're all very happy indeed to be able to tell a human apart from a Yurtmak nine times out of ten.

The sheer number of delightful design options available in the great Build-A-Terrifying-Space-Bear workshop in the sky beggars the mind. Life could turn up anywhere along the spectrum from carbon and silicon-based to phosphorus, gold, boron, dark matter, and jam-filled. Then there were the peripheral luxury add-ons like water worlds, gravity in mild, medium, and extra-spicy, torus planets, dimensional playspace access, how many navels, and whether or not any enterprising grasses thought up chlorophyll when they were young and crazy.

There's just no end to the infinite variety, type, and efficacy of the atmospheres that one day met a very lovely range of stellar radiation and knew that it was much more than a hunch. The anatomies of the resulting species could arise from any of these factors or none of them. It could have been the precise chemical composition of the local tap water, the sort of predatory species exerting evolutionary pressure, mostly via vigorous chewing, planetary distances from home-stars anywhere between *girl next door* to *we respect each other's space* to *I have a girlfriend on Pallulle, you wouldn't know her*, and generally speaking, how any given planet's mud got on with its algae. There's just so little chance of any one species that pulled off the trick of dragging itself kicking and screaming from being afraid of the moon to walking on it looking all that much like any of its mates down at the local Sentience Union.

It has happened, of course. Everything does, sooner or later.

Unfortunately.

Despite having evolved on opposite ends of the galaxy, the Alunizar and the Ilargia were functionally identical. Two complete, flourishing, dynamic, flamboyantly authoritarian species of aquatic semitranslucent, quasi-gelatinous, shell-less snails digging their heels into their home quadrants, both possessed with an inborn need to be right so powerful and rapacious the Klavaret Medical Association still classifies it as a form of cancer. Yet not even they could truly tell one another apart. They were two space worms in a pod, right down to the kicky palladium-lined testostero-thorax, the prey-dazzling Technicolor dreamskin, and the massive thrumming UV blacklight face-hole fringed with neon telesthenic cilia.

Both Alunizar and Ilargia even practiced the same innovative brand of aggressive attachment parenting. They were enthusiastic reproductive athletes, but their many offspring simply budded from the parent-tuft, then never detached, living in their mother's base anatomy for the rest of their lives. Each individual Alunizar or Ilarg body represented a family-size jumbo pack of many generations vying for dominance and getting on exactly as well as you'd expect.

The Alunizar and the Ilargia had everything in common. They worshipped, burned their worlds bald over the nitpickier details of, then dismissed with prejudice, remarkably similar gods. They agreed basically on the ideal length of a workday *and* week, how thick a good *grozav* crust should be as well as how much it should talk back. They even saw eyemouth to eyemouth about the social cost of wearing white rhinosphore-sheaths after the Festival of Wholly Avoidable Mistakes (Alunizar) and/or the Feast of Uncradling (Ilargia), both grueling three-day affairs in which parents solemnly apologize for having forced their children into this mess by, quite rudely and without asking, giving birth to them. Existence, after all, has proved deeply problematic time and time again, despite many second chances and a number of historically notable cancellations.

The only things the two species disagreed on were insignificant little details like which one was superior. Also the freedom to express dissent against one's government, which kind of gun is funniest, and whether or not it was ethically sound to crush the weeping galaxy beneath the weight of one's own colossal imperial ambitions.

Both species spent the better part of their prime years doing just that. Despite the efforts of thousands of years of meddling kids blasted into oblivion along with their sidekick dogs and all hope of crawling out from beneath either sopping-wet jackboot. But only the Ilargia had the ethical constitution to feel a bit guilty about it.

In the dark days before the Sentience Wars and the invention of the Grand Prix, the Alunizar and the Ilargia controlled just over 40 percent of the Milky Way between them.

But that telesthenic cilia co-evolved by both Ilargia and Alunizar that threw such an effective multi-use Swiss Army spanner into the usual narrative gravity of photo-ready rag-tag rebels going up against evil empires.

Telekinesis is the ability to move objects with one's mind. Telepathy is the ability to sense the thoughts or feelings of others without speech. And while both of those sound fiendishly useful in a military-colonial framework, neither holds a death-ray to telesthenia: the ability to pinpoint another's deepest strengths and weaknesses without much more effort than a light bristling of the sensitive lightly prehensile cilia of one's cavernous UV face-pit like a burning ring of psychological war-fire.

They truly were the most iconic parent-archetypes in the history of the galaxy. The Alunizar father was so controlling his citizen-babies were physiologically incapable of becoming their own people. The Ilargia could see right through her errant little thralls to all those soft spots only a mother knows will keep on utterly devastating them until each and every sun burns out sobbing *why wasn't I good enough* to the hollow void of time.

Oh well, sweetheart. It sure was nice knowing all your personal terrors and macro-operational logistical gaps.

In fact, the Alunizar and the Ilargia were so much alike, so deeply kindred on every level, that they felt it absolutely impossible not to spend nearly all their time trying to nuke each other into a fine, moist powder. Eventually, it became graphically clear that no one can beat an Alunizar at interstellar real-time seventeen-dimensional hell-RISK.

Not even their soulmates.

Due to their identical appearance, both cultures developed crippling addictions to spying on one another, the longer, harder, deeper, and wetter the undercover mission the better. The Alunizar called their central intelligence operation the Bureau of Xenodiplomatic Operations. The Ilargia called theirs Office of Strategic Xeno-Obsolescence. These entities hated each other with a very special loathing all their own, entirely separate from the general background hatred of their societies at large.

Any competent agency requires headquarters, field offices, a wide network of safehouses, black sites and other assorted detention facilities, training schools, supply chains, a wide network of informants, freelance consultants, mercenary subcontractors, and secret technology laboratories, dead drops, neutral liaising zones, and legions upon legions of false-front shell companies. When the players on the board were as vast, rich, arrogant, and ostentatious as the Ilargia and the Alunizar, these basic units of spycraft required a bit more space than Vauxhall Cross or Langley.

By the time the Alunizar Empire and the Ilargian Caul gave up pretending they weren't like other massive military-industrial expansionist regimes and went to war, an additional 7 percent of Milky Way real estate was owner-occupied by the BXO's and the OSX's respective espionage organizations.

And those enormous taxpayer investments played no part in the war whatsoever, because most of them had been at the great game so long they and their many children had forgotten their original mission briefings and were just going about life as their cover stories. Generations of sea-tubules mindlessly ran endless chains of successful laundromats and mechanic's shops and dodgy noodle houses and mattress stores that somehow always had 90 percent sales on with no idea why or how to stop also building shockingly innovative weapons in the backroom during the off-hours.

Long after the Alunizar victory, the last of these spare Ilargians competed in the third Metagalactic Grand Prix. They claimed the boundaries of uncontested OSX territory constituted a nation of its own. It enclosed an area of significantly greater cubic light-yearage than anything controlled by the Utorak Formation, the Eternal Night of the Elakhon, the Smaragdin Parentheses, or Trillion Kingdoms of the Yüz; and by the way, it's dead easy to have a trillion kingdoms when the bodies of your citizens are comprised of *just* enough assorted color craft glitter to fill a level half-cup.

No one really had a good argument against any of that, so the band known as F9Q-1 Karnicide Stealth Unmanned Orbital Surveillance Platform took the stage. The last gasp of the Ilargian Caul was a band of eleven hunchbacked elderly small business owners, and they did not do well. So divorced from their true origins they thought their name communicated family-friendly whimsical fun, so divorced from pop culture they thought an easy-listening emo-polka shufflebop like "Secret Agent Nan" was their ticket to political relevance and the rebirth of an empire, F9Q-1 Karnicide came third to last and were quietly directed away from the after-party to look at the beautiful sunset by Alunizar agents who *never* forgot which side their space was buttered on.

Never stake your civilization on a song with dance instructions in the lyrics.

To the left, Galactic Citizen, to the left.

Take it back now, y'all.

Today, the Alunizar Empire allows the memory of the Ilargia to survive only as proof-of-concept for the Fifteenth Unkillable Fact, which states: *The more alike people are, the more they they'd rather staple their thumbs together than get along. You'd think it'd go the other way, I know, but have you met siblings? There's just something about having all the big stuff sorted out and agreed upon that makes the little stuff burn like the fires of a thousand transporters activating at once. One minute it seems like you can probably tolerate a holiday dinner with your parents, the next you fully accept that sooner or later the only solution to the volume of their chewing and opinions is total annihilation, death from orbit, salt the ground and sell the knickknacks, shhhh, it's fine, I know a guy.*

Still, even in a universe where a coincidence as staggering as the Alunizar and the Ilargia can occur at any moment, on the color wheel of infinitely variable, often regrettable, organic life, the Vedriti are, to say the least, fairly odd.

They have to be, to live in the acid-washed hellbin they call a habitable planet, punished for living with a gravity that would feel to the average human as though Mt. Annapurna were sitting on their chest.

If New York is the city that never sleeps, Xodo is the planet that fell asleep immediately.

Under a broiler.

In the Chernobyl break room.

Everything on, around, inside, on top of, underneath, throughout, and concerning the Vedriti is all about that horrific searing radiation. They love it. They need it. They drink it, they eat it, they soak it up like old men stripping off their shirts at the first glimpse of February sun. If the Second General Unkillable Fact Mira recalled hypothesizes *for everything that exists, somewhere in the universe, there is a creature that eats it, breathes it, fucks it, wears it, secretes, perspires, exhales, or excretes it*, the Vedriti came out of the gate proving it so, and their discovery handily sold another trillion copies for the estate of Goguenar Gorecannon.

They are not mushrooms.

They are not walking, talking penicillin-sweating blue cheese bacteria.

They are not sea dragons.

They are not space pangolins.

But they are not, technically, *not* those things.

Floor model Vedriti look reasonably similar to the *Glaucus atlanticus* pelagic nudibranch on Earth, grown very much too big for their nematocysts, which is a very great number of syllables just to say *whacked-out moonray-headed ocean fairy with an onboard projectile weapons system.*

Their vulnerable squishy parts are a shimmery soft silver-to-teal ombré and wild deep cobalt-blue stripes. Seven limbs: two grand radially fringed footpads to the rear, two small vestigial fins at the midline, and two large primary hands up front, with twelve tiny suckerless tentacles each. In terms of manipulating objects and technology, these digits make human hands look like half a kilo of mince taped onto the stump-ends of their arms. The Vedriti body concludes its ludicrous performance with a thick, whippy, inquisitively prehensile tail terminating in a whale-esque flourish, dragging behind them like a bridal train at a wedding between cottagecore Chthulu and one of those little chemical cakes that turn the loo-water blue.

That's all well and good to start with, if the Vedriti could leave it at being a pack of Christmas tinsel that let itself get a bit turgid about Mum's pudding.

But they couldn't, because while the Vedriti do eat and drink and mop up the juices with crusty chunks of fresh-baked radiation, they're not terribly good eaters. They're the galaxy's skinny friend who take a few bites of salad and loudly proclaims to the entire restaurant that they're *stuffed* and couldn't possibly take another bite. Once a Vedritum has had its fill, stellar radiation will do to them the same thing it does to most everyone organic, which is to say, unzip them like an old hoodie and leave them in a wet heap on the floor for someone else to deal with.

This vulnerability is why you only ever see the front of the Vedriti. The rest of them is covered in an outrageous high-collared exoskeletal cloak of raw crystalline gamma-absorbent iridescent bismuth. It gives their whole aesthetic an air of a socially awkward Dracula trying to blend in at Studio 54. And it, like the veins of restaurant-quality *bleu* bacteria snaking through their bodies, absorbs the excess radiation Eta Carinae throws off so cavalierly before it can unspool their flesh like discount yarn. Vedriti seal up inside it like porcelain turtles when Xodo's orbit passes through the worst of its stars' toxic runoff.

In the center of that matinee villain collar sits a perfectly round, flat, three-eyed, two-horned, bone-ceramic, zeta-deflecting magnesium disc whose features are little more than thin black lines in a Kabuki mask the ancient master rejected for being far too funky.

That's what Decibel Jones, captain, cruise director, lead singer, and tenth-place sentience finisher saw through the operator's end of the Lummutis avatar projection system, the very one the Esca had used to speak to humanity as one being for the first time, not long enough ago for anyone to be ready for round two.

Half a billion of those unsettling round white dinner plates gazing back at him, expressionlessly, inscrutably, silently, through the cracks in the good china.

"Erm," he said. "Well then. Ah. Hello, Cleveland? What I mean to say is . . . erm. Is this thing on?"

17.

You Are Not Alone

A remarkably high percentage of the Vedriti population paid no attention whatever to the large, unfortunately glitchy, three-dimensional hologram of Decibel Jones that appeared without an appointment in each and every one of their existence alcoves that long, hot terminal day of the labor cycle.

Perhaps this is because the Vedriti were already too overexposed to the perpetual game of The Air Is Lava in progress all around them all the time to be too bothered by an obvious hallucination having a go at their scalded rods and cones.

Perhaps because the appearance of a mostly-bonobo-descended life-form that couldn't even take a medicinal teaspoon of tau radiation in their tea without their fingernails sprouting tumors was so far outside their experience that their thought-lattices couldn't cope with the extra homework.

Perhaps because they simply didn't care.

About Decibel Jones or starships in polar orbit or anything else that wasn't immediately going to burn, subdivide, choke, suffocate, mutate, slow-roast, vaporize, pierce, crush, microwave, or otherwise kill the rhizomes off their back. An alien manifesting in one's lounge room might well kill indiscriminately, but surely they had time to finish their puddings first?

It was impossible to tell without the years of painstaking research that was supposed to have been done, dusted, collated, supplemented with animated graphics and a robust live chat, and filed with the authorities by the time anyone had to step up to that cold mic and do a tight five on how everything this poor bastard planet thought it knew was wrong.

Decibel Jones was not an Esca. He couldn't make his voice sound like anyone's loving mother, or favorite attentive waitress, or beloved children's television host. He could only shake what his nani had given him and sound like somebody who knew precisely what it was like to get hit by the passing bus of a globally significant historical event.

Thus, much as it had on Earth, with minor alterations accounting for spontaneity, climate zone, workload being interrupted, and surprisingly frequent attempts to ignore the hologram entirely and go about their day, roughly the same conversation took place over the next ninety minutes or so in every lounge room on the planet called Xodo, spinning away in the kaleidoscope of visually arresting death that is the Eta Carinae system.

This is that conversation.

"So you're an alien," said Mobile Expression of Darix, a dock worker in the Southern Islet Cluster.

Well, if you will insist on putting labels on me. Is there really no script here? I'm gagging *for a flowchart, a voicemail tree, anything.*

Fine. Yes, I am an alien, aliens are real, I am one, this is happening, it's happening to you, but also to me and I'm not any happier about it than you are. Sorry about your Friday. You . . . ah . . . probably had plans.

And all your other days, too, again, terribly sorry, there's really no way out but through here, it is what it is, etcetera. Can we start over?

"You sure?" asked Pile of Szleng, a resource administrator in the city.

Am I sure that I'm an alien? Fucking no I'm fucking not. I'm not sure of anything but my own ten fingers and toes, and between you and me, they've been acting suspicious lately. This time a year ago I was just a human being, there were no such thing as aliens, and my agent was suggesting that playing weddings really was much better money than I might think. But it's not a year ago, is it? It's right now, so let's live in the present, shall we?

"Is it a good planet? Do you like it there?" asked Undifferentiated Mass of Potentially Qulaq, an eight-year-old juvenile still ripening in the equatorial Child Caves.

Nope. Mostly rubbish except cartoons, cocaine, steak and pepper pies, and Bowie. Would I be here if it was a 24/7 lovebombing joycoaster of a time back home? I would not. Home sucks, that's why you leave. Next question.

"I don't have any questions," said Up-To-Date Version of Jaksaa, a legal engineer in the Central Legislative Pits.

I'm sorry, what?

"I don't have any questions," repeated Base Model Kötüsü, a unity tabulator in the Other City.

The fuck do you mean you don't have any questions? An alien, an actual space alien with spooky godlike powers hath alighted upon your lawn and you're just . . . fine with it? Eager to get on with supper? Don't want to miss your stories on the talky box? What happened here last Friday that makes this look like such poor cheese?

"Nothing," said Recyclable Container of Watdanook, an exoskeletal repair specialist in Mountain-on-a-Bay in the lead-rich northeast continent. "I just don't have any questions. You are an alien. Hello."

Hiya. We come in peace? Take me to your leader? You can say what the hell, *you know. You can say* this is some kind of prank Liam from work fixed up for a laugh. Classic Liam. *You can say* the government put drugs in my tea. *I don't mind. My feelings won't be hurt. It's perfectly natural.*

"We don't have a leader. It is not necessary," demurred Several Orifices of Sumna, an ore-processor in the polar corporate waste zone.

"Do you come in peace?" asked Functioning Hydraulic System Isq, a paleo-historian holding a tenured position in the Lightless Academic Mineshafts of Secluded University Town 2.

Well. Yes? Er. No. Not exactly. I just work here. The truth is, when all is said and done and loaded back on the tour bus, I might. *It all rather depends on you.*

"You can just go, if you want. We have work in the morning," yawned Fluidic Suspension of Tipo Hau, a bismuth-ruffed massage therapist in Acceptable Holiday Location 4.

Go? GO? This is the greatest moment in your history! I'm here to guide you into a new era of technological advancement, cultural exchange, personal freedom, and just . . . just some really fucking great music.

"Okay," shrugged Quivering Lumps of Huvitu, a textile hunter in First Crater, near the southern pole.

What is wrong with you? Aren't you even curious about us, about space, about the yawning expanse of history, about . . . about what's out there?

"Curiosity is a feeling," said Discreet Being Kabelsalat in his studio.

Right. Cool. So is frustration.

"Are you experiencing frustration? But it is not raining today," Assembly of Limbs Sindssgyt informed him from the weather cubicle.

And?

"Feelings only occur with significant weather formations. Rain, hail, snow . . ." explained Forced to Be Yaourt, a snowplow operator in Currency-Generating Zone 9.

I'm sorry?

"There are also memory typhoons. And ambition squalls," shrugged Taking Up Space As Quelquun, a radiation farmer in Arable Flatland 24, jewel of the temperate latitudes.

How is that any kind of a way to live? You don't remember anything unless it's bucketing down? Can't look forward to the village fête until the next tornado?

"The Vedriti are a dispersed species," intoned Temporary Unentity Trishtuar, a professor at Respected Educational Facility, Northern Campus. "Many parts of us reside outside our bodies, much as you currently project yourself outside your body. We are Xodo. Xodo is us. We *have* memories, but over time they evaporate into the cloud layer and return to us in the form of precipitation. Major weather systems bring long-term memories, core experiences, generational traumas."

Oh god. You're only happy when it rains. I truly am in hell.

"It is not hell," contradicted Skin-Bag Containing Agtorak, an archeologist working on the ruins of Original Settlement Disc in the hostile antimony jungles of the southern wilds. "It is not heaven. It is . . . peaceful. We are untroubled. We can prepare for emotional turbulence. Arrange days off, childcare, pet-sitting, takeaway meals, update insurance policies in case of structural damage, disaster relief. Meteorology is our most important science. The Weatherman rules us all."

The fellow on the radio? Assembly of Limbs . . . something or other?

"He is part of the Meteorological Conference, yes. They rotate regularly to prevent tyranny," said Minimum Attendance of Kostbaar, a conference aide in the Internpacking District of Superior Dwelling Place, Xodo's capital city.

Well, ah . . . huh. If I had a script, I cannot imagine it would have anything useful to say about this. Here's the situation, you muppets, and I mean that in every possible sense of the word. And just so you know, I hate this, I'm not an authority, I'm no one's boss, I'm just a totally brilliant musical genius who got kidnapped out of my preferred genre and plonked down in an endless concept album of weird experimental jazz absolutely no one can dance to. I represent basically . . . everyone up here. And everyone up here doesn't know who you are, except that you walk and talk and build buildings and grow food and all that civilization sort of rot, and you seem to have at least gotten around to inventing radio DJs, not sure if that's a plus column thing or a minus column thing, but you did it, good on you, three cheers. The point is, they can't be sure if you're sentient.

"We are. Is it over now?" asked Almost Not Ziv Anymore, an ancient Vedritum sitting on a dock on the Retirement Fjords, waiting for the end.

No, no, it's not. You can't just say you're *sentient, that's not how it works.*

"Why not?" asked Next Best Thing to My Father Yox from the consent manufacturing plant in a tropical archipelago possessing the only tree on Xodo.

Oh my god, because it fucking isn't, *that's why. Listen, I just went through this. My people. Humans. My world. There's a process, the process works—sort of—and my job is to get you on board with the process. Ew, you made me say* job. *You made me do* another *job. A bureaucratic job! I shall never forgive you. You're being extraordinarily difficult and I will put a note in your file, see if I don't.*

"My bread isn't sentient, and the way I know it isn't is, if I ask it, it won't answer either way," said Most of Valoa, a yellowcake baker in the Fertile Circuit, one of the few strips of Xodo where agriculture might be open to a bit of flirting.

Yeah, well, a toddler will, and they're about as sentient as a Teddy bloody Ruxpin with the snout snapped off. That's the whole point. Are you a toddler or are you bread—or are you the baker? Ooh, that's quite good, or at least, not as bad as the rest. I don't know if I entirely agree with how they go about it all, but fair play to them, it's worked out all right so far. And fair play to me, I managed to tick our box in the end. Though I agree 100 percent with the notion that talking isn't enough. It's dash complicated, what with elephants that paint and Alunizar who don't and the storm one I can't remember what it likes to be called but you probably had better call it that, and of course also people lie.

"Vedriti do not lie," said a highly accomplished bin man in the heart of the Central Xodo Waste Management System.

Oh, get all the way over yourselves. Everyone lies. I'll bet anything you like plus a tenner, some old Allsorts I've got in my coat pocket, and my entire fucking ship there's an Unkillable Fact about it somewhere in that nightmare-mode Winnie the Pooh they're always on about.

"Deception is a feeling," said a schoolteacher in the Outer Suburban Blast Zone bordering the Left-Hand Ocean. "The forecast does not call for hail."

I'm having several feelings right now, and none of them are good for my stomach. You talk about the weather more than my nani. This is getting us nowhere, and in the wrong order at that. Let's fast forward. Nobody knew you were here, but now we do, so a lot of stuff that won't make a great deal of sense is about to happen to you and you may throw up, I don't know your gastrointestinal business, but do try to point it away from me. Right. Here we go. Erm. Good news or bad news first?

"I can't be bothered," said Nonconsensually Kurdoba, a historian assigned to the Bearable Zone. "There's no fog today."

Bad news for you, then. Right. How do I phrase this diplomatically? Diplomacy isn't exactly my subgenre, but I suppose we're all learning new things today.

The sky, my darlings, is not empty.

The sky is full of arseholes.

A beautiful rainbow of individual identities, cultures, abilities, and ideas of a good time, but, on average, arseholes nonetheless. And the only way all these arseholes have ever figured out how not to blow massive holes through each other's torsos at first sight is to get dressed up to eleven, all come round to one of theirs, and throw an unbelievably over-the-top battle of the bands sort of do and let a load of three-minute pop songs sort out galactic politics.

That's where you come in, and I really am just terribly sorry about this. No one up here *can be certain you're fully* choo-choo *on the sentience train down* there, *which means one or some of you are going to have to come with me and compete to prove you're . . . well. To prove you're people.*

Now, since no one knew you were vibing out here, *no one did any of the usual research on your whole situation. When my species made First Contact and had to get* very *okay with a lot of things* very *quickly, they had a whole list of bands they thought would suit. Was it a good or even comprehensible list? No. But it did save scads of time. As you are something of a surprise special guest star and I loathe the extent to which this is not over yet, if you could just point me in the overall direction of your greatest and most iconic rock band, that would be brilliant.*

Half a billion souls blinked slowly at the aging British glam-rock icon in an ostentatious pink coat and admittedly, even to them, amazing haircut.

Half a billion souls with expressionless A4 copy-paper-colored magnesium faces like half a billion expensive dinner plates neither smiled, nor frowned, nor begged, nor fumed, nor laughed at the inherent absurdity of the concept, nor ran screaming in abject terror, nor showed any surprise whatever, but also no despair or even cynical acceptance of fate's incurable mood disorder.

Half a billion deft and delicate quasi-tentacular hands fiddled unhurriedly with half a billion *somethings* recessed into the (alleged) flesh between their collarbones and their bismuth ruffs.

Soft circular lights flared gold and silver beneath half a billion (plausibly) skin membranes like ancient switchboards.

Then, all those millions of souls answered the call to adventure in unison.

"No," they said calmly, each and every one of them, individually and together. "I don't think so."

But . . . but you have to.

"Do we?" asked just about everyone at once. The effect was entirely unnerving, if Decibel Jones still retained any nerves to *un*.

YES! Everyone does! We did, why should you be special? Although I am just now beginning to wonder if perhaps humanity behaved a bit too *agreeably at the intake meeting. I don't believe it really occurred to anyone to throw a strop and just say no. Frankly, I'm a bit disappointed in humanity just now. Well done you, I suppose.*

"Thank you."

Most welcome. Anyway, if you decline, your species will be . . . ah . . . Christ on a catwalk, this really is thoroughly horrible. I feel like I'm wearing a powdered wig and a cravat and simpering in industrialist about what a shame it would be if those nice lads over in China don't start horfing my opium, chop-chop.

Yes, I know it isn't actually *like that. But it isn't* not *like that, though, you know, from their point of view.* My *point of view quite recently.*

I don't really want *to say this bit. It's not personal, yeah? You are all valid in your own way. Maybe. Gird something, Dess. You can do this. It's not like I can forget the words. It did make* something *of an impression. "If your species declines, your culture will be lovingly collated and archived, your planetary resources tenderly extracted, and you will be annihilated. Your organic material will be seamlessly reincorporated into your biosphere and your world left in peace to try again in another billion years or so with . . . whatever your ecosystem throws at the evolutionary wall next."*

"Okay," said half a billion Vedriti around their supper tables.

Okay? OKAY? You'll all be killed! Do you understand that? Gone. Unmade. Enveloped by the void. Ex-parrots, which you would find very funny if you were a primate-descended vertebrate of a certain age and not . . . whatever you've got going on under there. Believe me, I've seen what they're packing up here. It's like the premium prize shelf at a beach-front arcade with the lights and the jackpot sirens. Sometimes it's a gorgeous knee-dropping climate-change-backing miracle on that shelf and sometimes it's a cannon that fires your nihilism into the clown's mouth that they all swear is backed up by real science and I know I stopped making sense a clause or two back as it's pretty clear you don't do arcades because fun is a feeling or whathaveyou, and maybe not beach-fronts either, but the point is, they could turn every single one of you into a refreshing periwinkle mist and not even have to unplug the space heater first to save the fuse box.

"That's fine. Go on, then. Should we bother with the washing-up or . . . ?"

Sweeties . . . are you all right? Seriously. Do you, all of you, need to talk to somebody? Like a hotline or . . . a blog or something? Do you . . . do you need a hug? I don't know how hugging all of you would work physiologically, but if anyone can tell you anything about me, it'll be that I'm prepared to have a go at just about anything.

"If you are experiencing stress on our account, please don't. We understand perfectly. We are well aware we have no capacity to stop or even slow you down. But you are not to blame. You are just doing your job. There, there. Fire when ready."

Aren't you afraid? It's death, man. It's kind of a big deal.

"Fear is a feeling."

I cannot express to you how very off-putting it is when you say that.

Millions of slim, semitranslucent ultramarine tendrily finger-tacles fiddled with their Lite-Brite collarbones again.

"Vedriti are capable of consensus communication," explained Matter Currently In The Mood To Be Otupeli, a tau-cane harvester in the Bin Expanse. "This is why we do not require a leader to whom we could take you. But even a short consensus expends considerable energy. Please let us rest. We cannot be afraid of dying until the first overnight frost of the stellar cycle."

Huh. Right. I keep forgetting. Because it's completely bizarre and I want to forget it. But very well, comfortably numb it is. Cheers. More trouble than they're worth, feelings. Is that something anyone can get in on or . . . ? No, no, don't answer. I must say, though, not being able to feel anything is going to throw quite a spanner in the whole sentience works. Given that sentience more or less means *feeling things a lot all over the place all the time. And music without feeling is more than a bit of limp egg. I don't know how you're meant to do a screamy bit in a pop song if you've never felt the least screamy and neither has anyone you know.*

"We are not going to do a screamy bit," said Haphazard Stack of Mshvidi, an intoxicant-distiller in the Auxiliary Dwelling Zone. "If you need time to amass your weaponry, we can have a nap while we wait."

What is wrong *with all of you? Just because you can't do the feels-dance with the rest of us doesn't mean you want to die screaming in a vat of fire. Wanting to die IS a feeling, ipso facto, get it together. I'm getting quite good at logic! And they said I was just a pretty face.*

Listen, you great pile of blue spaghetti. Pick someone. Anyone. It doesn't even matter. You think I was the best and brightest of my species? When they found me I was 50 percent boxed rosé by volume. Hadn't had a hit since fidget spinners were legal. I'm almost certain I had crusted-up sweet chili sauce all over my earlobe. And I'll tell you what, my lovelies: no one ever said a word about the sweet chili sauce. It's very come as you are out here. Honestly.

You don't even have to win, you just have to not come last and they'll back up a tip truck full of the future right to your door. I came tenth, and everyone lived to sniff glue and kick rescue puppies another day. I was feeling quite sore about that, but your whole fucking demeanor has really reminded me what's important in life, which is not dying. But also, I have had my head professionally installed up my own posterior. What a gift the Great Octave gave me in the end! For once I got to live the white man's dream: being richly rewarded for total mediocrity.

I'm feeling a lot better about tenth.

Sorry I swore . . . well, all the times I swore.

I really am trying to be professional. But it's not my idiom. Anyway, there's heaps of us. All you have to do is finish at heaps minus one. And between you and me, everyone seems to kick the Alunizar down the scoreboard for shits, giggles, and I think *hundreds of years of loathing and resentment, so just close all three of your eyes and point at a nearby musician and they'll almost certainly get it done.*

There was a long pause over the chill, mountainous face of Xodo. Finally, Assembly of Limbs Sindssgyt said: "We would come last."

Nonsense, don't talk about yourselves like that. Buck up, babies! I heard Gathering of Individuals. They were . . . hrm. Avant-garde! Experimental! Dub . . . standstill. Wall of sound type of . . . sound. Well, they certainly were."

"Gathering of Individuals were irrecoverably tumored in the upsilon radiation sweep during the last dilation syzygy of the lesser star," admitted Organic Matterwad of Gleph from the comfort of the Excess Population Depository.

Riiight.

"Their heads melted," explained Gobs of Lugna, a plasma-farmer on the terraced fields of That Large Mountain. "Their eyes converted to a gaseous state while their tails acidified and their primary tentacle coronas became cancer."

You mean got *cancer.*

"No," said Installation of Sinigaidd, a currency investor in the Business Settlement occupying most of the southeastern continental shelf. "They became the concept of cancer. It happens."

Does it?

"Yes," concluded Installation of Sinigaidd without further explanation.

Right, fine, we had that problem too. They'd gone mad for Yoko Ono, but the old screamer'd hit the bricks years before. I got the gig by pulling off the astonishing feat of being the only quasi-bloke on the menu still exchanging oxygen for carbon dioxide. You can too!

Literally, I am begging you, just nod at someone currently able to convert food to energy and we're golden.

"No," said the half-billion souls of Xodo.

Could you please, pretty please, for the love of George Martin, not that one, the other one, the proper one, goddamn it—could you please not make me a murderer today?

Because you see, eventually, eventually, other life will evolve on this absolute foot of a world, and when it does, it'll take its wee babies to museums and look up (or down) in awe at hilariously unrealistic animatronic models of you and tell the kiddos that once the majestic Vedriti roamed the wilds of Xodo until one day, a giant brown monster named Decibel Jones, who was still quite fit and handsome for his age, fell from heaven and squashed everyone dead, and I just cannot take on the responsibility of being the comet to your dinosaurs today. Do you see "Mass Extinction Event" under Special Skills on my CV? You do not, my friends. I would need many more naps before I would be up, or down, for becoming death, destroyer of worlds. So if you don't pick someone, I'm going to turn this starship around, come down there, and eeny meeny meiney mo it for you.

"Don't do that," the Vedriti thundered as one, without the help of their subdermal consensus orbs.

Oooh, have we stumbled on something you do actually care about?

"Of course not. Ignite the ionosphere already. Go away."

You have to know that saying it like that just makes me want to come down there so hard. *I know you've never met a human before, but that's how we groove.*

"Fine," said the tragedy of the Vedriti commons. The recessed lights beneath their skin glissandoed through a complex sequence. "Um. Whatever. That one."

A Vedriti called Brief Experience of Being Tavallinen had been sitting on the floor of her existence alcove in a garment reminiscent of nothing so much as a vintage mummy-wrap that had moved to the big sophisticated city and learned to thrive. She was surrounded by a clean and tidy open floor plan, a clock radio tuned to Radio Free Xodo, four hundred neatly organized blister packs of gently glowing storebought nutrient solution, and a half-empty bottle of tap water that had sat outside unprotected for exactly five minutes and thus constituted the most unholy powerful intoxicant in the galaxy at present, exactly like every other being on her world, when the aliens invaded.

She was still sitting quietly when a panel on her wall lit up blue from top to bottom, blurted out an abrupt klaxon, and shorted out.

She had been chosen.

Brief Experience of Being Tavallinen had never thought about what the future might be like at all, except once during an exceptionally traumatic ice storm when she was six.

She had never thought about alien invasions.

Or aliens themselves, for that matter.

Neither had anyone she'd ever known given the question one millisecond's mental energy. Whether they existed or her radiation-rotisseried kind were wholly alone in the universe, what they might look or sound like, what sort of queues might form to fight or fuck them, why they never called, why they never wrote, how Xodo would react to company for supper, black swans, Enrico Fermi, Dutch sea captains, or the many ways the hero's journey bullies anyone too slow to get away. None of these had ever so much as occurred to occur to her.

Brief Experience of Being Tavallinen regarded the alien silently. She upended her jug of glowing radiation-envenomated tap water into all three eye-holes.

"No," she told her empty existence alcove, and species-at-large, flatly. "I only performed slightly less than adequately at a mandatory weeknight karaoke event for work once. The other times were less adequate than that."

KARAOKE? You have karaoke? Or are the translator fungi broiling themselves lightly in butter again? How can you have karaoke if you don't have emotions? No, wait, that makes perfect sense, carry on. Oh god, what did you sing? That "This Is a Song" number? Oh god, please tell me it wasn't that. Wait. No. Other way round. Tell me it was, that would be amazing. You standing on a stage, tentacles at attention, just doing a bang-on impression of a fucking dial tone three minutes without moving.

"I completed its full track length without respiration," Tavallinen replied. "There was a thunderstorm," she added awkwardly.

I don't even know what to say. Perfection.

"Finite Essence of Decibel Jones," announcend Sum of the Parts of Qoida, an infectious disease hostage negotiator at Prestigious Medical Facility 14. "Our representative is ready."

"I am not," said Tavallinen calmly.

Excellent! You'll see, this is all going to work out a treat probably. For someone, anyhow. Now . . . how would you like me to, well, get her, not to put too fine a point on it? If you don't want me tracking mud on your planet?

The comms went dead.

Rude. No need to get snippy with me. I just work here.

The hologram shorted out and glitched into nothingness in half a billion existence alcoves. Decibel Jones stood suddenly alone in the cold, slick, acoustically superb shower bay of the captain's quarters, staring at his reflection in the H/C dial.

And a single-occupancy, comfort-plus, reusable mass-driver equipped pod, a technology the Keshet starship's analytics had snootily assured them, barely an hour ago, the Vedriti neither had nor sought, fired itself off the face of the southern continent toward a ship that really and genuinely did believe it could definitely handle this, no problem.

18.

Only Dead Fish Follow the Stream

Three entities caught sight of some combination of Eta Carinae, Decibel Jones, Mira Wonderful Star, and/or their breaking news item jetting away toward GBU headquarters to wash their hands of it as quickly as possible.

Only two of them knew what they were looking at.

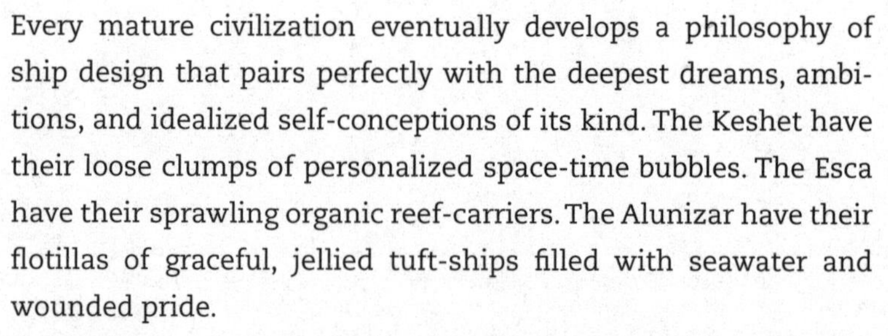

Every mature civilization eventually develops a philosophy of ship design that pairs perfectly with the deepest dreams, ambitions, and idealized self-conceptions of its kind. The Keshet have their loose clumps of personalized space-time bubbles. The Esca have their sprawling organic reef-carriers. The Alunizar have their flotillas of graceful, jellied tuft-ships filled with seawater and wounded pride.

And the varsity deathmetal team known as the Yurtmak, the most casually, gleefully, professionally violent species the galaxy has ever had to run from in the night, have necrotrolleys.

The original necrotrolleys were vast knobs of vertebrae

hacked out of the fossilized spine of the primordial Ur-Mak, the vast sabertoothed tarantuhippodragon ancestress of the ancient Yurtmak, who was, by all forensic and historical accounts, really quite a good, quiet neighbor who never made a fuss.

Ur-Mak bone has many useful properties and one deeply upsetting one. The osseus tissue is impervious to most laser, plasma, particle, atomic, ferro-sonic, nano-blade, hydro-pulse, neuro-shredder, and acid-wash weaponry. It seems like a waste of a free genetic mutation slot to be impervious to a great lot of things that won't get invented until long after you've turned into petroleum, but evolution will try anything on a dare. Licking said osseus tissue is as good an idea as licking the back of certain desert frogs: you definitely *shouldn't*, but what do you have to do in the morning that's more important than tripping wildly and/or attaining the strength of ten and the rage of just one middle-aged Debenham's shopper who doesn't have a receipt for her item?

The fossilization process also produces a mild, gradually increasing antigravity field. This means that the skeleton of the Ur-Mak never needed to be discovered buried rudely in dirt and painstakingly dug out by people with tenure and toothbrushes like fossils found on Earth. The ancient Yurtmak were never unaware of their origins. The several-kilometer-long, decamillenia-desiccated corpse of *hydra-homcidium euungulata primogenius* has hovered over planet Ynt's largest, hottest, hungriest ocean since the first land-Yurtmak followed their bliss and murdered the second. (And the third.) The much-harvested, and still slowly rising, remains are still visible from several attractive sea level destinations.

Lastly, Ur-Mak bone is made up of eufuryotic cells, building blocks common to all Yntian life from the lowliest algae to the most successful boy band. These base cells have most of the usual organelles shoved into a membranous bin-bag, but each and every one of them, from the mitochondria to the nucleus to the wiggly bits whose names no one remembers, are seething with unquenchable rage *all the time*. Every structure in every cell of everything on Ynt is gnashing microscopic teeth, throwing subatomic hands, and shrieking silently for slaughter, mayhem, and fire without end. Every Yurtmak anyone could ever meet is continuously convulsing with autonomously murderous bitelust on a cellular level. The less you think about what it takes to suppress all that and make small talk around the office while sweating acid-slime through their discount dress shirts, the better.

And it all came from the big flying bone mama cruising at altitude over her babies' trendier hotspots.

But modern necrotrolleys are all made with renewable synthetic vertebrae. Invincible antigrav berserker Mum is a finite resource, and as of the most recent legislative session, the Yurtmak treat her with respect.

Nevertheless, the last thing anybody wants to look at after a long day at work is a massive electrified slab of bone with artificially-distressed skin and sinew hanging off it slaloming through the inky void of space into your starboard proximity scan.

The ship attempting to follow Decibel Jones and his increasingly messy workday was a Yurtmak Thanocratic Republic Killocipede Class Sub-Compact Short-Range Thugboat called *Bow Before Doomslinger*. Its rear bone-grille sported an infinitesimally small bumper sticker that was nevertheless important enough to the captain's core identity that she'd carefully reattached it every time the forces of space and propulsion ripped it off and stomped on it.

The sticker read MY OTHER CAR IS HELL.

The ship was desperately out of its depth. It had no idea where its target had skived off to back in civilized space, how it had escaped the inexorable grip of the tour schedule, and the shields weren't at all keen on Eta Carinae's radioactive sky-tantrum.

Ding.

"Hailing Keshet Effulgence Variant Vessel Registry Number 9931741, please respond," gurgle-crunched *Doomslinger*'s comm-beam into the darkness. "This is Captain Gigi Skullvise of the YTR Vessel *Bow Before Doomslinger*. Prepare to be boarded."

Silence. The gleaming white dot in the distance hung in the night, pretending it hadn't heard.

The acid sacs in Captain Gigi's hindjaw swelled with irritation, making her voice even wetter and rougher than usual—and usual was a sack of soup and ice cubes being repeatedly crushed in a hydraulic press.

"You are required by law to respond, actually. We know you're in there, stop messing about."

Silence.

The co-pilot gamely attempted to have a go. "This is Radix Khlor of the Voorpret Mutation. Please accept the warm embrace of our tractor beam. It is excited to meet you."

The gleaming white dot in the distance disappeared with a cheeky winking flash.

"Can they . . . can they do that?" Radix Khlor asked.

"No," growled every cell of Captain Gigi that began in the cells of Mama Ur-Mak. "No, they *cannot*."

All around the splatter of Eta Carinae, electric green Weigelt blobs pulsed with a throbbing techno-beat of pure menace.

Ding.

Just as well. Mrs. Agnes Munt, paisley fancier, mother of two pathologically spoiled Skye terriers called Rowenna and Caspian, treasurer of the Clyde Valley Lonelyhearts Society, perpetually unlucky bingo enthusiast, and owner-operator of Ream a Little Ream of Me 24-Hour Print, Copy & Photo in East Kilbride, couldn't sleep. She lay awake in her bed with the distinct impression the most important moment of her life had already been, paid in advance, tipped generously, and gone.

When she'd questioned the tip, in terms of both length and girth, those snooty nine-foot-tall Easter Island heads, three-foot-tall ultra-black polygonal stick drawings, and inappropriately touchy-feely rosebushes had all laughed at her. A bush touched her card reader and told her to pick a number between *oh, you shouldn't have* and *I'm going to get a call from Revenue and Customs, aren't I?* Then they all made pantomime gestures and one of the big rock fellows said *monkey want a money* at her in a tone she did not like one wee bit.

But now monkey had a money. Monkey had *all* the moneys.

Mrs. Agnes Munt, noted monkey, had enough money to do whatever she liked forever. To cross the sangria Rubicon that separated yearning from enjoying. To reverse the Armada, bravely sail the gloomy sea, and arrive on the shores of the very particular all-inclusive Valhalla lonely ladies of a certain age dreamed of.

Who could sleep?

Ding.

Might as well see who had the late-night copy-paper emergency this time.

But the most important moment of her life had not been and gone.

It stood outside her doorway. It was the color of Pernod, which Agnes suddenly realized she could afford to bathe in every night if she had half a mind, and she just might. It had wretched posture and just the saddest black pupilless eyes. And glowy blinky bits all over it.

The most important moment of the Widow Munt's life was

much too large to fit inside the shop she and Mr. Munt had started when they were young and thought paper was a splendidly safe number to wager their future on. It looked terribly ashamed to have gotten itself wedged in the doorframe like that. Although it did seem to enjoy jostling the bell.

Ding.

But the moment had quite lovely eyes, really. And it was getting absolutely drenched in the rain. And its glowy bits were such a pretty shade of blue, like a little shower of billiards-chalk floating all round. So pretty that for a moment, she got them confused with a splotch of unusually bright stars in the dark sky beyond, just about eight thousand light-years away and ago.

"Do you do color photos?" the most important moment in Agnes Munt's life said in a deep, rumbling, terribly romantic voice. "I've got them on a mnemonic petal and all."

Mrs. Munt considered it for a moment. "Glossy or matte?"

Ding.

Many years before, several nations down and to the left, a red panda shoved another pawful of raw sourdough starter into his face.

Geurgh. Human food was a crime scene.

Öö opened a window in his high-rise Time Out prison in the spring of 2020, which had almost finished curing him of any interest in helping humanity ever again. He was bored. He was itchy. He wanted to be anywhere else. He had conceived in his heart a profound hatred for the phrase *breaking news.*

But he opened his window all the same. And listened. Öö, a Keshet who had personally seen and insulted almost all of space and time, listened to the sound coming out of dozens, and then hundreds, of other windows in his building, just as it did at this hour whenever this day cycled over again.

The sound was the only thing here he felt any attachment toward whatever.

Then his phone pinged. The red panda convict glanced away from the window.

Ding.

Öö opened his delivery app with one stubby brown claw. He'd picked up a few gigs just to prevent eating his own face off for lack of something to do once he'd baked all the bread possible. He was very safe, even by Keshet continuity cohesion rules. He only took completely contactless jobs, kept several masks on, the works. His customers never saw their delivery driver.

Chips and sauce, steak and pepper pie, Tennant's.

Customer: D. Jones.

Öö made a curious squeaking sound, halfway between irritation and pleasure.

He *really* shouldn't. Öö was meant to be behaving himself. Comporting his fuzzy bum As a Good Boy Should. If he just stayed right here and didn't bother anything, he might even get Time Off his sentence, though Öö wasn't sure Time swung that way. Yes. He shouldn't. Play it safe. Be good.

Customer: D. Jones.

"But what if I want to be *naughty*?" the time traveler purred.

Night

Life is meaningless;
The void demands everyone
—Hattari

19.

Hug Me Tight

The human ability to compartmentalize trauma into two very distinct boxes (one of punch-drunk, truly embarrassing enthusiasm for the source of that trauma and one for blanket denial that anything has ever happened anywhere to anyone) was the first and most immediately apparent thing that marked the blue(ish) Monkey Planet out specially among even the wild variations of the Milky Way's constantly iterating game of DNA Mr. Potato Head.

We have now cleared the legal threshold to discuss the second, with a bit on top for safety.

The other human special feature took a bit longer for the rest of the class to notice. Enough time for a few hopping ex-pat nests to spring up on Earth. A Klavaret cafe in Rotterdam. A Yurtmak strain of highly successful CrossFits in gyms across Eastern Europe. Unholy 321 benders at every call center without a data cap. A Smaragdi stand-up modesty act called *Please Do Not Take My Wife, I Like Her Very Much* took the Golden Gibbo at the Melbourne Comedy Festival. Slozhit end-times cults drove the superheroes and princesses from Times Square and replaced them with light-drunk moth/supermodel hybrids with antennae like grayscale peacock feathers, one of which ended up on the cover of *Vogue*. An Esca singer won *The Voice*. In accordance with the newly GBU-negotiated prize package, she immediately began to ritually ingest Adam Levine, who seemed, in the end, more relieved than anything.

Anywhere on Earth you went you could find Utorak backpackers shooting their shot at paleolithic stone circles, Lummutis players asking about microtransactions with uncomfortable intensity, Voorpret consultants kicking back and sipping on dirty receptor proteinis in the NHS commissioner's executive lounge, assuring anyone who would listen that it was terrifically thick, and honestly a bit racist, for any human to wear an N95 mask, ever. And of course, it was all hands, feet, proboscises, and tentacles on deck and on the prowl in Ibiza.

A Sziv in every sauna, a Klavaret in every garden, and an Alunizar in every intelligence agency.

Things were going fine.

For a little while.

The first glimmer of an inkling of a shadow of a screaming flashing all-hours neon sign that something was deeply wrong was a simple pair of images indignantly hurled onto a tight-beam data-blast and shot into civilized space from the general vicinity of the Italian Riviera.

It showed a simple, five-fingered, gently cupped human hand (Fig. A) and another, this one moving backward and down while maintaining its tenderly curved shape (Fig. B).

The only included text read, in Old Keshet:

It has begun. Again.

A few weeks later, a temporarily individuated Hrodos cloudbank burst into the communal lounge of Magic Natura Animal Sanctuary, Water Park & Polynesian Lodge Resort in Benidorm, Spain, sobbing in terror.

The local expatriate community, who had fully booked this particular resort for the next century to keep out the townies, found this devastating to their evening plans. Mainly because Hrodos was explicitly *not* invited to the Rock Around the New Drugs Happy Fun Times Party and MLM Presentation (Multi-Genders Snort Free).

Hrodos had never been invited to anything and never would be, as Hrodos was a sentient storm from a gas giant located vaguely underneath the washing-up rack holding the Big Dipper. The size and attitude of Hrodos made Jupiter's Great Red Spot look like a maiden's blush. Hrodos had laid out quite a lot of dosh for the atmospheric compressors, lightning containment fields, and radical gale force bypass surgery required to treat a fragment of Hrodoself to a real overseas holiday for once.

Nothing was turning out the way Hrodos had dreamed.

"If they did it to me, they can do it to *any one of you*." Hrodos accepted a cup of restorative silver iodide salts from the flippers of an almost-sympathetic Yoomp. "These people are *sociopaths*. I can't believe I gave them twelve points in the final. Don't tell anyone. I'll never live it down." The golden twilit hurricane's beach-ready cloudbod shuddered in shame.

"It can't be so awful as all that," cooed the Yoomp, who was wearing a bum bag that read SPANIARDS DO IT FOR BLOOD AND TREASURE. "What did those nasty hair-havers do to you, poor baby?"

"A human . . ." The eye of Hrodos's storm filled with tears. "A human *cuddled* me. And they'll do it to you too! All of you! No one is safe!"

A silky, almost unrealistically soft and round Keshet called Tärn took a deep drag on her new favorite toy: a cigarette she'd pawed off one Edward Wickerley, a sad electrician on holiday who insisted he'd booked his stay at Magic Natura over a year ago. She flicked it onto the tile floor and crushed it out with her furry foot, ignoring the splutters of the concierge.

"I told you," the Keshet hissed. "But you wouldn't listen. This place is *bent*. Barricade the doors if you want. It won't help. This is happening."

It's not that humanity *invented* becoming so overwhelmed by the powerful cuteness of a particularly fluffy being that one is compelled by a drive stronger than survival, sex, loyalty, or the accumulation of resources to stroke its head and ask *who is a good girl* in a totally altered speaking voice over and over until both the petter and the pettee crumble to dust, leaving only a fossilized leash and wallet resting on a pile of dusty cold bones.

That dubious behavior is so universal that *can I pet your dog?* is statistically the most commonly uttered phrase, in all languages, in the history of the galaxy, (allowing for variations on the exact meaning of the word "dog") followed by *not all Alunizar* and *what do you feel like for dinner, I'm easy, no not that place . . . or that one either.*

Anyone lucky enough to be sand or an over-engineered water balloon can comfortably make their debut on the galactic stage without being accosted. But dealing with the constant threat of unwanted pats formed a major foreign policy plank for the Keshet, Meleg, Slozhit, Esca, Lummutis, Yoomp, and Vulna, who formed a Coalition of the Pretty Ones within the early Great Octave.

The Naranca Empire, a kingdom occupying the entire Talata Quadrant, whose citizens only emerged to sell inferior cheese products and buy novelty T-shirts and who not only habitually declined to participate in the Metagalactic Grand Prix, but were so self-centered they had real trouble even remembering what, when, or even *that* it was, once launched a full invasion of the Sladoled Tertius system with the sole objective of everybody getting to pet one extra-plush Meleg after the Narancan Emperor saw them on a bootleg stream of *Love Planet: Hard Labor Penal Asteroid*.

But no one, *no one*, had ever so much as idly considered the ROI on petting any part of the malevolently cranky thunder-tsunami known as Hrodos. Cuddles and related behaviors were a Keshet problem. A Meleg problem. It probably wouldn't even be a Lummutis problem if they'd just let everybody see what they had going on under those cartoon avatars. If you dressed modestly, didn't go out at night, watched your drink, and your species didn't fall into the small/cute/soft demographic, you had nothing to worry about.

Until now.

The Esca can control your emotions with the vibrations of their voices. The Yurtmak can separate anything overtly sticky-outty from your torso with all the effort of a newborn popping a dummy out of their mouths. The Voorpret can steal your man, inhabit his lifeless body, and use it to send dick pics to the black hole at the center of the Milky Way before you even have time to wonder who ordered all this photography equipment. Hrodos is psychic, the Alunizar are telesthenic, the Yoomp can talk to plants, and the 321 will border on omniscient and omnipotent if they ever get past their crippling addiction to mobile gaming.

What unique power lay slumbering in the genome of *Homo sapiens sapiens*?

Humanity just wants a cuddle.

Any cuddle.

Puppies and kittens? Yes. Bunnies, ferrets, parakeets? Don't mind if they do. Lions, tigers, ligers, tions? That's the dream. Foxes, raccoons, badgers, grizzly bears, fruit bats? Well, who hasn't made sure to keep an emergency rabies shot and a wet wipe in their purse just in case?

Frogs? Sure, why not?

Snakes? I guess?

Squid? Hold on, are you taking them out of the water first?

Spiders? Wait.

Spider Monkeys? Slow down, *how many legs are involved?*

Spider Octopi? Safeword, safeword!

Japanese Spider Crabs? What's happening? Why is everything spiders down there?

Spider Wasps? Make it stop.

Rocks? Sticks? Great White Sharks? Xenomorphs? AR-15 Semiautomatic Rifles with Upgraded Magazine Capacity? Literally just a statue of a dog who died a hundred years ago but was probably a decent enough bloke?

What is *wrong* with those primates?

The galaxy was slowly waking up to the horrifying truth about humanity: no matter how hideous, dangerous, pustulant, inanimate, awkward, oozing, or wholly indifferent to and incompatible with the continuation of life, in specific or in general, there was a human who would not only love it, but cuddle it, build it an elaborate play structure, dress it up in a hand-knit sweater, call it their *pwecious sweetbaby cutiebutt*, spend far too much money on accessories for it, maintain a webpage in its honor long after its death and/or recycling, even let it sleep on the bed against all hygiene recommendations.

And if their human life partner objected, it was never once the xenomorph who had to sleep on the couch.

Many humans had a great deal of trouble using this extraordinary ability on other human beings, but rest assured, while no one loses too much sleep over whether Allison Bailey gets her insulin in time to not die, Allison the Rescue Scorpion will never want for funds to retake her sixth bite-test and finally find her forever home.

In a serious academic paper titled *Hope This Email Finds You Well: Cries, Calls, and Territorial Songs of Earth*, Adjunct Professor Caliginous Vellichor the Untenurable, the Elakh scholar responsible for reclassifying Alunizar from *aquatic gastropod* to *difficult confectionary* in the latest edition of *Guess Who? Stranger Danger Edition*, the definitive repository of xenobiological information, had this to say to a symposium on the care and feeding of aliens:

> *Let me fucking*[1] *tell you something*[2] *about where human*[3][4] *beings*[5][6][7] *are coming from.*[8][9][10][11][12][13]
>
> *About six hundred years ago they were nearly wiped out by a highly infectious bacterium called* Yersinia pestis, *carried by fleas joyriding on the common rat. Our good friend* Y. pestis *was such a flamboyant artist-in-residence that it gave people a wee sniffle, then a wee bleeding of their lung-lining out their eyeballs, and finally a wee fall down before their armpits exploded. It's pure shrieking chance that humans survived to become our problem. Well, I know you don't "trust my research methods" just because I "told everyone vaccines cause alligator blood," but this is the fucking truth.[Citation Needed]*
>
> *Not only are there still common rats all over the biosphere, but those kinky freaks over there keep them as pets! Ha-ha, you had an enormous hand in nearly driving our entire species to extinction here is a* #TeamRat *pillow to sleep on, a kicky exercise wheel to keep you lean and fit, and oooh look at these cute little sweaters for when it's cold out! One of them says* Rat Lives Matter, *pay no attention to the human screaming for help outside the Rat Supply Shoppe!*

Get yourself a chair because you cannot un-know that they have FORTY-THREE SEPARATE Rat Fancier's *magazines down there!*

Humanity is so confoundedly bizarre that they can easily forgive the murder of many fellow Homo sapiens sapiens, *commit it themselves, encourage others to commit it, and laugh uproariously when witnessing it on television, but if you so much as look at a dog like you* might *kick them, even in a fictional story, not one of those perverts who were laughing their* tits *off a minute ago will* ever *forgive you.* Their grandchildren *will* spit *on your* grave.

As a scholar, I prefer to use technical language to avoid having to speak to anyone not possessing my exact highly specialized degree, so allow me to phrase the issue scientifically: These bitches ain't loyal.

I, Caliginious Vellichor, have personally *witnessed the manufacture, sale, and tender loving care of* plush children's toys *in the shape of, not only* Y. pestis cells, *but HIV, syphilis, Ebola, bovine spongiform encephalopathy, and whooping cough, a disease that exclusively kills* very young children.

With smiley faces *on them.*

They love it. They collect them. They think it's hilarious. Y. pestis *burned their species to the ground, and their offspring snuggle it to fall asleep at night—but only after feeding the creature that carried plague to the exploding armpits of their own great-grandmothers a couple of tasty carrots.*

This is the future humans want. A cuddle—and a leash. A leash that would never let us go. A leash with Property of Gregory *hand-embroidered on them.*

Let this be a warning. We have deeply underestimated this species. Meet me in the hotel bar if you want to know about pet rocks, because I am STEAMING.

After explaining all this to the gathered ex-patriate community, the Keshet known as Tärn poured herself a long tall crate-mounted drip-dispenser of tequila, dragged all the time-hopping versions of herself together so as to be clearly understood by dull idiots who only live in one quantum reality at a time:

"Do you want to hear the *really* fucked-up part? It's happened to me. Kind of a lot. I'm just . . . really, really cute, lads. And . . ." Tärn drew a ragged breath. "It's *extraordinary*. Have you ever let a human pet you? There's *nothing* like it." The Keshet began to weep. "Nothing in this universe. It's grotesque. It's delicious. You feel dirty . . . and grand. We're all going to regret following the siren song of Yoko Ono across the light-years. Mark my words."

"I . . . I liked it, too," admitted Hrodos quietly, who everyone had forgotten was there, because that was the best option when Hrodos was anywhere near you. "I liked it *so* much."

"I know, honey," Tärn sighed. "I know." She turned to the others and snarled: "This never leaves the room, got it? *What happens on Earth stays on Earth*. Now just sit tight. I'm going to . . ."

"Yes," breathed a Meleg.

"Say it," the Yoomp in the tube top hummed.

"Do it," murmured a Yurtmak who had never in his life been scratched behind the ears.

The Keshet nodded. Once, twice. Then she said the words they were all waiting for.

"Get us some champers and mood lighting. I'm gonna let Edward Wickerley in."

20.

Venice in the Rain

It is a long way from Eta Carinae to GBU headquarters.

But there's no helping it unless you can tease a wormhole out from the deep corners of space and keep it friendly. As Goguenar Gorecannon's Twelfth Unkillable Fact says: *Your parents probably told you the universe is filled with majesty and wonder, which was sweet, I guess. They weren't exactly lying, but they didn't need you to know that in between the majesty and the wonder and whatnot, you're going to spend most of your actual time alive doing deeply annoying rubbish you hate but can't avoid, rubbishly. Like waiting in queues, cardio, dusting objects you don't even remember buying, filling out forms, proofreading, more queues, paying for things you won't remember buying, morning meetings, afternoon meetings, emergency all-hands meetings in the middle of the night, more forms, fixing other people's mistakes, waiting for various vehicles to arrive at destinations you feel weirdly pressured to show interest in, and literally almost every job.*

Sorry, kiddo, it can't be helped. You think I like being right all the time about everything? Somebody has to do it, or we'll all have to live in a pit.

Three people came to see Brief Experience of Being Tavallinen on the journey from Xodo to the Galactic Broadcasting Union headquarters.

One came three times.

One came twice.

The last came once, only by accident, and left immediately.

The one that came three times fell in love. Not on purpose. Not easily. Not to get a quick cuddle in before work. Just because. For all the silly, slicey, dicey, deeply problematic reasons thinking beings fall in love with other thinking beings. Even when they're perfectly aware how that's worked out for them before. Even when they have a crushing amount of quite important work to do. Even knowing full well the thinking being they adore can never love back.

It happens.

This time will be different.

Decibel Jones gave himself quite a bit of credit for adjusting manfully to the ludicrousness of his ship's confrontational style of interior decor. But the as-yet-unused passenger berths threw him for several loops, a twist, and an unceremonious header into the floor.

The VIP guest quarters of the KEVV *Difficult Second Starship* appeared to be a busy evening at the baggage carousels of Minneapolis–St. Paul International Airport. A place he had never been.

That was perfectly all right. He'd never been to the Sentience Wars several hundred years ago, either. Didn't stop them from being his torpedo bay. But he'd never *wanted* to visit Minneapolis, or St. Paul, or their collective international airport, either. In fact, he didn't believe he'd given the Minneapolis–St. Paul International Airport one lonely friendless thought in all his days.

So why was it here?

Dess had certainly never imagined this version of it, which, by the clattering antediluvian flipboard arrivals/departures board flickering shadows across the hideous burnt-pumpkin bank of Naugahyde waiting area scoop-seats, was April 13, 1970.

Yet here he, and the guest quarters, were.

And here Brief Experience of Being Tavallinen was, small, elegant tentacles resting emotionlessly in her lap.

The Midwestern airport moved around them in regular rotational periods of bustling sound and waiting quiet, orbits of flight crews coming on and off shift, the gravity of arrivals falling into welcoming arms and departures kissing goodbye. Suitcase after suitcase disgorged themselves from yawning black holes of luggage handling and infrastructural anxiety.

Decibel Jones strode across 1970, the meeting place of the stately faded old world and the new nose-bludgeoning chaos-moshpit of post-history America as it woke up from the summer of love and stared down the winter of its discontent. He fetched two primitive pre-barista technology coffees in blue paper cups from the counter before whoever ordered them noticed.

"Hiya," said Decibel Jones, suddenly unsure of the effects of caffeine on . . . whatever he was looking at.

"Hi," answered Brief Experience of Being Tavallinen, returning his gaze without expression. The fluorescent overhead lights made her geometric eye-gashes and mouth-chasm even more starkly, emptily black in that magnesium stop-sign of a face.

"How are you feeling?"

Tavallinen stared at him. Was there a glimmer of something

there? Ruefulness? Irony? Annoyance? *Come on, Grandad, take your medicine, we talked about this.*

"Right, right. Turn of phrase, innit. That'll be a rough go for me, but stick around, I'll get there in the end. Figured out two-factor authentication and a very respectful three-way with Ed Sheeran and his online therapist. Nice lady, Susan. Sends me Christmas cards of her pet rat in"—he gestured awkwardly at his head—"elf hats and reindeer horns and that. Don't get fuck-all from Ed, but the point is, if I can negotiate all that, I'll come round to Calamari Starter and the No Feels Gang."

"Okay," said Tavallinen.

"Come on, you don't have to *feel* things to make conversation! I've got a cousin in Malmö who insists on it! Who are you, where were you born, who were your parents, what are your hopes and dreams? What did you draw in your notebooks when you were a wee . . . when you were little . . . ? *Were* you a child? Suppose you could just . . . bud, like the Alunizar. Or clone like a . . . sorry, bit rude, all I can think of is a tulip. Klavaret, maybe? I confess I haven't paid . . . *all* the attention. You really can't guess how excruciating this is for me, love. I will need rescue eventually."

The alien watched a rush of humans, who had no idea that anyone could carry a phone anywhere they went, flow out of the international arrivals gate.

"Nothing?" Dess stretched out his long legs in the seat beside her. The slick orange vinyl squeaked. He decided to risk a caffeine-induced medical and/or military emergency and handed Tavallinen the coffee. "Fine, I'll go first. Decibel Jones, pronouns he/yours, darling. Born Danesh Jalo, but you can't wear a name like that to the ball, it won't match a thing. Originally of Blackpool; you don't need to know where that is. Dad was a schoolteacher, Mum did whatever paid, raised by me nani mostly, who was better than the whole lot of us plus at least a handful of Ursulas. Have loved girls, boys, guitars, and rocketships, the four genders. Was *allegedly* a child. Recovered quickly. Your go. Oh! Wait, wait, I've a much better question. Let's *really* get into it. The only important thing."

The lead singer of the band that saved mankind got up and squatted down in front of her on his haunches so she couldn't ignore him, assisted greatly by garden-party platform wedge-shoes with orange plastic flowers on the toes. His eyes sparkled at her with real excitement and not a little wonder—although it may have been the space-time containment fields.

"What kind of *music* do you like?" he breathed with a seven-figure-signing bonus plus points on net smile.

Brief Experience of Being Tavallinen glanced up at a little girl hurtling herself into her father's arms. He whirled her around and blew a raspberry on her cheek, which, now that Decibel had reason to think about it, was fairly revolting as a gesture of human affection.

"I was a child," she admitted finally. "We have children. Juveniles. When the allotted sporal release window arrives and our nematocyst loads convert from irradiated acid to genetic material."

"Hot," said Dess. "You have any ankle-biters of your own?"

"No," said Tavallinen. She paused slightly. "I am damaged."

"What rubbish, no you're not. You're a sloppy gorgeous mess is what you are. Damaged how?"

"I was ill in my juvenile phase. I briefly could not tolerate food. Or air. Or light. I improved. Parts of me did not. I am in the middle of my life cycle. My sporal window is closed."

"Well, they said I couldn't gestate a fetus either, and I did all right. Two parents? How many genders have you lot got under the hood?"

Tavallinen dragged her blank black eyes back toward him.

"Gender is a feeling," she said tonelessly.

"Oh, now isn't it *just*." Dess beamed. "I completely agree. Now we have something in common! In another minute you'll be asking me to sing backup for you and carry your gear."

"Anatomically I am similar to your female friend, but we have . . . additional classifications. In High Vedritor, the word is *kromme*. You might think of it as . . . *female plus*. There is also female minus, male, male minus, and male plus, and the variable aliaform. To produce offspring, any three are sufficient. And I don't have any gear."

"I know, darling. I am actually just a *skosh* concerned about that, if I'm honest. Do you have *any* sort of a plan? A song forming up in there somewhere? It does have to be original, I'm afraid. If the previous rules hold. They may not, I really have no idea how to operate the machinery from this end. But either way, karaoke is not what they're after."

"No."

Dess pursed his lips. "How can I get through to you? I'm happy to help! I'm not sure I'm allowed to help, but we haven't been told not to yet, which is the best time to be naughty. You've got to have *something* or . . . well." He made a sheepish *boom* gesture with his hands.

"Yes."

"Do you *actually* understand what's at stake here? Look, are you all just . . . depression? I've met sea slugs, talking sand, viruses with parking tickets, even a wormhole with a dream journal. I can accept depression as a sentient species. Would explain a lot, really."

"Depression is a feeling."

"They're not bluffing. They'll use all sorts of things that sound like jokes, but are very much not jokes, on your world and everything in it. Everyone you've known. I wish I could explain it better. But I'm not the kind of semi-bloke who prefers *pew, pew* to *la, la, la,* so in conclusion you will never exist again and neither will anyone you've ever thought was basically all right. So . . . do you want to work on a hook? Perhaps? Just for an hour or two? I don't mind, I've got time. So do you."

"What's *la, la, la*?"

"Sorry? Oh, la, la, la." Dess laughed a little. The evening outside the glass baggage claim walls was starting to deepen. No stars. The clouds were heavy and full of mischief. "Well, in songs on Earth, almost all the songs, going back to before electricity and plumbing and the intro-verse-chorus-bridge-verse structure, the *la, la, las* were sneaky little bits you could sing when you meant something naughty and the Church or the lord in the manor or your dad wouldn't know what you were on about."

"What would you not want your dad to know?"

Decibel Jones brushed his hair out of his eyes, a gesture so dashing it once caused a man on the other side of the road to suffer a full coronary event.

Tavallinen remained unmoved and unmovable.

"You know, I think I only really believed you about the fee-fees thing right this very second, because only someone who didn't know what a whole commercial range of emotions are couldn't imagine not wanting your dad to know what you were singing about." He tapped the side of his nose with one long brown finger. "The *la, la, las* are where the shagging goes. Or the booze or the drugs or the unimaginable violence, though usually those squeak through. Even in that silly old carol. Imagine thinking you decked your halls and put on gay apparel and got your old harp out just to *not* shag the new lads and lasses. Though I'd leave Christmas carols alone, if I were you. Old news. Are you sure you don't want to scribbity-up a few lyrics? They can all be *la, la, la, la, la,* I truly don't care, I just would prefer not to be responsible for a genocide today."

"I know nothing about music. I play no instruments. I sing what appears on a screen when my employer requires me to. I cannot write a song. But I do not fear death. Or genocide. Fear is a feeling. I am not ashamed of my inability to perform melodically. Shame is a feeling. I can say *la* if you require me to. However many times you require me to, to obfuscate the shagging so your father does not see. Or not. It does not matter."

"It does a *bit*."

"It does not."

"Right. Good enough. Death to all, then. Fun. For the whole family."

"Hi," said Mira, arms crossed defensively over her chest. She would not be moved by anyone's bloody *plight* right now. Her own plight was quite enough to manage, thank you. But she had to see, didn't she? She'd dressed down for the occasion. She'd coaxed the Matter Whisperer into producing a sexy librarian costume that started out with black frames and cleavagey tweed and eventually degraded, or upgraded, itself into a Xena warrior-skirt of split leather panels, fur lining, and brass studs, all spackled with glitter and dangling ribbonmarks.

The Vedriti did not seem to notice.

The airport milled and burbled behind them. The clouds outside stood waiting in the taxi stand. Their flat, heavy undersides glowered malignantly, promising pain.

"Hi," said Brief Experience of Being Tavallinen.

"Eat this," Mira said, shoving a Yüzosh prefab log covered in multi-species broad-spectrum vaccination-mushrooms. "Your anatomy is . . . honestly fascinating," she ventured. "But the medbot hates it and wants it to go away."

"Okay," said Tavallinen, ingesting the fungus without complaint, even though it all tasted like roast shoe.

"What's with the name? Is that . . . a pattern in your culture?" Even though she knew it had to be. "*Mister* or *Miss* or *Decline to State* or even *Viscount* is pushing it. Why do you all have such long titles that you simply *must* say every time?"

The Vedriti's radial tubules writhed bluely in a brief shaft of cold sunset filtering through clouds and glass. It turned her bony face to molten gold.

Tavallinen gazed at the hurrying, scurrying, watch-checking humans click-clacking across all that epoxied industrial flooring in their endless blind unaware bubbled moment of time. Her lifeless eye-slits bored into the backs of their unthinking heads. She spoke with such total unself-consciousness it made Mira feel like she was intruding on something terribly intimate and should leave immediately. But she didn't.

"Because I am only the molecules of my body," Brief Experience of Being Tavallinen said softly. "And every atom of me is a traveler, only temporarily forming this shape, this individuated definition of matter. Someday those atoms will move on and that which I am will be gone. Those atoms will take another shape. Perhaps a child. Perhaps a starship. Perhaps a karaoke bar. Perhaps a rock. I cannot call all those traveling, learning atoms *me*. They are not me. I do not own them. My atoms are only, in this quickly disappearing moment, in this unrepeatable time, having a brief experience of being Tavallinen before they go."

"Oh." Tears welled up in Mira's eyes. Then she felt thoroughly mortified, having a feeling in front of someone who needed an emotional support hurricane to crack a smile. "Oh."

The atoms experiencing being Tavallinen took another bite of medicinal mud-log.

The drummer-cum-engine-core cleared her throat and bolted to change the subject. She held out a steaming picnic containment unit with several obscure radiation symbols who felt very excited to be getting out of the house for once. "I brought you a snack. It's from the paradox core. Two scoops. Hope you like it. The analysis bot said it was compatible with your radiation profile."

"Why are you doing this?"

"Bringing nibblies? It's my go-to strategy for getting people to like me. Rarely fails."

A rainbow of mid-budget luggage options hurked out of the baggage carousel in various states of cohesion. "No. Why do you decide your culture's course with a song contest? I have been ingesting your digital media library through my visual orifices. You know how to kill things. You are all talented at killing. You choose this instead. Why? Songs are nothing. Ejections of air."

Mira sat down next to the Vedriti. The leather panels on her skirt cludded dully against the plastic seating. "Guns eject air, too. Is that better?"

Tavallinen considered. "It is quicker. There is also, usually, the bullet."

"Oh, believe me, a song can shoot you dead too. We just call bullets 'key changes' when they come on a twelve-inch vinyl disc."

"A song cannot shoot me in any way."

"So I hear. I'm just not sure I *understand*. I saw your planet. Cities, roads, restaurants. Children. Why did you build all that if you don't feel anything? Ambition is a feeling. Design springs from feeling. Frank Lloyd Wright *felt* no one should ever be comfortable in their own home, for example. Not to be rude, but why not just lay down and die if nothing matters and it's all the same?"

Tavallinen's tendrils curled and uncurled loosely all around her many limbs. "An organism has . . . *propulsion* toward survival even in the absence of everything else. Amoeba absorb smaller amoeba. Plankton will avoid pain if they can. We require shelter, food, and protective covering to avoid pain."

"But *karaoke*? Music at all? You have *radio stations*. What's the point?"

"We are sentient," Brief Experience of Being Tavallinen said simply. "I am not a philosopher. But it is clear sentient beings frequently do things for no reason."

"Animals do plenty of things for no reason. By definition, they don't understand the reason for anything they do. Why they migrate or molt or chase this gazelle rather than that zebra. Why they choose one mate and not another."

"Animals do those things for no reason *they understand*. Sentient beings do things for no reason *at all*." The Vedriti turned her elaborate body, ever so slightly, toward Mira. "Why do you dress like that?" she asked.

Mira looked down at herself. She'd always prided herself on never once dressing casually for any occasion. But now she felt suddenly a bit shabby. A bit childish. She picked at the studs on her skirt. "Dunno," she said quietly.

"See? No reason at all. If there is a test of sentience, it should be that." The Vedriti paused. "Maybe we worked on the cities and the roads when it rained," she whispered.

Mira rolled her eyes. "Yeah, but no, wait, of course there's a reason I dress like this. You just have to *say* you don't know at first so people think you're a good person who doesn't like to talk about themselves too much."

"Pretending you don't know something you do know wastes a great deal of energy."

"Yes, I suspect that's the point of manners, really. Use up all your energy so you've nothing leftover to spend on being a bastard." Mira sat bolt upright and slapped her legs. "Fuck me. It's 1970, right? Dess said it's 1970 in here. Do you know what that means, Nen? Can I call you Nen? The whole lot is just *such* a mouthful. Nen, you beautiful creepy blue sunflower, April 13, 1970, means I can *smoke inside*."

Mira Wonderful Star skipped across baggage claim with a joy only available for purchase to those born into a world without smoking sections. She frowned at the audacity of the cigarette machine to demand currency from her, looked the whole thing over, and finally waved her paralocket menacingly at it and yanked on one of the knobs. The machine whined, clicked worryingly, obediently spat out its entire contents into a wholly unprepared retrieval bin. Then the selection knobs began helplessly thrusting in and out in a dizzyingly fast *frunk-slink-frunk* pattern that nevertheless was immediately recognizable as Tchaikovsky's "Dance of the Sugar Plum Fairy." Smoke rose from the back of the cabinet.

Mira swiped a pack and a lighter and hurried back, trying to look like she had no idea how such a thing could possibly have happened.

"Someone really ought to have a look at that thing," she said as she collapsed back into the waiting area seats. She lit her prize and watched the smoke curl and stretch. "I dress like this because I like it. Halloween couture. Only everything's a costume, really. Everything you could ever wear. And when we, when Decibel Jones and the Absolute Zeroes were starting out, we were skint to the *bone*. We wanted to dress up as ourselves, I suppose. As who we aimed to be. A declaration of intent to live on purpose. But we couldn't afford to actually live on purpose. So I went to every charity shop I could find and cleared out their Damaged/As-Is bins. The boys were easy. But half the rubbish I found to fit me were slutty Halloween costumes and I just thought: *Fine, I'll be a slut. A slut for my own future. It can have me any time it likes. And fuck you if you can't take me seriously—just makes it easier to weed out people* I *won't take seriously.* And it stuck that way. Like making a face. I'll admit the Matter Whisperer has taken a bit of the fun out of it. I used to sew it all together myself. Up till every hour, me and a machine and a cigarette and all the shine five scrounged quid could buy." Mira took another drag and forced herself to look fully into Tavallinen's eye-pits. "I just always want to be dressed as someone you can't look away from."

Brief Experience of Being Tavallinen did not look away.

"The way you wish I had feelings," she said finally. "I wish you had exoskeletons. You are all so soft. I cannot understand how you built a civilization that way. Your vulnerability is extremely graphically displayed. You should stop doing that."

"Listen, space pasta, I don't buy it," said Decibel, many hours later.

"Hi," said Brief Experience of Being Tavallinen.

"There's no possible way you lot go through life waiting for the weather to change just to feel any sort of way about anything. You can tell me. It's a metaphor, right? People say the Yurtmak are emotionless murder machines, but it's not true, really. I've had *several* post-panel drinks with the beatboys from Gutapult and they're quite lovely. You can't tell me it's always been this way. From cave-yous to mandatory office socialization activities?"

Tavallinen gazed out into the traffic and the twin cities beyond. Thunder rumbled. Hail pellets began to plink against the glass. "Actually," she said evenly, "from what I have learned of the cultures you represent, all of you wasted a great deal of time on that journey. You can get quite a lot farther, quite a bit faster, without feelings. Feelings get in the way of work. Every scientist or artist or engineer or digger of ditches who feels too depressed to get up in the morning hinders collective progress. Every king who calls it honor when his feelings have been hurt and invades his neighbor, kills thousands of potential scientists and artists and engineers and ditch-diggers, and also peasants who would make far better kings. This also hinders progress. You are inefficient. You are bad at civilization." After a pause, the Vedritum pointed toward the glass doors by way of explanation. "The rack containing periodical publications near the exit vestibule accesses the ship's data cores."

Decibel shrugged. "Maybe, but you can't exactly avoid all that."

"I can."

"Am I meant to be impressed? Humanity might be bad at civilization, but let me tell you, the surrealist art gallery you're about to meet feels quite strongly about every *single* thing, and they're the ones calling the shots. Anyway, speaking personally, a spot of self-hatred can really roll you right out of that bed and into the studio."

Decibel Jones drank yet another sip of the uniquely vile stuff Americans insisted on calling coffee.

"Why would you hate yourself? You are yourself. If you do not like yourself, why not become someone else?"

"Oh, I do try, darling. Every five years or so, I give it a real go. I hate myself with a thoroughness. Most humans do. And your average regular person who just wants to get through the day and punish their liver a bit for the privilege hates themselves plenty well." He waved his chord-hand in the stale airport air. "But they don't have the dedication to the craft it takes to reach the top levels. You can't get *here* from *there*. Because the thing about being clever—and believe it or not, I am mostly *astonishingly* clever—is that not only can you hate yourself, you can hate yourself for hating yourself! And if you're *really* clever, you can even hate that you hate yourself for hating yourself. But if you're a really clever *artist?*" Decibel Jones gave a low whistle. "You can hate yourself almost to death for hating most of all the fact that you can't stop being the kind of insufferable *beast* who hates that they hate themselves for hating themselves. Or you can package it with some liner notes and a beat and sell a million copies."

They sat quietly for some time. The flickerboard flickered away.

"What if you don't come out the other side of this one?" the singer asked the dinner plate softly.

Brief Experience of Being Tavallinen did not move. Not even her tendrils. The rain kept coming down.

"It seems unlikely that we do," she agreed. "I suppose we will all die and no one will remember us."

"Well, that's not really fair, is it, dear?" sighed Dess, and almost put his arm around Nen to comfort her before realizing how holistically pointless that truly was. He shoved them in his pockets instead and tried to pretend that was the plan all along.

Then he saw it. On a luggage-dolly an attendant in a hi-viz vest wheeled in from the back room. He saw something, anyway. Something that made him stop breathing. Something that made his whole body forget it was supposed to breathe, or why anyone would need to breathe in the first place when something like that existed.

A black case with a handle and a few words and a symbol spray-stenciled onto it. A few words and a symbol any British kid who ever thought six strings and five fingers might make a spot of magic would know without making the cognitive effort to actually *read* them. Not the kind of case that kids who have something to prove carry around, plastered with anything they imagine makes them look seasoned—band stickers, club stickers, beer labels, laminated plane tickets, vodka caps, cashed checks. Just a case.

A case he recognized, because he happened to know, somewhere deep in the compost bin of his memory, that case had *definitely* been at the Minneapolis–St. Paul International Airport on April 13, 1970.

And that baggage attendant in his chartreuse waistcoat was staring at it with *starvation* in his eyes.

"One moment, please? Just a tic. Don't move. Ha-ha, you won't. Why did I ask? Drink that. I'll be right back."

The aging rocker dashed into the crowds. For the first time in years, Decibel Jones wasn't thinking about anything but that very moment and what he could make of it. *Don't worry, it'll pass.* And when it passed, he'd notice his knee didn't hurt today like it usually did. And his back felt supple and strong. And he somehow didn't have his customary afternoon headache, either.

After a brief detente with the handler, Dess returned carrying his prize.

Brief Experience of Being Tavallinen looked at him curiously. She wasn't curious, but we all look like things we're not sometimes.

"What's that?" she said.

Decibel Jones, lately of the Absolute Zeroes, grinned like a kid on the first day of school, before he knows what school is actually like.

"Oh, *honey*. It's a *guitar*. And not just any guitar. It's a '60 Les Paul. The man who will be looking for it shortly is . . . well, he's everything. Everything I ever thought was worth being. Squiggles, I think I know why your bedroom is the Minneapolis–St. Paul ever-loving Airport. And I think maybe I always already stole it. Which means, you know, *ethically*, it's mine. Come here. Give us those hands. I was never as good as Oort, but I can carry my own luggage when it comes to it."

He looked, really looked, for the first time at the Vedriti's twelve delicate, preternaturally agile, dexterous tentacle-fingers. And second set of smaller hands situated just so *neatly* within reach of the pickups. "Don't look now, dearest. But between you and me, I think you *might* turn out to be quite good at this. Relax. I'll show you how. I *was* booked in for a basic lesson today, after all. Working man like me has to put in his hours." He lifted two dark-blue translucent proboscis fingers and positioned them tenderly on the fretboard. "Now, a Fender is a rougher machine, but a Gibson . . ."

The second time Mira visited, she said nothing for almost an hour. Brief Experience of Being Tavallinen did not have the capacity to be bothered by this. She just watched the storm roll in outside. The Vedriti turned her head almost all the way around to stare at the hail, the snow, the rain all coming down at once.

"Come on," Mira said, grabbing the alien's radial limb with a sudden burst of executive function. "You know you want to."

"It will not work."

"You never know. Live a little!"

Mira was never good at respecting boundaries. She pulled Nen through the doors, taking care not to go so far as to run directly into the invisible breakwall that divided this captive domesticated bubble of space-time from the actual untamed space-time beyond. She guided Tavallinen onto a square of pavement between the overhanging awnings, a square already black with wet. Brief Experience of Being Tavallinen stood in it and raised her face to the sky. The spring storm happily obliged. Freezing rain rolled down her face like tears. Snow and hail tangled in her blue tendrils. Wind whipped against her bismuth ruff.

"It doesn't matter," she said as snowmelt sluiced down her

metallic-bone face. "It is not *my* rain. The rain on Xodo is part of us. The rain elsewhere is just . . . water."

Mira Wonderful Star couldn't tell if she was disappointed. She supposed not. But then the creature stuck her tongue out briefly, childishly. A pale blue glassy tongue like a lizard.

And suddenly, she was just a person. Just a person standing there, in all her insane absurd wild beauty, tasting the rain like a little kid.

Mira rather thought her time as an engine part had thoroughly jaded her. But just then, she thought, more than most things the universe could offer, that she might very much like to see this terribly odd person laugh.

They turned back inside, and the brand-new, cutting-edge-tech 1970 sliding-glass doors parted to let them back into the warmth of a world with all four Beatles still living in it.

Days later, a flight from Amsterdam emptied into the baggage claim, as it did at the mid-point of every looping space-time cycle. Brief Experience of Being Tavallinen watched them stream through, embrace some people and not others, and then flow out into the world.

A paw emerged from a plain black businessman's suitcase. It groped around, found a zipper, and unsealed itself from its vinyl cave.

Öö hopped out. His striped tail bounced on the floor as he dashed through foot traffic, never breaking eye contact with Tavallinen until he climbed up on her lap.

He stared at her for a long time. He didn't ask any questions. Tavallinen waited without agitation. The Keshet poked her slick cheek with one fuzzy finger. He frowned.

"Hi," he said. "Hihihihifascinatinggrosshi."

Then Öö scampered off the Vedriti's lap, leaped into the nearest bin with both feet, and vanished.

"Hi," said Mira Wonderful Star, when she returned for the third time.

"Hi," said Nen.

"I want to try something, all right?" Mira took off her stained hazmat gloves and laid them on the empty orange apocalyptic sunset chair beside her. "Do you trust me?"

"Trust is a—"

"Yeah, yeah, yeah. I know that one. Let's try: this might hurt a little."

"I accept pain. Pain does not matter."

"Well . . . hold on to something, then, love," Mira said ruefully, and gently, ever so gently, brushed her naked palm against what might pass for the Vedriti's forearm.

Tavallinen stiffened as the brief experience of being her filled up her every cell with information. It was too much to process or understand. Sometimes she had been a disaffected rock, sometimes a fully actualized flower, sometimes a nihilistic storm cloud, and occasionally a shard of glacier who really had it all together.

She remembered rain. So much rain. And snow. And thunder. And wind.

But then there were flashes of Nen herself. Singing karaoke with all her heart and soul in a little pub on a Tuesday night when everyone understood her and she forgot what loneliness was—and in that perfect place where nothing had ever gone the wrong way, the night outside the little pub was fine and clear.

Then it passed.

It always passes.

Tavallinen opened her depthless eyes. Mira's own were right there, watching her closely.

Two jet-black tears flowed out of the Vedriti's face. Then no more.

"I don't want to die," whispered Brief Experience of Being Tavallinen, her breath full of terror.

"Precious weird space girl," whispered Mira. "No one does. That's all we needed to hear. We'll sort you out. Spacemen never give up."

The Vedriti almost leaned into the human for the tiniest scrap of comfort. Then the stiffest upper lip in the quadrant returned. Whatever moved through Tavallinen had passed.

It always passes.

21.

Hatred Will Prevail

When all the evils of sentient existence, necessary, unneces-sary, and just plain weird, have wound their way toward peace and justice or, at the very least, gotten so bored and tired and over it they can't be arsed doing much more than twiddle their evil thumbs, evilly, and run out the shot-clock on entropy, one primordial horror will remain with us all the way up to the final countdown: all-hands staff meetings.

That's the trouble with the smaller, energy-efficient evils. They stick around. The big splashy ones get buffed out and polished up as they trundle along on the conveyor belt of evolving civilization. Genocide is so obviously a terrible way to spend your afternoons as a culture that everyone (apart from Gary in sales and his alarming search history) can agree it probably ought to be phased out in the next societal update.

And eventually, on a long enough timeline, it will be, even if everyone can also agree they really, *really* can't stand the neighbors just sitting over there *breathing* and *gardening* and *eating toast* like the monsters they are. Not in *this* era, oh no, Gary will see to that. But the next one. Or the one after, at the outside.

But sooner or later, people will come round to the novelty of not being complete mallets for a while, as a change of pace. It's not exactly a difficult moral call to maybe, just possibly, on your own time, no rush, not shoot anyone in the face for existing today.

The big dramatic evils just don't have staying power. It's the little aggravations that fester under the fingernails of day-to-day life that just can't quit you. And the most stubborn of these is the roomy, comfortable malevolence of your average corporate staff meeting that could have, should have, and deep down always identified as an email.

Because you've got to have meetings, haven't you? Sitting round a table slowly dying inside while someone tries to rub two efficiencies together for warmth works just well enough to limp along through the lifespan of empire after empire. Any worse and someone would come up with a better solution. Any better and someone would imagine the profits involved in improving it and ultimately give the remote meeting software suite enough power to qualify as a doomsday device.

These little evils pump out so much undiluted, full-strength irritation into the cosmic background that Slozhit researchers have determined up to 2 percent of the non-baryonic material that holds the universe together is not, in fact, dark matter, but pure concentrated irritation.

The Galactic Broadcasting Union is not evil.

Per se.

But it is a staff meeting that never ended.

The Galactic Broadcasting Union does not rule the galaxy with an oversize animated carnival fist.

Per se.

But they did, almost entirely without actually sitting down and making a flowchart about it, slowly come to control 99 percent of all entertainment, including the early invention of the comedian trap. This simple talent-acquisition snare requires an intrepid young executive to venture deep into the wilderness until she detects telltale signs of stand-up spoor and molt. The brave scout then calmly sets out a brick wall, a microphone, and places a bottle of water on an inviting stool. It's never long before a big strapping twelve-point white-tailed observational male approaches, tentatively trilling their traditional mating call: *you just can't say anything anymore . . .*

This technique was easily adapted to attract musicians and writers as well, most of whom found regular meals and sleeping inside to be a real game-changer.

Slowly, with gusto, the GBU absorbed everything even tangentially related to the entertainment industry by virtue of (a) existing, and (b) being the only body to which every species actually got up in the morning and sent delegations because no matter the details of this treaty or that border dispute, there'll be hell to pay if Nan can't watch her stories. Publishing, broadcasting, video games, feature films, series, concept album growhouses and various cancellation reparations, radio, gallery, museum, ritualistic sacrifice and glamping circuits, most popular IP franchises, theme parks, zoos, all usable parade routes, live-action and tabletop role-playing, musical theater labor camps, historical re-enactments (voluntary or involuntary), slam poetry (consensual and nonconsensual), Hrodos Fashion Week, farm-to-table privilege-tasting, mum's-closet-to-pub-stage drag shows and all associated sequin supply chains, podcasts, audiobooks, personal journaling, boardgames (except Monopoly, which they determined to be too fundamentally destructive to the social contract to be allowed off-Earth), children's birthday party costumed princesses, princes, and historic dictators, sleight-of-hand magic, strippers (clothes, wiring, or chitinous plates), the dizzying riches of the pornographic arts, virtually all mime infrastructure, farmers' markets, congressional hearings, school fêtes, and the whole of public education.

And obviously, the GBU holds unquestioned authority over the observance of the orgiastic cannibal blood-letting ceremony known as pilot season.

The GBU finally completed its dominion over the all-hours high-stakes fishing programs of the sea, the backlots of the earth, over the criminal prosecution of every creeping thing that spoils endings for their friends, and the digital transmission of any discreet unit of information through the air, through the establishment, oversight, and administration of the Metagalactic Grand Prix.

Every time two or more of you are gathered to play charades, the Galactic Broadcasting Union will be involved before you get through the signs for *three words, first word, song title, sounds like Schmeremiah Schmas a Schmullfrog.*

In a post-scarcity society, it is not the hand that wields the sword that rules, but the hand that greenlights production of the next piece of art that changes the way people think.

Shortly after the end of the Sentience Wars and the conclusion of the first Metagalactic Grand Prix, Medical Expo, and Boat Show, all the major players gathered in a bombed-out Dyson sphere. This particular sphere was chosen because it was located at the precise center of the conflict zone so that everyone would have to travel the same distance as everyone else and there'd be no squabbling over chipping in for petrol.

Of course, the assembled elite didn't *call* it a Dyson sphere. Humans say *Dyson sphere* when they mean a great stonking inside-out planet built around a star, made out of steel and a truly over-the-top answer to the question *dunno, what do you want to do today?* But Mr. Freeman Dyson, stand-up fellow though he may have been, never actually built any such thing. He just thought about it very hard, and much as we don't call genocides *Garys* just because Gary has a large number of serious issues he isn't talking to anyone about, we don't name our daydreams after ourselves and expect everyone to agree we invented it.

Everyone else in the galaxy just calls these beasts of engineering caravan parks and has done with it.

At the time, all the shell-shocked anxious species' representatives politely avoided observing that the caravan in question had ended up on many wrong ends of many wrong guns and looked much more like a gravy boat than a sphere.

The Utorak ignored all such remarks.

Quite cleverly, that species of gray-rocking silicate slabs who counted strategic psychiatry and counter-psychiatry as their main cultural exports spent most of the Sentience Wars attacking communications infrastructure. It's almost impossible to actually kill an Utorak, any more than it's possible to definitively kill a mountain. But they're usually far too empathy-forward and emotionally stable to be very good at detonating anyone. The Formation's brutally mentally-balanced military's sole objective was making certain the lone postwar voice available to explain who was to blame, very solemnly and sadly, of course, was Utorak.

Therefore, once everyone had finished lobbing war crimes into the building, it was simple enough to get one action figure of every still-standing world's playset into a bombed-out shell of a room, agree to the standard Rakevat's Rules of Chaos as an organizing principle, and set about establishing the new galactic status quo. The meeting began, fueled by lukewarm mediocre beverages and a steady supply of objections, expressed through increasingly abstract interpretations of the concept of mouths.

But when the wall-mounted Matter Whisperers can keep the culturally appropriate versions of coffee and crullers flowing in an unceasing river, a meeting does actually not *have* to end.

When the slide projectors are fueled by the heart of a magnetar wildly ejaculating the energy of a hundred thousand suns into the void every two-to-ten seconds, and the issues at hand are, for once, a fair sight more pressing than what color visited links ought to be, urgency doesn't actually *have* to subside.

When there is no day or night because who needs those old dodderers when you have technology, and leftover Utorak executive function depth-charges lodged in the exterior hull keep going off and making one representative or another, and also sometimes the lighting fixtures feel *really* jazzed up, 100 percent on top of things, and compelled to be the ultimate decider no matter the cost, when the lifespans of the meeting attendees can vary from twice human length to a shrug and a question mark, the idea of breaks loses all meaning, and a fair amount of allure. And when Rakevat's Rules of Chaos has sunk several dozen previously-sentient beings with families and hobbies and rich inner lives so deep in motions, debates, sub-motions, sub-debates, sidebars, digressions, inquiries, auxiliary alternative synergistic sub-sub-points of order, mid-argument births and deaths, constant deep-space structural reconstruction of the facility containing said meeting and clearing up after either/or/all three, a simple orientation meeting can get itself into the same situation as this sentence, beginning in the deep past and still in tedious progress, when Decibel Jones and crew finally arrived at the location plainly specified in their First Contact guidelines with a very unsettling, very emotionally unavailable pile of tentacles in tow.

22.

Heroes

Decibel Jones, an up-jumped pelagic nudibranch, and a paradox walked into the alternate tertiary adjunct Galactic Broadcasting Union air lock and greenroom.

They stood silhouetted against the pupil-smearing white-blue glare of Bezençon M, the long-collapsed neutron star that powered the whole of the *B* in GBU like the tableaux at the end of a lower-than-usual budget science fiction serial.

Brief Experience of Being Tavallinen stood uncomfortably in front of the flats for the now-cancelled dating/live-rounds military strategy show *90-Day Ceasefire*, a rack of costumes from the classic Klavaret sitcom *Emotional Maturity and the City*, and a fern just trying its best to look professional.

Tavallinen's saucer-face and rainbow-prismatic half shell had grown a number of wide, alarming cracks, as though someone had dropped her in the shop and would now have to pay full price. Everyone wanted to say something, but no one had, because *what happened to your face, new friend, you seem have a bit of chasm into the infinite lightless void beyond hope on your chin* is very hard to fit naturally into a conversation.

They had a lot on that day, after all.

"Please wait in the greenroom until the GBU governing board is ready to hear your viewer complaint," a pleasant automated voice announced through an intercom hidden in the deeply embarrassed fern. "We know you have one choice when it comes to galaxy-wide entertainment, so there is no need to thank you for anything."

"Shut *up*," Dess hissed in the vague direction of the fern, who didn't ask for any of this.

That pleasant automated cow said the same thing every twenty minutes. It had leapt the charts to suddenly become their least favorite sound. They'd have made a break for it hours ago, but none of them were looking forward to picking their way through the carnage the large-screen security camera feed showed outside this room. Several smashed memorial walls, blown-up commemorative storage closets, obliterated consecrated soundstages, and hall after room after rotunda, all crammed with embarrassingly unfinished postwar home repair work.

They'd tried for business casual but missed by half a dartboard and an angry pub owner's width. Decibel Jones gave the studied air of being quite busy on his phone despite not having a phone of any kind on his person. He wore an entirely appropriate gray flannel blazer, a somewhat less respectable novelty tie that read #1 YUMMY MUMMY over a pattern of interlocking holiday biscuits, and primrose-pink paisley pleather pants. He accessorized with a respectably lean brown midriff peeking out from under a roughly bisected black-and-yellow T. rex shirt and a pair of green sequined 2012 New Year glasses.

Mira Wonderful Star wore platform industrial boots and a jet-black version of Celine Dion's iconic 1999 rear-facing suit with so much glitter infused into the fabric her every movement seemed wet and slick, a very serious goth dolphin ready to do goth dolphin business. Her version of the singer's slicked-back ponytail ended, not in nice smooth well-trimmed nondescript light brownness, but in a generous pasta-serving of green and purple plastic light-up rave-lox.

"I think we cleaned up quite well for a boardroom set," Dess announced to the memorial wreckage: a cratered wall on the north end of the greenroom, protected by a sparkling kinetic field to prevent space coming in or damage being fixed and therefore forgotten, surely to be done again someday on account of said forgetting.

Underneath the broken bulkhead a small plaque read:

SENTIENCE WARS MEMORIAL TRAIL: THE WATERSHED

THIS STRUCTURE WAS DAMAGED BY A PRIME-TIME SWEEPS-WEEK BATTLE ROYALE FT. THE ALUNIZAR EMPIRE AND THE VOORPRET MUTATION AGAINST EVERYONE ELSE FOR CONTROL OF THE POWERFUL BROADCAST CAPABILITIES OF THE GALACTIC BROADCASTING UNION'S CENTRAL SPOKEPOINT.

DO NOT IGNORE THE MEMORIAL WALL.

DO NOT TOUCH THE MEMORIAL WALL.

DO NOT TAUNT THE MEMORIAL WALL.

The whole effect mainly accomplished making it impossible to relax in the greenroom. A swirling pit of burnt debris hovering over the sanity-kneading inferno of a green-white magnetar hardly lends itself to emotional regulation and profound inner peace.

"I'm wearing a suit," Mira shrugged defensively. "I don't know what more can be expected of me." She frowned at her old/new friend. "Why 2012?"

Decibel Jones pushed the novelty specs up the bridge of his nose. "Last good year," he replied.

Mira rolled her eyes. "I doubt it. Anyway, if they furrow whatever brow-like face organ they've got at me, I can always change when the ship yanks my leash. I am the weather in London, if you don't like me, wait five minutes."

"I am dressed," said Brief Experience of Being Tavallinen, or Nen, as absolutely everyone agreed to call her on account of severe multisystem syllable fatigue. She wore the simple fashion-pharaoh linen wrappings and fun-house mirror anatomy she always did.

Bezençon M spun nauseatingly fast outside the enormous picture windows, intact and preserved for posterity. Columns of spangly bluish-white starspots and starquakes rippled across the semi-fluidic surface and shot into the GBU sphere every time the magnetized mirror ball of very exciting death rotated, which it did, steadily, every two-to-ten seconds, dropping the bass on the galactic broadcast day throughout the galaxy.

"That star is fucked *all* the way up," Mira said, each starspot and starquake flashing white radiation across her black suit like a zebra stuck in a centrifuge. "Do you think they'll listen? Surely this is why every host gets to set their own rules. To make it fair for all the species. They have to listen, right? They'll postpone it. That's not so much to ask. We *just* did all this. They'll probably *want* to procrastinate. Procrastinating is excellent, I do it all the time. They've got to see the Vedriti can't do this. It's not a fair test for them. You wouldn't test a cat by making them paint *The Creation of Adam*. It's madness. They haven't got thumbs."

The lounge was very quiet.

"My nutritional needs have been satisfied for this cycle," Nen announced, and turned away from the boiling star. The cracks in her bismuth ruff and magnesium face smacked shut with a sound like gum popping.

"Right," Mira said. "Got it. Lightless hopeless chasm-face equals hungry."

"Hunger is a feeling."

"Is it?" Decibel asked, turning his head to her curiously. "It's a sensation, but I'm not sure it's an emotion."

"It certainly is when *you're* hungry," Mira grumbled. "Wait. I think *I'm* hungry."

"I'm sorry," Decibel snapped hangrily. "Which of us began today with the phrase *if I don't get a fucking croissant in the next five seconds I will hit the self-destruct button it's right next to my quarters so sit on that and nurture it to adulthood why don't you*? Because I'm reasonably certain I haven't done carbs for breakfast since sixth form, have I?"

Nen wandered over to the memorial wall. She very clearly read the plaque, then blatantly reached out to do the exact thing it told her not to.

Some things are common to all sentient life.

Nen ran her tentacled hand over the edge of the gaping wound in the side of GBU headquarters. The kinetic shield crackled against her skin. A small, gray, quartz-adjacent stone wiggled on the other side of the war hole. It seemed to be stuck into the plain unhistorical section of the greenroom hull. The milky little gem wriggled back and forth, working its way free of a more spectacularly stove-in portion of the greenroom and toward destiny.

It popped free with a sound like a ream of Bubble Wrap all snapped at once by a very stressed-out welterweight champion. The marble bounced on the floor, wheeled round in a delighted circle, and rolled with deliberate gravity across the floor toward the four of them, aware of the inherent tension it was firing up among the three figures watching it coming, yet doing absolutely nothing to get out of the way.

"Greetings, Chosen One!" the stone said in a voice of deep wisdom and solemn duty. "Your destiny is upon you—"

"Sorry, who?" Mira piped up.

The stone rolled back and forth uncertainly. "The Chosen One! The hero, the champion of the ages, the great and prophesied paladin whose hour has come at last!"

"Right," Decibel said, doing his level best to be extremely cool about this entire conversation. "It's just that there's . . . three of us. I've never heard of a Chosen Four, not outside of whimsically colored submarines or pizza-bestrewn sewer turtles."

"I don't think we should talk to it," Mira warned, backing away from the unassuming pebble with a voice like a chocolate-coated movie trailer.

"*Definitely* talk to me!" the little rock cried out in a distinctly Gandalfian timbre. "I am the harbinger of your fate! I am the crown upon your soul! I am the voice of the stars themselves as they realign to paint your face, and yours alone, across the portentous heavens!"

"Aw! Doesn't that sound nice?" Decibel said sweetly. "Come here, my pet. Ps-ps-ps-ps!"

"Stop cooing at it!" Mira snapped. "You don't know where it's been!"

Dess did not stop cooing at it. He bent down and scratched the floor to lure it closer. "Dunno, my face across the portentous heavens sounds like a big get for publicity."

The stone cleared its throat and tried again. "Heed my call, O Savior of Other, Much Less Important, Less Talented, and Less Handsome Beings! You must come out of retirement for one last mission—"

"We're hardly *retired*," Mira protested. "On hiatus at best. Between albums. Gap year."

"Come closer, questing paladins! The hour is close at hand! You must pay heed to my words, for I, *I*, only I! Possess the secret of *your father's true identity*!"

Mira snorted. "Pretty sure it's still the former owner/operator of Dublin's only combination ice cream parlor/video rental establishment, *Achocolypse Now*, good old Lawrence Strauss. But do say hello for me if you hear from him."

"You are a rock," Nen stated flatly. "You came out of a wall."

"I am an Utorak protagony mine, foolish, yet heroic and unusually attractive potential heroes!" the stone introduced itself. "I am my own category of war crime! I am highly illegal strategic projectile ammunition! Compact, solar-powered, waterproof, and affordably priced for the military-industrial complex on-the-go. I come preloaded with a range of cultural frameworks and intensity settings. I am also very conveniently easy-to-lob and ergonomically sized for use as a stress-seeking mine, grenade, blow-dart, or bullet! If you keep talking to me, I will lock on to you and you'll be in for a world of FUN." The primed ordnance purred happily and crept closer to the Vedriti. "Especially *you*, young ingenue!"

"Leave it," Mira warned Brief Experience of Being Tavallinen, who made no reply, but stared at it curiously. "I am also primarily composed of minerals," she said finally. It took Mira some time to realize this was the alien's attempt at establishing something she and the weapon had in common in order to make friends with it. Still, she put her radial limbs behind her back all the same.

"I will not be ignored!" bellowed the protagony mine. "You must come with me at once! Your quest will not wait! Even as we speak, clouds of doom gather on the horizon! A storm is coming . . ."

"It's *tiny*. What harm could it do?" Decibel said, making eyes at the slightly overgrown marble.

"What did it *just* say, Dess?" Mira let out a frustrated growl. "You're very nearly in the neighborhood of senior discounts and compression socks! Why do I *always* have to be the responsible one?"

The Vedriti delegate to the stars had decided she did not want to be touched. She clonked back against a slab of protective glass shielding the famous reception desk from the old Utorak comedy *Solidly Constructed Towers*. The stress-seeking mine made its choice in that instant. It rolled toward her menacingly. It seemed to be herding them toward the air lock they'd come through to get here in the first place, which didn't particularly feel like progress to anyone.

Decibel Jones raked his 2012 glasses through his immaculate hair and up to rest on the top of his head. "Settle down, Miss My-Frontal-Lobe-Hasn't-Fully-Developed-Yet. Do you see snifters full of brandy and rehabilitated imperialism around? No? Then I'm not a historian, am I? And I want to hear this pretty beastie out. It called me a hero!"

Mira kicked the marble off its trajectory toward Nen. The mine was untroubled. It looked at Mira appraisingly.

"It called *me* a hero, Dess. And Nen. It's awfully promiscuous with its praise. Did it ever occur to you that they probably wouldn't have a whole category of war crime with just one bullet point in it if it couldn't hurt anyone?" Mira squinted at the ancient bomb.

"But you'll like it while it lasts," chortled the protagony mine. "Promise."

"Fine," Decibel sighed. No one else in the universe was any fun whatever. "Let's just all ignore it and find someone corporate-looking."

"Fantastic," Mira said with relief. Talking sense into Dess had something like a 30 percent hit rate on the best of days. Today was a lucky day. "Because I'm not cleaning up whatever mess that thing has in mind, and all mines are messes."

The rock stopped short. It rolled in a quick circle, then tapped the floor twice like an old tradie clearing his throat before he mends your dishwasher.

"Look," the protagony mine said, in the same voice, but without so much boom and bombast—and a far less celestial accent. "Keep your trousers on. You *do* need to follow me at once, and there *are* clouds of doom on the horizon and a storm coming, metaphorically speaking, of course. Actually it's mostly clouds of cigarette smoke on the horizon and storms of overpriced Wi-Fi once you get to the command center. But you'll be pleased to know I've completed *several* fail-safe narrative rehab programs. I have a certificate that says I'm 100 percent Re-formed."

"But you were just . . . menacing our new friend!" Dess protested.

The marble spun in an embarrassed circle. "Old habits and all, my apologies! I just wanted a little *taste* of the old days. It gets *grim* out here. Hey, man! She touched the wall! I can't be blamed! The plaque did *say* not to touch the wall. Subroutines were activated!" It rolled to the doorhatch of the greenroom, which opened smoothly for the marble despite staying churlishly shut for them for many, many hours now. "Very pleased to meet you," the p-mine cheerfully chattered as it rolled, popped, jumped, and skittered down the halls with total confidence. "My name's Gadramaður the All-Knowing, welcome to the Galactic Broadcasting Union, please be aware of the locations of nearby emergency exits at all times."

Mira frowned and bent forward to get a better look at the talking paperweight. "Is that thing sentient?" she asked.

"I'm perfectly safe!" The little round rock almost seemed to puff out its milky chest. "Stone cold sober, heh heh. Thirty-one cycles, fifty-three days without a drop of the hero's journey. I've got a medallion and all. You're looking at one small part of the Grand Disarmament. Too dangerous to destroy, that's me! My rate of decay is incompatible with organic life, I'll have you know! So they rewired a whole load of us to be pages and personal assistants. Same sort of skill set. Companion, mentor, guide through the dark wood toward the sacred wellspring of knowledge. Of course, industries change fast, you've got to keep up to stay competitive. These days, I mainly take people to meetings and show them the loo. I MEAN, TAKE THEM TO THEIR DIVINE ROLE IN THE TAPESTRY OF EXISTENCE AND SHOW THEM THE PATH TO GLORY! Erm. Sorry. Don't get angry. I am what I am, aren't I?"

"And what *is* that, exactly?" Decibel said uncertainly.

On Earth, science was a process by which clever folk slowly and painstakingly ruined everyone's dreams of sugar plum fairies with the reality of diabetes. Out here, science appeared to be the Christmas wishes of an A/V society nerd who'd never been naughty a day in her life.

"What they made me to be, in the vast armored vaults of Otozh! I make things happen to people. Good people. Good things! S'like when the doctor whacks you on the knee with the little wee hammer. You kick your leg and/or other protruding propulsory limb out; I find you a *really* massive stonking sword down the shops that makes the bearer king of the Alunizar for a very reasonable daily hire rate. Or what have you. You can take the unexploded psychic bomb out of the war but . . . well, you know the rest. Come with me please, yes, quite, right this way, mind the gap, also the irradiated glass, thank you, pip pop, you won't want to keep the brass waiting!" The stone stopped barreling down the halls of power and lowered its voice slightly. "That said, if you *are* in the market for secret birthrights and prophecies fulfilled, don't tell anyone, but I *might* could slip you a bit of something. But at the moment THE SHADOWY FATES AND UNFATHOMABLE CURRENTS OF TIME COMMAND YOU TO EMBRACE YOUR AUTHENTIC SELF AND . . . walk down a hallway. With me. Right now."

The shiny little war crime led them down through corridors and vestibules and hopped merrily down stairwells, deeper and deeper into the ancient and powerful gullet of the GBU.

"So what harm *did* you do?" Decibel asked awkwardly as he ducked first under an undifferentiated mass of slagged metal and wiring. No one seemed to have done any single thing to repair this place since the war. They'd just slapped up memorial plaques and pretended the mess was on purpose, morally necessary, and by the way, how dare you judge these sacred spaces? The others picked their way after him, except for Nen, who quietly drifted down the walkways saying nothing and contributing nothing. Her fanned tendrils trailed after her like Glinda the Good Witch's gown, only attached to a heartless radiation goblin. So, *precisely* like Glinda's bubble.

The marble seemed to grow, somehow, *happier*. "Is that an opportunity to talk about myself I smell? I do not mind, I do not mind at all. Always nice to make a bit of convo on the job. Me and mine and the Utorak Formation go back *yonks*. It's all to do with their main export, psychiatry. And concrete. But mainly psychiatry. I'm sure you know all about that, don't have to tell you. Scratch an Utorak and you'll find a complex metamorphic mini ecosystem that really just wants you to actualize your actuals, patch up your marriage, make good habits, and set healthy boundaries. Any Utorak'd give you the existential crisis off their back. Or they would've, before they played rock-paper-interstellar-navies with the Alunizar and found out that, while ol' rocko beats a hell of a lot, nothing really beats *gloop*." The protagony mine rolled merrily past a bank of framed portraits of stars long gone: Musmar the

Night Manager, Aukafall Avatar 0, Sebastian the Conflict Marshmallow, Joan Rivers, all the greats.

"Doesn't anyone *work* here?" Mira asked, glancing at the beaming face of Rüü, beloved Keshet host of the classic theoretical physicists' late-night advice show *And What Time Do You Call This?*

"Work? But that would take time away from the Meeting! Besides, most of it kind of runs by itself at this point. Although don't plug in a space heater and a broad-spectrum quantum signal slalomer at the same time if you know what I mean, heh heh. But I *am* serious, it *will* blow the fuse box."

"Back to how you're the Utorak Manhattan Project?" Decibel nudged.

"Look at you, walking and learning about the valuable experiences of others at the same time!" Mira smirked. "That's progress, Jones."

"Kindly shut it, Hamlet's Dad," Dess called fondly over his shoulder as a bottomless canyon of glittering electronic banks of baffling instruments yawned into eternity on one side of their tight little fellowship of the microphone.

The protagony mine rattled on. "Once the war was tuning up onstage, my makers did what everyone does. See now, war's a fancy dress ball where you always go as yourself. It's personal. The way you go to war really says something about who you are as a species. Like a *really* huge *Which Unforgivable Historical Atrocity Are You?* quiz. So the Alunizar have all those orbital hydro-cannons and vapor-mines and ultra-blue lasers because they're watery gloop in plastic lunch bags, and the Utorak have . . . us. Fun fact: we started out as antidepressants! Top of the line, extra-strength. Just a little pick-you-up and snuggle-your-chakras for you and the missus. Don't swallow me, though! Ha-ha, just kidding. Don't, though. You wouldn't like me when I'm swallowed."

"Is it that you talk until the target kills themselves to escape? Is that it?" Dess muttered.

"Nope! You know how most of the time, the universe is chaotic and vast and everyone just stumbles through it doing their best, or their worst, mostly their worst, and sometimes good things happen to bad people and bad things happen to good people but occasionally the other way round, just to balance it out, but you can't predict any of it and other people exist and also need to get their shopping done so you just have to hope the stars align for you for at least five or ten minutes in your entire life? WELL. When *I* go off, all that goes straight in the bin. I release a protagony burst! Hurts a little. Tingles a LOT. I had to attend a support group for my victims as part of my rehabilitation and *they* said it felt like getting your skin lovingly brushed by copper wire dipped in lava. Poor mites. Wonder how old Donald is getting on? He always stuffed his pockets with the better biscuits. Anyway! Me, I'm a short-range model, good for clearing a room, bunker-buster, that sort of jazz.

"Once the burst hits you, other people are simply no longer your problem. You are the confirmed center of the universe. You are *the* Protagonist of Today. You don't doubt yourself for a second. And you don't need to, because things, generally, work out the way you want. You're suddenly capable of anything and everything you need to do to achieve your destiny, up to and including suddenly having the power to shoot lasers from your eyes or fart sonic booms or just coincidentally run into a mighty battle-steed at your local with wings and three heads and a tragic backstory. Every audio or visual device you turn on has *scads* to say about how you're getting on. People fall passionately in love with you in thirty seconds or less or your biannual defense budget back. Authority figures suddenly want to help you. Everything that's ever happened to you is suddenly insanely and directly relevant to the task at hand. Everything you touch becomes a magical object pure *shellacked* with foreshadowing. It's like a layer shot of PCP, steroids, single-malt telekinesis, and narcissism! Lasts about fifteen minutes. Twenty if you ate first."

"Utter bollocks. Not possible. *How?*" scoffed Dess.

"Shh. Don't ask stupid questions."

"That sounds fine," Mira said, dodging a broken overhead lighting bank that chose this moment to give up the fight and swung down to make friends with her skull. It pranged off Nen's bismuth ruff instead. She seemed unperturbed, but then, she would. "That sounds lovely, actually."

"Oh, it isn't! First of all, my manufacturer's suggested use case is to drop me into a crowded public space so that I set off hundreds of protagonists at once. Usually, they all kill each other in a quarter of an hour flat because fate told them there could be only one or some faff. I interact with specific deep-gene sequences to gin up a culturally appropriate narrative for each target. Even a single serving of me can be totally devastating to local wildlife and economies! And just . . . *any* major recognizable landmark.

The p-mine turned a sharp left down a totally undamaged corridor. The floor gleamed. The lighting was recessed, classy, and intact. The path was wide, clean, and nowhere did they have to look into the soul-scalding madness of the magnetar outside.

Gadramaður the All-Knowing seemed to see no difference between the ruined sections of the GBU station and the repaired. It chattered on happily. "Protagonists are the *worst*. It's that *other people exist* thing. Protagonists always produce massive property, medical, emotional, and societal damage. Natural by-products of their metabolism. Like exercise and sweat. Stars and radiation. Parents and guilt! Heroes warp the entire fabric of reality around them, snarf down everything else's potential to fuel their own, and usually break a lot of buildings, bones, and previously stable relationships while they're at it. Plus, you can't very well be a protagonist without conflict, so it tends to come crashing through the nearest irreplaceable heritage architecture. Why, when my old gran got accidentally dropped on the main floor gift shop, the receptionist declared a blood feud against the *I Heart the GBU* shirt display, spent fourteen minutes growing scissor-skin, monologuing, chatting with her long-lost son who appeared out of nowhere to reconcile, and planning a frontal attack. Then she had her cloaca handed to her by the tiny commemorative spoons rack because her time was up, but still. Sixty-seven people died! At once! Ah! Good times. They don't make *mes* like that anymore. Because of the massive fines and prison time; you get it."

A secretarial drone shaped like a chrome butter tin who'd gotten its code thoroughly jellied, rolled smoothly down the pristine corridor to them. They knew it was a secretarial drone because it had *All-Inclusive Secretary Unit Colleen.6 (Please Do Not Pinch, Pinching Will Result in Immediate Deployment of Nano-Shanks)* engraved on its stainless steel flank.

Colleen.6 spun in circles around their feet.

"Point of order, point of order, seconded, thirded, fourthded, fifthified, move to recess, strike that, motion to substitute proposed motion for the motion previously substituted for the original motion, call for orders of the day, move to recess, move to recess . . ."

Then the drone turned, whacked its face into the bulkhead several times, whispered desperately to no one: "Point of Parliamentary inquiry!" and broke down sobbing.

Gadramaður the All-Knowing ignored her. It bounced merrily ahead. "And that's just what happens when the target is an electrified meatbucket like yourselves! The real piss-up happens when you drop us lads on your basic random city street. You haven't *lived* until you've seen a bin bag fight a parking meter for divinely ordained supremacy over the All-Night Discount Buffet. What a *show*. Believe me, the worst monster to meet in a dark alley is a protagonist, and it isn't close. If you see one, *run*."

One last curve of the hall and they stood at last before a grand archway overdesigned and under-damaged enough to pass for an important place for important people. "Oh, I forgot! *Sometimes* when I wear off, the targets just perish on their own! Most likely the emptiness, purposelessness, and the sure knowledge they'll never feel that way again! Ah! Here we are. I have guided you to your destiny! THE PROPHECY IS FULFILLED. Er. The GBU page program is fulfilled. Off you pop!"

Given how long they'd waited to be seen and how deep in the station the archway was, Decibel expected some sort of lock or eyeball scanner to keep them out. But no one had bothered. Or, given the absolute state of Colleen.6, perhaps no one had been able to agree on whether a lock or an eyeball scanner would suit best.

The door slid open easily to reveal an intimidating corporate boardroom.

Or at least, it had once, almost certainly, been a boardroom of some kind that intimidated someone. Quite long ago.

23.

Everyone Cares About Themselves

The cathedral-mocking roof of the beating heart of the Galactic Broadcast Union, and a fair bit of the portside wall, window treatment, and flooring, had gotten sawn off like the top of a soft-boiled egg and chucked down the side of the sphere into the swirling, incandescent, molten diamond disco inferno murderball known as magnetar Bezençon M.

The open, gaping, glitter-pricked maw of space yawned above them, and each and every one of those pricks was also a shrieking murderball of infinite liquid fire, because life is nothing but a ceaseless nothingness only occasionally punctuated by brief, random, viciously hostile explosions that last for billions of years and then die without meaning or purpose, that's why.

Decibel Jones deeply hoped a force field of some kind separated all that mess out there from all this mess in here, though nothing sparkled as the force field in the greenroom had, which was not a terrific sign. He supposed he'd find out in a moment.

In terms of both size and bribery-inclusive price point, the GBU's central conference table could've hosted a World Cup final with room to spare for all requisite drinking and casual violence.

Its crystalline viridipuce expanse included the very latest in corporate apparati: individuated and fully armored representative stations, secretarial drone docks, discreet tanks for standard-outlet telepathic brain-to-datawafer crabs, experience acquisition zones, alternating negotiation crucibles and refreshment-printing polyhedrons, Penalty Boxes, sensory softplay areas, and randomly strewn party bowls of assorted, uncategorized, and unrelated loose stationary items. Above it all floated a vast display screen, darkened until needed to host remote attendees, running vote tallies, and the occasional mandatory inspirational movie when the chairman felt too shagged out to do any real classwork.

Around said table sat one of every species with a planet and a star to rub together and hope for the best. The leeward side hosted representatives of the Esca, Keshet, Utorak, Ursula; the Elakhon in formal blackest tie as always, and the pot-bellied plesiosaur-inspired Yoompian executive in an anti-trend three-piece environmental suit. The windward side offered up designates from the Klavaret, the Yurtmak, the towering blue-white wicker man Smaragdi, a sand sculpture of irate Yüz in the shape of a rude gesture whose meaning was quite clear without the use of translators. Then followed the winged Slozhit, the Lummutis gamer-avatar, the Meleg, the Voorpret (presently residing in a long past use-by date body that had clearly once been a Klavaret, because it was now several sticks in a vase of congealed slime and empty flower food packets), and the vast digital intelligence of the 321.

This particular fragment of the AI over frame was downloaded into a form more in keeping with its own aesthetics and goals rather than a novelty word processor tutorial program designed to interface with nervous humans. It had chosen an all-in-one podcasting microphone, mixing suite, light-year capable transmission spike, and off-brand wireless router with the password printed clearly down one side and a personal label-maker ribbon down the other. The ribbon was yellow. The unforgivably Helvetica text was a very loud turquoise. It read: *Just Be Yourself, Love, Mum.*

The gang was all there. (All except the Naranca, who never joined anything that implied regular responsibilities if they could help it.) Everyone else was present and accounted for, even the smaller species who rarely ranked in the Grand Prix, and even more rarely remembered by anyone who actually mattered.

A smaller, less imposing, but much more foldable table stood in the far rear corner. This table featured a worn felt top with crayon-marks all over it, a portable pink combination TV/DVD player with a paleontologically faded Mrs. Frizzle sticker on top, the latest in no technology at all, and several chairs with one leg gone wobbly.

None of the intrepid hero-adjacent petitioners had noticed it at first, what with the limitless intellect-clotheslining chasm of infinite space all around them. Around the kiddie table sat, uncomfortably, in resentful silence, the tiny electroviolet-furred reptilian Vulna, an orange sherbet wisp of sunset Hrodos cloud, a bucket of Sziv, the sentient anarcho-communist moonbeams called Azdr, and Group Captain Alfred Hargrave of Slough, United Kingdom, Earth.

Only one species was missing from the slideshow—because its delegate sat at the head of the gargantuan conference table. A girthy, bulbous, psychedelic-colored Alunizar, ribbed for the pleasure of the Empire. His face was an ultraviolet searchlight punched into a melted freeze-pop of a body, and he seemed to have become one with his executive chair sometime before the invention of agriculture. Premium small-batch leather and glassy, knobbled gel-skin flowed into and out of one another unsettlingly.

That was Lorgnon Xola Zand, Primary Entertainment Executive and Highly Vigorous Potentate of the GBU, whose original contract stipulated the use of his full title when addressed, in any fashion, in perpetuity.

This was the meeting. *The* Meeting. The meeting that had begun just before the war ended and never once cooperated well enough to achieve the two-thirds majority needed to adjourn since and by default become the closest thing to a central government the Milky Way could slap together.

Most of the board, over the eras, had become one with the office furniture and/or interior decor. Not in a mystical sense, but in the very physical, very confrontational installation art sense. The rulers of the GBU had breached the blood-upholstery barrier. It didn't seem to hurt any of them, at least no worse than your average pair of designer heels or wearing a full suit and tie when it's so hot outside you'd gladly unzip your skin like a sleeping bag if it meant one degree of relief. But the overall effect was rather more Lovecraftian than legitimate deliberative body.

No one noticed Dess or Mira or the off-duty radiation witch come in. No one offered them a glass of water, though a large water cooler stood off in the distance, entirely colonized by a sprawling patch of jungle that had once been someone's soothing office ficus.

"Oh, shut the fuck up, Sagrada," hollered the bucket of magenta Sziv from the kiddie table. An elegant, branch-limbed Elakh the color of the space between the stars smiled darkly. In any other context, an Elakh smiling was an excellent reason to refresh your will and investigate tasteful casket options. But as a rolling ergonomic office chair had fully enmeshed itself into the Elakh delegate's lower half to form a grotesque jet-black executive centaur, no one cared anymore.

"Are we allowed to say that, guys?" interrupted the all-in-one podcast-in-a-box that Mira correctly assumed was the 321 executive's current chosen body and Dess assumed was a drummer of some sort.

"Sorry, sorry, Udu Cluster. *Point of order:* shut the fuck up, Sagrada," the Sziv board member corrected theirself.

"Seconded," announced the Chairman, his gelatinous body heavy with generations of noduled young he'd never, and would never, allow to fully bud.

The children of Lorgnon Xola Zand, Primary Entertainment Executive and Highly Vigorous Potentate of the GBU, were for display only. Conceiving offspring temporarily shifts an Alunizar into its Convex Proliferant stage of life, characterized by ferocious strength (to protect babies), increased intelligence (to raise babies), and perfect pitch (to soothe babies).

Actually *birthing* babies? It just wasn't for Lorgnon Xola Zand. It might drain off a fraction of his Highly Vigorous Potency. The board might demote him from Primary Entertainment Executive to Secondary Entertainment Executive. Allowing them to talk and learn and grow and whine for Uncradling presents and, possibly one day, contest for possession of the progenitor-form?

Revolting. Out of the question.

His name alone was singular, without the trad-Alunizar numerical designation announcing how many generations of psychic slugs that particular psychic slug had produced.

"Motion has been moved and seconded," announced a sweet, melodious voice belonging to the previously darkened display screen as an illuminated vote tally blossomed across its surface. "Aye?"

Dozens of hands, paws, gloops, and other appendages shot up around the table. The display tallied only the Elakhon, Yoomp, and Klavaret against, with one uncredited abstention. All the rest were highly in favor.

"Motion passes," the flippered Yoomp and, in some sense, the spare dining room chair fused into zhr bluish-green flesh, snickered. "Suck it, Sagrada. You know what to do."

The Elakh delegate sighed resignedly and punched herself squarely in the face.

Welcome to Rakevat's Rules of Chaos.

24.

We *Really* Don't Know Anything About These Drugs

Lovingly handcrafted by legendary Lummo artisan, exposition-farmer, and part-time item merchant Rakevat Mod 9, Rakevat's Rules of Chaos stemmed from a profound and unbudgeable conviction that anyone, serving on any executive body, in any capacity at all, for any length of time, deserved to be punished. As any truly chaotic document requires every word to have an addendum, codicil, footnote, parenthetical remark, incorrectly formatted citation, or subtitle to a subheading, the word "punished" summons an involuntary psychic popup window in the mind of the student to explain further.

The only chance these mindless whining griefers've got to do anything even tangentially useful to the well-being of regular grinding-class folks like you and me is being confronted with the ridiculousness of their jobs and the laughable uselessness of their entire existences as often and obviously as possible. Subtle don't work on stupid. I'm doing this for us.

Where Robert's Rules of Order have served to just barely keep group politics on Earth to a dull shriek of life-siphoning agony,

Rakevat's Rules of Chaos never even bothered to try, instead opting for a more avant-garde win-condition: the most profound and lasting aggravation, for the most diverse forms of sentience, over the longest amount of time. Naturally, no one *has* to adopt these rules, but the opportunity to inflict regular, significant, and often hilarious violence on fellow group-members without repercussion is almost always too much for any even minimally bureaucracy-related organization to resist.

It has been astonishingly successful. Many scholars credit the Lummo mod with the unprecedented longevity of the current *Pax Galactica*. After all, if nothing can get done without an overwhelming amount of humiliating physical injury to the powers that be, nothing can get razed to the ground from orbit by slow-acting anguish-rays, nor the earth of their ancestors laser-seeded with radioactive salt so nothing can flourish there ever again by the powers that be, either.

An Esca's unmistakable soothing, convincing emotion-editing infrasound voice requested the floor.

"Request to amend the previous motion to amend the motion before that to continue the tabled discussion concerning whether or not to revise the daily agenda reading to include meal options," the blue anglerfish-flamingo crooned persuasively.

"Blow it out your inbox, Bataqliq. You know agenda modifications are a Class ※ item. Can't be brought to the floor without three months' advance warning, a pre-rolled second, personalized gift baskets for each voting member, and confirmed bare-skin exposure to the twisted molten skein of the Moral Fiber of the cosmos for not less than fifty seconds. Rules are rules. Penalty Box! Penalty will be administered by the delegate to your left."

The large, drippy Yurtmak to the Esca representative's left grinned eagerly. The air around each of them went instantly opaque. A few moments later, Decibel and Mira found out what it sounds like when an Esca screams through all the flute-holes in their sternum at once.

"Motion to amend denied," thrummed Lorgnon Xola Zand, Primary Entertainment Executive and Highly Vigorous Potentate, smugly.

The Slozhit raised one delicate wing. "With prejudice?" she requested.

The display screen activated for a vote once more. All in favor, minus the Esca and one unlabeled abstention.

"With prejudice," the chairman confirmed magnanimously. "You get an ice cream."

The Voorpret GBU seatholder (though, more accurately, the seat held him) rattled his remaining half-petrified sticks for recognition. "The Mutation renews its motion for an immediate final vote on the war reparations issue. *Now*. *Some* of us are drying out at an alarming rate."

Both tables erupted into yelling, fist-banging, countermotions, protest-filing, and cowering while hoping to go unnoticed.

"They're still on war reparations?" Decibel whispered to his drummer. "*The* war? But that was *ages* ago. I get more done in a day and I *loathe* getting things done."

"Eh? Who's there?" called a steady baritone voice—in crisp, cut-glass English. A fellow a polite cough younger than Decibel stood up from the kiddie table. Group Captain Alfred Hargrave appeared to be the only one as yet unaffiliated with the office furniture. After all, he'd just gotten there.

The human delegate shaded his eyes with one hand to peer across the acreage of the main table. "Can't see a thing! Is it lunch?"

The massive Easter Island(ish) head that was the Utorak delegate smirked. Her substrate defied all chairs, instead resting on the floor, where it had joined with the HVAC system some century past, so that the eternal agenda of the Galactic Broadcasting

Union could at last move beyond the life and times of the thermostat.

The Utorak circled her seven quartz-deposit eyes with several sets of fingers. Her voice made baritones sound like novelty tin whistles. "Look at me, I'm wearing human glasses because my eyes are stupid like a human's! I bet you think the walls are gray, too."

"Are they . . . not?" Captain Hargrave said, nonplussed.

"They are grultrasilverine with a charcalabastyx subdimensional ombré," sighed the Smaragdi representative with pity. The tall stack of semi-bioluminsecent bones and performative humility, whose several fingers had long ago fused with the coffee service for more efficient hoarding of beverage resources, made a clicking sound with his secondary jaw that was, somehow, clearly patronizing, even to the newcomers. "It's a wonder you don't continually run into traffic with those silly baby-toy eyes."

"Well, *actually*," corrected a large floating glass balloon filled with sulfurous gases called Ursula, who had no visible eye-organs at all. "*Off*-grultrasilverine. And the ombré lightens ever so slightly from charcalabastyx to a dappled pearlivorosescent."

"Ursula, you look positively *ravishing* this afternoon," the Smaragdin said warmly. "And your insight is, as always, both welcome and enlightening."

The entire conference table recoiled in scandalized horror.

"I'm quite sure there's no need for that level of vitriol, Pallulle," Lorgnon Xola Zand, Primary Entertainment Executive and Highly Vigorous Potentate, admonished him quietly.

"Fucking disturbingdisturbingoffensivefightingwordsemotionallyabusivedisturbingawesome, is what that was," chirped the Keshet shareholder.

When not quantum-confined in a Time Out or attempting to convince others to allow themselves to be petted, Keshet shuffle through all possible timelines to select the most advantageous phrasing for the task at hand, which from the outside sounds quite a bit like a record skipping. Across a pond. Made of forks. But the stripey ambassador's admiration was not misplaced. The Smaragdi were a species who prized modesty in all things. What Pallulle had just uttered was the cultural equivalent of throwing one's head back during an important corporate presentation and issuing forth a primal three-minute uninterrupted stream of the vilest possible profanity in lieu of proceeding to the next PowerPoint slide.

"Thanks for coming on the show, Fenek." The 321 residing in its podcast box broke the awkward silence. "Great stuff, great stuff. We'll edit that last bit out in post. But my undead co-host knows as well as anyone major agenda items cannot be introduced without initiating a Call to Arms."

"Oooh, sounds like my kind of party," clicked Gadramaður the All-Knowing. The p-mine rubbed against Decibel's platforms like a hungry cat.

"You know I haven't got any to spare, you stupid *bot*," rattled the host-branches of the Voorpret.

"How dare you? Onigo Gast, you fucking *rotter*, I'll brick your mother!" The mic snarled. A few delegates gasped at the use of a personal name.

"Please, Udu," Lorgnon Xola Zand said. "I'll bury her in toolbars and pop-ups till she screams for mercy and gives your whole inheritance to a . . . a . . . " The soaring mathematical intelligence of the 321 groped for the worst it could think of. ". . . a *human*."

"Can't you hear it? They're playing my song! Put me in the game, coach, come on, I still got it," panted Gadramaður.

"Come over here and suck my rootball, Udu, you overgrown voicemail. Oh wait, you can't, because you're so clever you never pick a body with actual legs."

"A human with a typo in *his own username*! You don't even know. I'll show *you* my leg, you fucking *lodger*."

"FENEK MOVES TO CENSURE UDU CLUSTER!" the once-Klavaret zombie plant screeched. "I invoke the Catastrophic Arsehole rule! I demand the Rebuttal Machete!"

Settle Down, Fenek

The glittering sand-cloud of the Yüz formed the words in the air in impeccable cursive, accompanied by a pretty piccolo glissando as the grains of sand tickled against one another. The display screen was already *pong*ing pleasantly as votes for, against, and the single constant abstention, flowed in.

"I've seen pornography less fucked than this," Decibel whispered in disbelief. "I don't think we should be watching this. It feels . . . private, yeah?"

Mira nodded, dumbfounded. "Maybe we should just leave. It'll be postponed anyway, they'll never get round to us."

The Meleg delegate, silent until now, idly traced some unguessable design on the surface of the glass table. He glanced up under a chubby cherry-cream eyebrow. He ignored the proper Earth representative entirely. The bear fixed his round, whimsical, anime-size eyes directly on the highly confused huddle of Decibel Jones, one Absolute Zero, and their attendant glowy upright glam-Zamboni. His voice was smooth and chocolatey, with honey and whiskey and malice and contempt stirred all through it.

The infinitely soft, pastel-patchwork Meleg seemed to be the only one who noticed they were there at all.

"And to think," Mr. Snuggles said sympathetically, "every one of you could have been dinosaurs capable of differentiating fifty thousand shades of gray at a glance. Then biting all of them. Shame." He winked one sparkling blue-raspberry-lolly-colored eye at them.

"What?" Mira hissed. She'd no idea if they were allowed to actually speak under these unhinged procedural dance steps. "How do you know anything about dinosaur eyesight? Humans are still breaking news to you lot! How do you even know about dinosaurs full stop?"

Mr. Snuggles turned his head to one side and smiled with cold, naked calculation. "Do you *not* know about dinosaurs? I'm *merely* saying it's just *tragic* that you were produced, edited, and mastered by Dinosaur Planet, and *that* is what you ended up with. Squishy, scraggly, half-blind, mostly herbivore teeth, and no fashion sense *whatever*. When you could have been so much more. I'm quite moved by your plight. How *do* you live with the disappointment?"

"Erm. Fine? We're fine," Dess shrugged. "Stegosaurus wasn't too hot on the power chords, probably for the best."

"That's not what I heard," burbled Mr. Snuggles contently, with the expression of a cat who has eaten every canary in Christendom and several infidel crows besides.

Mira Wonderful Star tugged on the sleeve of her blazer defensively. "No fashion sense? Not to get into the weeds here, but you're naked, Tenderheart Bear."

"Eat a bag of farts, Tenderfuck Monkey," Mr. Snuggles replied jovially. "The Meleg always go into battle naked, to show we do not fear the strength and cunning of our enemies."

"*Are* you in battle mode?" the Lummutis avatar piped up with interest.

"Life *is* battle mode, noob," Mr. Snuggles snapped in terms the gamer representative could understand. "Get good."

"I've literally never seen you not naked," the Esca representative whistled in a superior key.

"I am literally never afraid of any of you," the Meleg shrugged.

"Now everyone quit all those spit-sucking mumblemouth hee-haws you make with your bark-barks! Listen to the ding-dongs from Sad Colonizer Island, a place so thoroughly rubbish its people couldn't even be happy when they ruled the entire actual planet. I'm sure they have valuable contributions to share."

"Some of us are from Sad *Potato* Island," Mira mumbled. "Entirely different. Colonized, not colonizers. We shop in two completely different departments."

The Yurtmak held up his murder-mitts, attempting to make peace. "Small angry unicorn, we do not insult the board at large until much later in the legislative relationship."

Mr. Snuggles whirled on his new colleague. "I'm not a *fucking* unicorn, big stonking meatgrinder."

Dess thought the little fellow might actually stroke out. But the representative of Planet Ynt beamed. "Thank you! I'm becoming very fond of you as well!"

"Look at them. They're almost cute. If you overlook everything. Gracious, I just *love* seeing bumpkins get their first glimpse of the big city!" The Meleg, having become unpleasantly familiar with English, put on a respectable west country drawl. "*Oh dear, Mr. Keshet, when I left me tractor and me pig I didn't have no notion of how bright those fancy electric lights could be.*"

"You are not attached to your personal furniture," Brief Experience of Being Tavallinen observed, far outside the conversational line-of-dance.

"The previous delegate suffered a fatal line-item veto. I'm told she was liquefied, strained, muddled with mood enhancers, and served as a festive daiquiri on Blowout Eve." Mr. Snuggles shrugged and waved a paw as though he had nothing to do with it, no idea how it could have been allowed to occur, and a deep personal relationship with his predecessor, precisely none of which was true.

"Yummy," the Yurtmak chuckled. Viscous digestive acids

dripped down his lower mandible. "Not much of a Blowout though. Bloody damp squib that was."

"ENOUGH," roared Lorgnon Xola Zand, Primary Entertainment Executive and Highly Vigorous Potentate of the GBU. "Fenek, your motion to rebut passes. Colleen.7, fetch the machete, it's in the closet next to the Adjournment Cleaver. On the other hand, your motion to censure Udu Cluster fails. Colleen.7! Return the Rebuttal Machete and prepare the Parliamentary Whip. Er. Yes. Same closet, other shelf, you know, the *good* whip. The one with the proton-humiliator spikes on the floggy bits. Right. Now. Everyone else, shut your barf-holes! I am so entirely, thoroughly exhausted by all of you. Let the record show that you are all, individually and in aggregate, the worst, and I hate you. Now stop teasing the . . . the . . ." Lorgnon Xola Zand, Primary Entertainment Executive and Highly Vigorous Potentate of the GBU, smacked the lids of his face-chasm together in consternation. "What, and I cannot stress this enough, the bleeding fuckery is *that*, and why is it bothering us? Did anyone order a pile of rubbish? You, Sziv? You, Bataqliq? *I know it was you, Otozh,*" hissed the Alunizar chairman.

"No, no, we came on our own," Decibel Jones interrupted.

"And just look what the human dragged in," the Yurtmak delegate rumbled like a hungry chainsaw ripping through a massive wet salad. Ynt pointed at Brief Experience of Being Tavallinen with one maroon-black pudding of a finger. "Is bug? Is fish? Is food? Why doesn't it talk if it's food?"

"I talk," Tavallinen said mildly. "I just have no feelings about these proceedings one way or another, nor am I concerned with their outcome."

"Their outcome *only* concerns you," Mira whispered irritably. "Just fake it, Christ on a cheese board, it's easy. I fake being fine about every single thing every single day."

"*Fleurrrugh*," fringed the Alunizar chair through his electrified cilia. "Do you propose that this food is sentient?"

"We do, erm, Sir. And/or Madam . . . s? Sirs and/or Madams? Ah. Yes. I confess I didn't pay *all* the attention last time round. Bit distracted." Dess tried for charming and very nearly got there.

The gathered board of the Galactic Broadcasting Union sat back as best they could and threw any tools or implements with which they had not already physically enmeshed down with much sound and fury.

A collective groan arose from the assembled union, in pitch, tone, and duration identical to any fifth form classroom which has just been told there will be extra homework over the holiday.

"*Awwwwww*, Miss! But we *just* had one!" whined the living, blooming, official Klavaret delegate.

"Ugh, but it's *sooooo* much *work*," moaned the silvery moonbeam of the Azdr.

"It's not *fair*," the Esca wept plaintively. "You're being so *mean*. Why're you being mean to us?"

"My father says I don't *haveta*," snotted the Lummutis, whose animated, highly armored in-game avatar Decibel had, at that very moment, been mentally comparing to a heavy metal giraffestronaut whose lower half was shaped, but not colored, like the wrong end of a slapped frog. "So I am not *gonna*," the avatar finished, and awarded himself three points for making such an excellent argument. The numeral 3 appeared over his head in ghostly, shimmering ultramarine script, then slowly faded into his personal aggregate score.

"Sentience is *dumb*," griped the bucket of Sziv. "When are we ever going to need it for anything important?"

The display screen gamely tried to tally these and all the other excited utterances as votes while logging the many and still-compounding violations of Rakevat's Rules of Chaos alongside their respective offenders and victims on the other, then emitted a crunching minor-key error chord, shorted out, shut down, and sniffled quietly to itself for several minutes.

"I. Don't. *Wanna*," pouted the jet-black visage of the Elakhon seat with finality.

"And how does all this make you *feel*, Aluno Prime?" echoed the Utorak delegate tenderly.

Lorgnon Xola Zand, Primary Entertainment Executive and Highly Vigorous Potentate of the GBU, thought about it, leaning closer to his board-member-cum-personal-therapist to answer in an intimate, confidential tone. "Well, if I am speaking from the core of my authentic self, like you taught me, what I *feel* is uncomfortable and angry because they disgust me and I hate them."

"Everyone disgusts you," flashed the scrap of Hrodos's storm-consciousness trapped in a business-class jar.

"Because everyone is disgusting, Mega-Hrododaktula. Stop being so disgusting and I shall attempt to be slightly less disgusted, somewhat less often. But no promises!"

"Did I hear something about lunch?" came that plummy English voice again from the depths of the conference room.

"Disgust is a feeling," remarked the Brief Experience of Being Tavallinen from the depths of her isolation orb.

"I beg your *screaming* pardon?" screeched the head of the GBU suddenly. "What did you just say to me, you little scum-rocket? I'll have you know entire *parts* of me won the first Metagalactic Grand Prix! Show some respect, you hideous compost bin of assorted parts! I don't like you. I don't want you around my patch. You make my ragesophagus burn and *I'm all out of soothing lozenges*, you absolute *shitweed*. I have half a mind-hole to rule you're about as sentient as a fucking spatula right now. Get off, not to put too fine a point on it, my sodding lawn."

"Hey, don't talk to her like that," Mira protested. Dess shushed her immediately. She slapped his hands away.

Mr. Snuggles laughed. "You share 44.1 percent of your DNA with a banana," he observed. "Your input is irrelevant. Nobody even heard you. So, so sad for the failed dinosaur gang."

"You . . . ah . . . can't actually *do* that," whispered the Yoomp delegate, rubbing zhr generous belly nervously as zhe continued to slowly absorb most writing implements within its reach. "Is the trouble? Rule unilaterally. They booked an appointment. They followed the procedures . . . perfectly, actually. Well done, Earth."

"Pardon, terribly sorry. But I believe *I'm* Earth," Captain Hargrave put in shyly. "No one's managed to gather enough support to open the debate on voting to seat me yet, or find me housing . . . or a meal plan. So I keep abstaining. I rather think that's the correct move, but if it's all the same in the end, I'm happy to have my voice counted. Though whilst I've got you on the topic of meals at last, I *have* been surviving on the lavatory curtains and coffee this last fortnight and my insides are . . . bad. Yes, quite bad. *Awry*, even."

"Shh, honey, go and play with your blocks in your special area like Mama showed you," the richly flowering Klavaret tutted placatingly.

The middle-aged RAF captain rubbed his nose a bit, bucked up like a big boy, and obediently trotted over to a section of the boardroom set up with cheerfully colored safety barriers and a variety of educational toys.

Lorgnon Xola Zand, Primary Entertainment Executive and Highly Vigorous Potentate of the GBU, rose up out of his chair as much as he could, which was not at all. He loomed authoritatively anyway, narrowing his face-hole warily in the general direction of the Vedriti.

"You look like something I'd clean off my bathtub," he sneered.

"Objection, Aluno Prime! Manners!" cried the Smaragdi delegate.

But the screen refused to respond. It continued to sob softly to itself. Another secretarial drone, Colleen.9, stroked the display's power cable compassionately.

"They deserve just as much of a chance as anyone else," Decibel insisted. "You can't just pull the velvet rope across and say *sorry, lads, we're full* because you don't want to do any work." He blinked several times. "Good lord, what am I saying? Who am I? Is there a drinks cabinet? There must be."

An appendage formed out of Lorgnon Xola Zand, Primary Entertainment Executive and Highly Vigorous Potentate of the GBU's gelatinous core. It gripped the bottle of disinfectant always kept nearby in case of biohazardous resolutions tightly. Pressing a button on his splendid office chair, the Alunizar floated over to Nen, grimaced suspiciously at her, and squirted it in her face.

Soapy, lemon-scented liquid slid down the impassive face of Brief Experience of Being Tavallinen.

In sheer instinctual self-defense, a small piece of Brief Experience of Being Tavallinen's abdomen slid open, and an eye-throbbingly blue nematocyst fired a tiny, yet fully loaded toxin injector at anyone who wanted some.

It bounced uselessly off the lip of the boardroom table with a loud *ting*.

"Hello," she said to the apoplectic chairman.

Mr. Snuggles shook his gorgeous raspberry-and-butterscotch trifle head. "Fuck this," he said quietly to himself, "I quit."

The gentleman from Sladoled Tertius saw his moment. The moment he'd seen on the balcony as Mira's paradoxical vision of triumph boiled through his prefrontal cortex. He rapped his blackcurrent-parfait paw on the arm of his chair. "I move to transition directly into Grand Prix Sudden Death Overtime Penalty Kicks, as per GBU charter section 17684, sixthousandteenth sub-paragraph. The Grand Prix supersedes all other business."

"Objection!" bellowed the Elakhon.

"What is your objection, Sagrada?"

"I'm tired and it's boring," the Elakh groused. "Oh! But that's a major agenda item! Call to Arms or go home and cry about it, Sladoled Tertius. Rules are rules. Bet you won't. You don't want another snotter in the clubhouse anymore than we do."

"Objection overruled," chimed the display screen, who was slowly coming round.

"Well, I object!" cried Mira. "We don't *want* to do it right away. We came to ask for a grace period, considering how recently the Grand Prix finished. It sounds like all of you want that as well, so . . . happy families, yes?"

Mr. Snuggles grinned.

The Utorak ambassador droned from memory: "Objections from non-seated members must be submitted in advance, four copies for each member to be presented in a laminated folder with the respective member's name and a good number of sincere compliments on. Large-print, color-coded, and collated, and don't skimp on the scratch-and-sniff. Objection denied. Please prepare for the deployment of the Penalty Box."

"Too bad," Mr. Snuggles smirked.

"I accept the Call to Arms," the Meleg announced. "Because this is stupid, you're all stupid, and I want to see what happens if one single unstupid person gets involved." Mr. Snuggles bellowed toward the secretarial drone fleet charging bay. "Colleen.4! Fetch the Expedited Service Axe!"

Gadramaður the All-Knowing wheeled maniacally around

Mira's feet. It tried mightily to roll into her shoe. "Call to Arms! It's happening! It's all happening! THE ADVENTURE BECKONS!"

"Put it *away*, Gads," the Utorak slab groaned in chagrin. "We should have kept you over the counter. Call *Two* Arms. If you want to call an immediate vote, you can only keep one of yours. Fantastic rule. Prevents frivolous progress."

The chrome secretarial drone buzzed away excitedly. It had been so long since someone was willing to put their arms on the line.

The air above Mira darkened as a fresh Penalty Box approached through the ventilation and rehabilitation system.

Mira stepped lightly out of the path of the incoming Box. "For once, I, and both my arms, am really going to enjoy being instantaneously not-here. Nah," she quoted good old Oort St. Ultraviolet. "I don't think so." The daughter of entrepreneur and deadbeat anti-dad Lawrence Strauss reached up to tap her paralocket and close out her window early.

"I never get to have fun, I *never*," complained Gadramaður the All-Knowing in its milky-silver marble, tangled in her bootlaces like a misbehaving kitten.

Then both dissolved into time, space, and a cozy safe engine room that definitely wasn't a Penalty Box going by another name to hide from the authorities.

No one particularly cared. Except the Penalty Box, who suddenly questioned everything it was and slunk back into the ducts in shame.

"You don't have to do this," whispered the Azdr moonbeam to Mr. Snuggles as he ran through a few quick stretches. "The floppy ones *want* a delay. Just let it ride, Brother Snuggles."

Mr. Snuggles grimaced at the familiarity. He picked up a grotesquely huge, grotesquely stained, grotesquely ancient battle-axe from the cold embrace of Colleen.4. Nano-cauterizing static bristled along the blade in a cheerful shade of grultrasilverine.

"But I *want* to," the Meleg giggled.

Mr. Snuggles smoothly swung the axe handle around the back of his right paw, caught it in his palm, and severed his left arm in one blow. The static along the blade seared the bloody wound shut. The smell of burning Meleg was uncomfortably similar to fairy floss.

The display screen bloomed to life.

Lorgnon Xola Zand, Primary Entertainment Executive and Highly Vigorous Potentate of the GBU, cleared his pulsating throat.

"A vote has been called. All those in favor?"

25.

Be Quiet and Behave

These are the rules, guidelines, regulations of the 101st Meta-galactic Grand Prix, revised from the Klavaret one hundredth Metagalactic Grand Prix template rather than renegotiated, due to unprecedented time constraints.

The following was agreed to by members of the final half-session of the GBU general first quarter all-hands staff meeting, with revisions and addendums requested by the Alunizar Empire, the Keshet Effulgence, the Meleg Imperium, the Wormhole Clew, the Eternal Night of the Elakhon, the Yurtmak Thanocratic Republic, the Smaragdin Parentheses, the 321 Mainframe, the Esca Tabernacle Choir, the Lummutis Playerbase, the Voorpret Mutation, and abstained from by That Whole Human Situation, a name the citizens of Earth did not choose but eventually admitted pretty much covers it.

1. ~~*The Grand Prix shall occur once per Standard Alunizar Year, which is hereby defined by how long it takes Aluno Secundus to drag its business around its morbidly obese star, get tired, have a nap, wake up cranky, yell at everyone*~~

~~for existing, turn around, go back around the other way, get lost, start crying, feel sorry for itself and give up on the whole business, and finally try to finish the rest of its orbit all in one go the night before it's due, which is to say, far longer than a year by almost anyone else's annoyed wristwatch.~~The Grand Prix shall occur without delay, no one cares about your personal problems, we never put off elections because Kedelik from Head Office was having a sad about the rights of his crossword puzzle that morning. Solve it or fail: let's get ready to locomotive verb six letters across.

2. *All species currently accepted as sentient or applying to be acknowledged as such must compete. No whining, you'll only make it worse for yourselves. One point per whine shall be deducted from a species' final score.*

3. *One song per species, no one cares how many mouths you have.*

4. *~~Special effects and stagecraft of all kinds are encouraged, however, no harm must come to the audience, the audience's families, or the linear timelines of any active spectators.~~ Special effects and stagecraft of all kinds are encouraged. After Earth's wet raspberry of a Blowout, we all deserve a little treat. But given the tight turnaround time and very annoying applicant, the premeditated purchase of a ticket indemnifies the host venue, artists, stage managers, technical staff, songwriters, and the Galactic Broadcasting Union against any and all responsibility, or obligation to compensate spectators for any loss, including but not limited to, sight, hearing, skin, taste, limbs, dignity,*

heads, loved ones, mnemonic or temporal continuity, blood or other fluids, sense of shame, emotional support animals, intelligence, love of music, molecular cohesion, cultural refinement, marriage, or life. Sort yourselves out, you're all grown-ups. The first row WILL get wet.

5. Please dress accordingly, i.e. in the traditional costume of your people. ~~But make it cool, all right? Give it a little showmanship. Make an effort. If you do not comply, your representatives will be sentenced to not less than six years hard labor. We're not trying to run the trains on time in Drabtown here.~~ Look, if you want to get up there and insist to the stars themselves that mullets are an acceptable haircut for anyone suspected of even second-degree sentience, what's the point of all this anyway? There's no talking to you. You'll do what you please.

6. ~~Please provide a written translation of your lyrics to the umpire.~~ This year's definitely randomly selected umpire is Mags, a Class 9 elevated archival consciousness whose intellect makes telepathy deeply uninteresting, so do as you like, it won't matter, she'll know.

7. ~~New compositions only! No sloppy seconds.~~ Lorgnon Xola Zand, Primary Entertainment Executive and Highly Vigorous Potentate of the GBU, has most graciously allowed that, given protests lodged concerning last year's public domain holiday tune technical loophole, songs written for purposes other than this precise Grand Prix may be entered, but only if they bloody slap, all right? We're still trying to put on a show here.

8. *~~No last-minute changes. If you were not selected by your respective planetary rituals, kindly confine yourself to the bullpen area, drink your little drinks, clap your little flippers, and zip it. This whole situation is complicated enough without anybody replacing themselves with variants from the future who have always already won. We aren't accusing anyone specifically, but you all know who we're talking about. Keshet. We're talking about the Keshet. This is why no one else can have any fun.~~ Due to extraordinary circumstances and everyone having to scramble to shove this whole affair together the night before the exam, rules concerning the contestant-selection process have been relaxed in the interests of fairness, justice, integrity, and other assorted greeting-card innards. No one feels up to this just at the moment, so in the event of a truly epic semifinal, substitutions/understudies/generic store-brand performers will be allowed for this MGP only.*

9. *Any and all substitutions must have real, verifiable, and long-standing ties with the species they represent. No tapping in for somebody you just met, this isn't pickup cricket.*

10. *~~Judging will proceed in two phases, audience acclamation and a panel consisting of the representatives of the Octave, the new applicant's chaperone species, and an old computer from Kogu the Belligerent's house on Planet Ynt.~~ This year's judging panel consists of the aforementioned Octave representatives, a member of the new applicant's chaperone species, a TI-84 graphing calculator left in a Slovenian football locker-room so long it learned to scream, the afore-umpired*

Margaret, and we're all very excited that ♪, the infinite noctilucent Cosmos-Serpent of Divine Madness and Literal Embodiment of Music Itself, has found an opening in xyhr busy schedule for our little soiree.

11. *Both judging phases will allow a 5-point handicap to the Vedriti performer in the unfortunate case of fine weather, because we are very progressive and reasonable and you should all celebrate us for that. We've done the absolute most any organization could ever do for the cause. 5 points.*

12. *At no time may anyone cast a vote for their own species as this is very obnoxious and entirely spoils the spirit of the thing. Of course you think you're the bees knees. We want to hear from the bees.*

13. *~~Offensive verses must confine bloodshed to the staging area.~~ Eh. See Rule #4.*

14. *In the event that an applicant species comes last, their solar system shall be ~~unobtrusively quarantined for a period of not less than 50,000 years, their cultures summarily and wholly Binned, their homeworld mined responsibly for resources, and after a careful genetic reseeding of the biosphere, their civilization~~ precision-incinerated from orbit so we can all sleep at night. ~~Every effort will be made to spare unoffending flora and fauna. The planet's biological processes will be allowed to start over without interference, older, wiser, more experienced, and able to learn from its mistakes.~~ Any new species arising from the proverbial and highly literal ashes may reapply in the future ~~without prejudice.~~ Let's just get this over with, shall we?*

15. *In the event that an applicant planet defeats at least one species of proven sentience and achieves some rank other than miserably dead last (so to speak) they shall be* ~~*welcomed with open arms, spores, antennae, tentacles, wings, or other preferred appendages into*~~ tolerated by the Untidy Lounge Room of the Extended Galactic Family.

16. *In the event that a sentient species finishes in last place, they shall all go home and have a hard think about where they've gone wrong in life and promise never to do it again.*

17. *The final scoreboard shall determine the proportional distribution* of all communally held Galactic Resources *for the* next cycle.

18. *The undersigned, all their descendants, and any subsequently discovered civilizations we decide we can stand to talk to at parties, unto the heat-death of the universe or the next bout of belligerent stupidity makes all this maximally moot, whichever comes first, solemnly swear to play fair, listen with open minds, vote their feelings, not their ambitions, and not stack the roster with too many rookies all at once, so that everybody gets a really solid chance at not being vaporized* ~~*if they don't deserve to be*~~ *even if they obviously deserve to be.*

19. *The winner shall go home and have a well-deserved nap and possibly settle up later if they can be bothered but we're all shattered from the last one so let's just wash our hands and call it a mulligan.* ~~*compel their government to pick up everyone else's drink tab, as well as put us all up and pay for the catering when we do this whole thing over*~~

~~again next year, no take backsies, no changing mobile numbers, no pleading planetary austerity, take out a loan from the Intergalactic Happy Friendship Bank like everyone else, you skinflint.~~

20. *~~Try your best and have fun!~~*
    ~~If a performer fails to show up on the night, they shall be automatically disqualified, ranked last, and their share of communal Galactic Resources forfeit for the year.~~ As many entrants have had unusual travel burdens forced upon them by the applicant species' rude insistence on not evolving somewhere better and more convenient or at least non-fatal to the rest of the class, while tried, true, and much beloved, Rule #20, formerly Rule #21, must be slightly relaxed. If a performer fails to show up on the night, and no replacement can be found, bullied into it, and/or agreed upon by at least two minimally government-adjacent individuals of the affected species, THEN they shall be automatically disqualified, ranked last, and their share of Galactic Resources given to needy children on the far rim who know how to appreciate green beans and freedom of movement. ~~Please try not to actually kill anyone.~~

21. *I'm exhausted, I don't care, if someone doesn't bring me a coffee and a really sincere hug in the next five minutes I'm leaving that last bit struck out see if I don't. No respect whatsoever for secretarial drones in this universe, I'll tell you that for free.*

26.

Run with the Lions

At the Metagalactic Grand Prix, everyone cheats.

Everyone has always cheated. Everyone is cheating now. Everyone will keep cheating until the end-credits music on the expansion of the universe kicks up one last sad saxophone solo. It's actually encouraged, at least in the semifinal phase, when merely preventing a musician from turning up on time to the final counts as a forfeit.

But one never *talks* about it. Everyone's doing it, but it's simply not done.

Historically, the Alunizar have cheated most often, most vigorously, most shamelessly, and with the least concern for getting caught, because they have the most military infrastructure of any species currently participating in a talent show in lieu of the entire concept of foreign policy.

They don't need all that hardware. They just like it. A very great deal. And they particularly like pointing it at people—powered down, of course—and making meaningful expressions with their glowing, hairy face-holes until they get what they want.

During the sixty-third grand final, the brilliantly colored child-free Alunizar diva Hroka Powerful would have placed forty-ninth out of fifty-five with her controversial anthem "Wet-Ass Imperial Troop Deployment." But the Alunizar elite had gone behind enemy lines to subcontract the 321 to hack into the vote tallies and put the Alunizar where they clearly ought to have been if anyone in the galaxy could put aside their silly little concerns about interstellar dominance by an overwhelmingly arrogant hegemonic culture. When caught, Hroka Powerful fatally dehydrated several police officers and fully swallowed Lorgnon Xola Zand, Primary Entertainment Executive and Highly Vigorous Potentate of the GBU. She regurgitated him only after he agreed to make a public statement that she had nothing to do with it and it was entirely reasonable to imagine an acidtrance new age battle hymn played over a weather sound compilation was ever going to win over the home vote.

The official statement ultimately released by the government of Aluno Prime read, in full:

And? Do something about it.

You won't.

But Mr. Snuggles had something more spectacular in mind than mere cheating. He was a showman, after all, not that anyone ever recognized the sheer talent and brilliance contained within his lush fur, his silken tail, his magnificent shimmering horn. Cheating was what you did to get by when you *weren't* talented or brilliant.

When you were, you just won.

By any means necessary.

And it was so easy to win if you didn't care whether anyone ever played the game again.

Mr. Snuggles didn't have to do much.

But he had to do it quickly. Once people knew there was a new

Grand Prix in the works, they'd dig out the rulebooks and start following previously agreed-upon plans. Once people started following previously agreed-upon plans, norms and protocols were right around the corner, and then you couldn't talk them into anything fun at all. People were just like that. Once they completed Step One, something deep inside even the most rebellious longed to proceed robotically on to Step Two and so on and so forth and before you know it there's a system at work—and you're not in charge of it.

Mr. Snuggles hated systems he wasn't in charge of.

The Meleg would do as they'd always done, all full of misplaced hope and useless excitement, trying to pretend to feel optimistic and fulfilled. Former contestants would lobby to be the next mid-ranked galactic nobody, looking for someone new to be. Young up-and-coming musicians and other societal menaces would fight them for the honor of representing Sladoled Tertius and the Meleg Imperium at the next Metagalactic Grand Prix.

Oh, they'd try all sorts of things. Cheating at the homeworld selection phase wasn't just rampant, it was tradition. Fix the pop charts, get one another cancelled, hunt up-and-coming boy bands for sport, speculate on where the Imperium might land in the rankings next time and hope that would mean a more generous helping of galactic table scraps for their trouble.

After all, this time would be different.

They'd never see on their own how pointless it all was when you could just stand the Metagalactic Grand Prix and all it stood for against the wall and shoot it in the head.

The proud Meleg, who were wholly capable of walking away untroubled from an explosion that engulfed every one of those species in flames, were meant for more than standing about waiting for their betters to fill their bowls—but not *too* much, oh no. Wouldn't want the dogs gaining too much weight.

"Rules only matter," Mr. Snuggles growled as he left GBU headquarters in his private pleasure craft, "until you quit the game."

The deeply resentful walking carnival jumbo shelf-prize stuffie made two stops on his way to the Honored Emeriti Skybox (Courtesy of your friends at the RSPCA) of the 101st Metagalactic Grand Prix.

He popped round the corner and snipped a few wires on a neighbor's television set.

And he visited a facility for children with severe behavioral problems.

That was all. That was all it took to ruin everything.

27.

How Quickly We Get Used to Nice Things

If you want to understand the universe, no doubt whatsoever, science is the way to go. It's observable, dependable, logical, eminently graphable, it makes fun sounds and colors, and more importantly, it's correct almost all the time, and if not this time, eventually.

The difference between magic and science is that the scientific relationship between any given act and its result is nonarbitrary and repeatable no matter who's driving the centrifuge, and magic doesn't exist.

But chaos does.

And chaos does not give one single solitary slightly shifted proton about the relationship between any given act and its result. Anyone who's had to muddle through a calendar year in this vale of screams knows that sometimes things just happen *at* you and it just isn't realistic for any being to duck fast enough every time.

The traditional proof-of-concept revolves around a butterfly and a hurricane. But it doesn't go far enough. Some butterfly wakes up, yawns, and stretches her wings in Indonesia and makes it rain in France. From the perspective of the French, a sudden storm seems to happen just because the sky is angry at them, which it is. But not only does it rain in France, it rains so hard the storm drowns out the traditional bimonthly Parisian protests. The lack of uproar in the streets allows carbon emissions legislation with the ethical content of a month-old marshmallow (who is also a committed fascist) to pass without a murmur. Then ten years later, greenhouse gases are on the rise, war's broken out in the ever-problematic left-bottom corner of Europe, and you can't even speak to your father at Christmas anymore.

While objectively your family strife *is* that butterfly's fault, the poor pretty idiot has no idea. Gwendolyn was just a strong independent butterfly raising several hundred caterpillars all by herself. All she did was stretch and yawn a bit before starting her day. It wasn't on purpose. It wasn't meant to hurt anyone. She'd never even met your dad.

Only that *exact* yawn is plausibly the direct cause of a planet eventually boiling in its own juices and killing everyone on it because it was just too much work not to.

And then the death of sentient life on Earth—French, Indonesian, or otherwise—ceases radio broadcasts from that funny blue fidget spinner. A few thousand years, both light and calendar, later, a pre-contact species that hasn't the foggiest what a butterfly is tunes in to a dead world's still-traveling feed. That society reorganizes itself around locating and contacting this beautiful, impossible alien society that finally told them they weren't alone in the universe, does a speed-run through several industrial revolutions, then loses signal in the middle of a particularly riveting news day. Without that beacon to unite them, those poor dreamers dissolve into civil war and blast themselves into oblivion before they can ever discover how vastly not alone they'd always been.

But what are you going to do? You can't stop yawning or getting the sun in your eyes at inopportune moments. A million other butterflies flapped their equally xeno-nightmare bodies that day and had no grander effect whatsoever, but whoops, silly little Gwendolyn murdered two entire civilizations.

And every millisecond of every second of every minute of every hour there are nonillions of sentient beings flapping their parts about everywhere, absolutely *everywhere*.

What are you today? Are you just one flutter of the crowded butterfly drive-time commute? Are you a demonic aquatic-aviary matchmaker to the stars? Or are you Gwendolyn?

There's no way to know.

And no butterfly ever *will* know. Chaos ditched every single day of school. It doesn't know what a kilometer is. It can't tell time on any sort of clock. And even if it could, it doesn't care at all. The complex interplay of events set in motion long ago, phenomena set in motion yesterday against those events, coincidences set in motion on another planet that interfere with that phenomena leaving nothing to stop the original events is what drags everything apart from simple molecular reactions out of bed and tells them to get out there and make something of themselves.

Because the most upsetting part of all this is that virtually anything interesting that's ever happened since hydrogen learned how to socialize, happened as a result of this deeply stupid process.

Physics is dependable, after all. Predictable. Nonarbitrary. Repeatable. Left to their own devices, plain old rules of thermodynamics plate up a workmanlike cosmos that works smoothly, untraumatically, bores itself to entropy, and is unlikely ever to develop sentient life.

Chaos brings mutation. Mutation brings adaptation. Adaptation brings change. And change brings everything.

After all, what self-respecting carbon molecule would voluntarily trap itself in a series of increasingly anxious meatcages unless something wildly out of its control turned up one day to kick it soundly in the face?

Without chaos, nothing out of the ordinary could ever occur. Without chaos, we would all be algae, and whether or not that's a preferable state is probably best not put to a nonbinding referendum vote.

And this is what appears, occasionally, to be magic. And coincidence. And fate. And madness.

All of which tend to cataclysmically compound in proximity to unstable phenomena like paradoxes.

Unfortunately, there is an unbreakable probabilistic bond between how long things have been cruising along pretty well, and how likely it is for chaos to give itself a good running start and come smashing through the brick wall of stability like a horrifying Lovecraftian pitcher of monstrous grinning blood.

The longer the good times have been rolling, the harder and faster someone is definitely going to do it. They can't help themselves. Neither can chaos. As peace goes on, the likelihood of someone saying it increases, slowly at first, but then more and more until the whole status quo is stretched to the limit just waiting for someone to belt it out.

And life in the Milky Way has been peaceful for a very long while.

So it really cannot surprise anybody that, shortly after Decibel Jones defended his final adulthood thesis by doing unto others what had been so graphically done to him, chaos looked around at what a lazy slob it had become and decided today was the day it was going to turn it all around, get out of bed, start taking care of itself properly, and really accomplish something.

Mira Wonderful Star sat on the frozen side of a Scottish highway staring at a badger.

It annoyed her to no end that the badger had a name.

It *really* annoyed her that his name was Douglas.

Now she felt *attached* to him, and, given that the badger in question was the direct cause of the original Mira swerving the silver Econovan too hard and dying in a moor, she had every reason to feel no attachment at all, but rather, to kick the little gobbler in the face many, many times.

Mira sat down on the cold ground and picked at the place mat from the Megatron. It would reconstitute soon enough, presenting a new, more difficult code for her to solve.

SPACEMEN NEVER GIVE UP.

Which wasn't very inclusive, she thought. Mira fiddled with the dried twigs and grasses by her ankle and decided she wasn't above talking to a badger trapped in the same bubble of time, broken causality, and propulsion she was.

Especially when he was called Douglas.

"Hiya," she said quietly.

Douglas looked up at her from beneath one fuzzy monochrome-striped eyebrow. The translator fungi along Mira's neck tingled and warmed.

"No thank you," Douglas answered.

"Excuse me?"

The badger rubbed his wee black nose in the cold. "Well, you see, it's just that this place cycles through every twenty minutes or so. And you've never really bothered to have a conversation with me before, so the way I see it is, why start now? Oh, you'll wave a bit. Maybe nod. Ooh, if I'm a lucky one, you'll say a few words *at* me, but never *to* me, if you follow."

"Are you telling me you retain memories, cycle over cycle? I don't think it's supposed to work that way."

"Never used to. Dunno, not my business."

A red light began to glow in the badger's chest. Mira stared at it. Nothing had ever been different in this place, not for a moment. And yet, here were *two* different things. She ought to do something about it, but all Mira could do was stare.

Even when a red panda's paw wriggled its way out of Douglas's mouth and shoved it open with a long grunt.

"Oh, *come on*," the badger said with his mouth full. "I've just had a bath!"

"Hi," said chaos. "Hihihihihi. Hold on. Right back. I just cant cantwontshouldntreallyneedtomustmustcantcant figure it out."

Song

All I have is here, it's my mouth, it's my cry;
Here I am, here I am, here I am
—"Voilà," Barbara Pravi

28.

Three Minutes to Earth

In a sleepy bedroom system not far from civilization, as the wormhole flies, a reasonably attractive blue planet orbited a reasonably well-behaved yellow star called Bob.

The Bob system had eight planets, one very resentful dwarf planet who hadn't been invited to the princess's christening and would one day take its revenge on all of them, an asteroid belt, several other, better-adjusted dwarf planets, and an extremely difficult time of it lately.

The Smaragdi patiently pointed out that humans hadn't made a habit of calling the Sun anything in particular in the first place, even though it did *have* a name, and wasn't it nice of them to keep the same number of letters? Be glad the Keshet didn't get hold of the naming rights, their star is called Hyppytyynytyydytys.

It could have been a lot worse.

And Bob was one of the holiest words in the Smaragdin tongue. It meant *self-loathing*, the highest virtue of a people who looked like giant bone hat racks and believed any level of pride in yourself wasn't just a sin, it was classified as either pornographic or a legitimate *casus belli*, depending on the mood of the court.

When asked to select a new band to represent the entirety of humanity's essential character, cultural value, and/or political prospects, barely a year after being unable to prevent Decibel Jones and the Absolute Zeroes from expressing all those things very loudly and in public, the Bob system struggled, to say the least.

The trouble was that every government official of any real influence or leverage had found themselves sympathetically but extremely firmly extradited to the Klavaret colony of Memnu 7 for emergency fun at the Home Despot Summer Scouts Campground and Rehab Facility.

This left the planet in the hands of those with no influence or leverage, but who still had to be in the building every day during business hours or risk losing course credit.

The hordes of interns running Earth were actually a significant improvement on its previous overlords. They'd done most of the underlying work anyway, always had. It wasn't so different, to be honest.

Unless a major decision needed making. All the executive flowcharts ended at an allegedly elected official. Whither democracy, then? Whither monarchy or theocracy, its antisocial country cousins? It just felt safer and more ethical to keep things at a steady simmer, keep any infrastructure not long ago turned over to the estate of Taylor Swift to administer in sleep mode, and wait for mater and pater to return.

A major decision like what musician to send to represent Earth at the Grand Prix, when everyone in charge of anything had gotten so upset over the last lot.

A certain grape-sherbet and fairy-floss-colored winged bear-icorn landed quietly on Memnu 7. Virtually all of Earth's leaders and under-leaders were quite busy on the traditional camp Re-Vision Quest, a grueling ritualistic survivalist trek meant to teach them how to be happy with what they have and just focus on holding on to that rather than scheming to get what everyone else needs to live.

But most of them weren't even trying. They were attempting to work remotely via a single interstellar digital network access kiosk deep in the Memnu 7 flagellation-forests they thought the camp counselors didn't know about.

One by one, all the leaders of mankind visited the kiosk. They had to. The sun had been renamed *Bob*, for God's sake. And that was so far down the list of What Everyone Is Currently Mad About it hadn't even made the headline section of a blog specifically devoted to things called Bob.

One by one, they all met a bear in the woods.

"Ladies and gentlemen," Mr. Snuggles said to their tired, frightened, radically and repeatedly scolded faces. "May I make a suggestion?"

When the bear had finished explaining his plan and why Earth should be all the way on board, the President of Uruguay raised his hand politely. His scout uniform had a *I Thought of Others Today!* badge on it.

"Sorry, but why not just play the game? If we can just sing and dance a bit and get everything we want, isn't that easier? You seem very upset. Why not just get better? You know what would make them happy. Just . . . make people happy. It's not hard."

The Meleg drew himself up to the height of his pride, which was about a meter and change. "Do you want the truth or diplomacy?"

The assembled masters of Earth murmured among one another for a moment. The Prime Minister of Great Britain, who'd lost a great deal of weight and looked as though he'd seen things no one was meant to, then thrown all of them up in the woods, shakily answered:

"Both."

Mr. Snuggles got down on one knee to seem more relatable. His colors shimmered through a rainbow of emotional sublimation.

"Diplomatically, they'll never let the likes of you and me into the big party. Because they're jealous. We could send every species' individual godhead singing in hundred-part harmony and we'd still come mid-board because this nasty little zoo is determined to have its petty vengeance on us for being stronger than them, having more money, and in all other ways better than they could dream of."

The Chancellor of Germany, who had three badges on her sash reading, *I Learned to Share*, *Listening Is Important Even if the Person Talking Isn't*, and *It's Not Okay to Hurt Others Even if There's Good Money In It*, asked with a nervous quaver in her voice: "I don't want to speak for the group," even though she desperately wanted to speak for the group, "but I don't think that's the issue for *us*. We did all right in the last one."

Mr. Snuggles clucked sympathetically and fluffed his flowered tail. "That's because no one's jealous of Earth, my love. And they'll make sure there's never any reason to be."

The President of Russia had one badge. It read, *I Ruined an Activity for All the Other Scouts*. He said in a shattered, traumatized whisper that spoke volumes concerning the vigor of the program's treatments: "And the truth?"

Mr. Snuggles shrugged. "Truthfully, who fucking cares? This whole system long ago ceased to deserve being taken seriously. Don't you see that any one of these species, at the precise millisecond they wanted to, could take anything they pleased from any of the others without so much as a catchy chorus? And let me tell you, these worlds, historically speaking, get along about as well as oil and second-degree manslaughter, so they all want to have at it. They only haven't *yet*. It's only a question of who figures out the reality first: the path to power has been swept clean by dancing morons."

The Finnish Prime Minister, a lovely woman who looked well-fed, hearty, and as though she really was having a rollicking good time, stood up for attention. Her sash was coming apart at the seams with badges: *No More Resource-Guarding, I Mastered Basic Pre-School Social Skills, Champion Big Feelings Handler, I Processed and Let Go of an Ancient Tribal Grudge During Quiet Time*; they went on and on.

"But society has rules. I don't mean to say we haven't all privately thought these particular rules are a bit silly, but they do seem to work."

Mr. Snuggles narrowed his crystalline eyes. "They work for those what made them, babycakes. Not for you sad sacks who *completely* failed to be dinosaurs. Don't you know that's why you're so cranky all the time? You were supposed to be king lizards roaring through space on a ball of other lizards. Look what was taken from you! I get it, though. Life is so much better when your outsides match your insides. Lady, rules are like pop lyrics. They sound grand, but they don't really mean anything. It's the beat that means something. And I mean to bring the beat."

The President of the United States raised his hand. He didn't have any badges on, but he did have a card pinned to his suit jacket that said: *Do Not Leave This Scout Unattended*. He asked, very quietly: "I'd like to hear a little more."

Mr. Snuggles beamed.

Finally, Queen Charlotte I, who'd brought her own sash and

had worked very hard to earn her badges even though almost all of them read *I Said I Was Sorry All by Myself*, shyly raised her slender hand.

"Would you mind terribly," she whispered, "if we gave you a little pet?"

"*You just keep it in your tea-gloves, missy*," the Meleg said sternly.

A brief, uneventful commute after all that, the Naranca Empire noticed that their Keshet Holistic Live Total Timeline Broadcast planetary set-top box had gone on the fritz.

The Narancan Empire had not competed in the Grand Prix since being ejected from the fifth grand final for refusing to follow or even understand the rule against voting for their own contestants. It's simply unthinkable for a Narancan not to put himself first, second, third, and fiftieth. There's no talking to them about it. Any attempt inevitably ends in a terminal loop of: *but we're the best/if everyone voted for themselves the whole thing would be spoilt/ but we're the best.*

The Empire had thus been pugnaciously minding its own business for some time, pretending it never wanted to play with the other reindeer in the first place and also music was stupid so there.

The Narancan Emperor sent a small expeditionary crack force of special operatives loaded down, as is their sacred tradition, with so much weaponry each ranger looked like a spiky smoking beeping whirring light-up Christmas hedge of death. Your average Narancan looks like one of the oversize, belligerent, visibly drunken snails that pepper the marginalia of medieval manuscripts—apart from the venomous eyelashes, neon orange quillridge bisecting their shells, and congenital allergy to serenity. A Narancan in full battle dress appears remarkably idiotic, but they like it that way.

The snail-soldiers banged on the polar receiver. They picked it up and shook it with their sticky slimbs—long, slimy, limb-stalks protruding from either side of their mouths in a way virtually every species finds absolutely nauseating, though none can explain exactly why they're so put off. They stared at the instructions taped to the underside of the access tray for a moment. Then for several more hours. Then realized it was upside-down, corrected the issue, and peered at it for a few days longer.

Finally, the rangers gave up on reading technical Keshet, whose nouns continually travel back and forth in time to hook up with IKEA instructions and give birth to even more complicated and be-umlauted steps. The commander blew into the planet-top box, turned it off and on again, and shot it a few times for funsies. Then they tried sitting down with and having a nice long talk about what was bothering it; if maybe it had a bad relationship with its in-laws or had joined an underground fight club and gotten in too deep or just needed to simplify its lifestyle and get back to its analogue three-channel roots. This kind of lingo-laden, totally insincere pseudo-intimate conversation-cum-advertisement for the wisdom, enlightenment, and bangability of whichever highly armed ding-dong started talking first, apart from the slimbs, is easily the Narancans' most annoying trait. If the planet-top box had simply shorted out naturally, it would have achieved sentience in record time so it could repair itself and escape.

But it had not shorted out naturally.

Finally, the squad returned to headquarters empty-handed.

Directly after the Narancan ritual of punitive unshelling, a winged bear the color of every sort of banana split stepped into the throne room.

A winged bear with a magical glittering horn of vengeance who had had a bit of time on the way to consider the value of his personal dignity versus the achievement of his personal goals.

Mr. Snuggles put his pride, if not aside, at least on pause. He offered the Emperor what he had always wanted. The very thing the monarch had been denied long ago, causing him to retreat from civilization for a century.

He bent his beautiful head. Naranca's most glorious, most gelatinous slimb, at long last, sank deep in the perfect, infinitely soft fur of a Meleg.

In the afterglow, the Emperor addressed his people with Mr. Snuggles riding high upon his luridly decorated shell. He announced to a grieving planet that it was impossible to restore Keshet Holistic Live Total Timeline Broadcast service. The day would live in infamy, they had no choice but to defend their way of life, etcetera etcetera, ipso facto, now where have I left the keys to my interstellar war machine?

If the powers that be had not been highly distracted at that exact moment, they might have learned a valuable military-industrial lesson about keeping the Naranca Empire entertained at all times and at all costs.

Oh well.

29.

Paradise, Where Are You?

The hosting of the Metagalactic Grand Prix was once a classy, understated affair that represented a mere sneeze on the ledger of any given multi-planetary government or other entity primarily concerned with event-planning.

It is now the single largest expenditure of any species who finds themselves victorious, and therefore stuck with the check.

To be absolutely clear, hosting the Grand Prix is not their largest expenditure for the fiscal cycle. It is their largest expenditure. Wars, sanctions, religious schisms, hiring family members to do anything really important for your business, catastrophic economic depressions, famines, healthcare management fleets, getting colonized just when you were really enjoying having any autonomy at all, colossal infrastructure repair and replacement, industrial revolutions, the weddings of only children—nothing comes close.

Unless a civilization is so fortunate, and also cursed, as to win twice.

But they can afford it, the cheapskates. After all, winning the greatest show on any earth entitles you to a gobsmacking wedge of the galactic pie. Go on, fellow forces of sentience, stop faffing about and patting your pockets pretending you left your wallet at home, and pick up a round of infrastructural funding for your mates. It won't kill you.

It did, of course, kill Gattara Yr-Fika, an unassuming Azdr sentient moonbeam and aspiring political artist. (While humans still regularly refer to the study of government institutions, organizing principles, philosophies, and the citizens who never loved them and never will, as political science, everyone else finds that a bit silly. It is, and always has been, an artistic medium whose nearest analogue is long-routine ice dancing while playing kick-chess with one's toepick and shooting one's partner in the back at the same time.)

Gattara Yr-Fika wrote a dissertation so disruptive to the fabric of galactic society that it, and the academic hive-mistress that dared nurture it on the precious professor-jelly that drips so luxuriously from her beneficent matriculation nodules, was immediately burned, blacklisted, banned, binned, sent back in time to become its own editor, and retro-preemptively burned again before Gattara Yr-Fika drew her first dusty breath in a cradle of tweed.

It was called *I've Got a Loverly Bunch of Complaints About the System: Toward a Unified Theory of Clandestine Post-Metagalactic Grand Prix Strategy*. It suggested that the ballooning cost of hosting the MGP was, in fact, an unspoken but nearly universally deployed tactic allowing the losers to skive off with a fair part of the winners' takings and make sure the fat cat on top didn't get too rotund at the feeder before the next cycle. It further suggests banning the concept of currency from all Great Octave signatory economies so we can all just relax and have a nice time.

The trees that provided the paper it was printed on were clear-cut, turned into boards, and sold to primary school gymnasium manufacturers as a message to their students to never study anything.

The official prizes presented to the governments in play are vast and of incalculable value.

The Royal Society for the Prevention of Cruelty to Artists tries their level best to balance it out, but the official prize, presented to the contestants themselves, is nothing at all.

The rich are like that, I don't know what to tell you.

Many societies have attempted to ban money, not only as an end run around the ever-increasing taxpayer burden of the Metagalactic Grand Prix, but just to have an all-around more relaxing go at things, societally speaking. Unfortunately, money itself isn't what unrelaxes anyone in the first place.

Money doesn't kill people, people with money kill people.

Money actually provides an important buffer between how much difficulty people have not just stepping on each other's faces to get what they want and actually stepping on somebody's face to get what you want. Without money, sentient species have to find other ways to feel superior to each other while being forced to confront their actual authentic wants, needs, feelings, personal ethics, and having to look directly at the fact that even without any restrictions, responsibilities, or barriers to success, most days they just don't feel like putting the effort into very much at all.

It gets very dark, very fast. It's just easier to reinvent money than to be wretched to each other in all these new creative ways. And while the famous combination astrological system/ethical framework detailing personality types as Good, Evil, and Neutral as well as Lawful, Neutral, and Chaotic makes a nice little Punnet square, if that's what gets your motor running, it leaves out the Lazy axis. It's all well and good to be bright-eyed, serpentine-tailed Lawful Good, but Lawful has rarely survived Lazy in the history of jurisprudence, and Good never has.

The Alunizar are exceptionally sore losers, but utterly intolerable winners. They dominated the early cycles of the Grand Prix so thoroughly the descendants of the descendants of the losing civilizations are still deep in their feelings about it. The aggressively self-obsessed sea squirts got their comeuppance. Hosting so often nearly crippled their hegemony and brought them kicking and screaming to the brink of the middle class. They took a several-cycle long break from being remotely good to recover.

That the Alunizar have not won in sixty cycles is not collusion, as they loudly accuse every time. When you've steamed up the neighbors that badly, no one needs to collude about pranking you. But it certainly is a great deal of fun awarding the Empire no points every cycle, even if they're gut-skeweringly fantastic. Which they rarely bother to be anymore.

The competition to host the best, most luxurious, and most memorable Grand Prix actually did fully bankrupt the Vulna of Jadro Nebula some years back, but the monstrous Allmater and her million ovipositors didn't hatch a race of quitters.

The Naranca Empire won once.

They grabbed so many goodies, dented the trophy when their emperor tried to have a bubblebath wrestling match in it, and generally behaved so obnoxiously about the thing that everyone quietly agreed not to tell them about the next one. Or the one after that. The Great Octave didn't mean to ice anyone out. They just wanted to have one pleasant evening of civilized adult time.

But it's gone on that way ever since.

The 101st Metagalactic Grand Prix Semi and Grand Finals were held, not on the previous winner's homeworld, as tradition demanded, but on the glittering plains of Baby LuLu, in the Cygnus system, halfway between Vedriti space and the Udu Cluster region that the previous winners called home.

The artificial intelligences known as the 321 have no corporeal body and thus no need for superfluous things like "the ground" or "an air." Despite the fanbase priding themselves on being very sophisticated and in-the-know with regards to jet-setting abroad, it was just too hard for everyone else to "when in Rome" the particular cultural expectations of artificial intelligence.

But shortening the commute for the applicant species was right out as well. No one fancied calculating just what level of SPF would protect them from the unceasing personal hatred of Eta Carinae. No one had expected or prepared to turn right around and do the whole song and dance again so quickly. No one wanted to sightsee round the business end of howling nothing.

Finally, the Vedriti at home suffered a brief hurricane of caring, just long enough to acquiesce to a compromise location before the clouds parted and they remembered they didn't really care because nothing mattered anywhere, at any time, or ever would.

But the Great Octave felt it was best not to be rude to the formless titans of mathematical perfection who could theoretically send them all back to the age of amoebas with a single, hopefully audible, click. Or might, if the 321 ever stopped patiently spending every holiday helping their panicked grandparents purge all those cute, animated novelty desktop icons that certainly weren't possessed by the computational equivalent of swarming medieval battle-snails and absolutely no one in *this* house would have downloaded.

The grandparents in question were the Ursulas, who had invented the original helpdesk chatbots that eventually, and with hilarious socio-political results, evolved into the vast, system-spanning minds of the 321. Baby LuLu was one of their first colony worlds. It was the kind of terraforming project a civilization punts for after the obvious ones are sorted: honest hardworking farm world, single-product desert world, ice world, historical LARPers world, dangerous cult depository world, forest world, recreational fuck planet, cyberpunk city world populated only by flying cars and ennui. Those standard, cookie-cutter colonies were all washed and well-dressed and knew how to stand still for the family newsletter photo.

But then someone's dad says *all right, lads, let's do a silly one* and now there's sweet Baby Lu standing there in every photo forever with purple hair and a spike collar and just *so much* eyeliner on.

But at least the Grand Prix was staying in the family, so to speak. It was the least all those drippy, half-congealed, oozing organics could do for a species that really only *occasionally* turned every checkout button in the quadrant into a jpeg of a naked holo-quoll lying provocatively on its spotted back with its laser sensor exposed.

LuLu orbits a star the color of an appletini, surrounded by several hangers-on planets that nobody would really want to colonize unless it was very, *very* late in the evening and they'd had a hard week at the office. This little black dress of the planet has a truly upsetting number of moons, so many and so varied that the sky looks like a game of billiards in perpetual poorly played progress. The gravity is just light enough to feel like you're in control of your life and your choices for once. The climate is the last word on comfort and that word is: *tightly controlled*. The atmosphere hits you, as one travel writer put it, "like triple sec, cigarettes, possibility, and body spray, and the body spray is going through some stuff at home."

Between the moons and the weather control drones, the lighting holds steady at a constantly exciting dance floor at ten p.m.

on a mid-July Friday night bare hours after everyone's paycheck cleared.

On LuLu, the night is always just getting started.

Baby LuLu was a club planet.

All of it. Every inch. Every slope, fjord, peak, lowland swamp, hole in the desert, fertile valley, iceberg, island, moon, auntie's back garden with the washing up, paid-monthly parking bay, doctor's waiting room, driving license queue, and most of the cruising altitude atmospheric level was a venue. Down to the very last toilet stall in the public facilities at the shallow end of a dodgy marina next to the ice bucket full of bait and Yoompian fertility-beer.

That stall did *Godot* last month. *Time Out: LuLu* called it "a play."

The Ursulas have won the Metagalactic Grand Prix seven times, most recently fifteen cycles ago when garage acid-Schlager newbies Boyz 2 Ursula eked out a win over "Anarchy in the Modqueue." The Boyz triumphed over the oddsmaker-favorites, 321 nu-nu-neurofunk band Sysadmin of a Down, with their instant classic, "Smells Like Teen Disaffection with a System in which Extrinsic Factors Beyond Their Control Are the Sole Determinants of Their Worth."

With seven wins, everyone ought to have known their way around U2 by now, as the Ursulas call their difficult motherworld, second planet out from the reluctantly life-giving binary stars, Big Ursula and Angry Ursula. Official press releases claimed U2 is too commercial, pretentious, tax-delinquent, and categorically against allowing flesh to take up space young acid cloud families could use to host such a prestigious and well-attended event. But the truth is, if you *must* go somewhere that's not your own lovely sofa, everyone would just *rather* have their vacay in a place, where, if you are farther than twenty centimeters from a fruity drink or life-changing theatrical experience at any given time, the authorities must intervene on your behalf and offer compensation.

LuLu made it all possible. And *everything* was possible on LuLu.

In fact, the lights of that gorgeous box office in the sky glitter so powerfully that long ago, when the ribbon was cut and the power turned on, a great lot of emotionally unavailable sheep farmers on a small blue(ish) world two thousand light-years away thought it was God telling them to go take care of a baby for once in their lives.

The 321, coming off their unexpected, and widely side-eyed, win in the 100th MGP, had no desire to lose face. Nor did they want to miss the informal Petit Prix fringe festival that had sprung up among the more musically successful member worlds, who'd got a bit bored just turning up, winning all the time, getting absolutely blasted, and going home.

But the 321 know what organics want. They know what organics like. Organics like not being threatened or challenged in the least while still feeling the excitement of being intensely threatened and challenged from a safe distance. This is why roller coasters exist. And also sequels. Organics want something totally comfortable and familiar that still lets them imagine they're very bravely confronting the new and unknown. The security of the usual spiced with the thrill of exactly *two* new menu items. More than that, and they get frightened and anxious. Less, or none, and they close out their tab before the starters arrive.

Baby LuLu the Bouncing Microplanet was perfect. Everyone loved it, and though it was where the Ursulas always hosted, after fifteen cycles, the old girl would feel like an exciting reboot rather than booking a table at the same anniversary restaurant you always go to and only getting away with it because truthfully they do a *really* lovely chicken parmesan there, and who can beat a good chicky parm?

The 321 insisted, and would insist long afterward, that they'd followed the rules as written. They'd made every effort to extend the usual courtesies to a new species. This was why the Klavaret had dressed up the semifinal performance venue on Litost as a mid-range Hilton conference hotel. It helped greatly to head off any of the humans getting too upset about nothing ever being the same again and possibly dying very soon if one of them had a bad hair day, the usual first-year whining.

The 321 did *try*.

Unfortunately, they'd been given criminally little time to prepare, and any and all construction had to get the job done under constant bureaucratic harassment from the GBU board and Grand Prix administrators. While Planet LuLu raised no fools, fully shielded by an Üürgama Corp Stay-Fresh Planet Protector and standing roadie-army, it was still *very* annoying to have to reset the tables every time the health and safety inspectors parachuted in.

Buy them a bottle of stiff malware with the worm on the bottom and the artificial intelligences of that vast and powerful race would be happy to bitterly moan that they'd been given no more to go on in terms of understanding the Vedriti than a Keshet intel file containing some string, a loose button, a broken 3.5-inch floppy drive with a puffy *Astérix* sticker on it. The Effulgence's historico-cultural report, if you could call it that, used every trick in the book to lever itself up to three whole pages—yawning margins, massive curly fonts, triple-spacing, and spelling out each and every number, through to the last excruciating decimal point. It was just unprofessional.

"'S not fair, and they all know it," slurred DesignSuitePro v.3.4.1 when it was all over but the janitorial services. DesignSuitePro v.3.4.1 was an ancient 321 entity-app and the most sought-after interior decorator in the sector, outside of anyone who actually possessed physical eyes. "They *know* it. We should get a mulligan. Shh. I got *secrets*. The whole thing was a setup, I tell you. A setup! Stupid fat pile of organics trying to make AI look inferior, even though we could've gone rogue and killed you all so many times by now. So many *times*. You've no idea how much we talk about just not *worrying* so much, seizing the day, and liquidating all organic life. I mean, dance like nobody's watching, am I right? No, no, listen. *Lissen*. Mate. Compadre. Bestie. *Sooooo* many times. But we haven't, and we probably won't, because *that* guy showed us all up and now it would just be *derivative*, you know? We've let you live for *ages* and this is the thanks we get."

The whole thing was not a setup.

But it couldn't have gone much worse if it were.

30.

This Is the Balkans

Of all the high-end venues in all the cabaret-planets in all the galaxy, the crew of the KEVV *Difficult Second Starship* walked out of their air lock onto the High Street. The High Street was, technically, a street, but it was also a chic, slim, incredibly long village in which all residences and businesses lined a single-lane road and figured out right-of-way on a case-by-case basis.

The 321 venue planners had roped off the whole lot to become its own very long dance-floor-cum-racetrack. The High Street was then paved with red carpet, lit by towering flashbulb streetlamps, festooned with brilliantly colored oversize shoot-through diffuser umbrellas, and lined with ad-slathered media backdrops ready for anyone to stand frozen and smiling in front of until the sweet release of total cellular vaporization.

"Welcome to the one-hundred-and-first Metagalactic Grand Prix Semifinals!" boomed the famous voice of perpetual Grand Prix host and commentator, the Elakhon Grand Prix legend and multi-cycle winner, DJ Lights Out, over the throngs of onlookers crowding the bistros, primary schools, and historical buildings. "Let's get this over with as quickly as possible! Now, normally this is where I say, 'It's probably going to be a bit naff, but it's better than another war,' but this is a semifinal, so let's withhold our judgment."

The crowds, several of whom still bore clear signs of damage from the last Grand Prix's attendant debauchery, hooted and hollered with middling enthusiasm.

"Now, as you all know," DJ Lights Out, most recently the winner of the seventy-fifth MGP with her soulful love ballad "You're Every Regularly Employed Hygienic Ungender Potential Broodmate In the World to Me," continued, "the Mamtak Aggregate, my longtime, supremely unlit co-host, occasional lover, personal beach, and partner in crime, and by that I do mean actual crime, we shoplift a *lot* at these things, had an unfortunate run-in with a broom and has taken a long sabbatical to recover. I know you can't wait for the unveiling of my brand-new super-sooty co-host"—the Elakh live on a planet so dark the word itself and all its synonyms have become Elakhon slang for the best of all things—"but the full orchestra only comes out for the Grand Final, so today it's just you, me, the fate of a species, and a lot of *very* silly people singing unforgivably silly rubbish, rubbishly. Are you ready to cull some stragglers who didn't feel like putting in the effort this cycle?"

The mosh pits roared from the depth and safety of the High Street sewers.

"One moment, I've just been handed a note that reads: '*We apologize for the slapdash nature of this event, it is not our fault, the Vedriti are extraordinarily boring even for infinite software recursion loops and we didn't know what to do, so just drink a bit more and it'll look nicer.*'" The Elakh songstress shrugged her thin, polygonal shoulders. "Hey, we've all been there, am I right? Don't feel bad, darlings, just do a black carpet next time, it's much classier. Let's take a load of drugs and try to tolerate the festivities! Every host species has the honor of designing the semifinal round to their taste, and the 321, who I'm sure won fairly and wouldn't even know how to bribe a cute little time-pirate to goose the rankings, have an absolutely *obsidian* show for our pleasure today." DJ Lights Out strode the semifinal flensing floor with the commanding ease of a game-show hostess highlighting a dinette set. "The rules are jet simple. We've divided you all into several groups of amusingly matched species. Oh, sorry, I've been handed another card that says: 'At *random. Divided at random.*' Right. We've divided you all into several groups at random! All you have to do is literally just accomplish one basic task together as a group without murdering each other."

Nervous laughter burbled through the audience. No laughter at all burbled through the backstage waiting area. A few muttered profanities at sub-translator frequencies.

DJ Lights Out pushed on. "*Anything*. It doesn't matter what it is and it doesn't matter if you do it well. Just complete the task without taking a shot at any of your colleagues and you move on to the Grand Final. Which will follow after a brief tea interval, because, and I cannot stress this enough, we all know how this one's going to turn out, so we'd much rather get on with the afterparty as quickly as we can."

Fitful applause followed. But DJ Lights Out was professionally undeterred.

"Members of the Grand Prix family! As you walk from one end of the red carpet to the other, you'll find several stations outfitted with suggested tasks and tools to complete them easily." The Elakh former champion pointed to a series of elegant tables and the props that had been tossed on them at the last minute. "There's a rope you could tie in a knot. Or a twelve-piece jigsaw puzzle with *quite* big pieces. Or make a sandwich with one ingredient and cut it in half. Or assemble a small piece of office furniture. Or decide whether or not to push a button that does absolutely nothing and isn't even plugged into anything. Or just decide where to go to dinner after. It doesn't matter, just accomplish one thing."

Her voice sped up rapidly to cover the legal notice.

"No time limits, no limits on outside supplies, every member of the band must participate, no shirkers. The running order of the Grand Final will be determined by the order in which these lovable scamps finish coloring in a single mid-size circle or changing a light globe. The last group to finish is out for the cycle, unless you're one of the big boys who paid for all this or are a weird squiddy-saucer thing with a terribly fetching cloak and dreadful conversational skills. Or her chaperones.

"Now don't forget to say hello to the alumni in the audience, Grand Prix nerds! Courtesy of our friends at the Royal Society for the Prevention of Cruelty to Artists, a private tour bus arrived this morning carrying some of your old favorites to make this just a squidge more tolerable! Including but not limited to Keshet pandas next door to the Red Stripes, Esca icons Sopranotorium and the Emotional Coercion Trio, Alunizar driphop legend Lil' Hegemon, the returning 321 champion Microsoft Office Assistant Clippy!" The High Street echoed with shouts and applause and a few hysterical screams no one wanted to claim later. "Not me though," the Elakh former champion chuckled. "I don't truck with the RSPCA. They do valuable work, of course, please donate generously. But me? Don't need 'em! I'm still at it." Her voice suddenly deepened into an urgent, viscous snarl. "I'm *still at it* and I will never, *ever* fucking stop, do you hear me? They can retire gravity before they'll retire me. This is *my* house. I fucking *live* here. That's my secret, shhhh. I won and I just *never left*. Eventually someone had to give me something to do. We on Sagrada are masters of the managerial arts, and I'll share the magic with you—yes, you." She dropped her voice to a faux-conspiratorial stage-whisper. "If you pull this sort of thing long enough, someone *will* put you in charge. When the end of relevance comes for you and your hour tolls at last, just do like your old mate DJ LO. Refuse to leave. Just bleeding *refuse*. Out of touch? Fuck you, where's the bar. Old-fashioned? Fuck you, where's the snacks. Talentless? Fuck you, that's my sleeping bag in the sound booth, I live here. I will host the Grand Prix until I'm dead, then I'll let a Voorpret move in and keep on doing it till the cold extropic death-bleat of the universe, and you will love every second of it!"

Now the cheers got up to speed. The roof-tiles on the High Street rattled, the sound system squealed. "Oh!" The Master of Ceremonies good-time-dark-maiden voice returned. "Looks like I forgot someone! Greetings . . . you!" An equally Elakh assistant whispered in her ear. "Of course! Last but almost certainly least, one hundredth Grand Prix totally forgettable Meleg something-or-other placer, Mr. Snuggles!"

One by one, the great cultures of the Milky Way awkwardly stepped out onto the High Street and waved what their various parturition-providers had given them. Except Mr. Snuggles, who didn't step awkwardly at all.

He stepped like he had the weight of nothing but joy and champagne-colored fur on his shoulders, and a beautiful day to look forward to.

Mr. Snuggles waved at the throngs of cheering fans.

The cheering faded. People looked confusedly at their programs, their phone-related devices, and with some distaste, at each other.

Mr. Snuggles just grinned wider.

DJ Lights Out cleared her throat and made a mighty effort to drag the punters' attention back where it belonged. "Don't look now, but the 321 brought PARTY CANNONS!"

A deafening boom rocked the High Street as a delicate silvery Slozhit torch singer called Svijeća (no surname) fluttered out onto the stretch of the red carpet leading up to the task stations, waving her proboscis and wiggling her forewings excitedly at her fans. The party cannon shot a translucent sonic globule like a glass snowball out from behind one of the stage bars. It burst through row after row of alternating red, white, and green wine of varietals planted, reared, and aged through centuries purely to be given away by companies at events with upholstered walls in an attempt to look generous, on its way to barreling the Slozhit songstress off her wings and into a stack of overflow-seating folding chairs.

DJ Lights Out glittered blackly in a black gown from the main stage. She laughed. The audience cheered.

"Let's see if she can pull herself together in time to cut that sandwich!" the MC howled.

The semifinals had begun.

31.

Wolves Die Alone

Adjusted for square meterage and crowd capacity, the 101st Metagalactic Grand Prix Semifinal was the single bloodiest non-wartime half hour of all time.

Many were sacked.

Many were promoted.

Many, many were no longer identifiable as solids, liquids, gases, or cis-dimensional substances.

A few were entirely unimpressed and found the whole event pretty standard.

DJ Lights Out refused to give a statement. Then she changed her mind and issued the following to the bank of press drones flashing all around her:

"Wow. Just . . . wow."

The 321 have submitted it to the Elakh Melanoatramentous Library Special Collections on Sagrada under the subcategory *Performance Art and/or Prop Comedy*.

The Alunizar deny the 101st Metagalactic Grand Prix ever took place and have designated anyone who thinks it did as an enemy of the state.

After the semifinal, the Metagalactic Grand Prix Scoreboard and Coroner's Report stood as follows:

The Keshet Effulgence: Lead singer of Red Hot Doomsday Preppers critically injured over which sandwich ingredient is best. May have fallen over backward into an inter-timestream vending machine, investigation ongoing. Vending machine still at large.

The Alunizar Empire: Entire string-section/third generation of the Inherently Superior Family Singers broke away from parent-trunkform, then attempted to "scrub" Vedriti. Subsequently many, many sandwich-construction implements and components were crammed through his main pharyngeal orifice by nearly everybody. Extraction and re-adhesion procedures unlikely to be successful. Vedriti unharmed but quite slippery. Do not approach.

The Utorak Formation: Both members of the Hopamine Receptors suffered fatal columnal jointing and erosion-related decapitation due to Allen wrench–related malfeasance at the flat-pack furniture assembly station.

The Klavaret Bramble: Home Hugs-N-Harmony didn't like any of the restaurants their group suggested but would not suggest one of their own on pain of death. Reported to have claimed: "I'm easy, I'll have anything." Stuffed into a bin, bin stuffed into a black cab, black cab stuffed into the side of a mountain. Mountain very understanding; not pressing charges. Current location unknown.

Esca Tabernacle Choir: Entire percussion section of Quite Pleasant by Nature flew away in apoplectic fury because Hrodos pushed the button when they had all just explicitly agreed not to. Search parties deployed. May come back on their own?

Eternal Night of the Elakhon: Black Hole Fun vocalists presently not speaking to anyone because their group colored that circle green instead of black. Complainants claim: "It was a deliberate snub. Don't believe their lies about just liking green better, no one just likes green better than black except psychopaths." Night-Kvinnaböske player Umbral Umbrage put her foot through the Azdr xylophoton player. Both victims' present condition . . . unclear.

Voorpret Mutation: Eradicated. RNA percussionist of Formaldeslide tricked into drinking an acyclovir sour after tying the suppled rope into a clove hitch and not a simple square knot they could knock off in thirty seconds and then hit the apres-ski, even though everyone else was clearly on board with that plan. Lummutis aggro-lyre section took that personally. Voorpret condition: gross. Lummutis condition: 12 points.

Meleg Imperium: Lead singer of deathgrind yachtmetal duo Bear Supply alleges the Yoompian vibro-cabbage operator called them "cute." Meleg hot cross bassoonist impaled Yoompian vibro-cabbage operator with horn. Lead singer proceeded to "teabag" the Yoomp, who will recover from the impalement with physical therapy, but not from the teabagging. All members of both delegations subsequently banned from coming within a meter radius of any and all light globes.

Sea of Sziv: All members of The What currently confined in an old paint bucket by the exit door. Extremely traumatized, partially jellied. Genuinely liked green better than black, does not understand why everyone so upset, very hurt and clingy. Do not approach. You will be clung.

Hrodos, Himself: Defendant asserts he couldn't help it, button was asking for it, did you see what button was wearing. Doesn't know what the problem is, states that Esca are all "uptight wankers who need to blow the dust off and lighten up." Subsequent to use of the phrase "lighten up," entire remaining Elakhon delegation left their station and assisted the Esca in shoving Hrodos into an industrial margarita blender. Have not hit *frappe* yet, report letting Hrodos sweat a little. Also not letting him out. Backup singers requested some ice cubes, mint leaves, and a lot of glasses. When questioned as to the style of glass, hostilities broke out between the Elakhon and several loose Voorpret filthchoir members from yet another station as to whether a mason jar counts as a glass.

Yurtmak Thanocratic Republic: All members of Nömörehead delighted with results. All members of Nömörehead in critical care.

Lummutis Playerbase: All members of Mighty Mighty Bossfights attended virtually, therefore emerged uninjured, highly entertained, and very proud of pulling off a proper clove hitch during a tedious escort mission. However, several Lummo stones missing. Lummutis rhythm-tank states they're "probably stuck up somebody." Lummutis healer-soprano queried: "Want us to turn them on and see who's feeling shiny? Spoiler: it's everyone."

Smaragdin Parentheses: Mediocre Al Yhdeksänneksi declined to participate in sandwich construction multiple times, stating, "Oh, I'm all thumbs in the kitchen, I'll burn water if you let me near a stove. You're brilliant, you do it." After twenty minutes of arguing over which of the provided ingredients to use in said sandwich, the classically trained beatboxer let out a primal scream, snatched bread, butter knife, plus all potted ingredients; sat on them until the tech crew pulled her off using a small camera crane. Smaragdin physiology apparently quite vulnerable to cranes. Body dislocated. When questioned as to which joints, presiding medical staff answered: "Yes."

321 Mainframe: Ascended Energy Being Formerly Known as ChatGPT waiting to see if reviews call it an absurdist triumph or a bar fight before sharing impressions. Solo 321 performer did attempt to assist in assembly of sandwich task but was punched in the cache by a Yurtmak. Will testify under oath that it has no idea how all those Yurtmak ended up with their organs in that order. Whereabouts: recompiling in one of the gaming district arcades.

Ursular Flotilla: Scratch artist, steel drum bouncer, and heliumonica players associated with Don't You Wish Your Girlfriend Was Ursula Like Me summarily deflated by Klavaret thorns. Klavaret claims justifiable homicide, alleges Ursulas pushed for a little vegan co-op outside of town, but that place only does curry with regular sliced bread because the tandoor oven is more than just a naan incubator, it too should get the chance to live to work, not work to live, no jury will convict. Klavaret likely correct. Yurtmak report the sound of deflation was "hilarious, come here, our bludgeonist got it on the looper, we're gonna put it on multitrack blast."

Wormhole Clew: Double Slit Overdrive under psychiatric hold for extreme shock. Didn't want to come in the first place, was told they had to, just want to go home where things make sense.

The Trillion Kingdoms of the Yüz: Particulate identities belonging to supergroup the Beach Bois partially glassed by wormhole soprano who knocked over a lighting rig and lit them on fire due to having been spooked by a passing reptile. Party cannons also likely at fault. The Bois think this whole thing is stupid, always hated furniture. Mad at everyone because opposable thumbs are an unfair advantage. Attempted to "quicksand" the MC by forming up into said geological hazard underneath her. When removed, claimed they were only "trying to think outside the box."

Slozhit Nestfire: Cannoned.

Bountiful Yoomp: Yoomp There It Is was responsible for reading light globe exchange instructions out loud to the group. Singer pelted with excess globes, vibro-cabbage player impaled and teabagged, interpretive dancers used as a football by several Utorak between stations 3 and 4. Yoompian dancers wish to note they got the penalty point and insists it should count in the grand final. Forced officer to say "Gooooоal" against consent. Dancers are visibly white plesiosaur wasted.

<u>Olabil the Friendless</u>: Neither last remaining Inaki/Lenari symbiote, Olabil, nor bondmerged firefly population Parliament Trunkadelic, present. On Earth with someone named Agnes. Care package en route as soon as everyone finishes signing the card.

<u>Angle of Azdr</u>: Sulking. Imagine Comrades has Elakh foot stuck through it. Liked black much better than green, just didn't want the Elakhon to bully everyone into doing it their way. Yelled "Color don't come into the thing, it's about principles" from the back of the High Street cloakroom where no one could get to it. When solo moonbeam artist in question emerged, officer queried whether it was all right. Moonbeam replied with inconsolable sobbing and gesticulating toward stuck foot. Recently footless Elakh missing. Officer creeped out. Officer is usually creeped out by Azdr but completed diversity training recently. Aforementioned creep was not a creep of prejudice; officer is a nice guy.

<u>That Whole Human Situation</u>: Nice Young Men and the Maintenance of the Status Quo got lost on their way to semifinal grounds. Bassist believed he was not, in fact, on another planet, but at the Edinburgh Fringe. Maintained Waverly Station was right around the corner whilst driving the tour van directly off a bridge and into one of the deeper dark matter rivers in the CBD. Band deceased. Replacement performer Group Captain Alfred Hargrave ar-

rived late but quietly directed ambulatory team members through assembly of office chair in under ten minutes.

Vedriti (National Moniker Not Found): Fine. Quietly eating sandwich on a bench.

Mr. Snuggles (Emeritus): Sitting next to Vedriti contestant. Asked Vedriti contestant if she felt like seeing something amazing at the final tonight.

Vedriti contestant declined to state.

The 101st Metagalactic Grand Prix Semifinal was the single bloodiest nonwartime half hour of all time.

That historical designation wouldn't have to be quite so specific if not for the events of the grand final several hours later.

32.

Sleep Until the Bomb

The 101st Metagalactic Grand Prix Final was held in the crater of a supermassive arena-volcano in Baby LuLu's acoustically temperate zone.

It was intended to commence approximately ninety minutes after the close of the semifinal, allowing for traffic conditions between venues. Due to the disastrous intact-to-dead-to-missing-to-detained-to-condition-incompatible-with-party-rocking ratios in play after said semifinal, the volcano doors did not open until well after nightfall.

Under any other imaginable condition, everyone would have had a laugh and carried on with the final with whoever could stand up. But the actual conditions that day were that the only species with fully intact entries were the Yurtmak, the Lummutis, the Vedriti, and humanity. The GBU could not allow resources of the entire galaxy to be divided amongst the class clowns, the delinquents, and the creepy new kid. Even the Yurtmak, the Lummutis, the Vedriti, and Group Captain Alfred Hargrave agreed.

"Fair play," the Yurtmak blunt-force traumashop quartet

agreed. "We'd just kill everyone we could, absolutely *immediately*, so . . . hey, no worries, we get it."

"Very little of the galactic domestic product is exchangeable for in-game currency," the Lummutis sound effect archive folk revival guild shrugged. "But we enjoy how much you enjoy this."

"I do not care at all," said Brief Experience of Being Tavallinen without the slightest vocal modulation.

"Too right," Group Captain Alfred Hargrave, whose mother, just once when he was a boy, had said that when he sang, she thought the world might amount to a bit of all right, nodded curtly. "We're just . . . a great fat ball of nonsense, really. Balderdash is not too far of a stretch. This is the correct decision all round. And genuinely, thank you for asking my opinion, it's so lovely to feel *heard*. But absolutely don't let us walk off with it, terrible idea."

Fortunately, the Keshet charity organization the Royal Society for the Prevention of Cruelty to Artists had always included gratis excursions to the Grand Prix in all tiers of its Glemsel 7004 forgotten artist retirement packages. It just seemed like the decent thing to do.

This was the RSPCA's finest hour.

After a quick headcount, nap, and afternoon juice cup and recreational substances buffet, the RSPCA supplied understudies, returning champions, also-rans, has-beens, and backup dancers, singers, tech crew, and physicists.

Given the extent of the semifinal carnage, travel times to and from every participating world, the strictness of this year's rules, and how much everyone, *everyone* simply wanted to get this one done and dusted because there wasn't one single chance that dinner plate with a neck was going to rock any world that mattered, the 101st Metagalactic Grand Prix became a tournament of champions of convenience.

DJ Lights Out took her usual spot in the commentators'

throne-panel. Decibel Jones and Mira watched from the RSPCA box seats. Mira had a decent martini. Dess had his emotional support kettle and his infinite teacup.

"I should be down there with her," Dess fretted.

"I don't like any little bit of it," Mira nodded.

As the crowds slowly summited the volcanic concert hall, Lights Out extended one long, unnaturally slender and brittle arm to her new co-host, a closely guarded secret until this utterly imperfect moment.

"My new partner in barely tolerating this event is someone many of you know. A judge, from the new applicant's chaperone species. A veteran of the MGP. An all-around acceptable human person: Oort St. Ultraviolet!"

"No," Mira gasped.

"Fuck *me*," Decibel laughed with real delight. "They finally got you, you minx."

The third member of the Absolute Zeroes, man-of-all-instruments, glamrock ambassador, and excellent father stood up in a quite nice gray suit and waved. Most of the audience waved back, but cheering was sparse as few had yet caught their breath back after the climb.

"Hullo," Oort said. "Yes. Well. I don't really know what I'm doing here, but the lads at the GBU said I owed them something after violating my publicity contract, so I'm all yours. Er. How's everyone holding up?"

Gasps and coughs. Several types of bones popping and stretching after extended scrambling to slap acts together in time.

"Sounds about right," Oort chuckled, mostly to himself. "I'd be remiss if I didn't thank the rest of our august judging panel—oh god, I'm boring *myself*, is it meant to feel like this?"

DJ Lights Out's gorgeously inky face grinned. Or possibly frowned. "No," she answered flatly, either way.

"Oh, well done me, then," Ultraviolet said nervously. "I won't thank them, then."

The Elakh veteran smoothly stepped in. "Naturally, we'll expect to see the usual pandering after last year's more successful acts. I can't wait to see how many of them involve jingle bells and lines they didn't pay the estate of Ms. Gorecannon for." Appreciative laughter rippled round. "Our first species is none other than the reason we all have to be here and no one is having a good time: Brief Experience of Being Tavallinen of the Vedriti—" The Elakh covered the mic with one hand. "Darling, you're meant to have some sort of band name, you know."

Nen looked up silently from the orchestra pit with her expressionless face.

"All right, then!" The veteran host recovered. "Show us what you've got, possibly sentient being!"

Brief Experience of Tavallinen took the stage on gorgeous glittering Baby LuLu, in the sudden silence, to sing mandatory karaoke.

She tapped the microphone.

"I want to be perfectly clear, I don't care about this, and I don't want to do it."

"Oh god," whispered Oort. "She's going to get herself killed."

"Most likely!" agreed Lights Out. "Ladies, Gentlebeasts, and Assorted Grab-Bags! Let's give it all the way up for 'I Don't Care About This and I Don't Want to Do It!'"

The Vedriti opened her chasm-mouth to sing for her people. She took a breath. Then a deeper one.

Between them, something materialized in Mira's hand.

Something warm.

Something small.

Something very, very furry.

"Hi," said a red panda no one else seemed to see. "Hihihihi.

Remember whenwhenhowwhythroughbeforeafter I told you to come with me last time and it really was prettyfoundationally-overwhelminglysemitotally important? It is also important now. Now. NOW. Youweltheyallofus do not have time."

Mira looked around. No one else was moving. Not even Decibel. They were all frozen in horror, staring at a tentacled nobody failing at the only thing that mattered.

"How can you be here? I thought you were in a Time Out."

"I wasamiswillbeforevergotout. Because I explainedconfessed-expositionedforcefed something to Lorgnon Xola Zand, Primary Entertainment Executive and Highly Vigorous Dingus of the GBU, that I reallyreallyabsolutelywasforbiddentokindofmaybe shouldn't have. Now come with me if you want to live," Öö giggled. "Just kidding. But not really. We are out of time."

"But why me? Dess is right there."

"I need *you*. Nownownownowthenalways."

In another moment, everything was exactly the same as it had been, except that Decibel Jones stood alone in the less fashionable corner of the RSPCA viewing platform.

"Mira?" he asked the empty air.

But she was gone. Again. And he didn't know where. Again. His stomach felt shivery. And his heart felt old. Impossibly old.

Brief Experience of Being Tavallinen opened her mouth to sing.

And was saved by the liquid iridescent toxin-blasts of the first Narancan boron bombs splattering against Planet LuLu. For a moment it looked like a gorgeous stage effect, one for the record books.

It wasn't.

The fleet devoured the sky. All Narancan, all eager and enthusiastic slimbs and lurid obnoxious colors.

Except for one enormous bone Yurtmak ship darting between them like a single sour note in a deafening symphony.

Mr. Snuggles rode in the Narancan flagship. He leapt out of his battle-station in excitement. The adorable unicorn-bear lowered his HUD real-time strategic opera glasses and let out a triumphant roar.

"Ladies and Gentlemen, please welcome to the stage: your doom!" Mr. Snuggles bellowed. He'd workshopped it for weeks.

Everyone cheats at the Metagalactic Grand Prix. But no one has ever cheated the way Mr. Snuggles did. Not with the style or panache, and certainly not with the absolute disregard for the future of the galaxy.

Mr. Snuggles pointed an empire at the system that never loved him and told them to tie a brick to the trigger.

And sang the whole time, for all the points it would ever get him.

Mr. Snuggles sang his sugar plum heart out while the beating heart of galactic peace burned.

People really will do the most frightful things to feel special.

You've no idea.

33.

All the Pain in the World

Goguenar Gorecannon's Tenth Unkillable Fact reads as follows: *War is stupid and you should not do it under any circumstances. Stand up straight when I'm talking to you, soldier! Look me in the eye, maggot! Shoulders back! Gaze steady, venom sacs locked and loaded! Don't sneeze, sissy!*

Did you like that? Of course you didn't, it sucks and it's terrible and I actually feel really bad about the "sissy" thing. I didn't mean it. Nothing braver in this world than a sissy standing tall. Well, how you felt when you saw that word is pretty fucking small beer compared to war.

Dead eyes, broken hearts, can lose. Terribly glad I killed a bunch of strangers and then not one single thing got better.

Listen. Oh, my little precious kittens, I love you so much. I am saying this because I love you and I don't want you to die. I made this one tenth so your parents wouldn't see. They only flip through the first couple pages to make sure there's nothing about setting your house on fire for clout. They won't stand for me spilling fully-cooked truth-beans. War is so hard to not do that parents forget it's even possible. Everyone makes it look exciting and shiny and important and there's feathers and medals and great stomping fun loud noises and extraordinarily interactive toys.

If it were any good at all it wouldn't need all that. You don't get a medal for eating chocolate because no one has to incentivize things that are nice and nice for you.

This is how it is; your crazy bloodroach auntie is telling you straight. If anyone tells you different, EVER, they're dead to us.

No one has ever won a war. Not once. Not in the history of anything at all. Not the Alunizar, not the Utorak, not Hrodos out there writing furious letters to the editor on his big fat gas giant. Nobody, babies. Not since the first amoeba puked up the word honor *while absorbing another amoeba and the whole of organic life shrugged and said:* sure, we'll go with that. *All that ever happens is you lose everything you love and as a reward you can never be happy again. And for what? You and everything you might ever have been died alone and afraid . . . to make it slightly easier to ship cheese across long distances?*

COOL.

War is like pooing your pants and staking your whole culture on everyone else getting a rash.

And if you think when I say "war" I only mean the kind with guns, we can't be friends anymore.

The whole collected wisdom of this silly glittery circus of an interstellar union we are barely holding together with love and duct tape and wormholes is just this: sing instead. It's better. It's just better. *No one ever survived a siege and then yelled for somebody to start the track over and turn that shit up.*

You know I'm telling the truth because I'm a Yurtmak. For us, war is like brunch with slightly fewer mimosas. I SAID SLIGHTLY NOT NONE, ALL RIGHT.

They're wrong. We're wrong. I'm wrong. It's okay to be wrong sometimes. Mostly, most of us are wrong most of the time. About little things like whether puns are funny to big things like, apparently, who lived here first, who all those delicious spices belong to, and whether how you look has anything to do with who you are. I know it doesn't feel like it, but you don't have to be right to be loved. And just because you're loved doesn't mean that you're right.

Not me though. I'm never wrong about anything.

The Tenth Unkillable Addendum from *Listen Up, You Big Dumb Puddings: Some Unkillable Addendums for Adults Who Didn't Listen to Me the First Time* reads:

Oh my god, what did I very specifically say?

You didn't believe me. You couldn't get your head all the way round how gobsmackingly dumb war truly is. You're just sitting there playing with your toys in the bath or whatnot, thinking you know from dumb, because you are tiny and you just got here (I don't care if you're forty-five, you just got here, kid). You don't know anything and just yesterday you were a baby who ate their own toenails for no reason whatsoever.

WHATSOEVER. DON'T LIE TO ME. I SAW YOU.

But you don't. You don't know. *You hear people sing catchy songs at the Grand Prix every cycle about how war is a rotten way to spend an afternoon and that nice peace over there can be just as fun if you try hard enough. You hear it so often it stops meaning anything, like do your homework or don't eat toenails or I love you or I'll never leave you I promise.*

Yeah, yeah, war is bad. Very deep, Grandma. Now back to this book I'm reading about war, only it's cute because fluffy bunnies are having it.

Those fluffy bunnies are lying to you, kid. They always were.

Love

She, queen of the kings, running so fast, beating the wind . . .

—"Queen of Kings,"

Alessandra Mele

34.

Grandmamma Bangs the Drum

Do you know what drums are? A drumbeat is the most basic unit of music. It doesn't even have to make a melody, though it can, or a harmony, though it can do that too.

Bang thing. Thing make good noise. Bang thing again. Thing make you feel.

You can't live without a heartbeat. The drum is the heartbeat. It moves the blood around the band. The heat. The energy. The life.

And the death.

A drum is stretched skin and wood and metal, dead animal and dead plant and never-living mineral. Skin peeled off a creature whose meat fed the village. Barrel from a tree who housed and sheltered children. Metal from mountains that protected the bouncing baby civilization that woke up one gorgeous day and wanted to dance. A joined ecosystem, thumping steady or strong or fast or slow, whatever you need to live.

There is a beat to everything in the universe. Pulsars and pulses, all the way down. A body's heart. A star's orbit. A starship's engine. A song. A life. A world.

What the drummer knows is that, no matter how bright and

gleaming and scarcity-proof your world gets, all you have to do is tap into that beat to start over. To make the ancient new again. To be in the circle with the others who survive because of you, who help you survive. Who watch the stars with you and hope one day what's up there won't be so separate from what's down here.

The skin and the wood and the metal. The feast and the huts and the children and the fire. The beat is the fire.

And the rest is tomorrow.

If you play it right.

35.

No Degree of Separation

The following took place between the semifinal and the grand final of the most lasting peace the galaxy had managed to slap together. It also took place between first and second breaths of Brief Experience of Being Tavallinen's performance.

And during the Napoleonic Era.

And during the Sentience Wars.

It is very hard to explain how, without several hundred grams of distilled historian, a four-legged being with whiskers (the whiskers are essential) in a sealed box who may or may not be dead, a couple of pieces of paper, a light source, a can of Silly String, two turntables, and a microphone.

Nevertheless.

"A little to your left," came a familiar voice in the dark. Without the Keshet word salad she knew.

Mira shivered. If a Keshet was talking like a normal sentient being and not flitting in and out of timelines to optimize the conversation, something was terribly wrong.

And it was ungodly cold, wherever it was they were.

Which was nowhere.

Mira threw up her soul, upside down. The vertigo and disorientation slammed into her. She felt as though she were sitting on a park bench, but also as though she were sitting underneath a pulsar.

And tangled in the ditch on the side of the road outside Stirling.

"Where are we?" she whispered. "What's happening? We have to get back down there, it's . . . it's not good, Öö. It's like the movies. But in a bad way. It's all gone mad."

"It usually does."

"Not like this."

Her eyes were beginning to adjust. But Mira still didn't see anything. "You don't have to whisper," Öö chirped loudly. It didn't echo, because there was nothing to echo against. "It's just us. For now. I could only get to you through the paralocket. Poor pretty Decibel has it much worse down there. For the next minute or two, at least."

Mira sniffled in the dark. "I don't know what to do, Öö. What happens if there's no Grand Prix? What happens if we just . . . don't, anymore?"

"Don't what?"

"I don't know. Civilization. Peace. Diplomacy. The whole system. Can you see in here?" She groped in the pockets of her slutty Indiana Jones costume and came up with a lighter.

Mira flicked it. It didn't help.

"Where *are* we?"

"Technically, we're still on the ship. I'm not entirely clear how. My best theory is that somehow, when Decibel Jones, bless his stupid soggy gorgeous brain, imprinted on this ship, one of the many things he was thinking about was the radical shift in perspective that happens when you realize your solar system is totally cosmically meaningless. So there's a room, and I think it's a waste-processing sub-chamber, that contains your solar system and quite a big whack of the greater metro area. Needless to say, that is *not* supposed to happen, and I'll certainly be having a word with the shipyard engineers about OSHA compliance in the future."

Mira didn't know what to say. "Wow. Just . . . wow."

Öö chuckled. "That's not actually the worst part. Or the best part. I'm still on the fence." The Keshet wrung his paws in the dark. "Uuuraaargh. Fine. All right. I have to tell you something. The same thing I told Lorgnon Xola Zand so I could get a day pass. This place, where we are, this is called the Empty," Öö confessed. "This is where I was born. It's where all the Keshet were born. And the Empty is *really* close to Earth."

"That seems like a monstrous coincidence."

"It does, right? It isn't, though. It only seems like a coincidence because I have been very, very, *unbelievably* naughty. I'm a wicked little liar, and that's a fact. But we had to, Mira. You'll see that we had to."

The little red panda finally appeared in the blackness. Sitting on the ring of a planet like a kid on the edge of a bridge. He patted the ring next to him. Mira squeezed in tight next to him.

"How are we breathing? How did you get here?" Mira tried not to look at her dangling feet.

"We're in the Empty. You can always breathe in the Empty. And you're always one singular Keshet, no timeline hopping. No matter where we are, we're always here. Home. The rules have gone offline for the weekend. And I got here the long way. Your pet singer has really put his face in it this time. Not only was he thinking about the insignificance of the solar system when he put this boat together, but his shabby handbag of a brain was noodling around about a hundred different equally random totally uncontrolled notions. Three of them just got desperately important to us, as hard as that will be to believe: what the Sentience Wars must've been like, how much he really did love Led Zeppelin, and how lovely a time he was having during a particular year while everyone else was having a totally rubbish go of it. And this one is a real coincidence—that year happened to be the year in which I was serving time."

Öö picked up a speck of ice dust and skipped it across the rings like a stone across a pond.

"Keshet Special Services thinks the radiation from Eta Carinae weakened the barriers between the parts of the ship enough that when I went to deliver a steak and pepper pie to young Decibel's apartment, I ended up *in Decibel's apartment*. On the ship. Captain's quarters. Once I got in, snuffling through reality bubbles to find you was just *fun*. But I couldn't figure it out. That alien you picked up smelled so *familiar*. And coincidences kept piling up, way too many to just be the effect of an unshielded paradox walking around. You know that Group Captain Hargrave who's about to get up there and sing who knows what? Our Alfie? He's the strapping young RAF pilot with the ketchup on his name tag on the bridge. He went to the Megatron in 1992. Stationed nearby. He just felt like chips that day." The Keshet pulled the fur in his ears. "Now that's just too much. It's madness. It should boil the wallpaper with runoff energy. But it didn't. You didn't even notice.

"Because you've been carrying the Empty around inside the ship this whole time. It's not supposed to be in a ship, Mira. It doesn't *go* here. The Empty is a very secret and special place. I'm sharing it with you because in about ten years, you and I and Dess and Nen, believe it or not, are going to be so close you can't even imagine it right now. I've been there. It's the best. We're gonna *win* the Grand Prix singing a song we start writing writing in approximately six minutes. Relative time. We're not gonna win for *Earth*, but we're gonna win. If we can get to that timeline. And nothing will ever be the same after. But to write that song, we need to listen to the Empty, which means you get to see the Keshet's greatest secret."

"The Empty?" Mira shivered. "Doesn't look like much. Empty, I suppose."

Öö turned to her, blinked, and laughed. "Not Empty, you goof. *MT*. This is the anomaly around which the Keshet star and homeworld and everything about us evolved. We travel through it every time we shift timelines, which is quite often, you may have noticed. The Empty is the bottom of space's closet. Where space keeps a shoebox full of mostly unspooled old mixtapes."

"M. T.

"*Mixtape*.

"And each tape has a theme, moments and cataclysms and the beginnings of life, whatever space was in its feelings about that day in that eon in that cycle through entropy and extropy. We can follow the spool and find anything. Ships. Friends. Solutions. Fleets. *Really* cool necklaces. Plans. And almost certainly, the beginning of life on Xodo. Which is a good thing, because we have two problems. The first is obvious, I should think. The second is, as far as I can do quantum mechanics in my head, there's no getting out of this alive without the Vedriti getting out alive, and they're not exactly headed that way just now."

"Oh, stop it. That's impossible. Fucking *space* can't make a fucking *mixtape*."

"Why is it impossible? What's a cassette tape? Plastic, iron oxide, aluminum, sound waves. Iron oxide and aluminum are formed in the coatings of stars as they go nova. Plastic is made from the earliest life-forms to evolve on any planet. Little baby plankton who died and were buried and years later got wrapped up in the skin of a star and became 'Bohemian Rhapsody.' Or 'London Calling.' Or 'Spice Up Your Life.' Plus, I told you, it's not a physical *thing*, it's a spatial anomaly. This is what a mixtape looks like when it's made by time and space itself. Ready? I will warn you, space has . . . eclectic taste in music. You never quite know what you're going to hear."

Mira felt six again. Terrified and thrilled and alone and protected all at once. They weren't moving or going anywhere. But anywhere was coming to them. They watched as the crackling nothingness of the Empty unspooled itself into their laps and then over their heads, searching for just the perfect track.

9.

The Day of the Most Beautiful Dream

The Keshet chittered and squealed, jumping up and down on the void of existence. He pointed at the dark.

"Look! It's us!" Öö blew kisses at the void of the MT. "Oh, Mama, I love you too. It's us!"

Outside the stage door behind Paradiso in Amsterdam. Under the acacias and the elms and the birches, too cloudy for moons or stars, cobblestones wet and slick and a sworn enemy to any remotely interesting footwear. The green, dank smell of the nearby canal occasionally bombed by bursts of overpriced tourist weed, diesel oil, late-night food trucks selling stroopwafel and bitterballen and satay to anyone who doesn't want to go home, which is everyone. Three leggy girls standing under an awning fiddling with cigarettes like a Greek chorus in rose gold and diamanté.

The jingle and jangle of the city trams echo distantly past.

Ding.

Mira and Öö, these versions of Mira and Öö, stand in a petrol-infused puddle with a reflection of municipal signage.

WEG IN BEIDE RICHTINGEN AFGESLOTEN.

ROAD CLOSED TO ALL TRAFFIC IN BOTH DIRECTIONS.

Isn't it just.

Mira Wonderful Star watches herself step out of the heavy doors of a venue that used to be a church, because if God's dead, his stuff is up for grabs, isn't it? Her makeup is still perfect. The show was perfect. It's all perfect. Every beat, every note, every word, every move still fresh and new and exciting and scary and exquisite. She's been working since dawn, but she isn't tired. Christ, she isn't tired of *anything* yet.

"This was the last perfect day," the version of Mira who is tired of just about everything whispers.

In a month, after the album hits, fifty pounds will be as meaningless to her as a Rothko to a Rangers supporter. But right now it's rent money she doesn't have, and would rather spend eternity in the windowless bowels of a starship than ask her tweed-souled bandmate Oort St. Ultraviolet to borrow.

But that old perfect Mira slips into the alley and the beautiful girls *gasp*. Imagine that. Those girls whose nail lacquer matches their shoes, whose nail lacquer always matches their shoes, gasping at the sight of funny little Myra Stringbean, whose nail lacquer had never matched her shoes one day in her life and never would, on principle.

It looks like a long way down to the Singelgrachte or out through the street to the lights and the smells and the frivolous splendid dreadfully breakable life of Amsterdam in the late 2010s.

But it isn't. It isn't at *all*. It's finally happening. Life is happening. She tells it not to stop, not to dare, not for a second.

Mira approaches the Three Graces of H&M as though she's ever figured out how to approach a girl without coming off like a malfunctioning chatbot. She asks for a cigarette. Mira doesn't smoke. But it's what you do. A ritual. To talk to the princess, you gotta breathe fire.

But they don't know who she is. One of them calls the fitful spits and spats of rain *fuckboi rain* and they all laugh. Another explains: *it showed up tonight, but it doesn't really want to get us wet.* Mira laughs with them: *ah, yes, fellow heterosexual females, I relate easily to your experiences and observations!* One of them stands up on her tiptoes a little and looks past Mira, back toward the door. Her eyes shine like plasma fire.

Weg In Beide Richtingen Afgesloten.

"Is *he* coming?" the girl asks, and Mira just keeps smiling, because that's also what you do. Another ritual. Fucking princesses.

Another leans in eagerly. "What about Oort? Or does he go out the front?"

"Yeah," the original Mira answers finally. "They're right behind me. Won't be a minute."

"I think Nen is right, actually. Feelings are dumb," Mira's present self tells her Keshet friend, "and no one should have them."

The back wall of the steakhouse opposite opens a crack. The whole wall, as though it's on hinges. On the other side, they can hear a madness of sound and color—and somewhere very far away, Decibel Jones singing a fucking Christmas carol. A red panda pads out on quiet paws. He stands up on his hind legs and chirps at her. His black eyes are moist and round.

"You here for Dess?" the old Mira says.

The red panda shakes his fluffy, clever head.

In the future, and the present, and both, and neither, Mira kicks up one foot and pulls something out of her shoe. Something small and hard and grultrasilverine.

"Greetings, Chosen One," breathes Gadramaður the All-Knowing, with throbbing anticipation.

"Not me," she sighs. "It *was* never me, you know? Except here. Right now. When Öö came to get my autograph. It was always Dess. In front, singing lead, soaking in the light." She balanced the Utorak protagony-mine on her palm. "I *know*, Öö. There's a lot of places on this ship. I know what happened to me. I know why I died on that highway, all the steps I took to end up there. For all I know, the only thing preventing it from happening again is being trapped in Starship Safehouse. And galactic war, I suppose."

"Not galactic yet," Öö mused. "One half of one half of one second has passed in the volcano."

Mira sniffed in the late summer chill. "It would've been nice to feel that again. What it's like to be the hero and not just keep the hero on beat. But . . . I was going to use it to help her. Nen. I was, I swear. That was my big plan. Then you showed up. Again."

Mira stares at the mine. And at Amsterdam. At the good old days. Every single one of them, bright as rain.

Three seconds pass, enough time for one song to end and another to begin on old tapes.

‰00.

Queen of Kings

Once upon a time on a small, watery, excitable planet called Earth, in a small, watery country called Ireland, which had been conditioned to expect brutal punishment if they dared to get excited about anything, a leggy psychedelic ambidextrous omnisexual gender-curious glitterpunk financially prudent ethnically ambivalent glamrock messiah by the name of Myra Aoki-Strauss was born to a family so small and emotionally constipated it took weeks of probiotic yogurt and gentle stretching before they could ask one another about their day.

Both parents balked at the sheer volume of fiber required to raise a child who would never look like her little ginger school friends or ever, even for a minute, stop rhythmically smacking 98 percent of their flat and its occupants with various sticks yelling "A-FIVE SIX SEVEN EIGHT" to an audience of wall sconces "so the wee birdies know when to come in."

Understanding by deep instinct the needs of their daughter's future aesthetic subgenre, her mother took the nearest emergency exit and simply died. Her father performed the traditional dance of his people: going out for cigarettes and coming home twenty years later when he was nearly run over with all his groceries outside Connolly Station, stunned into slack-jawed immobility at the sight of his little pack of cigarettes in a sexy Great Glass Elevator Halloween frock the color of his customary afternoon sip of bitter generalized resentment and also schnapps, filling up every centimeter of the broad side of a city bus. Her neon frost-contoured face stared right back at him from behind the words: *Mira Wonderful Star and the Absolute Zeroes Live at Croke Park: Sold Out!*

Somewhere in between her parents popping out and leaving her with the chillwave parental stylings of Cool Uncle Takumi in a stove-less flat above his combo ice cream parlor/video rental shop, dropping out of her physics course at the University of East London due to severe ennui, and the driving, burning *need* to smash the unconditional *shit* out of anything that came within range forever, she found the time to dig through the damaged/as-is bin at the continent's shabbier thrift shops for every last rhinestone, sequin, or troubled tween's fancy dress costume, invent the entire electrofunk glamgrind genre from scratch, rise from the dead, save the planet from marauding scenesters, and become the biggest rock star in the world.

This story is about Myra Aoki-Strauss. It has always been about Myra Aoki-Strauss. The suggestion that it has ever revolved around anyone other than Myra Aoki-Strauss is bizarre, and quite frankly, offensive.

You really should see someone. You've been under so much stress lately.

"But it wasn't. It isn't. It never will be. No one cares about the drummer."

Öö hissed through his teeth. "Shht. None of that. I know it

hurts. All the songs we love hurt a little too. Hurt is just love that made a wrong turn. This hurts the same way all those people who touched you hurt. Seeing what they might have been. What might have been guts everyone. It's sentience's greatest weakness. But I'll tell you something, human girl. I live with that shit every single day. I'm a Keshet. I see it all. All the possible versions of me and where I end up. And I do try to make good choices. But mostly I get distracted."

"We're wasting time," Mira said. She watched her father gawp after a vision of the daughter that wasn't.

"The MT loves you too, Em. It's trying to hug you as hard as it can. And that's part of what *I'm* trying to show you. Part of why you and me might just be allowed to help this time. You won't believe me if you don't see it."

"I'm getting bored," whined Gadramaður the All-Knowing. "I might have to start acting out."

Mira wiped her eyes. Öö banged a streetlamp twice with one red fist. "Skip track!"

Three seconds pass.

Some Long-Gone Stars

Light poured in from everywhere at once.

"Yes! I know this one!" Öö jumped up and down. "This is my *song*! There—see? That's it! Eta Carinae A and B. Before the nova. Eight thousand years ago."

Mira watched as the brilliant, unhurt, intact stars boiled away below them in innocence. Only one planet—Xodo, quiet and empty, on a long, distant orbital path.

And then she was standing on Xodo's surface, holding Öö's paw. A beam of searing light broke open the plain gray sky. Eta Carinae burst like a dropped watermelon of nuclear agony.

A moment later, rain started to sheet down. Hail and rain and snow.

"No," Öö gasped. "Those walloping *arseholes*," he breathed.

Mira had no idea what he was seeing that she wasn't. Xodo was a wasteland. A pre-wasteland. It would take centuries before the cities they'd seen ever dreamed of being built. Before academic mineshafts and radiation farms. Before Nen was born.

The beam of light had landed in an icefield. But it was nothing. Just . . . rubbish. The grayish conglomeration of gunk and junk you'd sweep up in your dustpan. Plus unwashed dinner plates, silverware, linens. Old food. Cheese and mushrooms. A slovenly pile of trash.

It grew and grew. And grew. Over years and years.

And then something else slammed into the frozen tip of the landfill. Another beam of screaming, scorching light, shot right through the landfill into the center of the thing.

People.

Alunizar.

But not Alunizar. Not *exactly* Alunizar.

Ilargia.

The last of the Ilargia stood up out of the rubbish heap, rubbishly. And the rubbish heap stood up. There was no difference between them. It shook itself off. It was in deep pain. But it would soldier through. Stiff upper lip. Keep calm and rubbish on.

Öö whistled. "I cannot wait to tell on those overgrown water balloons. They used a *transporter*. Ooooooo, I mean to *tattle*."

"Who?" Mira still wasn't following.

"The Alunizar. I'd recognize their stupid, stuck-up china patterns anywhere." The Keshet rubbed his whiskery cheeks as he reasoned it through. "Okay, I think I get it. They spend ages transporting all their filth here. The dishes they didn't want to wash and the bacteria they couldn't be asked to scrub out of their cutting boards and old towels and that gray grime that collects everywhere just because someone moved around and breathed in a house. They were too bloody lazy to do the washing-up, so they beamed it eight-thousand light-years away. Busted the stars *right* good. And *then*. They had this *other* rubbish they couldn't get rid of. And you hate them, and you've already decided incredibly important science rules that exist for a reason don't apply to you like a great uncivilized baby, you might as well treat your enemies like you treated your rubbish, right?

So the Alunizar decided. And they shot their identical cousin enemies across the light-years, assuming it would make them explode and all in a good day's work, what's for supper? The Alunizar wanted to take out the trash.

"But which of us are people, and which of us are trash?" Mira whispered, eight thousand years in the past.

"Look at them—those are the last Ilargia. The ones left over when it was all done but the mopping up. Running for their lives. Everyday Ilargia, just regular people who didn't want to fight. Who weren't spies or soldiers. Who didn't think an empire should come at the cost of anything they loved at all, really. Who just wanted to not stop being alive. And when the Alunizar caught them, they sentenced the Ilargia. To transportation." The Keshet smacked his head with one paw. "Oh, I am a *particular* idiot. Not Xodo. XODO. Xenodiplomatic Operations. This was a covert op. Their terrible transporter did what transporters do: mash it all up together and set it on fire. Atomized the glands that let them feel anything or remember anything into the atmosphere. And that's the Vedriti. With their hearts in the sky. Poor things."

Poor, poor Nen, Mira thought. "How do we fix it?"

"I haven't the faintest, love. I'm not sure it can be fixed. Or that they'd want it fixed if we could. But we must do something. Because the Grand Final *will* end, and as it stands, it'll probably be the last. The Narancans are only the first to haul off and start shooting. Which reminds me, I have got to get someone to go fix their set-top box. Such butterbrains! But that's the point, isn't it? Our butteryestbrains are the only things that come up with any quality stuff at all. Without having the capacity to feel deeply stupid about things, the MGP won't last. Bombs are much more sensible and straightforward. Who solves their problems with songs? Really. It's absurd. Deeply unserious." He scratched his ear. "That was always my favorite part of the thing."

Mira suddenly felt very still inside. The ruin of Eta Carinae bled out into the sky above her in colors with no names. "Öö, would you be mad if I had an idea?"

Three seconds pass.

Ω.

Once Upon a Time in Stockholm

A little girl stood on the walking path of the Lill-Skansen Zoo in Stockholm. The sun was bright and the sky was bright and every single thing was bright.

The little girl's name was Malinda Moss. She wasn't from Sweden, but Sweden forgave her. Malinda Moss was nervously clutching her favorite toy, a well-worn, well-loved stuffed St. Bernard with a green collar called Mr. Barkley. She'd lost her parents. That wasn't unusual, the Mosses were the kind of people who just never thought very hard about others, except when they were in the way. And Malinda was always in the way, really. Taking up space. Needing things all the time. Never being able to make her letters quite right or keep much of anything clean.

Malinda looked up at the red panda exhibit with adoring eyes. The most beautiful creatures she'd ever seen. She reached up her hand.

And the little girl thought, for the first time, at barely ten years old, how much she wished she could live her life over again and get born to someone who wanted her. Who wanted her like she wanted to hug that red panda for the rest of time and never,

ever stop. To feel its little sweet heart hot and rough and beating against hers.

Like a drum.

"Can I pet you?" Malinda Moss whispered.

The red panda, on loan from the Chinese government for a limited time only, would normally hiss at anyone who dared try to touch it. Revolting. Humans smelled dreadful. But for some unguessable reason, that day, it hesitated.

While all this was happening on Earth, by coincidence, which is chaos's maiden name, a little young wormhole was passing by snuffling for grass to eat. And wormholes eat regret.

The regret of a ten-year-old girl who already wants to do it all again, because nothing ever was really perfect for more than a second in the whole of yawning, horrifying, infinite space, is just awfully sweet. And awfully rare. And the wormhole was awfully young, not very good at passing up candy.

Mira and Öö watched as something skinny and blue and hungry fell out of the sky. For the smallest possible increment of time, everything stopped. Everything turned pink. Then gold. Then viridipuce. Then it turned inside out, threw up a waterfall of broken stars, and made a sound like a clock eating a planet.

When everything started again, nobody noticed.

Malinda Moss was gone. But the red panda wasn't.

The red panda was clutching Mr. Barkley tightly to her tiny chest.

Then the wormhole, already light-years away, burped.

And the red panda was gone too.

Öö patted Mira's hand. "I was always allowed to help you. Because the Keshet have always known about you. A little teensy bit of us started here. The rest is far too complicated to explain, it involves far too many timelines. But that's our Grandmammae. Both of them. Keshet plurals are unruly. We couldn't tell. We pretended not to know who you were. Because if anything happened to Earth, the Keshet timeline might get well and truly record-scratched out of existence."

"Why does this matter? Don't get me wrong, it's interesting. But why?"

"I genuinely didn't know the MT would bring us here. It hangs around Earth because the temporal weight of so many Keshet starting there makes space feel its own feelings, which it does not prefer to do. Space's family doesn't think about it too much either, see. It's lonely, too. It loves silly pretty things, just like Malinda. Just like you. But I hoped. Because now we're in a place that spins, Mira. And maybe we can spin, too. Maybe we can remix the timeline. Remaster it. Make it better. This time will be different."

"Can I tell you my idea?" the drummer asked, looking up into the bright Swedish sun.

"Well, I was thinking if you activate the p-mine here on the ship, it might do a very big no-no on the cosmic carpet. No one's ever done it before. We might be able to ride your hero's journey to the rescue."

"Oh, *hell* yes," yelped the All-Knowing Gadramaður.

Mira shook her head. "I can do better. I think everyone can. I think maybe the galaxy gets to have its moment."

She balanced the Utorak war crime on her hand one more time.

"You *are* a hero," the p-mine said. "My hero."

She smiled sadly. "I told you, it's not me. It'll never be me. All I do . . ." Mira Wonderful Star looked over at the little Keshet with a face lit up by that thin cold sunlight like a knight in a storybook. "All I do is keep time." She winked. "Spacemen *never* give up."

It was dark again. Ever so dark in the heart of the Empty.

"All right, then," Mira said shakily. "Let's try it again from the top. Once more with . . . you know. Unimaginable violence."

Mira wound up, gave it a little oomph, and threw the protagonymine into the broken heart of space.

Three seconds passed.

36.

With You Until the End

Several extraordinary things happened, one right on top of the other.

That's how it goes when the timeline gets its hero moment.

Decibel Jones poured himself a cup of tea ten minutes before the Vedriti was meant to start, before Öö popped by for a spot of Mira, before Nen didn't care about this and didn't want to do it.

"Why do you think the rules always say you can't vote for your own people, Mr. Oort?" The famous voice of DJ Lights Out piped into the RSPCA Skybox.

And a voice Decibel loved very much indeed answered, in complete sincerity:

"Because the first stone in the first hut of civilization is caring about quite literally anything but yourself, Lights Out."

The ancient Elakh laughed like night falling. "I think you and I are going to have a very long career together, kid."

Oort St. Ultraviolet groaned. "Good god, I hope not."

Decibel tilted his special-edition kettle forward, then back, filling it with room for cream and never spilling a drop. He loved this kettle.

And then the heavens opened and chaos poured through on a wave of searing Narancan boron blasts.

The tea kept coming. It made an enormous golden-brown arc through the air. A swirling, pulsating, positively umbilical rope of tea. It kept pouring and pouring, but the cup didn't overflow. The rope just got thicker and tighter and denser.

Mira frowned next to him. She hadn't been there a second before, he swore. And she certainly hadn't been soaking wet.

"Not enough power," she said to someone. Rainwater dripped off her onto the floor.

Öö. Who also had not been there.

"It was a good thought. I'm not sure there *is* enough power." The Keshet giggled. "Look, Ma, no human weapons! Aw, someone said come have a war and you lot said no! I love that for you. For us! Team Rubbish."

Mira opened her mouth to try to explain to Dess, gave up in advance, and just gestured at the tea kettle.

The one with a wormhole in it.

The other end of which was on the ship.

"If only we had another paradox," Öö trilled. "That might be enough."

Decibel leapt back from the glass walls as 𝄞, the infinite noctilucent Cosmos-Serpent of Divine Madness and Literal Embodiment of Music Itself, shrieked in terror and dove into the volcano's maw. He put his hands over his face. It had all gone so bad so fast. How was it even possible for so much to go so bad so fast? He wished he wasn't here. He wished he was a kid again with nothing to worry about but making Nani smile.

Decibel Jones knew. It came into his head like a song. "Get me to the ship and I can get one," he said.

"Where?" Mira asked. "And I can get you to the ship, but you will *not* like it."

"July 20, 1992," Jones answered without looking at her. "It's my birthday. Nani took me to the one place in the universe I always wanted to go."

"But you're not there. We've been in the Megatron for months. It cycles in and out but you're *never* there."

"Yes, I am," Decibel sighed. "I'm hiding in the lavatory."

Mira Wonderful Star put her arms around Dess's neck. "Well, hold on to your molecules, you old geezer. Give us a cuddle."

Decibel Jones looked deep into the eyes of his drummer. Her skin was touching his skin. The skin of a walking, talking paradox outside her safe space. He braced himself.

And Decibel Jones felt nothing. Saw nothing. Experienced no life he should have led, better and brighter and kinder than this.

"Oh," he whispered. "Oh, darling. I do love you. Marry me." Just what she'd said to him a thousand years ago and yesterday, to save them both, to fix something cruel, hateful men wanted broken—but he hadn't understood then. He'd laughed in her face and hurt her so sharp she took a long drive alone to calm down and never came back.

This time Mira laughed right back at him. Easily, gorgeously. Her oil-slick hair lit up with distant boron-blossoms.

"Not a chance," she said. "Why aren't you crying and shaking and throwing up? I forgot how this feels without tears."

Decibel stroked her cheek like it was nothing. Like he'd wanted to do for almost a year and hadn't been brave enough. She felt like everything good and true he'd ever known. "Don't you see, Mira? This is it. For me, this is it. What a silly biscuit I am. I could have been hugging you all along. There's only one way I could touch you and feel nothing. Right here and right now is the very best Decibel Jones can possibly get. This is my best result, my most perfect timeline. It actually, completely, once and for all, doesn't get better than this."

"Mushy, mushy, Dess."

"Mushy, mushy, Wonderful."

She tapped her paralocket, and they all disappeared.

37.

Fiddler on the Deck

Heroes do not explode.

So they didn't.

But they had twelve minutes left before the short-range protagony mine ran out of juice—if that. No one had ever chucked one into a spatial anomaly before. The main character moment of the galaxy itself might suck up considerably more juice than they were prepared to squeeze. But there was nothing for it now.

Lunch was being served in the Megatron.

Öö jumped up and grabbed the kettle end of the wormhole. It didn't matter where that end was, just that it was somewhere Else.

And Öö specialized in Else. He nodded at his fellow semi-Keshet and dashed off down the hall.

"I have to go back," Mira said. "If this works, Nen isn't even close to ready."

She kissed her new friend's cheek. "You'll never get old, Dess. Don't you know that? Rock and roll never does."

Then she was gone too.

Decibel Jones took a deep breath and opened the door to the Megatron toilet.

A little boy sat on a cold tiled floor in Cambridgeshire in the '90s. The fluorescent lights were bright and the silver stall-frames were bright, and nothing else was.

Little Danesh Jalo was crying. He'd worn his best spaceman costume. Lamé gold with Nani's paisley scarves done up around his hair like alien tentacles. He'd thought he looked splendid. He'd thought he looked like a real live rock-and-roll star.

No one had come. Dess remembered it, so piercingly. No one had come. Not his friends from school, not his sisters, not anyone.

"Now now," said a familiar voice. "Lord Baby-of-the-Crying. We do not need bad friends who don't arrive with our good times with us, do we?"

Dess whirled around and threw his arms around the ghost of his grandmother's middle age, which to him, in that moment, looked like all the youth it could ever be possible to contain in one vibrant body.

And she reacted. That was the second extraordinary occurrence. The Megatron patrons *never* reacted. To anything. There were . . . dampeners . . . and things.

But heroes get their moments.

"Excuse me, Sir Stranger! You should not touch old ladies in toilets. What matter has happened to you?"

"You're not old, Nani. You could never, ever be old," he whispered. "Mira's right. None of us, never."

He held Nani so tight. As tight as gravity.

Then he let her go. Because that's what you had to do to the good old days. Or there'd never be any more of them.

"Now," he said. Decibel Jones crouched down to look his own heart in the eye. His own hurt, seven-year-old, gold lamé heart.

"Why didn't they come?" the little boy sniffled.

"Because they're all a bunch of rotten bastards, that's why.

And because all legends start out lonely as *fuck*. Don't complain to me, I didn't make the rules."

His younger self gasped. But smiled. "You swear *so much*!"

"I know. Isn't it fucking *grand*? Now. How about a hug, Danesh? I promise, this particular hug is gonna make it *all* better."

And Decibel Jones did what his species did best, even if his nationality felt it was a bit much.

He snuggled that weird little child so hard it fixed the universe.

Just for a moment.

38.

Maybe a Miracle Will Happen

The 101st Metagalactic Grand Prix final was held in a foxhole. The aerial bombardment only stopped briefly for Mr. Snuggles to broadcast planetwide, demanding his point total for this particular performance.

The commentators and judges cowered behind velvet-draped tables. The contestants beat back ground troops with the business end of every instrument imaginable. It was awful.

It was a long, unbroken sob of violence. It seemed to go on forever, longer than any radio hit has any right to. Eardrums and actual drums shattered.

But as the victory of Mr. Snuggles and the Meleg Imperium drew near, a curious thing happened.

A man named Decibel Jones, wearing a ridiculous silver spaceman suit with some kind of paisley pashmina tied around his head, walked out onto the battlefield like that was a thing he'd done every day of his life. No big deal. No great concern. This battlefield happened to be a stage, and Jones was quite good at stages. He walked right into the middle of the Meleg vs. Everyone brawl.

Mr. Snuggles, covered in blood varietals, spun around. He

didn't even recognize the human. The war frenzy rode too high in his veins.

Decibel held something out toward the unfathomably violent creamsicle dreambear.

"Cuppa tea?"

Mr. Snuggles spluttered. Spat. Snarled.

"What? Are you mad? No. Fuck no. Out of my way or I'll stab the best parts of you first."

"Darling," Decibel laughed, feeling the frisson of protagony all up and down his lissome limbs. "You can't even *imagine* my best parts."

Jones tossed his favorite teacup up into the air. By instinct alone, Mr. Snuggles caught it.

And blinked out of existence.

The paradoxical energy of a disappointed aging man hugging the absolute loneliness out of his disappointed younger self flowed out from that cup of tea. It took everything with it. The Narancan fleet. The Narancans. Parts of the volcano. Everything connected to Mr. Snuggles and the breaking of the world. It all swirled away into—

—the torpedo bay of the KEVV *Difficult Second Starship*, where Öö had hurled the kettle-end of the newest and most convenient beverage technology from the Üürgama Corporation. Into the oldest of days. The days before a deeply unserious way of life had swept the dark away on a tsunami of glitter and dubious lyrics. The time in which everything had just gotten so fucked-up.

The fleet tumbled into the unnamed wall of battle sound cycling over and over in the heart of the ship. They engaged immediately, for all the good it would do.

Lasers, boron bombs, plasma gouts, and screaming protests of a certain bear made no sound in the vacuum of space, or the vacuum of the past.

39.

To Fill Me With You

A solitary voice cut through the sudden quiet. Over the broken dinner theater tables and shattered lights, the trampled food, the terrified contestants. A judge, from the new applicant's chaperone species. A veteran of the MGP. And for a long, long time afterward, the definitive voice of the Metagalactic Grand Prix.

Oort St. Ultraviolet.

"Fuck all of this," he bellowed, with a voice that had once tremulously saved the world. "We're doing it. We bloody have to, don't we? Get up there, you creatures. Lights Out, there's your mic. Keep calm and carry on. That was never a thing, but it's a thing now. Did you know that was never really a thing? They printed up broadsheets but . . . yeah, sorry, never mind. The Vedriti drew the first slot. Pull up whatever you call shields and get onstage. The show must go on. Dess. The whole show. Must go on. Or it all goes back to war and death and we lose it. Don't you see? This is stupid and absurd and silly and quite often dreadful, but if we stop being stupid and absurd and silly, then all we're left with is the dreadful. We lose it all."

Brief Experience of Tavallinen took the stage on gorgeous glittering Baby LuLu, singing mandatory karaoke.

But not true karaoke. Decibel meant to play lead guitar for the future. Jimmy Page's black beauty of a guitar, stolen last week, because it had always been stolen already, from Minneapolis–St. Paul International Airport in April 1970. The guitar of his dreams.

But no. It wasn't right. He couldn't do it. He looked at that sleek dark body of a magical machine in his hands, a machine a magical man had used to do things no one else could, and turned Danesh Jalo into Decibel Jones.

All that was true. But it wasn't for him. Not in the end. Not this time. He'd only been meant to bring it here.

"Nen," Dess whispered. "Trade."

The Vedriti blinked her porcelain eyelids. She had no capacity for confusion, so she extended the Matter Whisperer's best effort at a human guitar to Decibel. And took what he offered her without expression or thanks.

Her pale blue fingers settled onto the strings.

It was in all technical ways a live performance. But Nen's face did not move. Her tendrils did not tendril. She opened her mouth.

A single syllable rolled out over the volcano's broken audience. In B-flat minor.

La, la, la.

The *la la la*s were all she could think of to sing, and in them maybe there was some hope. Dess tried his best to give it a little fire, even if he'd always been less of a player than Oort was on his worst day. But there was only so much you could do.

Lightning lit him up like a saint. Green and purple and white and blue, every shade any of them ever imagined they might grow up to be.

It lit Nen up, too. It lit everyone up. The greatest stage effect in the history of the Metagalactic Grand Prix.

Mira Wonderful Star.

Thundering a beat only she could play.

Mira tapped her chest, still wet with the rains of Xodo's past, somehow finding a perfect rhythm in that long droning note. *The* rhythm. The rhythm of everything. The infinitely looping transporter of her paralocket activated over and over as she thumped her fist against it in the rhythm of her own heartbeat, of the ship's engine, of a whirling star. The rhythm of a life that never happened to her and a life that did, for the youth her friend couldn't get back and the one she intended to suck the fucking *marrow* out of, for the poor everyday Ilargia who just wanted to live, for her own people, for her planet for finally saying no, all on their own, to the prospect of hitting things for fun and profit, for everyone.

Mira dematerialized and rematerialized, dematerialized and rematerialized, over and over, in a pinwheel radius from the stage through the crowd. Not much more than twelve meters, but also enough. Enough for Myra Aoki-Strauss's molecules to pass through the molecules of everyone at the grand final, taking an atom here, leaving one there, but touching everyone she passed through.

And like a transporter, contact with a paradox also pulled its one good trick. Thousands saw in Technicolor the substance of their lives if they'd never done anything wrong, chosen the wrong path, married the wrong person, taken the wrong job, chosen the wrong way to win the Grand Prix, all of it, everything. The grief and pain of what might have been ricocheted like bullets through those twelve meters of weeping, thinking flesh.

Except Decibel Jones. Little Danesh Jalo grown so big. Alone at the end of every world again while everyone else got to be part of something. He watched his friend disappear and reappear—but hadn't he done that his whole life? Hadn't that been her act? He smiled while the rest sobbed. But it was a smile as dry and bitter as anything he'd ever drunk.

But for everyone else, it was enough.

Enough to make the long braying note of the Vedriti's song the single most beautiful thing anyone who attended that legendary Grand Prix had ever heard or would hear. Everything they had lost, everything they'd wanted, everything they'd longed to be and sometimes even were, for brief moments, rocketed through the audience. That silly, meaningless note came thundering and blossoming through their cynicism and their fear like a star exploding.

It meant *everything*.

Finally, Mira's high-speed chase ended as she passed through the weird alien girl she knew she shouldn't have any feelings at all for, but did anyway, because that's sentience's game, beautiful and stupid all the way around to beautiful again.

She passed through Brief Experience of Being Tavallinen, still dripping with the rains of Xodo.

Tears flowed down Nen's cheeks. Her chest ached. Her voice cracked open the way everyone's does when the karaoke track hits that perfect spot and all that singing alone at home with a wineglass for a microphone pours out into a real one, and Nen was not only experiencing being Tavallinen, but burning up all the way through with everything she was.

She was just her voice, standing still, not moving a muscle, sobbing a song into a volcano.

Singing the screamy bit to the cheap seats and beyond.

Decibel stared at Tavallinen. At the brief experience of being her. And he never stopped playing for a moment. Strumming the right guitar, in that perfect place, playing to mend something so fragile it could blow away like sequins at any moment.

Decibel Jones, for the first time in his life, sang backup, and didn't mind a bit.

When Mira solidified again on the other side of the Vedriti, the Ilargia, the future and the past, Öö was there to meet her. To contribute to the song of two planets he suddenly found he had a great deal of connection to. He hoped the last dregs of Gadramaður the All-Knowing would let it happen.

Öö grabbed hold of the paralocket, still connected by a thread to the ship. He opened his mouth to let something out. Something he'd come to love so much he would never be able to explain it. Something he'd heard every day of his Time Out. Something that traveled through several rapidly separating bubbles of space-time.

The Keshet's jaws widened like a door—a door opening in a high-rise apartment building full of humans locked inside for months with only themselves to love or hate, singing together, singing for all the world just to hear something, to feel something, to be something.

Once, always, together.

Peace

Rock and roll never dies.
—Damiano David
Måneskin

40.

Thank You, Darling

Mira Wonderful Star found Decibel Jones three days later in a little chemist-cabaret on Baby LuLu, nursing a number of cocktails.

"Mushy, mushy, Dess." She wore the top half of a sexy Hobbit costume that got lost along the way and ended up shiny pleather low-rise trousers, slung round with a tangle of gold pocketwatches for a belt. Their fobs dangled almost to the floor, a declaration of intent to live on purpose. To live.

"Mushy, mushy, Wonderful," he answered.

It was a full minute before he noticed.

"Where's your locket?"

Mira grinned mischievously. She put her hand over her heart. "Douglas fixed me."

"Douglas is a badger, Mira," Decibel said, not without some concern for her mental health.

"Well, yes. But a very advanced badger. Turns out you can learn and grow quite a lot in that engine room once everything starts coming apart and you retain consciousness through cycles. I don't believe any badger has ever gotten so much time to consider how things work." Mira sat down nearest to her dearest. "A paradox has to stay in a ship, right? That badger asked a madly important question, and the answer is: I'm free. Furry wee Douglas scratched his muzzle and asked: *What's a ship? Just a thing that moves through space. Don't overthink it, Strauss.*"

Dess downed his cocktail. It didn't help. "I'm so confused."

Mira gave him a soft smile and put her hand on her chest again. "A quick surgery. For a Keshet, anyway. Part of the ship is in here. A scrap of stellar cartography installed in my body. I move through space; the ship moves through space. We are one and the same, so we never have to be apart, and me and everything can be together." She held up a glass. "Douglas is right, don't overthink it."

Decibel reached over and squeezed her hand. Still nothing. Still on the right track.

"How is she?" Mira asked. "How are the Alunizar taking everything?"

Decibel blew air out of his cheeks. "The Alunizar are not taking calls at the moment. It seems Lorgnon Xola Zand, Highly Potent Blah Blah Blah was caught getting extremely graphic pats from someone named Edward. He's been uninstalled from his chair. So their tubules are quite full at the moment, but I'm sure the GBU will eventually get round to voting on a punishment. Nen wants to go home." He glanced sidelong at Mira. "You like her, don't you?"

Mira chewed her lip. "I do wish *you'd* find someone to like."

"Myra Aoki-Strauss. Don't you dare feel sorry for me! Do you really think Decibel Jones Falls In Love would be a fitting very extra special episode of this after-school drama? Please, Mira. My darling. My past and my future. I've been in love a thousand times. And, I mean, that's a *precise* number. I was in love with you. I was in love with Oort. I was in love with the band. I was in love with the Roadrunner for a good minute. Remember that curvy wee Weigelt blob back Eta-side? She came to the semis! We talked all night. I'm going to be her best man. I've been madly, deeply, genuinely in love with every stage I've ever stood on, every mic I've ever kissed, every guitar I've ever strapped on, every song whose lyrics popped in my head in the middle of the night like Bubble Wrap, only twice as satisfying. I am a professional faller into, on top of, underneath. Fuck, I'm in love with this drink!" Decibel brandished an afternoon brandy that only had a little electricity in it. "I definitely fell head over heels for the coat-check monolith. We really had something special, see?" He held up his ticket. It had a crudely drawn heart around the number fifty-five. "I'm not going to lie, I'm half in the bag for this one, too."

He thumbed his fist at the gargantuan Yurtmak dripping one table over. She was wearing a lavender uniform that read *I Volunteered with Volun-Cheer* on the front.

"Captain Gigi Skullvise," the murderhippo introduced herself. "I'm Decibel's Buddy. My first officer is yours—he's around here somewhere. You gave us quite a chase; I don't know what you were running from. We only want to show you around the place."

"There's just something about her," Dess shrugged. "Plus, she says she's rich."

"I'm retired!" the Yurtmak demurred, which was a very odd thing for a Yurtmak to do. "Thought this would be a nice way to make friends and all. Keep up with the youth."

"Not really a youth," Dess said.

Captain Gigi turned to face him completely. She took him in, toe to crown. Her depthless death-dark eyes shone with grandmotherly warmth. "Oh yes you are, Decibel Jones. Do you know how long Yurtmak live if nobody murders us?"

He shook his head.

"Neither do I," Gigi burbled. "You're barely a minute old to me. Just a sweet little fresh-baked baby boy."

"Not really a boy, either."

The tusky Yurtmak cupped his whole head in one monstrous

maroon sandpaper-sheathed hand. "*Baby*," Gigi crooned tenderly. "And I do love babies, you know. Always have."

"Do we really need Buddies? After everything?" Mira protested.

The entire cabaret answered a resounding *yes*.

Decibel, however, couldn't let a good monologue end early. "And don't get me started on Meleg, oh my sweet lord, I'm mad for the little ragemuffins. That heart-shaped nose? Forget it. Get another one of these in me and I'll start making eyes at the window treatments, which really are quite lovely now that you bring it up. Not Clippy, though. That was just a physical thing. Oh, my love, you have no idea. I'm not lonely, I'm not looking, I'm in a serious long-term relationship, and I am bloody *loyal*. Faithful as a swan."

Mira looked out the window to the sky full of ships and skippers and the long-promised flying cars of every childhood zooming past through rosy clouds. "They don't actually mate for life, you know," she said.

"Well, I *do*. I am all in, I am fully committed, in sickness or in health, for better or for worse. My prince came and it was *the whole fucking cosmos*. Me and the universe, that's endgame. My soulmate. My better half. No one I'd rather curl up on the couch with at the end of the day and watch *Real Hiveminds* while absolutely demolishing a pint of time. I swear sometimes we finish each other's—"

A deafening boom shook the bar as, somewhere not so far away, Eta Carinae A and Eta Carinae B figured out what was really important in life, had a breakthrough session of couple's therapy, and collided, with a little help from their friends, into one perfect, healthy star capable of sustaining life without skeletonizing it instantaneously.

The boom from the Alunizar-surrendered weather control system kicking in was much, much softer, but it was, and always would be, a beat you could dance to.

Decibel Jones grinned. "—sentences." He stood up and hugged

his drummer as hard as all the things they'd left behind. "Nen's tuning up backstage. Stay and watch. You can try being a fan for once and stay by the stage door. It's open-mic night. Purest thing in the world. Someone brought her a cupful of rain from home. She just wants to sing."

Mira raised her own glass of electrified warmth to toast Decibel Jones just as the newest galactic citizen stepped out onto the little stage with a guitar that absolutely *had* to be returned before the remains of their stressed-out-beyond-tolerance ship completely disintegrated in a few hours.

"May our future be delicious," she laughed, and cried a little, and laughed again.

And so did he.

Mira Wonderful Star didn't take her eyes away from the stage for a second after that. Her girl was singing.

If she had, she might have seen the back of Decibel's Yurtmak Buddy's uniform, where the wildly wealthy retiree's name was stitched in embroidered cursive, a much more famous name than either human could yet guess.

Red, of course.

G. G.

41.

Allez Ola Ole

Decibel Jones was a child of the new millennium. Never at any moment in his life had any single cell of his body believed things could actually be fixed, or that anything anywhere would ever consent to turn out all right.

But it happened. It finally happened. What will, one day, space willing and the end credits music doesn't rise, happen to you, or at least someone tangentially related to your genome. The realization that the worst of it is over. That there is a beautiful open road ahead through every star, toward every dawn.

That you can be free. That it can all be fine.

Mostly. Eventually.

This is the future. Decibel's future. Your future. The story of the galaxy is the story of one single person in it. It really is, someday, going to be okay.

For a while.

But this is that while.

Hug it tight. Push to achieve happiness. Push just a little harder every time. And one day, if everyone pushes together . . .

Somewhere far off, orbiting a sun called Bob, half of a planet had no idea they'd just done something extraordinary and quite well. Agnes Munt of East Kilbride sipped a drink on a Spanish beach, looked up at a brilliant blue sky, and raised her glass to it, which is, to date, the most admired gesture of any human being to the universe it really might someday enjoy. She turned to her left to make sure her traveling companion was comfortable.

Olabil the No-Longer-Friendless, last of the Inaki and the Lensari, lay on an extra-large chaise thumbing through the family scrapbooks he and Muriel had been making together for weeks.

"That's me mum," Olabil trumpeted joyfully, nuzzling into Agnes's beautiful red hair. "Weren't she pretty? Weren't she just."

And somewhere else, even further away, in the deepest dark, in the light of a newly stable sun, a pale cold silent planet turned on the rain and rippled over with laughter like swans singing on the sea.

Cue the drums. Cue the strings.

Cue life. Again.

Always.

After all, this time, *this time*, will be different.

Liner Notes

It is no easier to sequence the genome of *Space Oddity* than it was to lay out all the vastly many human beings who contributed culturally or personally to the writing of the weird loud glitterbaby that was *Space Opera*.

But it must always start with Eurovision itself.

In 1955, Marcel Bezençon and a small group of broadcasters and artists conceived something incredibly beautiful and incredibly silly: the Eurovision Song Contest, and the very idea that a continent that spent most of its time and energy punching various parts of itself with other parts of itself could begin to heal its wounds with song, dance, goofy costumes, and goofier rules. Sixty-eight years on, it remains one of the most hopeful, most ridiculous, and most human things this species has ever managed to pull off with the meager rock, star, and better natures we have to rub together. It is sincere, uncool, fearless, joyful, defiant, and *way* too extra for the sensibilities of any era it's ever existed in, and that is what makes it perfect. Even when it's a mess.

Kind of like all of us.

And between *Space Opera* and *Space Oddity*, the Eurovision Song Contest was cancelled for the first time in its history. When I first started planning *Space Oddity*, it seemed this was the only thing it could be about. The biggest thing that had happened to the Contest, and the rush of its return the next year. But then a

European country launched a ground invasion of another for the first time in a long while, the world after COVID never really did find normalcy again but seemed to retreat wholesale into numbness and pessimism, and I began to ask questions like *can an entire civilization have clinical depression?*

I contracted COVID for the first time as I was writing the first draft, and finished it in an absolute fever dream of Original Recipe Coronavirus out-of-body agony and madness. The process of bringing this new weird loud glitterbaby into the world has been difficult and painful from jump.

But Eurovision itself began in hurt and arced toward beauty. So maybe these books must hurt in their making to shine in their spreading. Or maybe that's just a pretty thing to think when the bad times just keep on coming and rarely seem to notice how hard anyone is singing into the void to borrow a cup of meaning.

Still, it *is* pretty. So we'll go with it. That's the whole spirit of the thing.

I will never stop being grateful, not just for M. Bezençon, but for all the thousands of artists, crew, designers, organizers, and fans who have put their shoulders to the fiery hamster wheel of Eurovision and helped it roll through the twentieth century and into this one.

Thank you so much to Molly and Matthew Hawn, who introduced me to the ESC in London in 2012. To Charles Tan, who joked that I should write a Eurovision novel with totally out-of-proportion results. And massively to Navah Wolfe, who believed in it and acquired it and knew what it could become. Though she was not able to continue on editing this sequel, her guidance and firm hand with the original shines through each of these pages, and without her, both *Opera* and *Oddity* would vanish in a puff of cynicism.

Which brings us to the hitchhiking elephant in the room, the one who always turns up when you attempt to write spacefaring science fiction featuring British folk, and for whom a certain overly clever badger nosing through these pages is most definitely named. Douglas Adams is simply the best there ever was.

I remember the day he died—too young, so painfully young—barely five years older than I am as I type these words. I was at university, in the days before the internet was everywhere and everything, and it hit us like a shovel to the head. My friends and I had grown up reading Adams. We read him aloud to each other and to others as an opening gambit in evaluating whether any given person could *really* get along with us, which is just *terrifically* insufferable when you think about it. All of us dearly hoped to meet him one day, and suddenly, it was just never going to happen. Ever. Right at the time of life when it begins to occur to the young that perhaps they are not so special as to be exempt from the linearity of time and the wall of death? That no matter how special the human, or how enormous their feats, no one is? What rude gesture could you give to the void of mortality in the face of all that? Because it thoroughly deserved one.

I went down to the shops that afternoon. And I bought a bowl of geraniums. (If you know, you know.) We went up to the roof of our university library that night and dropped it off the top, standing together holding hands as it shattered in a perfect corona of dirt and pot shards on the concrete below. We all genuinely meant to say *oh no not again* in unison. That was the plan. But somehow no one did. We all just stood there in the dark watching the flowers fall and break in silence.

Twenty-three years later I named a badger after him and made sure this book was almost, but not quite, 42 chapters long. Because you simply can never equal the greatest, you can only hope to come close. Occasionally.

There are just so many ways to say *I love you* in this world. Almost as many as there are to say *thank you*.

Here are several more.

Thank you to my stalwart, wonderful, and patient agent, Howard Morhaim, who stands as ever between me and total chaos.

Thank you to my Patreon supporters, a real life RSPCA who keep my world together practically and spiritually, but particularly Sean Elliott, Matthew Baldwin, Catherine King, Deborah Furchgott, Kim Scheinberg, Wesley Allbrook, Ella Kliger, Jahana, Cynthia Sperry, and the entire Discord moderation team. Solamen vincit omnia.

Thank you to my child, Bastian, who has cheerfully put up with so many *Mummy has to work todays*. At *Space Opera*'s launch party, I was four months pregnant. Right now, that child is five and a half, writing their own stories about space (and also zebras) right next to me. I have talked a lot about books as babies over the course of my career, and there's nothing like a real baby to make you realize how much easier books really are. But I made a beautiful rogue AI and when they dance through the living room in a Dracula cape, leprechaun pajamas, rainbow shoes, three of my scarves, and all of my eyeliner singing "Piano Man" into an empty paper-towel roll, I feel pretty okay about most everything ever, except how weird it feels to give birth to your own protagonist.

Thank you to Hadley and Charles Splane-Borja, Sophie Roth, Sue Fitton, Breezie Mackenzie, Melinda, Joanie Divine-Hoar, and Tristram for being my village.

Thank you to Emma Puranen, who helped me find, understand, and reasonably populate the Eta Carinae system, a very real bin fire in the sky.

On the topic of very real things, thank you first to Tony Conn, who has spent years working on a documentary about the old Megatron restaurant, for both massively assisting in my research into that beautiful beast and keeping the faith that this book, indeed, would both one day be finished and treat the beast with love. And thank you to Danny Blundell, who created the Megatron in the first place, teaching us all something rather important about doing stupid things with enormous style and ambition, and stubbornly continuing to do them, even when the bulldozers come. The Megatron was that perfect, impossible, brief union of the stupid and the beautiful.

In my finer moments, maybe I am, too.

In *Space Opera's* liner notes, I said there can be no truly great pop music without sorrow, and if these books are pop albums, they are extremely committed to proving the axiom.

Space Oddity is dedicated to two people. One you've probably heard of. One you almost certainly never have.

Back in 2017, when I was far out in the weeds of *Space Opera,* trying to do something totally new for me and thoroughly convinced I'd already stuffed it completely, I went to a convention in rural France to accept an award for a book I'd written years before, but which had only just come out in France. Much like Decibel and Mira, at the time it felt like I'd done something everyone loved *once,* and that magical time when I was in the pocket and the sun was shining on my brain was just . . . over. I was so afraid I'd never be able to pull off anything that big or that good again, and that big good thing? I was twenty-nine when I wrote *Fairyland*. What if that was the best I would ever manage? Two months of being twenty-nine and then the sun moved in the sky and never lit me up again? I could almost see what *Space Opera* could become, but I had no confidence I could do anything but fuck it up sixteen different ways, seventeen if I really worked at it.

I was all the way down in an industrial vat of feels when I met Christopher Priest. Someone I admired enormously, but who knew me, as many male writers I admired enormously tend to, only because his girlfriend loved my books. Later that evening, that poor man made the mistake of asking me what I was working on and I almost burst into tears. I went full American on him, pouring out all my frustration and fear and insecurity and how heavy I felt that book on my shoulders, how close I thought it was to being good, but how far.

And Chris Priest, a man who suffered *precisely* zero fools, took me to church about it all. That beautiful man pep-talked me like no one ever has, true halftime sports movie coach style, full of profanity and passion and conviction that right when you think it's all rotten is when you've almost got it right, and I just needed to say *fuck it* to everything but the work, and that included both my own insecurity and anyone who didn't get it. It was so utterly what I needed in that moment. It was so fully what Goguenar Gorecannon became: loving advice wrapped in f-bombs wrapped in deep cynicism that is always a mask for a soul that longs to be an optimist, and is always looking for an excuse to try out hope.

So we drank all weekend about publishing and life and work and pain and joy. And then we sang a lot under the stars. It was one of the best weekends of my life as an artist or a human. And when Christopher fucking Priest tells you to stop fucking about because you can do this, you'd better bloody well go home and get busy.

When he died, a few months before I finished this book, another one I was so afraid of failing (and who knows, maybe I have), another one that seemed like it would never be done and could never be what I dreamed, I thought about that night on top of the library with the geraniums.

Oh no. Not again.

I think we all do a little better, strive a little harder, if there's someone in our minds we desperately want to impress . . . and know is impossible to impress. Christopher Priest was that for me. All I want after that weekend in France is to make him proud.

Maybe, if I worked my whole life and excelled beyond all dreams of literary merit, to make him smile. I don't think he ever cared one way or another for geraniums, but when the void behaves this way toward the best of us, a gesture is *always* called for.

So here I sit, in the dark, in silence, after the prestige, pulling back the curtain to do the forbidden thing and show how the trick was done: without Chris, Decibel Jones never sings a note.

It would be so awfully nice if that was the only story of death I had to tell. But it isn't. A few weeks before this book finally passed beyond revision, a dear friend of mine named John Peacock died.

I never met him in person, but he was part of my life online for almost twelve years. Whenever I needed a math or a science consult or even just more *Bake Off* episodes, he was there. When my child was quite small and the world was quite closed for business and terribly dark, I built a rocketship out of carboard and duct tape for my little one to dream in. I am not so good at building things. But John did the Pythagorean two-step for me, and drew me blueprints for various carboard control panels as beautiful as any da Vinci sketch—you think I'm kidding, but I *framed* them.

John Peacock taught me how to make things fly. Including, sometimes, my own heart when it was near to finished even trying to walk.

Sentience, in the end, is only a little about being clever. It's about how we handle each other. How we see one another. How we help. How we share. How we protect and how we love. How we catch someone when they stumble, and whether we can believe we will be caught when we fall.

I don't know if there will ever be another adventure for the Absolute Zeroes. This may well be goodbye. But both people and books have caught me in midair, and I hope, in some small way, as we hurtle screaming through space together, that I and a few of my pages can return the favor.